"If we're going to be spending the next few days together," he said, "we're going to have to come up with some ground rules. Number one: stop overthinking everything. Number two: stop trying to fix me. I'm not broken. And number three…"

"Yes?"

"I want it clear from the outset that if I kiss you, it won't be because I'm trying to get back at Jenna or trying to distract you from talking. It's because you're hot, and I'm alive, and I want to."

The air sucked out of her lungs with each word that passed over his lips, and she stood there, her feet glued to the pavement, winded and light-headed and incandescently hopeful.

"Oh?" she said, her body leaning toward his of its own accord.

His gaze dropped to her mouth which flooded with anticipation.

"Just so we're clear," he said.

"Got it." Her mouth parted as the air grew light and fast in her lungs. "Are you gonna kiss me now?"

His teeth nipped at his bottom lip again, and she nearly combusted despite the cool, night air. "I was thinking about it."

He smiled, a slow grin that drew her closer by some invisible thread.

She slanted her lips toward his ear. "Rule number one," she murmured. "Stop overthinking everything."

She didn't have time to pull back as his head turned and his mouth claimed hers.

When life and love take a detour...

The Runaway Cupcake Queen

Cheri Allan

~ Book One ~
A Lucky Charm Romance

Five Oaks Books

This is a work of fiction. Names, characters, places and incidents are either the product of the author's imagination or are used fictitiously, and any resemblance to actual persons, living or dead, business establishments, events or locales is entirely coincidental.

The Runaway Cupcake Queen

Publishing History
First Five Oaks Books Edition, 2019
Print ISBN: 978-0-9904815-9-1
Digital ISBN: 978-0-9904815-8-4

Published in the United States of America

Acknowledgements

My bottomless thanks to my family for cheerfully stepping over dust bunnies and bringing me snacks. To my dearest Plot Bunnies who, in a fit of optimism, have helped me plan for what I'll write after this, because there *will* be more. And to Charis. If not for her tough love and encouragement, this book would still be sitting in an unfinished mess on my hard drive. Should we ever bake together, you get to lick the spoon.

Other Titles by Cheri Allan

Luck of the Draw
Stacking the Deck
All or Nothing
Deal Me In

For all the...

late-bloomers,
dog-lovers,
cupcake-eaters,
adventure-seekers,
procrastinators and
love-makers.
Take the detour.
Pet the dog.
Eat the cupcake.
Love.

CHAPTER 1

Helen ran into the bathroom stall, snatched a tampon disposal baggie from the dispenser and held it to her face. *Oh, sweet mother of sunshine.* She swayed as another wave of dizziness hit her and sucked hard on the bag. The outer ladies' room door creaked open.

"Helen? You okay?"

Ivy's voice echoed in the tiny bathroom, breathless and concerned. As she should be. Helen leaned dangerously near a full-blown panic attack here. She'd never had one, mind you, but she'd never been this close to near total public humiliation before. How had she gotten herself into this? More to the point, how could she get herself *out?*

She yanked the baggie away from her face to speak. "A 'love bus,' Ivy? Seriously? No. That's not going to happen. No way."

"Marcia was brainstorming," Ivy soothed in that tone of voice you use with timid woodland animals and people perched on the edges of bridges. "You know how she is. Come out so we can talk. I'm sure she's willing to negotiate the specifics."

"She brainstormed on live TV!" Helen leaned heavily against the bathroom stall door. The traitorous latch gave way, and she swung out, heels, evening gown, paper bag and all. "She can't take that back. It's out there now. My employees have seen that. My banker. My own father!" The bag poofed in and out with each breath.

Ivy petted her hair. "It's all right. It's just nerves. You'll be amazing as the new lead of the show. I know it's crazy-making and Marcia comes up with things that may be a little out of your comfort zone, but you've got this. America loves you. I'm sure she'll be willing to tweak things. We can make it tasteful. You'll see."

Despite Ivy's reassurances, Helen couldn't help but feel that Marcia Powers, bless her heart, was talking out of her ass. The host and producer of the hit reality dating show *Happily Ever After* was high on a cocktail of adrenaline and endorphins and couldn't be trusted, obviously, to be reasonable.

Meanwhile, Helen's pageant smile felt permanently frozen in place. She'd dropped everything—her business, her relationships, her gym membership—and put her suffocating but stable existence on hold to take a chance that signing on as a contestant on *Happily Ever After* was her moment to break free, to breathe, to put the long years of living to please everyone else on the back burner for a change. Instead, she'd just been dumped for a second time in as many months then left alone and *freezing* on a stupid bandstand in freaking New Hampshire in *March* which was clearly a stone's throw from the Arctic Circle and... Dear Jesus, where was she? Right. Forced to smile and pretend the whole hell in a handbasket disaster was fine—*just fine!*

Well, it wasn't fine. Not by a longshot.

Helen wanted to believe Ivy. With every cold, miserable, tired fiber of her being, she wanted to believe the rejection and humiliation of this entire experience was well and truly behind her and everything ahead would be sunshine and roses. But, standing on that frigid bandstand watching someone else get the prize she'd worked so hard for sucked as much as being the runner up for Miss Alabama. She wasn't nineteen anymore, but she still needed a moment of privacy to collect herself.

"It took everything I had to stand out there and pretend everything was okay. But it's not. *I'm* not. This whole," she waved the bag wildly until Ivy grabbed her fist in self-preservation, *"thing* is too much. You know I put on the brave face, but this is the real me telling you: I. Don't. Want. This. Anymore."

Just then the ladies' room door slammed open. Marcia Powers burst in, her face and clothes smudged with ashes from the garage explosion that had rocked the small downtown of Sugar Falls, making the live finale of the show *all the more* dramatic. Helen's head reeled. She would have believed it was all some over-the-top, staged reality-show drama if she hadn't felt the jolt of the blast, choked on the smoke, and seen the fiery debris with her very own eyes. Thankfully, no one had been injured. It still felt a fitting metaphor for her life, dumped not only in front of a cheering crowd of townspeople but the entire live viewing audience of *Happily Ever After.* She was a mess, shaken, and in second place, but, hey, she was alive!

Before going off the air, Marcia had teased Helen as the lead for the upcoming season—along with new and outrageous details—and Helen had fled the bandstand, disoriented by the dark, the crowd, and the flashing lights. She'd held it together, smiling and waving at the blur of camera flashes and faces, and run toward the sign promising "hot coffee" like a beacon in a stormy sea.

Her teeth chattered, and she rubbed her hand over the bare skin exposed above the sling holding her left arm. She would never, ever, be warm again. Ever.

"For the love of God," Marcia said, smoothing Helen's flyaway hair. "You're a mess. Ivy, go get her some water or that sweet tea crap she's always asking for. Sweetheart, pull yourself together. What's happened to you? There are a hundred cell phone cameras on the other side of that door waiting to capture the excited face of the next lead and you're hiding? You've got to bring back my southern belle."

Helen grabbed the bag from Ivy's hand and held it to her face again.

"I just need a moment," she said into the bag.

Marcia squeezed her fist around the bag and yanked it away. "We are standing in the crapper of the *Gas & Go*, Helen. You can have all the 'moments,'" she air-quoted this, "you want as soon as we get back to the hotel. This place stinks. Literally."

The door opened a crack, and Nick, Marcia's lead cameraman and new fiancé, poked his head in. "Everything all right in here?"

Marcia grabbed his elbow and yanked him into their improvised office space. "Tell her, Nick. Tell her America is going to eat her up with a spoon. Tell her that whatever has her spooked is just hunger or fatigue or smoke inhalation…"

"You're a fan favorite," he said. "And the camera loves you."

Marcia smacked his shoulder. "Of course, it loves her! She's a goddess! That hair. That body. That accent. Hell, you blink at a man, Helen, and he's got a hard-on. Isn't that right, Nick?" Marcia turned to be sure he was listening. "Be honest. Doesn't Helen here make you tent your pants?"

"Um." Nick stared at Helen, surely in a mirror of her own horrified expression.

Marcia smacked him in the shoulder again. "Oh, he won't say on account of being so loyal and in love with me, but he would totally admit it if he weren't. I mean, look at you! Freakin' sex appeal on a stick! And the sympathy you'll get after the way you handled yourself tonight, all gracious and shit. Our ratings will go through the roof!" She punctuated each of these last words with the stab of a scarlet fingernail to Helen's chest. "America wants to see you get your own happy ending, Helen from Heaven, Alabama, and I intend to deliver."

Helen looked Marcia in the eye. "You promised them a *sex bus*."

3

"I did no such thing. I gave them a vision. Viewers need something to latch onto, and they'll love the whole female empowerment thing of you hand-picking your own men. We've never done that before."

"You're the match-maker. Shouldn't you do the picking?"

Marcia waved away this technicality. "I narrow things down, but you're in control, Helen. I can't make love happen. I can only set the stage. Give it an opportunity to happen."

She didn't feel in control. Of any of this. "But a sex bus?"

"You keep saying that. I don't think you understand the vision." Marcia wrapped an arm over Helen's shoulders. "Picture this: A glittering, golden tour bus traveling from city to city all the way from New Hampshire to Alabama. We'll hold a casting call in every major city down the East Coast, and you, Helen Walker, will get to personally hand-pick men to fill your very own *Trojan Bus of Love!*" She spread her hands in the air as if she could conjure the horrifying image. It worked. "Get it? Helen of Troy? Trojan? Oh God!" Marcia swung around. "I just thought of a brilliant endorsement opportunity here. Ivy! Make a note to see if we can get a sponsor for our Trojan bus tour, will you? You know what I'm talking about." Marcia winked like she'd been subtle. Helen felt the blood rush from her head again.

"It's the bus, isn't it? You think it's too much. A bit obvious." Marcia glanced at her reflection in the tiny warped restroom mirror and smoothed a silken black hair back into place while ignoring the ash smudge on her cheek.

"Yes."

"Fine. Maybe gold is a little... blingy. We'll make it more feminine. How about soft pink? Is that better?"

"Pink?" Helen wheezed. "As in *flesh-colored?*"

They all paused to imagine it. Nick snorted. "Sweetheart, I think you might want to stick with gold," he said.

"Ya think?" Marcia said, clearly annoyed she wasn't getting anywhere. "Helen, honey. Relax. You've got this."

Helen pulled back from the trio, the paper bag falling from her fingertips to the dingy vinyl floor. Her head seemed to be shaking of its own volition. The scents of unventilated toilet stalls and chemical cleaner slammed into her.

She flattened her back against the cold concrete block wall, a fitting place to rest her crushed romantic dreams and weary idealism.

All she'd wanted was to see a few things in this world before settling down in life like everyone expected. And, yes, she was well aware that going on a reality show came with its own financial benefits and social media attention, but that's how the world worked. It wasn't like she was asking to be made a fool of in the Liberace Bus of Bad Taste. All she wanted was to do her part to take the bakeries to the next level of success. Then, who knows? Maybe she'd finally get the chance to leave Heaven, if not forever, at least for a little while. Not that Travis, her business partner, knew any of that, but he had to know she'd been pushing at the seams of life for a while. What woman put her life on hold to go on reality TV if she didn't want something to change? But if she couldn't find happiness and freedom, precisely, she at least wanted to retain a sliver of self-respect.

And zero-calorie sweet tea, of course, because who wouldn't?

"I'm not going back out there tonight," she said. "I'll just stay here," her gaze bounced around the cramped restroom, "until everyone goes home, and then I'll slip out. Y'all can go back to the hotel. I'll be fine."

They all looked at one another as if telepathically debating the feasibility of the plan.

Marcia sucked in a long breath and let it out slowly. "I hate to be harsh, sweetheart, but you signed a contract. You can't hide in here forever. You have obligations. Also, we have to do your ITM before we can call it a night." Marcia was referring to the 'In The Moment' interviews meant to reflect the emotions and state of mind of the cast members as they reacted to the events of the show. This could take hours.

Helen looked longingly up at the small window high on the concrete wall. A tiny, unreachable portal to freedom.

She caught her reflection in the warped mirror, barely recognizing herself. The *Happily Ever After* makeup team had done her up tonight—her left arm still trapped in a sling following her harrowing rescue of a puppy from the path of a speeding car just days before. Her dark hair piled elegantly on top of her head in a sweeping up-do that might have been lovely in other circumstances but here... her eyelids were too glittery. Her lips too red. Everything about her looked desperate and forced.

It revealed far too much.

The hard truth of the matter was she *had* chosen this path. She'd made the decisions and signed on the dotted lines every step of the way. This was her bed, so to speak, and she must lay in it. Or, heaven help her, ride in it.

She spun away from the mirror and sucked in a long, shuddering breath then flashed a smile to prove she was all right. "I apologize. I'm just overwhelmed. It's been a long day. Forgive me?"

Ivy inched toward Helen. "Let me just call makeup. You're still looking a little manic. We'll clean you up and get you over to the inn as soon as we can."

Helen nodded.

"That's a good girl," Marcia said.

Helen side-eyed Marcia. She hated when folks called her a girl.

Hell, a girl wouldn't already be making plans to chug the bottle of champagne she knew would be waiting in her hotel room, because that's exactly what she planned, *thankyouverymuch*. She was a woman. An overwhelmed, tired, frustrated, pissed off woman who had reached the end of her proverbial rope.

Ten minutes later, she stepped into the blinding light of dozens of camera flashes as she made the short walk of shame across the snowy town common to the Inn at Sugar Falls.

Helen crossed the lobby, passed a handful of lingering crew members, and silently climbed the stairwell that led to the second floor.

Ivy trailed her as if she might bolt.

Wise woman.

Helen allowed Ivy to open the door to her suite. See? She could do this after all. She'd had years of practice sublimating her true feelings and holding her head so high and steady a cup of tea in a saucer wouldn't spill, and she had the pictures to prove it.

"Can I get you anything before we start ITMs?" Ivy asked.

Helen shook her head. She eyed the champagne on the small table by the window. "I'm fine. Thank you."

Ivy's eyes skimmed her ever-present clipboard. "Ten minutes."

Helen pressed the door shut and closed her eyes. Ten minutes wasn't a lot of time to regain one's dignity.

She wiggled her foot to ease the ache in her arch. She would have loved to kick off the ridiculous strappy heels she was wearing, but then she'd have to struggle to put them back on again, and this dress wasn't exactly designed for flexibility. She grabbed the cushy white robe with the inn's logo on the pocket, wrapped it over her shoulders for warmth, and crossed to the window.

Her room overlooked the small, quaint town common of Sugar Falls. Normally it looked like a throwback to some Norman Rockwell painting. Tonight, the detritus of television production littered the common and blocked the streets with vehicles, reporters, and equipment. The lights of Lucky's Pub down the way glowed along with the rhythmic pulsing of emergency lights. She wondered how long before the rescue and clean-up crews were done containing the site of the explosion that had flattened the old mechanic's garage earlier that evening.

As wild as it had all been, none of that had stopped the *Happily Ever After* live finale. Helen stared at the now-empty bandstand where Ian and Bailey had declared their love for one another. Helen had been forced to stand and watch like the ex-girlfriend everyone worried—and secretly hoped—would cause a scene.

She turned her back to the window. The bottle of champagne sat in a silver ice bucket, a pair of crystal flutes beside it as if anyone else were going to be celebrating this ridiculous night with her. She tucked the bottle under her sling, unscrewed the cap and poured herself a glass.

Bubbles bounced around on her tongue. For cheap champagne it went down surprisingly easy. She refilled her glass.

All too soon, Ivy knocked on the door to collect her.

Helen emptied her glass. "Let's get this over with."

Her stomach growled as she made her way through the darkened hallways of the inn to the room they'd set up for the ITMs. They had a pair of wing chairs set together. Behind that stood dark bookshelves pulled into the room to make it look like a gentleman's library instead of the storage area it clearly was under other circumstances. Helen glanced at the cases of toilet paper the crew had tucked just out of view. Fitting. They put a nice veneer on it, but the crap was always just out of view.

Helen closed her eyes, and the room went pleasantly dark. She waited for everyone to get organized and take their place. Lordy, she was tired. Tired of everything, of course, but being on reality TV meant a whole 'nother level of tired. You were always 'on,' always conscious of the cameras lying in wait like eager paparazzi, hoping to take an unflattering photo or clip of unguarded dialogue to exploit out of context.

It was no accident that Helen Walker of Heaven, Alabama, was still America's sweetheart southern belle. That kind of image took work. Faux serenity and 24/7 charm didn't just come out of nowhere. You had to store that crap up and let it ooze out slowly, like honey on a cold day.

Helen snapped to attention as Ivy clicked her pen repeatedly.

"Okay. Single camera tonight. No wardrobe changes. We've got a few things to cover, but once we've got it all, we can call it a wrap and get to bed."

Helen slipped off her robe, lay it on a side table out of view of the camera, and waited for the stylist to fix her hair just so. She hoped they'd blot her lips. They didn't. The camera guys adjusted the lighting, asked her to sit closer to the edge of her seat, as if she needed prompting to be ready to flee. She straightened her shoulders. Marcia stood just behind the camera motioning with her hand.

"Okay, I need you to tell us what you were feeling when you realized Ian was proposing to Bailey."

Helen nodded. She'd expected this. She smiled with an air of bittersweet tragedy at the camera. At least in this, it was real. As much as the outward setting and backdrops were orchestrated and manufactured, the emotions were genuine. "I'm sure y'all can understand, it's not easy seeing you're the runner up for someone's affection, and to be honest. It hurt. I thought Ian and I had a connection. No, I know we did, but I'm looking for more than a connection in a partner. I feel like we were good friends, but I want more than that. I deserve more than that." She shrugged, and it hurt. Her injured shoulder *and* her heart. "I deserve someone who nurtures me, body and soul, you know? Somebody who will fight for me. Sacrifice for me." She glanced at the ceiling as tears threatened which had nothing at all to do with Ian or Bailey or this blasted show. Why wouldn't they ever allow her to hold a tissue? "I want to be someone's number one."

A tear escaped and slid down her face and she reflexively swallowed trying to stem the tide.

"Brilliant!" Marcia cut in, swearing enthusiastically. "That's fantastic. Can you do that again, but this time tell me whether you ever saw Ian as your future husband. And... *go*."

Helen nodded and began again. "It's not easy knowing you're the runner up for someone's—"

Marcia cut her off. "Throw in that y'all again. Didn't she say y'all the first time? Show your southern. People love that shit."

Helen held her shoulders rigid, sucked in a breath, and started again, "Y'all can probably understand how hard it is seeing you're the runner up for someone's affections..."

After what felt like an eternity but had probably been no more than twenty minutes, Marcia decided to take things in a new direction. "I want you to talk about how we plan to cast this season. Give them a teaser for it."

Helen turned toward the camera. "This season I will be made to ride in a golden penis-mobile from—"

"*Cut!* Time out. *Penis*-mobile? That's what you think of it?"

"I would say that's fairly accurate."

Marcia threw her hands up. She did that a lot. "I cannot believe you're still freaking out over this."

"I cannot believe you can't see how embarrassing it is to parade around in a giant bus promoting condoms."

Marcia ignored the semi-shocked gasps of the crew. Frankly, Helen was surprised they had any reaction after all they'd seen over the years.

"Our viewership is 63 percent comprised of the 18-34-year-old demographic, and let me tell you, those folks are having sex. Lots of it. Promoting condom use is being a responsible role model. Did you think of that?"

"My widowed father will be watching this. Did you think of that?"

Helen's skin hummed with frustration. How could no one else see how outrageous this was? She glanced to Ivy for support only to have her avert her eyes and click her pen.

Marcia clapped her hands. "We're taking a fifteen-minute break, people. Helen? A word in the hallway?"

Helen mutinously grabbed her robe and followed Marcia into the dark paneled hallway. Marcia shut the door.

She didn't even wait for Marcia to start. "I agreed to be the lead, because you told me, no, you *promised* me you wouldn't force me to do anything I truly objected to doing. Well, I object. This is me objecting."

"I announced it on live TV. I can't exactly take it back."

Helen paced down the hall, her heels clicking on the hardwood floor. "That's not my problem. Go ahead and do your bus tour, but leave me out of it!"

When Marcia's casting director had reached out to her all those months ago, Helen had grabbed the opportunity with both hands and taken a bite like it was the apple in the garden and she was starved. But while tasty at first, tonight it had damn near choked her. The show wasn't an escape. It was a very public and humiliating boomerang poised to send her right back to where she started. She was prepared to walk home to Alabama, impractical footwear and all, to avoid going down this road any further.

"Do I need to remind you you signed a contract?"

"I'll hire a lawyer. I'll find a loophole."

"You don't think the show has lawyers? Oh, sweetheart, don't threaten. It's not an attractive color on you."

Helen stopped and stared at Marcia. She thought hard about the reasons she'd initially agreed to do the show. She reminded herself of Travis's excitement over getting national PR for the bakeries, Aunt Iris's horror at the idea of Helen's "prostituting herself for profit" (which, frankly, was a checkmark in the pro column,) and the outside possibility that she might actually make a connection with someone.

But, she wanted a man who wanted her for herself—not someone who saw her as a trophy or, as in Travis's case, a foregone conclusion in the inevitable march toward death.

"I do *not* want the kind of man that would willingly ride in a bus like that," she said, hands on hips.

"Helen, I hate to break it to you, but most men would find it an honor to travel in a—what did you call it?—penis-mobile."

"This is not a joke."

"I'm not joking."

Helen stared, aghast. How could she reason with people like this? "I need some air," she declared.

"You know I'm right," Marcia said.

Helen pulled her robe tight around herself and stalked toward the back door. The last thing she heard was Marcia yelling, "twelve minutes!" to anyone within earshot as the heavy door to the service entrance slammed in her wake.

She sucked in the cold night air. Twelve minutes? Marcia could take her twelve minutes and shove it.

Helen stomped down the short set of metal stairs, nearly falling on her backside in the process. She skittered across the pavement covered in half-melted patches of ice and compacted snow with choppy steps, muttering her frustration to the empty, frozen space between the river, a dumpster, and the inn's poorly lit parking lot.

As if *she* were the one being unreasonable! Her eyes ached from lack of sleep and too many tears, and she felt raw and exposed and, frankly, *used*. She could already see the kind of tabloid headlines Marcia's ridiculous idea would inspire. *Pageant Girl Turns Porn Star*. Or, *Beauty's Busload of Bachelors*. Tabloids were big on alliteration and hyperbole, as the *Rejected but Returning Reality Star* knew all too well.

The opportunity to vent and mumble expletives in private felt good, but it was still too cold to linger. Helen made her way back up the little metal steps to the door and pulled.

She pulled again.

"Y'all have got to be kidding."

She yanked a third time, then knocked. Given its location in the building, she realized no one could hear her, and she had zero interest cooling her heels, literally, waiting for someone to eventually find her.

She descended to the parking lot. Well, she could march to the main entrance up the left-hand alley crowded with news vans or hope there was another entrance on the far right of the building.

Far right of the building won. Helen's heels slipped on the patches of ice again as she grumbled over insufficient lighting. She reached the corner. Peering through a scramble of bushes, she could just make out a hotel employee putting out a cigarette, opening a door, and entering the inn. Perfect.

Helen picked her way through branches that snatched at her hair and caught the hem of her dress. Hopefully makeup and wardrobe wouldn't have a fit about her appearance. She broke free of the hedge, retying her robe when a flash of light temporarily blinded her.

"Helen! Helen Walker! Look here!" Another flash, and then shouts. *Oh, sweet mother of sunshine. You have* got *to be kidding.*

Helen turned toward the bushes again, but the sound of footsteps had her rethinking that escape route. Instead, she dashed toward a parking lot which was also dimly lit—thank you, Jesus, for small favors—and zig-zagged through the cars, grabbing onto side mirrors and the occasional door handle to keep herself upright. She huddled, crouched, beside a car when a faint light flashed across the hood like a searchlight.

Helen rolled her eyes. Really? They were using their cellphones to find her? Could they not leave her in peace?

She heard the crunch of footsteps on the edge of the lot, new voices intermingling with the first ones. She picked a stick out of her hair before it impaled her eyeball and considered her options. One, she could show herself in all her disheveled glory and let the tabloids say what they may, or, two, she could wait the suckers out.

They'd fanned out on the far side of the lot, and she crept along the car she was hiding beside as mulled over what to do. She grasped the handle of the next car, but instead of steadying her, it gave way and swung open.

"Son of a peacock!" Helen hissed to herself as her feet shot out from under her, and she slammed onto her back, sliding half under the now open door, staring in shocked surprise at the night sky.

It took a moment for her to take stock of the situation. The icy, gritty ground pressed against her neck and right forearm, and melting snow chilled her bum. Perfect. Just. Flippin'. Perfect.

Who doesn't lock their doors in this day and age?

The open door, though, gave Helen an idea.

As new voices joined those of the paparazzi, Helen made a split-second decision. She scrambled into the open car, snicked the door shut, and crouched low in the back seat. She'd just wait for them to give up then slink back to the inn and put this whole night behind her.

She crouched lower as footsteps neared the car and prayed she was enough out of sight. They wouldn't look *in* the car, would they? Oh, Lordy, they were close though.

The driver's door opened, a backpack landed on the seat inches from her face, and a man sat down with a heavy sigh. He slammed the door shut.

CHAPTER 2

All he wanted was to close his eyes.

Jack Adams muttered to himself about the asshats wandering around like vultures who hadn't had enough excitement for one evening. He hadn't asked what or who they were looking for. He had miles to put between him and this circus, and he wasn't interested in more delays.

He grabbed his keys from the visor, stuck them in the ignition, and allowed himself the luxury of closing his eyes for a moment.

A feather-light touch grazed his shoulder.

Jack's eyes flew open, and he thought he caught a glimpse of movement in the back seat in the rearview mirror. He lurched forward, landed on the horn, then apologized through the windshield to the guy standing fifteen feet away who, no doubt, thought he was an idiot for jumping over a random shadow in the car.

"I'm sorry. I didn't mean to startle you."

Jack lurched again, but he avoided the horn this time.

A woman? A woman was in his car?

Wait…

He tried to turn around, but his seatbelt held him in place.

Her. It was that southern chick who'd lost out to his half-sister on that show. He swung his head back and forth, searching the parking lot for answers. "Why are you in my car? Is this some sort of publicity stunt? Are we being filmed?"

"I sincerely hope not." She laughed weakly. At least he thought it was a laugh. It sounded sort of like a cat with a hairball, dark humor with a hint of hysteria. "No. I promise. I needed some air, but the door was locked…"

"Could we fast-forward to the part where you explain what you're doing in my car?" he said through gritted teeth.

"I'm hiding," she whispered. "I'm Helen Walker, by the way."

"I'd guessed that."

"You're Bailey's brother, right? You work at Lucky's? We've met."

He remembered. It was hard to forget a woman like Helen Walker, especially now that she was crouched in the backseat of his car like a fugitive.

"Anyway, I fell, because your door wasn't locked. And the paparazzi were swarming. So, here I am."

She made it sound like it was his fault she was in his car uninvited.

"Okay," he said. "Get out."

"Now?" she hissed. "Are they gone?"

He watched as several more figures joined the search. "No."

She went silent.

"Well," he said, "you can't stay here. I'm leaving. As in driving away, leaving." He started the engine to prove his point.

"Maybe you could just drive as far as the entrance, so I can get past these guys and get back inside? Would you do that? I'd be so grateful."

Fine.

He nodded, smiled with perverse satisfaction when he blinded one of the guys with his headlights, and pulled out of his spot.

He was promptly blocked by two guys with cameras.

"Hey, have you seen a woman in a white robe?"

He shook his head. Technically, it wasn't a lie. He hadn't seen what she was wearing since seeing her on the live feed playing on the big screen TV at Lucky's Pub less than an hour ago.

"Thanks, man," the guy said.

Jack pulled forward, and the guy's eyes widened with recognition.

"She's here!" he shouted. "In the car! She's in the car!"

Shit.

Jack gunned it, but more figures swarmed into view, blocking the lane beside the inn. He yanked the wheel to the right, gravel spewing as he bumped over potholes behind neighboring buildings then lurched back onto Main Street again.

"What's going on?" Helen asked, her voice a bit panicky.

"They were blocking the road by the inn."

"So, we're driving the opposite direction?"

Emergency vehicles blocked the route through downtown. He took a left, swinging his car back toward the common, around parked vehicles and television production crews.

"Good God. Could you quit swerving?"

"This car doesn't exactly have a small turning radius, Princess."

Dammit.

He looked across the common at the front of the inn where at least a couple dozen people with cameras were positioned as if guarding the gates of the castle. They shouted at him when they recognized his car, which, let's face it, wasn't built to blend in.

He gunned the engine and aimed for his only available exit.

"What are you doing?" she gasped, peering over the back seat.

"Improvising."

"By leaving town?"

"Do you want me to stop now?"

"No," she said, surprising him with her conviction. "Keep going."

"How far?"

She peered through the back window as vehicles pulled out of parking spots to follow them.

"How far do you think? Until we've lost them!"

CHAPTER 3

Jack pulled into an open spot next to a tractor-trailer and cut the engine. He yawned and leaned his head back to look in the rearview mirror. A streetlight illuminated the back seat.

His silver emergency blanket crinkled and lowered, revealing tangled dark hair and wide eyes.

"Did I fall asleep?"

"Yup."

"Champagne does that to me." She yawned widely. "Did we lose them?"

"A while ago."

"What do you mean a while ago?" She looked around. A slight frown marred her beauty queen features. "Where are we?"

"Just outside of Albany."

"New York? Why are we in New York? Why wasn't I consulted about this?"

He shoved open his door. "You were sleeping."

"So, wake me up!"

"I tried. Several times. You sleep like the dead." He peered back in at her from outside. "Consider yourself awake."

She flung her own door open and lurched out far less gracefully than he would have predicted. "You can't just kidnap a person like that and drive them across state lines," she sputtered.

"Technically, you were a stowaway, so…"

"But *New York?*"

He ran an exhausted hand through his hair. "Look. You weren't specific. I was tired and not interested in driving all over creation…"

"So, drive to your *house* or something. I could have had a car from the show come get me there. Why didn't you drive home like a normal person?"

Okay, now he was getting annoyed. He'd done her a favor, and all he was getting was grief?

"Because, Princess, I'm not going home. I tried to tell you that, but you told me to shut up then started snoring again."

She stared at him in horror. "I do *not* snore."

"I beg to differ. Anyway, I'm headed to Pennsylvania for a friend's wedding. Driving you and your hot mess of a drama parade on a detour wasn't part of the itinerary. We're only a few hours outside of Sugar Falls. Just call somebody. I'd love to stay and chat, but I have to use the facilities."

She looked toward the diner, then back at him. "I think I may have to," she motioned with her head, "too."

"Go ahead. Free country and all that." He turned toward the diner.

"Wait. What if somebody recognizes me?"

He sighed. "I doubt the average trucker watches the show."

"You're probably right," she agreed. She shrugged out of his emergency blanket and stuffed it into the back seat. She turned toward him.

He paused. "What in hell are you wearing?"

"I should think it obvious." He stared at the dirty, oversized hotel bathrobe, a silver sequined evening gown peeking from the bottom. "You look like you're on a bender."

"Then I should fit right in at a twenty-four-hour truck-stop diner."

He looked down. "You'll need shoes."

"Oh, Lordy." She turned and bent to retrieve what he guessed were her shoes from the back seat. She struggled to shove her feet into the strappy contraptions while balancing against the side of the car. They weren't the kind of footwear you often saw in late March in New England, but who was he to judge?

He waited while she pulled herself together, and when she seemed done, he strode toward the diner, her little heels clicking on the pavement behind him.

The intermingled scents of coffee and fried food made his stomach growl as he held the door open. Sure, he could have eaten at Lucky's before leaving, but the same menu gets tiresome after a couple or fifteen years. Also, it was nice for someone else to do the cooking for a change.

"Bathrooms are in the back," he said, pointing toward a sign over a hallway on the far end of the restaurant.

Her fingers gripped the edges of her robe a little tighter, and she lifted her chin a fraction before walking ahead of him past the handful of customers seated around the long counter.

17

"No drugs or sex in the bathroom."

Jack paused and swiveled toward the voice. A middle-aged woman stood just behind the counter. The vertical lines of one too many cigarettes framed her lips.

He held his palms up. "No worries. I'm clean."

The waitress motioned with the pot of coffee she held in her hand. "I was talking to her."

"Me?" A squeak came out of the Princess's mouth, her cheeks turning a shade best described as shrimp-stuffed flamingo. Jack almost felt sorry for her. Almost. But this was the same woman who'd stowed away in the back of his car, then snapped at him when he was only trying to rescue her, so the jury was still out.

"I don't do drugs or sex," she said.

"Pity," murmured Jack half to himself as he stifled a chuckle.

She gave him side-eye then brushed a lock of tangled dark hair from her face. "I know this looks... unusual... but I had a flat tire, and this... gentleman... kindly offered to drive me home."

Jack stared at her. Wow. Lying came *super* easy to this chick. "I didn't exactly offer," he corrected.

The waitress frowned. "What's with the bathrobe?"

"I forgot my coat. This was in my luggage. I got it dirty trying to change the tire. But it was complimentary. I didn't steal it. I swear."

The waitress eyed the 'Inn at Sugar Falls' logo on the breast pocket as the Princess not so subtly put her hand over it to hold the lapel closed.

"Five minutes. You two take any longer, I'm calling the cops. We run a clean place here."

Jack gave a mock salute and nudged his stowaway ahead of him. "You're the world's worst liar," he said. "Pro tip: less is more. No one believes you didn't steal that robe."

"I didn't. I swear on my mama's grave. It's not like I've had a chance to return it."

He stopped outside the restroom doors. "So, what's your name again? Hannah? Ellen?"

"Helen."

"Close." They stared at each other a moment, a less than pleasing odor seeping into the hallway from one of the restrooms. "So, ah, Helen, you're not going to need any help in there or anything, are you?"

"Lord, no."

"Good, because I wasn't sure what with the sling and all."

She glanced down as if she'd forgotten she was wearing it. "I bruised my rotator cuff, so keeping it still makes it hurt less, but it's safe to move it. I'm supposed to move it, actually, but the show wanted me to keep the sling on to remind people I'd been hurt."

Jack rocked back on his heels. "Well, four minutes and thirty seconds. I don't think she was kidding."

Helen nodded. When she emerged four minutes and twenty-nine seconds later, she looked slightly less like the woman who'd passed out in his back seat and lightly snored for two hours. She'd obviously washed a few of the dirt smudges from her face and finger-combed her hair. Her robe now belted the other way, half-hiding the logo, and she'd taken off her sling.

He turned toward the restaurant.

"Wait," she said.

He turned back.

"What happens now?" she asked.

"I eat and then I sleep and then I leave."

"But what happens to me?"

He shrugged, exhaustion a physical weight in his bones. "No idea."

Her fingers grabbed his elbow as he moved to walk away again.

"You can't just drive me across state lines and abandon me."

He looked down at her fingers, the knuckles turning white as she dug them into to his shirt. "I fail to see how you stowing away in my car, which has got to be trespassing or something, is in any way my fault or problem."

He found and sat down in a corner booth and pulled a menu from the holder on the wall. She stood above him. "Please take me back. They'll think I ran away."

"Didn't you? Hmm. Home fries and cheese-steak omelet or the Manager's Special?"

"No, I did not. This is all a mistake. People will be worried about me. What time is it, anyway?"

"Manager's Special, it is." He folded the menu and tucked it back in the holder. "Listen. I don't mean to sound unfeeling, but it's been a long night, a long drive, and I did not sign up for the drama that very obviously follows you wherever you go. I apologize for not being predictable, but it wasn't like we had a lot of time to discuss travel plans. I'm headed to a friend's wedding, and if I drove you back to Sugar Falls now, I'd lose a solid day of the few bachelor days he has left." He pulled out his cell phone. "It's two a.m."

She stared at him, aghast, whether at being told 'no' or the time, he wasn't sure.

He handed her his cell phone.

"Thank you." She took it, her tongue darting out to touch her lip as she frowned at the screen. Little worry lines appeared on her forehead.

"What now?" he asked, not really wanting an answer.

"I don't know who to call."

"How about those people you were so concerned would be looking for you?"

Her eyes welled with actual tears. "I don't know their numbers."

"Then call someone else."

She glanced out the windows along the front of the diner, the outside lights creating a cocoon of darkness beyond the edges of the parking lot. "They won't be awake at this hour."

"Then don't call." He waved over the waitress to give his order.

The waitress glared at Helen. "If you ain't eatin' you'll have to leave. No loitering."

Helen slid into the booth opposite Jack, her cheeks hot with color. He placed his order.

"And the lady?" Clearly this was meant as a loosely descriptive term.

Helen clasped her hands on the tabletop. "Just water for me, thank you."

"She'll have scrambled eggs, wheat toast and coffee."

"Or sweet tea if you have it."

The waitress gave Helen a deadpan look. "Coffee it is."

When she'd gone, Helen looked up at Jack. "You don't have to buy me food."

"Do you have cash on you? I thought not."

"It's still awful kind of you."

"Think what you want." He leaned his head back and closed his eyes. "Call your family," he said a few minutes later.

"What?"

He opened one eye. "Just call someone. Anyone. They'll be sending out the National Guard otherwise."

She nodded. A few moments later he heard her soft voice. "Travis? It's me, Helen. Sorry to wake you…. No, I'm fine. I mean, not totally fine. I'm in a bit of a pickle. No, I'm not in jail. Why would you think I'm in jail? I'm in New York. The state, not the city… I don't know the town. No, I'm with someone. Would he let me call you if I were abducted? I don't remember." She covered the phone with her palm. "I'm sorry. What's your name again?"

"Jack," he said.

She put the phone back up to her face. "Jack-something. Yes, I know it's the middle of the night. Could you just contact— No, they don't know

20

I'm here, that's what I'm trying to tell you. I did *not* run away. I'm— *Would you listen?"*

Jack opened his eyes again. Even soft-spoken Helen apparently had her limits.

"I need you to contact the show somehow and let them know I'm safe, and I just need to be picked up." She frowned. "I know full well I signed a contract. Yes, I'm aware of that, too. You make it sound like I did this on purpose. Fine. Please let them know I'll be in touch." She slid the phone across the table.

"Trouble in paradise?"

She let out a huff. "I did not do this on purpose. Why does everyone keep saying that?"

Jack repocketed his phone. "Maybe because it looks really, really suspicious?"

"It's not my fault. People were *chasing me.*"

He shrugged and closed his eyes again. He didn't feel like making chit-chat when he could be sleeping.

The waitress delivered their coffee and tossed a handful of creamers onto the table from the bottom of her apron. Jack ignored them and took a tentative sip. Hot. Hot, but good. He glanced at his companion. She sat with arms hugging herself, staring at the coffee.

"Sweet tea isn't a thing around here, you know that, right?" He ventured another sip.

Her eyes met his. "I'm aware."

"Do you not like coffee or something?"

"I like coffee. I just can't drink it. It stains my teeth."

"That's what toothpaste is for."

"Do you know how many people in this country see my teeth on a weekly basis?"

He rolled his eyes and was saved from further ridiculousness by the waitress delivering their food. She set the plates down and squinted at Helen. "Don't I know you from somewhere?"

Helen turned a little gray. "I'm not from around here."

"I could swear you look familiar."

"I have one of those faces."

Jack stifled a bark of laughter. Helen having "one of those faces" was the biggest lie yet. She had the face of a Greek goddess all wide, dark eyes and classic features. There was nothing forgettable about her. At all.

The waitress *humphed* and walked away.

"That was close." Helen shifted away from the other customers, as if turning her back would hide the fact that there was a gorgeous brunette in

21

a silver evening gown and hotel bathrobe at a truck stop at two-thirty in the morning. "And you said no one would recognize me."

He dug into his omelet. "My bad."

CHAPTER 4

They ate in silence, Helen finally caving in and taking a few sips of bitter coffee. She didn't care to antagonize the waitress by asking for a glass of water, too. That nasty woman would probably spit in it.

Jack's fork clattered onto his empty plate. He glanced up. "Done?"

"Yes. Thank you."

He flipped over the slip the waitress had left on the end of their table and drew a few bills out of his wallet. "Well, good luck to you."

"You're leaving?"

"We've been over this. Yes." He scooted toward the outside of the booth and heaved a sigh. "Look, I'm sympathetic, but it's been a long night."

"Y'all think you've had a long night? I've been hog-tied into this dress for more hours than I can count. That was the first actual meal I've had since yesterday morning. I've been paraded on live national television in frigid temperatures while I watched your sister get engaged, and now I'm expected to not make waves and smile sweetly while riding up and down the coast in a penis-mobile!" She couldn't believe she'd uttered that out loud, but Lord forgive her, she was tired of filtering every last word she breathed.

He paused, clearly thrown by her outburst. "I'm sorry. A what?"

"*The Trojan Bus of Love.* Marcia's decided she wants to shake things up this season, so she's having me pick up men in a gold-colored bus in every city from here to Alabama."

He actually laughed. "That's awesome."

"No. It's horrifying. It's demeaning. It's… sweet mother of sunshine," she took a breath, "it's what's going to happen. There's no getting out of it, is there? I'll have to do this."

"Oh, well."

"Oh, well? *Oh, well?* That's all you have to say? You're the reason I'm here right now, and all you have to say is, 'Oh, well?'"

23

"Seems to me you don't exactly want to be *there* either, so... you're welcome."

He ran a hand through the too-long dark-blonde shock of hair that habitually fell into his vision. "Though I don't suppose I blame you for getting cold feet. It can't be easy being dumped on national television."

Finally, a bit of compassion. "No. It's not."

"I wouldn't stress about it. You can take your pick of the hottest dumb guys from here to Miami, write a best-selling book about your experience and have a gaggle of gorgeous, low-IQ babies with him."

She felt her mouth flop open.

He smirked.

"This isn't funny," she said.

"Hell, yeah, it is."

She shimmied out of the booth and stood before him, back straight and head high. "I don't know why I thought you would help."

"That makes two of us, sweetheart."

She watched him stride toward the exit before she realized he meant it. He really and truly meant to leave. *Without her.*

"Wait." She hurried after him, hating herself for the tight grasp she already had on his elbow. "Do you think I want to be in this position? I don't belong here. I can't breathe here. My lungs physically hurt from the cold. This... the show... the paparazzi... it's gotten out of control." She couldn't quite hide the catch that halted her words.

"Look. I'm sorry the fame is wearing thin, but no one forced you to go on the show. Or sign on for more of it. No one can *make* you ride in a penis-mobile unless you agree to it."

He was right. Helen hated to admit it, but he was absolutely right.

She didn't have to go back—not if he'd take her with him.

She dropped her grip on his arm. "Take me with you," she said.

Jack let out one startled bark of laughter, then sobered. "You're kidding." He pushed open the diner door.

Helen avoided eye contact with the squat, unshaven man on a nearby stool, and hurried to catch up. "Why not?"

He didn't even have the decency to look at her to reply. "Because, you're a needy, hot mess, that's why."

She squared her shoulders and hissed at his retreating back. "You think you've got me pegged, don't you? You think you know all there is to know about me from what you've seen on TV, but you'd be wrong." She raised her chin, her throat tight. "You'd be dead wrong."

She was a second away from letting the door swing shut between them, her dignity held together by a thread, when his palm shot out to hold it open. His voice slammed into her low and lazy.

"Would I?" His eyes slid down her like a knife blade. "You're a southern pageant girl who hates the cold, wants everyone to like her, and has had everything handed to her on a silver platter including the business that made her famous enough to catch the eye of the *Happily Ever After* casting agents. Except you can't quite put your finger on why your life isn't all you'd hoped for, so you ditched your boyfriend and your employees and signed up for a reality dating show only to realize that real life is real life even when it's on fake TV. Then, when your would-be fiancé up and fell in love with someone else, it made you doubt yourself and your looks and your worth because you are, by all accounts, perfect in every conceivable way, and while you've put on a brave face and tried to appear serene about it all for the cameras, you're reeling inside. So now you're embarrassed and you want to quit, because you've looked in the mirror and realized that no amount of makeup can hide those dark circles under yours eyes, but the last thing you want is to do the walk of shame all the way back to Georgia in yesterday's evening gown or on a gold bus, so you ran away the first opportunity you got, counting on your southern charm to bend me around your pinky finger. Am I right?"

Her hand rose to touch the area under her eyes before she forced it to drop, emotion hot in her gut. "Alabama," she said.

"What?"

"I'm from Alabama, not Georgia."

He had the nerve to shrug. "Accent sounds the same to me."

He let the door swing closed between them.

Her breath came short and fast as she watched his retreating backside through the glass. *How dare he?* She yanked tight the collar of her robe, too many unladylike retorts fighting for permission to hurl themselves through his cruel, cold-blooded, smirking heart.

"For your information," she said, shoving the door open and running around to stand in front of him. "I do not have a boyfriend. I would never have gone on the show if I had."

He stared at her. Assessing. Her eyelids twitched. Fine. Perhaps that wasn't the most cutting thing she could have come back with, but she was fired up, and the words were all crashing into each other in her brain.

"Well," he drawled, "surprises never cease."

He shrugged and brushed by her, the heat and scent of his body tumbling through her senses along with the adrenaline he'd worked up with his hateful speech.

His hateful, spot-on speech.

"That's it? You insult me and then walk away? You are a horrible man," she breathed. "With no compassion or common decency."

"Then why would you want to spend another second in my company?"

"I don't."

He nodded, gave a mock, two-fingered salute and closed the distance between him and his car.

Her heart hammered in her chest. Anger mixed with nausea in her gut as she looked up at the pitch-black sky. She hadn't felt this alone since her mom had gone to live with Jesus.

She pressed her lips together to still them. For weeks after her mother's death, folks kept asking her what she planned next, as if she'd been able to envision a future without her mother in it and had only been waiting on her calendar to open up to get on with life.

"I don't know what comes next," she whispered aloud, horrified she'd just admitted such a secret truth in front of this man who clearly didn't care.

She hugged herself, gutted, as she stared at his rigid back. He had the door of his car open. She breathed in the cold night air, a panic attack one heartbeat away. She wasn't even sure he'd heard.

"Look," he said, more softly now but without turning around. "I don't know what you want me to say. If you're looking for somebody who can save you, you've got the wrong guy. Just go back in and call somebody to pick you up."

She took a step closer. "If I go back in there and ask for a ride, that waitress will figure out who I am. Do you know what they'll do to me in the tabloids if they find out I—"

"Ran away?" he asked over the open driver's side door.

"You know it wasn't like that."

"Look, I'm exhausted, so I'm going to get in my car, close my eyes, take a nap, and be on my merry way. You're a big girl. You can fend for yourself."

She watched, aghast, as he got in and closed the car door.

"I'll pay you."

He rolled down the window. "What?"

"I said, I'll pay you."

"You'll pay me," he repeated, as if she was shaking him down instead of offering him money.

"Fifty dollars," she said.

He looked at her, his cool blue eyes skimming over her like she was a slightly bruised peach at the grocery. "I'm not driving all the way back to Sugar Falls and definitely not for fifty bucks."

"You don't have to take me back. Just don't leave me *here*. You know that waitress will figure out who I am, and the crazy will start all over again."

He let out a long breath while Helen held her own hostage in her chest. "You're not that famous," he said. Then he started rolling up the window.

"Five hundred," she gasped, grabbing the open pane with her freezing fingers. "Please." She forced the word through her lips, because of course this wretched night would end with her literally begging a virtual stranger not to leave her stranded in a skanky truck-stop parking lot. "At least take me someplace I can have a moment to catch my breath."

His mouth was a flat line as he stared at her, his blue eyes unreadable. For a second she wondered if he'd close her fingers in the window. She wouldn't put it past him. "Get in," he finally said.

She scrambled around the front of the car and into the passenger seat before he could change his mind, her dignity trampled shreds at her feet.

"Of course, I can't pay you up front on account of my not having a purse or anything."

He rolled his eyes.

She avoided his gaze as she pulled her seatbelt into place and buckled in. It was one of those old-fashioned kind that only went across your lap. Her heart pounded a thousand beats per minute. Relief and anxiety and excitement warred within her. This all felt adventurous and a little bit wrong and the part of her that had always, always done the expected felt a teeny bit triumphant in an utterly exhausted sort of way.

She risked a glance over at him. He had his head resting on the seat back, his arms crossed, and his eyes closed.

"Aren't we leaving?" she asked.

"I need to rest my eyes for a bit."

"I just offered you five hundred dollars to take me out of here."

"I will."

"When?"

"Do you want me to fall asleep at the wheel? When I'm not so tired."

"When do you suppose that will be?"

"No time soon unless you stop jabbering."

She clamped her lips shut and hugged herself. "Could you at least run the engine? It's freezing in here."

He rolled his head to look at her. "Where do you expect me to go? I can't drive without sleep."

"There must be a hotel nearby."

"I'm not paying for a hotel."

"I'll pay for it."

He jammed the keys in the ignition and started the car. "Let me guess. You'll owe me for that, too."

She didn't answer. Why argue when he was right?

Twenty minutes later, they pulled into a nearly empty parking lot.

"Here?" she asked, looking at the dingy sign reading 'Shady Greens Motel.' It looked more shady than green. Several cars huddled together as if for warmth.

"It has a vacancy."

"Shocker."

He laughed. "There's also free wifi and a twenty-four-hour front desk. It's three in the morning. I'm not driving any further."

Dear sweet God in heaven. She was at a motel in a town she couldn't identify with a man she didn't know. The enormity of the poor life choices she'd managed to string together in one evening finally hit home.

"May I borrow your cell phone?" she asked.

He wordlessly handed it to her then opened his door.

She got out, took photos of the car, the license plate, and the motel sign, punched in some numbers, then handed it back to him.

His jaw hung open. "Seriously? People are going to think I abducted you for real. Who did you send those to?"

"My business partner. And he already knows you haven't abducted me, because I told him so."

"If a S.W.A.T. team breaks down the door, I'm using you as a human shield."

"Fair enough."

A few minutes later, he'd obtained a key from the office for the unit on the far end of the building. Helen followed him into the room and stopped short. She hadn't seen this much harvest gold upholstery since watching re-runs of *The Brady Bunch* as a kid. "Thank you. I'll be sure to come get you when I wake up."

He closed the door. "No need. You want window or door side? I'm not picky."

"This isn't a romance novel. We are not sleeping in the same bed."

"You can sleep on the floor for all I care, but I'm not paying for a bed I'm not sleeping in. I'll take the window." He sat on the edge of said bed to take off his shoes.

"You're not paying for the bed. I am. If it weren't for me, you'd be sleeping in your car right now."

"If it weren't for you, I'd actually be sleeping. My credit card. My bed. Trust me, Princess, I'm too tired to be any danger to you even if I wanted to be. Which I don't."

He leaned back, fully clothed, and stretched out on top of the covers. He crossed his legs at the ankle, folded his hands behind his head and closed his eyes.

Her feet felt glued to the fraying carpet beneath them. She supposed she had two choices: sleep standing up or trust him to continue to be the uninterested jerk he'd shown himself to be thus far.

She carefully pulled off her shoes, turned up the thermostat, and slid under the covers, facing away from him. She heard a soft snore from his side of the bed then closed her eyes and fell asleep.

CHAPTER 5

"Wake up. Time to get moving."

Helen turned toward the voice. "What time is it?"

"Time to roll."

She pushed herself upright and blinked against the light from the window. A carton of powdered doughnuts and a couple of to-go cups sat on the small desk. "Are we on some sort of schedule? I didn't think check-out was until eleven."

Jack stood at the window overlooking a scraggly patch of woods and bit into a powdered donut. White speckles littered his dark tee like confetti.

"I don't like the look of the forecast. I want to keep ahead of this storm system."

Helen swiped a hand down her face and found one of her false eyelashes stuck to her cheek. Lovely. "I'll just use the ladies' room if that's all right by you."

"Have at it. I've already showered."

And dressed. And gone out and back. Apparently, she'd slept through it all. She'd always been a deep sleeper, but this was ridiculous.

She clicked the bathroom door shut behind her and waited for her eyes to adjust to the light. *Oh, sweet mother of sunshine.* She stared in horror at her reflection. Glittered eye shadow formed raccoon-like circles around her eyes, her other eyelash was nowhere to be found, and her hair stood out like she'd been caught in the rain without her Aqua Net. One hair extension dangled raggedly from the side of her head. So much for worrying she might tempt him to act ungentlemanly. She was lucky he hadn't run screaming for the hills.

She grabbed a washcloth and set to work.

When she emerged a few minutes later, she'd scrubbed her face clean, carefully unclipped her hair extensions and tucked them into her robe pocket, and finger-combed the rest as best she could. Jack stood at the window, a frown sharpening his features. He glanced up and stared.

"What?" she said.

His frown deepened. "You look…"

"What?"

"I don't know. Normal. I mean, like a regular person."

"As opposed to?"

"Fake."

Gee, thanks.

He squinted. "Didn't you have more hair before?"

"Extensions," she mumbled. "They itch. I took them out." She skittered a palm over her head hoping the thinning patches that had developed from the stress of filming weren't showing.

He nodded, his continued assessment making her nerves dance. "I like you more this way."

She frowned. No one had asked for his opinion.

He held out the box. "Doughnut?"

There was no telling the next time she'd have a chance to eat, so she took the few steps toward him and peered in.

"Go ahead. I won't put it on your tab."

She glanced up at him. Bright blue eyes met hers. She couldn't tell if he was joking or not. "Thank you," she said, pinching a doughnut between her fingers and cupping her other hand beneath it.

She took a bite, powdered sugar poofing into the air and sprinkling to the carpet.

He wiped sugar off his shirt with his palm. The movement drew her eyes to his chest and the way his throat moved when he spoke. "So," he said, leaning back against the window ledge, "what now?"

She brushed the corners of her mouth and looked away. *Good question.*

"I don't know. I hadn't thought further than getting out of there."

"Not to point out the obvious, but that seems to be a recurring theme with you."

"If you're looking for your money, I've already said I don't have it on me."

He held up a hand. "Don't get your panties in a twist. I'm not going to hold you to it, but I'm leaving, and it's my credit card paying for this room. So, figure out how you're getting home, because you can't stay here."

Helen swallowed, the dry doughnut threatening to stick in her throat. She picked up the other coffee and took a sip.

"Where are you going again?" she asked, stalling for time.

"Pennsylvania. I have a friend getting married a week from Friday, so no matter what, I've got to hit the road." He held out his cell phone. "Just call the show and tell them to send someone to pick you up."

"It's not like Marcia Powers has her cell number in the directory."

"Call the inn, then."

She took the phone, searched for the number of the Inn at Sugar Falls and dialed. She sat heavily on the edge of the bed. Someone picked up. Helen asked to be put through to Ivy, Marcia's assistant. She was connected almost immediately.

"Yes?"

"Ivy, this is Helen."

Helen heard a sharp intake of breath. "*Oh. My. God.* What the hell are you trying to do to me? I'm literally dying here, Helen. D-Y-I-N-G."

"Marcia?"

"Damn straight. You've gotten Ivy in enough trouble."

"I'm so sorry." Helen moved toward the door so Jack wouldn't hear Marcia scolding her like a child.

"You should be." Marcia spewed a string of curse words then took an audible deep breath. "First you disappear, and we think you've been kidnapped, and then your family calls to tell us you've called them and accidentally driven to... where the hell are you?"

"New York."

"Who accidentally drives to New York? How does that even happen? No. Don't tell me. I don't even care right now."

"It was cold. I got locked out. The pap—"

"Whatever. I've sent a car to get you. Should be there any minute. You get in it and get your ass back here, and we'll forget any of this ever happened."

"But you don't know where I am," Helen said. "*I* don't even know where I am."

"Are you drunk? High? You sent pictures of the motel to that Travis of yours and he had the good sense to forward them to us. Are you sure you're not kidnapped? Because I'd forgive you if you were. Say pizza if you're in trouble."

Helen glanced up. Jack stood at the far window facing out. She'd surely inconvenienced him enough.

"It wasn't on purpose. I swear."

"Just get in the car and get back here. And for the love of God, don't let any more paparazzi see you."

"I understand. Again, I'm so sorry."

The line went dead.

Jack turned toward her. "Well?"

She avoided eye contact, instead letting her gaze slip away from his, her attention skimming over the day-old stubble that roughened his cheeks, the light smear of confectioner's sugar like a jet stream across his chest.

She thought about the car coming to retrieve her. Marcia's barely suppressed anger. It made her pulse lurch wildly. She'd agreed to appear on the show to get away and clear her head and see the world, but now she felt more trapped than ever. As soon as she returned to Sugar Falls, the clock would start ticking.

She'd have eight weeks of filming, a month or two of promotional commitments, and then it would be over. She'd be home again. Forever.

Helen had no illusions she'd meet the man of her dreams on reality TV. It had never been about that anyway. She'd jumped at the chance to get out and experience new adventures, and Travis had seemed excited for the publicity. He wanted to take the bakeries national, he said. Helen's job was to get folks excited about franchising, then go home, settle down, make babies, and have the life everyone always wanted for her.

Everyone, that is, except for her.

She'd been raised in a community that took care of its own, and there was nothing they wanted more than to take care of sweet, motherless Helen Walker. She'd make them beautiful grandchildren and would sit on all their beautification committees and bake the *best* cakes for church suppers. Everyone wanted her to find Mr. Right, and if he didn't exist out there, why, hadn't Travis Dean always said he'd do right by her if she let him?

She could go home, find her place in Heaven and blend so seamlessly into the fabric of their shared lives she wouldn't know where they ended and she began. Just part of the fabric. Just a thread woven into history like family names in a Bible.

The thing about threads is you never noticed them until one of them snagged and pulled out of place. The question was, now that she'd been snagged, would she let them—Marcia, Travis, Ivy, Iris—smooth her back in place, or would she snip herself free?

Free.

Maybe climbing into Jack's car wasn't an accident. Maybe it was fate.

Her mother had always insisted there were no accidents in life. Everything happens for a reason. Helen had struggled with that. What reason could there be to strike down a mother in her prime? What greater plan could possibly include cancer and grief and a lonely teen who only ever wanted to eat a cupcake without everyone around her second-guessing that she was eating her feelings? Sometimes you just wanted a damn cupcake.

Well. Even if she didn't believe in fate, Helen believed in opportunity. She held out Jack's cell phone.

"Are they coming?" he asked.

Her tongue darted out to her lips to smooth the way for the words she was about to speak. Her gaze met Jack's then bounced away. "I'm afraid not."

He swore. "What?"

"Marcia said, 'You got yourself into this, you can get yourself out.' She said I need to find my own way home to… to Alabama." Helen's cheeks grew hot and she held her breath, pressing her lips together, waiting for him to call her out on her lie, to smooth her back into place.

"Your own way home?" He muttered several unflattering things which Marcia probably deserved at some point in history but hadn't earned in this particular instance. "Unbelievable." He shoved a hand through the shock of hair that kept falling into his eyes and pinned Helen with his ice-blue gaze. "So now you become my problem? Is that it?"

"I don't want to burden you."

He gestured toward her. "Like I can leave you on the side of the road dressed like that."

Guilt made her fidget. She sent a silent prayer to Jesus to forgive her for lying, but really, it wasn't like she was murdering or committing adultery or anything. She mentally reviewed the commandments. Surely the Lord would forgive her for fibbing when the alternative was driving up and down the coast in a gold-encrusted traveling monument to sex.

She thought about going home, the unendurable mix of sympathetic words and unspoken I-told-you-so's dogging her every step for having dared to buck the status quo to go on a—gasp—dating show. She knew the old ladies were just lining up to shake their heads and mutter how being dumped on national TV was clearly God's commentary on her life choices.

She didn't want anyone's sympathy or self-righteousness. She just wanted to be left alone. To lick her wounded ego and figure out what came next when despite all the advantages in life, she'd found herself like a boomerang hurling itself into the sky but always destined to return where it started from.

If she had to do the show, she'd do it on her own terms, and that did not include a bus of love no matter what the color. When she was ready, she'd call Marcia back. The show could just as easily pick her up in Pennsylvania as here. And it wasn't as if she was inconveniencing Jack. She wasn't even asking him to go out of his way.

He'd probably welcome the company.

She swallowed, blinked rapidly, and forced a tear pooling in her eye to spill onto her cheek.

"Oh, Chr— Don't do that. Don't go and get all weepy. I'm not an absolute ass."

"I never said you were." Another tear slid followed the first and she swiped at it for dramatic effect. The tears were real, born mostly out of frustration, but she wasn't above using them.

He grabbed the box of tissues off the desk and shoved it toward her. "Fine. Until you can figure something else out, you can ride with me."

"Thank you." She dabbed her eyes with the scratchy corner of a tissue as relief swarmed her.

"For now."

"I never meant for any of this to happen," she said.

"Your kind never does."

She didn't ask him to elaborate. She knew what he meant.

A few minutes later, she hurried across the empty parking lot to Jack's car as he returned their room key. A steely gray sky obscured the sun and chilled her to the core as she pulled open the passenger door. Her heart slammed against her ribs as she buckled, silently imploring him to hurry and be on their way.

Instead, he strode toward the car, squinting at a sky that didn't even have the decency to let a ray of warming sun through. He opened the back door and rummaged in his hiking pack for a couple of minutes before pulling a very wrinkled flannel shirt out. He shrugged into it, then slid behind the wheel.

He pulled out his phone to set it between them.

"Can I borrow this?" she asked. "To navigate."

"I know the way once I find the interstate."

"I can keep an eye on the weather."

"Sure." He shrugged and started the car.

His phone was still warm from where it had been stored in his back pocket. Her mind helpfully conjured the memory of the outline of this very phone in Jack's back pocket as he'd walked away from her with that lanky cowboy swagger the night before. She wondered if he'd ever ridden a horse. She imagined he'd look good on one. Her fingers curled around the phone before the thinking part of her brain caught up and froze in shock. She dropped the phone into her lap, aghast at her reaction and glanced over to see if he'd noticed. What sort of woman would be attracted to *him?*

Surely, she was overtired. That must be it.

"Ready?" he asked again.

She nodded, afraid she'd blurt out the truth if she opened her lips. That she'd lied. That Jack had come closer to knowing the truth about her than even her own family. That in their brief acquaintance, some primitive part of her had responded to his whisking her away from, if not, physical danger, at least psychological discomfort, and had formed an unholy attraction to gruff men in flannel shirts.

How had it come to this? How did someone like her—successful entrepreneur, Helen Walker of Heaven, Alabama—end up at a seedy motel in a stained evening gown admiring the ass of a man who openly disliked her? Never in her life had she felt so confused and alone.

Surely, he *must* know. He couldn't actually believe that Marcia would leave her to fend for herself. She was the lead of the season! The central character of a popular franchise with scores of employees. He couldn't really believe Marcia would leave her return to chance, could he?

And yet, he seemed to. Helen watched as he glanced up and down the near empty road, his mouth a grim line as he pulled the car out of the parking lot. She stilled and held her breath tight in her chest.

A black SUV with rear-tinted windows passed them going in the opposite direction.

She picked up Jack's phone and muted it.

His lips twisted to one side and he met her gaze briefly before turning his attention back to the road. "Warm enough?" he asked.

Helen let the air seep out of her lungs. "Yes, thank you."

A crease appeared near his right eye, and he flashed a small grin. "That would ring a little more true if your lips weren't turning blue."

"I meant, I'll be fine."

"Once the engine warms up, I'll get you some heat."

"Thank you." She touched his arm and offered a light squeeze of gratitude. His eyes flew to hers. "I'm sorry. I forget you northerners don't like to be touched."

His eyebrow lifted a tiny fraction, but he didn't say anything, just moved his arm from under her hand to fiddle with a knob on the dashboard.

She turned toward the side window before he could see her eyes well with real tears this time. Lordy, she was a mess. She shouldn't think of this as an escape. It was merely a reprieve. Soon enough, it would all catch up with her.

"Is this our turn?" Jack's voice startled her from her thoughts.

She peered out the window. "Yes. Yes, turn here."

"I thought you were navigating. I don't want to end up in Canada."

"Is that even possible? I don't have my passport."

He flashed her a small smile. "Relax. I'm kidding. We're hours from the border."

"Oh."

Rain spat at the windshield. Jack turned on the wipers. He flashed her another not-quite-smile. "For the record," he said, "I would have done it for fifty."

CHAPTER 6

Helen shifted in her seat. Jack hadn't said a word for miles. She wouldn't even know he was breathing except for the fact he hadn't passed out.

Meanwhile, all she seemed to be able to focus on was her own respiration. She practiced the conscious inhalations and exhalations the way Mrs. Greenbow, her pageant coach, had taught her to do. *In. Hold. Out. Hold. In. Hold. Out. Hold. Oxygenate your brain. Stand straight, neck long, shoulders soft. Show me that smile. There ya go, honey…*

Helen stared, unseeing at the passing scenery. She had no idea where they were going aside from some town in Pennsylvania and no sense of how long it would take to get there. Everything north of Virginia was smushed together in a mental map of "north" populated by dots you reached via plane called "New York," "Chicago," and "Boston."

"How long until we get there?" she asked.

Brilliant blue eyes pivoted her way, dropping to the phone in her lap, before focusing back on the road. "Hours."

Right. She was meant to use technology rather than speak with a live person? "I know how to use a map, but that doesn't tell me how many rest stops you plan to take."

"Only those that are necessary. Why? Do you have to…?"

"*No.* No." She'd only wanted to fill the silence, not discuss bathroom needs. "I meant. It's a long drive, and you might want to stretch your legs."

"We've been on the road all of twenty minutes. I'm good."

She rolled her shoulder a bit to ease the ache that seemed to settle in with inactivity and turned toward the side window again. She didn't do well with awkward silences. There was too much time to think. Her stomach growled audibly.

Jack's lips pursed with laughter. "There's a protein bar in the glove box. Have at it."

"I'll be fine."

Her stomach disagreed.

"I'm sorry." She rummaged for the protein bar, tore it open, and took a bite.

She chewed and swallowed politely.

"It's been in there a while," he said, his lips curving. "You don't have to finish it if it's no good."

"It's fine," she lied, taking a second bite to prove it.

"You're practically gagging."

"It's just a little stale."

"When did it expire?"

She peered at the wrapper. "Three years ago? I've had worse." Bits of protein bar crumbled on her tongue. Great. Now she was thirsty.

He snatched the bar out of her hands and tossed it over his shoulder into the back seat. "I didn't think it was that old."

"It was fine."

He gave her a look. "Spit it into a napkin. You're turning green around the gills."

She gamely tried to swallow, failed. "A lady never spits," she said, holding her palm over her mouth in case her body forcefully rejected the rancid crumbs knocking against her teeth.

Jack's leg tensed as he slammed the brake and pulled to the side of the road. "Spit it out."

She opened the door before they were even fully stopped.

A few moments later, satisfied her gag reflex wouldn't betray her, she settled in her seat again. He handed her a water bottle. "You should have said something."

"And be told I'm a stuck-up Princess? No thanks."

"I suppose I deserve that." He cleared his throat. He flashed her a wry grin. "Start over?"

"I'd rather not relive any part of the last few weeks if it's all the same to you, but thanks for the water." She swished and swallowed.

He chuckled, a warm, lively sound like the crackle of a fire. She hated that she liked it. "I guess I don't blame you." His gaze raked over her, and she felt every inch of her too-tight gown. "If it helps, you handled it well. Kept it classy."

"Did I have a choice? I wasn't going to spit it out onto your dashboard."

"I was talking about the last few weeks, and yes, you always have a choice." He pulled the car back onto the road.

She wished she believed that. She wished it felt that way and her life didn't feel so predetermined she could already have her headstone engraved save for the date.

"You chose to go on the show. To hide in my car." His lips tilted. "To steal a bathrobe."

"I did not... Ah. You're making a joke again, aren't you? Anyway, it's not as if I can undo any of it."

"As my dad once said, 'You can't undo stupid choices, but you can choose not to repeat them.'" He grinned. "I was barely eighteen when he shared that little nugget, but it's stood the test of time, don't you think?"

She nodded. "*Mmm.*"

"It wasn't a dissimilar situation," he said. "I'd run away, too."

She glanced at him. He didn't seem to be joking anymore. She wasn't sure how to follow that up. "You've gotten chatty all of a sudden."

"Have I?"

"Yes."

He glanced at the road. "Thinking, I guess."

They road in silence for a bit.

"Why did you go back? To the show?" he asked. "After Ian dumped you the first time, why put yourself through it all again? Chances weren't high he'd reconsider. You're smart enough to know that."

Gee, he didn't think she was a complete idiot. "I was under contract. We're paid for every episode we appear in." She shrugged and winced as her shoulder tightened. "I never expected to get back together with Ian."

"No?"

"No."

"So, you did it for the money."

"No. I mean, yes, money is great, but unless you're the lead, it doesn't pay that much. I did it mainly for the experience and exposure."

"Ah. To build your personal 'brand.'" He used air quotes. How irritating.

"No, for my *business*. My partner and I have been talking about taking the bakeries national. Offering franchises. The show seemed a chance to gain name recognition, explore our options going forward."

"That's a relief. Thinking you'll find your husband on reality TV seems pathetic. No offense."

Helen forced a smile. *Offense taken.* "I suppose it does."

His eyes widened a fraction. "Jesus. You thought you would."

"No. I mean, sure, it's possible. It's happened for other couples."

"Yeah, it *could* happen, but it's not likely. Even if you look like you."

She laughed without humor. "Thanks."

"It takes more than a few weeks to fall for someone."

"An intense environment like the show accelerates feelings. Some say a month on the show is like a year of dating in the real world. And you can't argue the show's track record. Even Ian ended up engaged. Just not to me."

"Being engaged doesn't mean a couple will end up together in the long run."

"You don't think Ian and Bailey will marry?"

"I do, but they come from the same town. They have a lot more in common than most couples on that show. It's not like expecting you and me to get together because we're both hot. It's not how things work."

She choked on her own surprise. Did he just say she was hot? "You think you're hot?" she said, instead.

He slanted those baby blues her way. Damn him. He knew he was good looking. "You looking for receipts? Because I've got receipts."

"No... That's... I believe you."

His tongue darted to his lips.

Helen blew out. *Exhale. Hold. Inhale. Hold.*

"But, seriously, isn't that what the show does? Throws together a bunch of attractive people hoping sparks fly and not worrying if they have anything in common, just playing the numbers game?" he asked.

"How do you know we don't have anything in common? We don't know each other well enough to say that. I don't even know what your hair feels like."

She swallowed the rest of that thought, because, let's be honest, she had no idea where that was going. "I mean," she stammered, "there are a thousand little details we don't know about each other, and knowledge builds intimacy, and that's what the show does." She ended it in a rush of word salad.

He looked at her, then back at the road, then back at her. "Touch my hair then."

"What?"

"Touch my hair. Then you'll know."

"You're driving."

"Too much intimacy?" he taunted.

She reached out and smoothed the hair above his ear. *Silky.* She pulled back her hand and pressed it to the seat.

"So, does this mean we're engaged?" he asked, slanting her a sly grin. "Because I kind of liked it."

"You're making fun of me."

"A little."

"That what just an example. Yes, the challenges force couples to get to know those details quickly, which weeds out chemistry mismatches, but it's not just a bunch of hot people thrown together.

"Before we're even cast, we have to complete compatibility questionnaires, criminal background checks, health screenings. They even want your credit score to know how much debt you carry."

"Weeding out the criminals and grifters... how romantic."

"All I'm saying is it isn't as random as throwing a bunch of horny people together."

"*Mmm*," he said. "Which would make for riveting TV, but that's not what your show claims to deliver, all 'lasting love' and all."

She slid him side-eye. "My parents met as counselors at a youth camp. They got engaged a month after they met, married six months later, and they were together until the day she died. People can fall fast under the right circumstances. It's not unheard of."

A small pulse throbbed at the base of his throat. She watched the subtle movement out of the corner of her eye.

"Maybe that's the exception to the rule," she continued, "but why couldn't I be the exception? Why couldn't you? Why should we just accept that life sucks and then you die?"

"Says the woman in a dirty bathrobe on a random road trip with a stranger."

She squared her shoulders. "I am rocking this look."

He laughed, and it seeped past her defenses to warm the cold places inside her. "Damn right, you are," he said.

"No one can do miserable better than a beauty queen on the run."

"The Runaway Cupcake Queen does have a certain ring to it."

"Not that I'm running," she corrected. "Because I'm not."

"Right." His grin faded. "About that..."

Helen stilled.

"One way or another, we're going to have to work out what happens at the end of this. Pennsylvania isn't Alabama."

"I know." She just needed time to regroup. To talk to her family. To figure out what day of the week it was and renegotiate a few things with the show. "I'll make some calls. You don't have to worry about me."

He looked doubtful but let it go.

She rested her head on the seatback, looked out the window, and pretended she had a plan.

She must have fallen asleep, because she woke to a drumming rainfall, the drops sliding diagonally across her side window. Jack turned up the wipers. It was then she saw the tiny ice crystals accumulating on the edge of the windshield. She sat up straighter.

"You're awake? Good. Would you mind checking the temperature?"

"I'm sorry?"

"Check the weather app on my phone. I want to know how close to freezing we're getting." He cursed under his breath. "I was hoping we'd outrun this."

Helen didn't need to ask what he meant. The large purple and blue amoeba on the radar map on his phone weather app told her all she needed to know about what they were unlikely to outrun.

"How bad are the roads?" she asked.

"Not great." His eyes sliced her way, the same blue that'd been on the radar. "We should probably find a place to wait it out."

"Of course." Visions of jack-knifed tractor-trailers and massive traffic pileups from voyeuristic watching of the Weather Channel flashed across her mind. The first snow she'd ever seen was a catastrophic dusting on I-75.

He took the next exit, which appeared to be positioned exactly in the middle of nowhere.

"Take a right," she said. "I see a sign for a coffee place."

"You don't drink coffee."

"No, but that tells me there's enough of a population density for services."

"Good thinking."

"Don't sound so surprised."

He didn't apologize, just flashed her a smile and fiddled with the defroster knob.

"Watch out," she cried.

She pointed as a deer bounded in front of the car traveling in front of them. The car managed to avoid the deer, but fishtailed, swerved wildly, then bounced into the ditch at the side of the road.

Jack swore under his breath as he drove past.

"Pull over. Pull over," she cried, smacking him on the shoulder with her hand. "It's old people."

"I see," he said. "Stop hitting me. I can't just slam my brakes. It's icy." He eased the car to a stop and unbuckled.

"I'll go, too," she said. "They'll be less worried being approached by a woman."

"I'm not going to mug them."

"I didn't say that, but they don't know you." She pushed open her door. Sleet stabbed her cheeks as she tugged the robe's collar up around her face. "Smile," she prompted as they made their way back down the road. "Don't look so…"

"Myself? Got it."

Jack took her elbow to steady her, and Helen's heart rose in her throat as they approached the car lodged at an angle in the ditch, the passenger door shoved tight against the embankment.

The driver's window eased open, and Helen bent down to peer into the car. She gasped, her hand flying to her mouth at the sight of the gooey, red mass splattered across the dashboard and inside of the windshield.

"Oh my God," she breathed.

Jack peered over her shoulder and winced. "What a waste."

An older woman in the passenger seat held a large foil baking pan aloft, her eyes wide with shock. "I tried to hold it," she said, "but he swerved to avoid the deer, then we bounced…"

The man in the driver's seat grunted. "I told you to put it in the trunk."

The woman glared at the man. "The way you drive?"

"I'm not the one wearing a tray of lasagna."

"If you hadn't slammed the brakes, I'd be fine."

"I'm not about to hit a deer. Carl's collection is big enough."

"Don't make jokes at a time like this."

"His whole life was a joke."

Jack glanced back at his own car. "So, ah, can we help in some way?"

The man heaved a sigh. "If you wouldn't mind calling a tow truck, there's no cell service out here."

The woman leaned across the man, chunks of lasagna falling into the crack between the seats. "That's a lie. He forgot to charge his phone again. You never charge it," she accused.

"Because there's no service out here. No point in charging it. I don't know why you bought me the damned thing. Who am I gonna call? We're always together."

Jack met Helen's gaze then glanced up and down the deserted roadway. "Can I give you a ride somewhere?"

"That would be wonderful," said the woman. "I'm Martha. My husband, Larry." She balanced the lasagna tray on the dashboard to reach across her husband to shake hands through the window. "If we leave now, we can still make the funeral."

Jack swiped the smear of tomato sauce left on his palm on the leg of his jeans.

"Oh, I'm sorry for your loss," Helen interjected.

"Don't be," said Larry. He shoved at the driver's door, hauled himself out, and shook his head at his wife. "I'm only sorry we'll all be forced to eat whatever your Aunt Betty comes up with. I told you we should have called a caterer." Martha followed, gracelessly crawling over the driver's seat and out the door. Sauce dripped to the ground and stained the icy roadway like a crime scene.

"No one's forcing you to eat anything," Martha said. She swiped at her dress. "Maybe I should stay. I'll make a mess of your car if I ride like this."

"Sure. You're worried about *his* car."

"You can borrow my robe," Helen said, stripping down to her gown. Sleet slid down her cleavage. "I insist. As you can see, it's already stained, so no need to worry about protecting it. It'll keep you covered for now."

Martha gaped, bubblegum-pink lips forming a large '*oh*.' "Aren't you sweet? Maybe Betty will have something I can borrow when we get there."

Helen helped Martha into the robe, and they piled into the car. Jack eased onto the road again. "Where to?"

"Downtown," Larry said.

"We need to pick up Betty," Martha said. "And I need to change."

"It's too far," Larry insisted. "Just drop us downtown. Someone else can get Betty."

"Everyone else is traveling by now. She'll miss the funeral," Martha said.

"She's old. She won't remember."

Martha gasped.

"It's no trouble," Helen insisted.

"I need to change clothes," Martha shot back at her husband.

Jack looked about to ditch his own car to end the arguing. "We're happy to take you to Betty's house and then to the funeral, but for the love of God could someone tell me which direction I should be driving?"

Martha glared at her husband. "Take the next left."

Ten minutes later, they arrived at Happy Horizons Senior Living. Martha invited them in to warm up and stretch their legs. They made their way through the covered portico to the entrance. Betty buzzed them up.

Martha stared at Helen's dress as they waited for the elevator. "I take it we caught you on your way somewhere fancy."

Jack leaned in. "That's yesterday's outfit."

Martha went wide-eyed. "Oh. I see."

Helen glared at Jack. "It's not like that at all."

He fought a grin. "Not like what?"

"You make it sound like the walk of shame."

Martha patted Helen's arm. "I was young once, too. I'm not going to judge. I've very sex-positive."

Helen's face went hot. "There's nothing to judge. If you're implying that he and I… that I and this man…"

"Aw, honey, don't get all uptight. Martha's cool with it." Jack winked.

"It's a lovely dress," Martha said, "but maybe a little impractical for this time of year."

Jack followed Martha's gaze, his eyes snapping up to Helen's. "Um, yeah. You do seem chilled."

"I'm always cold," Helen grumbled, rubbing her palms on her arms.

"You seem particularly cold," Jack enunciated. "I'll give you my shirt."

"I'm fine," she said, boarding the elevator. She didn't want Jack's body-heat warmed shirt on her bare arms. Definitely, certainly not.

Martha leaned close to Helen, speaking loud enough for all to hear. "He means we can all see your titties, dear."

Helen's face burned like the sun. She glanced down, crossed her arms and swung to face the elevator wall. Jack wordlessly held out his shirt.

"I'll thank you to not laugh," she muttered.

"Was I laughing? My bad."

They exited on the third floor, Martha and Larry hurrying ahead, Helen still struggling to get the shirt over her bum shoulder. Jack reached out. "Let me help," he said, taking hold of the flapping shirt and easing it over her shoulder.

"Good manners insist I thank you."

"In my defense, I wasn't the one who used the word titties."

"You just did."

"Well, I mean, it's out there now. Exposed. Might as well accept it." Her face became a supernova. "Come on. We're all adults. Martha is sex-positive. We're all happy campers."

"You're enjoying this."

His eyes danced. "Most definitely."

She strode toward the open apartment door with all the dignity she could summon.

~ * ~

Jack stepped into the apartment in time to see a tiny woman with a shock of white hair banging cupboard doors in her kitchen. "Have you seen my fried onions? Where are my fried onions? I know I bought some."

Martha waved through the passthrough. "I'll help you in a minute, but I need to borrow a dress."

Betty stopped and stared at their little group clustered in her living room. "Who are all you people? What are you doing in my apartment?"

"This is Jack and Helen," Martha said. "We had some car trouble. They gave us a ride."

"Of course, you did. Haven't I told you to get rid of that old car?"

"There's nothing wrong with my car," Larry said.

"Not now, Larry," said Martha. "Betty, don't fuss about the onions. I have lasagna all over me."

Martha opened the robe.

Betty gasped. "Oh, my heavens!"

"I know. An entire tray."

"It's a good thing I made a double batch of my American Chop Suey. Enough for everyone to have seconds. Let's get you a clean dress." Without another word, she turned and started down the hall, Martha following.

A timer pinged. Jack went to the kitchen and opened the oven door. "Smells done. You think I should take it out before it burns?"

Larry snorted.

Martha bustled back into the kitchen, running a quick hand down her fresh dress to smooth it. "It could use a bit of ironing, but there's no time. Oh dear, is the casserole too hot to carry? We'll just have to leave it. Driving will be slow, so we should get going." She gripped Larry's elbow and propelled him toward the door.

Larry stood at the door, keys in hand, Martha beside him.

"It won't be too hot," Helen insisted. "Jack, find a cookie sheet and insulate it with that kitchen towel."

Martha waved a hand. "Don't trouble yourself. We'll make do with what the others bring."

"It's no trouble. You go to enough church suppers, you learn a trick or two."

Helen slid the casserole onto the towel-lined cookie sheet and set another cookie sheet on top. "There. We're good to go." She paused. "Aw. You have a kitty? I love animals."

Martha stopped in the doorway and turned with a puzzled look. "Animals aren't allowed here. Why?"

"Nothing. My mistake."

The others stepped into the hall, but Helen sank her fingers into Jack's arm and held him back. She motioned to a tiny row of empty cans perched on the edge of the sink. "She doesn't have a cat," she mouthed.

Jack looked at the cans. He could just make out the words "…savory beef bits in gravy." He looked at Helen then down at the casserole

"This is a lot of casserole," he said.

"You don't think she would have…"

"No." He paused then said more emphatically. "*No.* Besides, even if she did, would it really hurt anyone?"

Helen blanched. "You can't mean to let people eat this?"

"I don't see it as our business."

"It's food. That's definitely our business. Never mind. I'll fix it." She swept out and left him to close the door for himself.

They were well on the way to the funeral when Helen leaned over the back seat. "You know, Betty, maybe we should stop at the grocery store for those fried onions after all. We have time."

Jack cast her a look, startled. "Really?"

"*Mmm*," she said. "They'd definitely finish the dish. By the way, is there a kitchen at this funeral home?"

"Yes. We're holding the reception at the parish hall," Martha said. "We just renovated a couple of years ago."

"Wonderful. You may not know this, but Jack and I are professional cooks. We'd be happy to help out so you can put your energies elsewhere."

"We would?" Jack asked.

"You would?" Martha and Larry asked simultaneously.

Helen turned toward the road again. "Absolutely. And don't forget to stop for those fried onions, Jack."

Two minutes later they'd arrived at the local grocery. Helen sprang into action. "Grab a buggy and don't dawdle."

Jack trailed after her. "I'm sorry?"

She pointed. "A buggy. Grab a buggy. We don't have a lot of time, and I'm not exactly inconspicuous."

Jack grabbed a shopping cart and shoved it through the slushy parking lot. "Why do I need a cart? And if you really think that old bat put cat food in the casserole, why dress it up with fried onions?"

Helen paused just outside the door. "We are not buying fried onions. We're getting supplies to make something edible, and you're going to trip on the way into that parish hall with that casserole if I have to stick my food out and take you down myself."

She turned and entered the store.

In that moment he fell a little bit in lust with Helen Walker.

He caught up with her in the produce aisle. "When did you hatch this plan?"

"About three seconds after I saw the empty cans of cat food. Try to keep up."

Twenty minutes and a crap-load of grocery bags later, they were back at the car. "I'm so sorry," Helen said with a tone of regret, "I couldn't find the fried onions anywhere, so we picked up a few extra supplies hoping that might round things out."

"What would we have done without you?" Martha asked with a note of genuine gratitude.

Helen glanced at Jack. "Don't you dare answer that," she murmured.

Jack offered to drop off Helen and the food at the parish hall and take the others on to the church. They soon pulled into a parking lot, the low, squat building less than heavenly or uplifting.

Jack hopped out to retrieve the cat food casserole from Betty.

"The stewards said they'd have it unlocked," Martha said.

Jack nudged the car door closed and squinted against the icy pellets hitting his face. Helen came abreast of him. "Okay. You know the plan," she said.

"We don't know for sure she put cat food in it."

Helen's hand gripped his elbow and the tray wobbled in his grasp. "There's enough circumstantial evidence to suggest she did.

"*Oh!*" she cried. A moment later, one of her feet flew up into Jack's peripheral vision. He tensed with disbelief as her grip tightened on his elbow, her body weight slammed into his, and the slick pavement pulled them both to the ground. Hard.

Jack swore. A wet warmth penetrated his jeans, and he turned toward Helen, his palms pushing off the gritty, icy pavement beneath them. "What the hell?" he ground out.

"You weren't tripping," she said.

She had the nerve to half smile as she stood, gently swiping the remains of Betty's casserole off her gown as if it were no more than a few pieces of lint instead of gobs of sauce-laden macaroni.

Jack lurched to his feet. "You're insane. Now we're both covered in this shit."

She plucked a gooey brown bit from his front and held it in his face. "This is why I did it. *Cat food.*"

He swatted her hand aside. "Couldn't you just throw it in the trash after they were gone and told them you dropped it?"

"I could have, but you were being argumentative. Never argue with a Walker."

He turned back toward the car as three sets of eyes stared on in horror. "I'm sorry!" he called out. "We'll fix this, I promise!"

Jack watched Helen disappear into the hall, exhaled long and slow and trudged back to the car for the rest of the groceries. "Hey, Martha. Can I borrow that bathrobe?"

~ * ~

Ten minutes later, the kitchen door slammed open ushering in a gust of cold air. Jack stood in the doorway, scowling, his backpack slung over his shoulder, the Bathrobe of Doom bleeding bits of Italian food on the threshold.

"Was that entirely necessary?" he demanded.

"Maybe not necessary," she said, "but definitely satisfying." Her hands shook with laughter as she poured baby carrots into a colander to rinse.

"What did I do to deserve that?"

"You embarrassed me in the elevator."

"So, you body-slammed me onto pavement for it?"

"That part was an accident. I only meant for you to drop the casserole. These shoes aren't designed for winter weather, and you have an iron grip." She glanced up. "I'm sorry. Truly."

"I'm going to find a bathroom to change."

She froze as his palm flattened on the door to the parish hall. "You might want to prepare yourself," she said.

"For wha—?" He gave the door a shove, then swung back toward her with a horrified expression. "What in holy hell is out here?"

"It appears to be taxidermy," she said, wiping her hands and following him as he stepped into the main reception hall to peer at the item displayed by a window.

He squinted at the figure. "Is that a weasel's head on a fox's body?"

"It's a Fweasel, yes." She pointed to a small card on the table. "See? Dated 1992. Apparently, Larry's brother was quite the artist."

Jack's gaze swung to hers. "The cat food casserole is making a *lot* more sense now. You're telling me this freakish thing has been haunting somebody's living room for three decades?"

"So it would seem." She fought to press her lips into a neutral line.

He followed her gaze, literally jumping back into her as he turned. "What the…?" He tiptoed closer to the *thing* on display in the center of the room. He shook his head back and forth. "This. Is. Not. Right."

"It appears to be his *piece de resistance*, both creation and commentary."

"*It* being a…?"

"Portunk. According to the card, it is technically a skun-tur-pine. 'As smelly, dumb and prickly as most of my relatives. Except for Martha whose brownies are dry by edible.'"

Jack swung to face her. "For real?"

"It appears to be the artist's own handwriting. I have no reason to question its authenticity."

"This family is whacked."

"I think it's creative."

"Someone has literally created a Franken-animal out of a turkey, a skunk, and a porcupine, and you call it 'creative?'"

"It says in his obituary it was his way of giving road-kill new life. There's a whole photo-board of his life's work and articles about his creations on a table by the coat room."

He backed toward the door to the kitchen, turned, and emitted a choked sound.

"The squirrel diorama kind of sneaks up on you, doesn't it?"

His eyes slid back to her. "They are wearing clothes."

"Their injuries were often too severe, so his wife helped sew them outfits. Aren't they darling enjoying their little picnic? He was quite skilled. I read he often gave them as gifts to other…" She hiccupped and clapped a palm over her mouth. "…nature lovers," she mumbled. Her eyes began to water, and she swung away from him with a sweeping arm. "It's quite beautiful when you think of it."

"I can't believe you aren't freaked out by this."

"I think it's lovely," she snorted before swinging back toward him and grasping his arm for balance. "Oh, sweet Jesus. *I'm dying.* Who does this? Whose mind works this way? If you could have heard my scream when I first came in here. But your face…" She gasped. "So worth it."

"One of them is holding a banjo."

"I know," she said, tears streaming now. "*I know.* Be thankful they only brought choice pieces for the reception. I read he was quite prolific in his later years."

Her laughter subsided and they stood in silence a few moments.

Jack quietly pulled a handful of something from the pocket of the robe and draped it over one of the squirrels. "There," he said. "That's better."

Helen snatched back her hair extension.

He snickered. "So, what now?" he asked.

"Get back to cooking."

"I vote we get out now before we're next."

"They had an eccentric relative. It's not their fault. With all these place settings they're clearly expecting a crowd. We have to do something to replace the casserole you dropped."

"The one you made me drop."

She looked at him. "It was not fit for human consumption and standing here arguing is only wasting time."

"I can't cook with you like this. You stink."

"It's Betty's casserole. You smell the same."

His gaze zeroed in on her elbow. "And you tore the sleeve of my favorite shirt."

"I didn't mean to."

He pulled aside the torn fabric. The red smear underneath was not tomato sauce. His eyes snapped back up to hers. "You know you're bleeding, right?"

"I assumed I probably was."

"Jesus, woman. Why didn't you say something instead of yakking about Freddie the Taxidermist?"

"What would be the point? That robe was the only clean thing I had."

He nudged the small of her back. "Come on. I must have something for you in my pack that isn't blood-stained and covered in cat food."

She unbuttoned the shirt he'd loaned her earlier and paused outside the ladies' room door as Jack pulled some items out of his pack.

"These should fit if you cinch them up," he said.

"I'll make it work."

She clutched the fresh clothes tight to her chest trying to avoid the splatters the shirt hadn't covered. "But, um, I could use a hand."

He'd had his own hand on the opposing door and glanced up, his gaze bouncing off hers as she turned to show him her back. Her face flushed with heat and something she recognized as awareness.

"You want me to unzip you?"

"If you don't mind."

He stepped closer, the warmth of his fingertips a shock to her even thought she'd been expecting it. He fumbled a moment, struggling with the tiny zipper before setting his own clothes on his pack and freeing both hands.

She shivered, not from cold for once, and closed her eyes. It was like being in a romance novel except for the stench of heated cat food and the franken-display in the next room.

"It's stuck," he said, tugging her around by the zipper. "And microscopic. How the hell did they get you into this?"

She sucked in a breath and stood straighter in hopes it might free the zipper. "Pull the fabric toward the zipper so it has some give," she suggested.

"How? You're poured into this thing."

"It's not that tight." It was.

His hands paused, and she felt him vibrate with a laughter that sent another shiver through her. "I can see your stomach growl through it."

The thought of him looking at her that closely made her think of him looking at her in the elevator. Her skin grew warm. "Oh, for Pete's sake."

He started tugging again. "I swear, it's not budging. Short of cutting it off you, I think you're stuck for now."

She sucked in a breath, the idea of slicing through the designer gown giving her heart palpitations, but, honestly, she was going to have to pay for it one way or another. "Tear it."

"What?"

"Tear it. Then it won't look like it was on purpose, like it happened when I fell."

"You're going to tell the show that this dress spontaneously burst open when you fell?"

"Do you have any better ideas?"

He reached forward and placed both hands on her shoulders and looked her in the eye. "They're going to know. You're a terrible liar."

She nodded, wondering if he was telling her he knew she'd lied to him, but then realized they were still talking about the gown. Her breath hung suspended in her chest as his eyes bore into hers. She turned away, he gripped the thin fabric at each shoulder and yanked.

Helen blinked, her hands flying to hold the fabric to her chest as a rush of air cooled her exposed back. "Thank you," she said facing him again.

"My pleasure." He cleared his throat and wet his lips. "I mean, no problem."

"I'll go change now."

His gaze slid down to the clothes clutched to her chest, the front of her gown pooling at the edges of her grip. His lips tilted in a half grin. "Really hope those fit."

She nodded and stepped backward into the ladies' room. As soon as she closed the door, she let her gown puddle at her feet. She quickly washed up and unfolded the pile of clothes Jack had given her. A plain long-sleeved tee. A pair of lightweight sweats. And a pair of thin boxer briefs.

Helen blinked at the underwear then at the thong she'd had on under the second-skin gown. She jumped at the sound of a knock on the door.

"Everything fit?" Jack asked.

She coughed and heat flooded her as she stood on the other side of the door holding *his underwear*. "I was just about to get dressed."

"They're clean," he said, his voice a low rumble through the door. "In case you were wondering."

Her face flamed hotter. "I assumed they would be."

She avoided her reflection in the mirror over the sink as she pondered whether she was more comfortable going commando or wearing this man's underwear. Neither option felt ideal. She decided she was done being prudish about it and stepped into the boxers. The soft fabric slid up her thighs, and the fact that she liked the feel of them made her want to rip them off. It was one thing to borrow the man's clothes, it was another to put her nether parts near where his had once been—the separation of a laundry pod and a few gallons of water not-withstanding.

She quickly finished dressing, wrapped her high heels in the ruined gown and stepped out into the hall. Jack was waiting.

"Look what I found in Lost and Found," he said.

He held up a pair of ladies' chenille bedroom slippers. The kind grandmother's wear.

"Somebody lost a pair of slippers? Here?"

"You want to know their provenance, or you want to wear them?"

"Wearing. Gratefully. Thank you." She snatched the slippers from his hand and slid them on. Yes, they belonged to a stranger, and, yes, they were pink, but she was currently wearing this man's uber-comfortable underwear, so her bar was already embarrassingly low.

"Shall we get started?" she asked.

She didn't wait for him but hightailed it to the kitchen, rolling up her sleeves as she walked. "You get the pasta water boiling, and open the beans, and I'll lay out the tray of nibbles."

She pulled a jumbo package of beef franks out of a bag, cut them all into one-inch chunks and tossed the lot into a large pot. "Add the beans to that."

"I see we're going highbrow," he said.

"We are cooking for a crowd. We used to serve this a lot at the homeless shelter."

"That's right. You're a regular do-gooder."

She paused and gave him a look. "I believe in charity work."

"Whatever makes you feel good about yourself."

He set a large pot under the faucet to fill and began opening cans of baked beans.

"I don't do it to feel good about myself. I do it because it's the right thing to do."

"And looks good on your resume. Oh, don't give me that look. I know how these things work. The beauty pageant stuff. The *Happily Ever After* show. They want a noble backstory to paint you like the patron saint of good deeds because it makes you likeable. It's fine. Just be honest about it."

She stiffened. "I am being honest about it. Some of the people I've met at the shelter were the kindest, most hard-working—"

"—drug addicts you've ever met."

He glanced up at her through those impossibly long gold lashes. "You know I'm right."

"Not all of them."

"It's not all sweetness and light. Some of those folks were just out for a free meal. It's fair to say so."

"Of course, they were. Why *else* would you go to a soup kitchen?" She poured the beans he'd opened into the pot with a *plop*. "Charity work feels good, and maybe my being there showing them a kindness helped them rethink their life choices. You never know."

"I'd rethink my life choices if you served me this."

She made a face at him. "Why are you being so hateful?"

"I'm not. I'm just a realist." He stopped and slanted a cocky smile her way. "Tell me, is my kindness helping you rethink your life choices?"

She bit her lip. His tone was serious, but his eyes were laughing at her.

"I think I'm on the road to ruin, to be honest," she quipped.

He laughed. She liked it.

With the beans started, she piled baby carrots on a large plastic tray while Jack dumped pickles, olives and an oversized bottle of ranch dressing into bowls. Helen rinsed the grapes and set them to drain while slicing a large block of cheddar into bite-sized chunks. "Is the pasta water boiling yet?"

Jack raised an eyebrow. "It's been on the burner two minutes."

She glanced around and heaved a sigh. "I wish we had time to make cornbread."

"We have dinner rolls."

"It's not the same. Beanie wieners are always served with cornbread. Not that you'd know the difference. 'Course if I were really making them right, I'd have some kidney beans and chopped onion, yellow mustard, brown sugar..."

"That sounds disgusting."

"You eat poutine. *That's* disgusting."

"Poutine is Canadian."

"As a Yankee once said to me—close enough."

He smiled, a crinkling around his eyes more than anything. "You're a lot snarkier than I thought you were."

"We call it sass where I'm from."

"You surprise me. You've got some backbone."

"Never mistake a soft approach with weakness. As President Roosevelt said, 'Speak softly and carry a big stick.'"

"And she's smart."

"Summa cum laude," she said.

"God bless you."

She glanced up at him. "It means I graduated with highest honors."

"I know," he said, turning back to chopping broccoli. "That was a joke. I'm not as dumb as you think I am."

"I never said you were dumb."

But in all fairness, he was a thirty-something line cook in a pub who drove a guy's guy classic car and dressed in jeans and flannel shirts. He wasn't striking her as a Harvard alum.

"I got into college," he said. "More than one. I just didn't go." He piled the broccoli on the platter with the carrots.

"Why ever not?"

A muscle near his eye twitched. "Poor life choices," he said with a smirk that told her that was all she was going to hear on the subject. "So, what's your degree in?"

"Hospitality Management"

"Not culinary school, eh?"

"I'm from the South. Cooking is in our blood."

He side-eyed the pot of hotdogs and beans.

"It's comfort food," she said. His smile widened. "Stop. I'm not defending myself to you right now. We have mouths to feed. Now, grate me a mess of that cheddar. I'll start a roux for the mac and cheese. Did we get flour? We didn't get flour, did we?" She opened and slammed cupboard doors in quick succession. "Praise be. Flour! All right... you set out the trays of starters and prep the rolls for heating. I'll tend the beanie weanies and make the mac and cheese. I need some of that butter... Why are you just standing there?"

"You're growing on me," he said.

Something fluttered inside her, but she tamped it down. "Of course, I am. Now grate the cheese."

"Yes, ma'am. Grating. Finding a grater." He located a grater and bowl and set to work.

"No lolly-gagging. We have mouths to feed."

She opened the tubs of cookies and arranged them on a tray. "What do we have for drinks?"

"I started coffee and hot water urns while you were changing."

"You did?"

"This isn't my first rodeo. Whoever set the tables had already prepped them. I just had to plug them in and turn them on. There's creamer in the fridge, too. I already checked."

"We should set out ice water." She pulled some plastic pitchers from a cupboard and started dispensing ice from the refrigerator door into each, then carried them in her good hand to the sink to fill.

Jack collected them two per fist and walked to the door to the hall. "We may just pull this off," he said.

"We make a good team," she said. She ducked her head and turned away to hide her grin lest he get a big head over it.

Thirty minutes later...

"We're out of cheese," Jack dropped an empty serving tray on the counter. Bits of cracker skittered off onto the floor.

"Already?"

"They're a hungry lot. Is that mac and cheese ready yet?"

"Yeah. If you could lift the pot." Jack lifted, and she shoveled it into a serving pan.

"How many people are out there?" she asked.

"A shocking number given it's a funeral for an old guy during an ice storm."

"I hope we have enough."

"We're fine. A couple other people brought food, too." Helen side-eyed him. "It looks safe," he said, backing toward the door.

Helen reminded herself to breathe and smoothed her palm down the Christmas apron she'd found hanging in the broom closet. She poured another box of crackers onto the tray and added grapes.

She felt badly leaving Jack to do all the running back and forth. Surely, she could sneak out and back without anyone recognizing her. Pasting on a smile, she pushed into the reception hall, tray in hand.

A tiny woman with thick ankles and a loud floral dress approached the Portunk figure. "Thank you for coming," she squeaked as the room quieted to hear her. "It means so much that you're here to celebrate Carl's life with me. And now, I would like to follow through on his final wishes. I hope you cherish these mementoes as he cherished each and every one of you." She dabbed at her eye with her thumb.

"The first gift is Chippy. One of Carl's earliest works…"

The widow, Nan, proceeded to terrify various relatives with Carl's parting gifts.

Helen slid the cracker tray into an open spot on the buffet table and caught Jack's eye. Nan picked up Fweasel next and started rambling on about "new life" and "creative inspiration" as those she walked past averted their eyes and coughed into their napkins.

"Denny always had a sense of humor, so Carl wanted to honor that." A man, presumably Denny, visibly paled. "But in the end, he decided Denny's cat, would probably attack Fweasel, so Carl asked me to give him to Pat."

This carried on through several more items, including the individual figures in the squirrel diorama until the treasures had taken residence on each table like morbid centerpieces.

"Finally, Portunk," she said standing next to the center display. "You all know Portunk is the culmination of years of work. Not only was it technically challenging but each animal was symbolic. This piece won him an Honorable Mention at the bi-annual chamber of commerce art show, so I almost hate to part with it." She sniffed. "But it was Carl's wish. And so," she reverently cupped Portunk, "I give it to his only brother, Larry." She held it toward Larry like Simba holding his firstborn.

"I don't want it."

Nan's hold on Portunk wavered. "You don't mean that."

"Hell, yes, I do. Look at it. It's a freak and so was Carl. I refuse to continue this farce. Nobody wants his crazy crap."

Martha gripped Larry's sleeve. "We love it, Nan."

"It's demented. And she's just as whacko for enabling him."

"*Larry.*"

Nan pulled Portunk toward her, as if to shield it. "Carl was a gifted artist. Everyone appreciates his gifts. Why, Pat was so moved, she cried!"

Martha stepped toward Nan. "We love it, and we're honored to make a place in our home for it. Him. Her?" Martha made as if to accept the creature.

Larry body-blocked his wife. "Over my dead body is that thing coming into my house."

Martha reached around him to grip the figure with both hands. "Don't let grief make you say things you don't mean. We're taking him." She tugged. Larry tried to pry her fingers off.

Betty stood and put her hands on her hips. "How come Larry and Martha get Portuck? They don't even want him."

"Yes, we do," Martha insisted.

Helen took a tentative step forward, not knowing what she intended to do but wanting it to stop.

"Don't," Jack warned.

"We have to do something," she said.

"No one ever asks me what I want," complained Betty to the room in general.

Nan tugged the creature back from Martha. "If you don't want it, you don't deserve it."

Helen hurried forward. "Ladies, I'm sure we can work this out."

"There's nothing to work out," Martha insisted. "We're taking it home. It was Carl's dying wish."

"Never mind *my* wishes," whined Betty.

"See?" said Helen, reaching out to steady Portunk as both women pulled it toward them. "No need to fight about it."

"I'm not fighting. I'm— *Oh!*"

Martha suddenly stumbled into Larry, Betty tumbled backward, landing on the floor, and Portunk took flight, landing in the middle of a nearby table, a spray of baked beans from someone's plate streaming into the air like a fountain of legumes.

Helen stood, speechless, and stared at the single stuffed turkey leg in her hand. Blood pooled in her feet, making them immovable when every other fiber of her being screamed for her to flee. This. Was. Not. Good.

She lowered the turkey leg to her side as if that would somehow make it less noticeable. "I'm so—"

"Jesus Christ," someone mumbled. "She's just ripped Portunk's leg off."

"It was an accident," Helen whispered. She gingerly took hold of Nan's limp hand and pressed the appendage into her palm. "A terrible accident." She pressed Nan's fingers closed around the turkey leg.

The room fell silent, everyone collectively holding their breath as if gauging what the correct response to a taxidermy brawl at a funeral reception should be.

Jack murmured loud enough for everyone to hear, "Too bad it didn't have pig feet, right? I hear pigs can fly."

Helen turned on Jack. "How can you make jokes at a time like this?" she whispered.

Jack shrugged. "Just trying to help."

She turned back to the table where Portunk lay sprawled in a plate of baked beans. "Please don't be upset. We'll just clean him up and, uh…"

A stuffed squirrel flew overhead and landed on the table next to Portunk. "Pig pile!" shouted a small voice.

"Emily!" scolded a shocked adult.

Suddenly, all hell broke loose. A half dozen other kids scrambled out of their seats, grabbed stuffed rodents off the tables and began tossing them in the air, running around pretending they were fighting each other, and generally ignoring the reverence of the occasion.

"Look what you've started," Helen accused Jack as parents rushed their children and dead squirrels whizzed past. Nan's fingers went slack. The turkey leg hit the floor with a soft thud.

"What *I* started? I didn't dismember Portunk. May he rest in peace."

Helen glared at Jack. "He's not *dead*. Just not fully intact."

"Not dead?" Jack laughed. "Do you hear yourself? Portunk is the definition of *dead*."

"Cayden!" a father bellowed. "Do not chase your sister with that squirrel!"

Nan sank into a chair like a forgotten ragdoll. A mother tried to tug a calico-clad squirrel out of her toddler's hands as the child insisted it was her new "baby." Several teenagers stood in the corner, cackling with laughter and holding up their cell phones to record it all.

Larry clapped Jack on the back. "Best. Funeral. Ever."

Helen gaped, horrified at the turn of events. How could people behave like this? A man was dead. His life's work was being mocked.

A squirrel smacked her in the chest. Helen stared at it as it lay on the vinyl floor at her feet, its tiny straw hat unraveling at the edge. She bent to pick it up, cupping its little broken body in her palm.

A toddler ran past shouting that his squirrel was Super Squirrel. He made airplane noises.

Helen looked up, surprised that Jack was blurry. Her heart felt hot and heavy in her chest as she stared at dozens of strangers, laughing, *at a funeral.*

"Hey," Helen heard one of the teens from across the room, "isn't she from that show? The one who was dumped?"

Her vision blurred even more, and she clutched Jack's arm. "We have to go."

"Now?"

"*Now.*" She tugged harder, her feet leaden like a dream you can't wake from. "*They're videotaping me.*"

Jack followed the direction in which she was subtly waving the squirrel and swore. "Get in the kitchen."

She nodded, plucked a random water pitcher off the buffet table and fled to the kitchen.

Jack came through the door a few moments later. "Grab your things. We're leaving."

"What about Larry and Martha?"

"I told them we had to go."

"But the teens…"

"I said they were mistaken, that you get that all the time, but they're not stupid. They heard your accent. And you look like… you. My guess is they've already posted photos of you holding that… Seriously? Can you not let go of that thing already?"

She stared with surprise at the squirrel still in her grip and dropped it to the counter.

"Let's go."

She grabbed her ruined evening gown and shoes and hurried to his car.

Ice-cold water seeped through the fabric of her slippers.

Jack pulled onto the highway heading south, slush drumming the car's wheel-wells. The gray sky matched Helen's mood as the adrenaline of their flight gave way to a familiar ache inside her. She clung to the hard-worn familiarity of it, like the stiff support of a wooden church pew, bracing her, stopping her from falling even as it offered scant comfort. "That was horrible," she finally said.

"No kidding. Is your life always like this?"

"I'm sorry?"

"Don't give me that shocked face. You are literally the poster child for freakish, no-one-would-believe-it-unless-they-were-there events. This is exactly your life."

"I have never been a party to such a spectacle."

"You act like you were an unwitting observer. If it weren't for your interference, none of this would've happened."

"Are you actually blaming me for that? I did *not* cause that brawl. If anything, I probably saved them from food poisoning."

"I'm beginning to think cat food casserole is a treasured family recipe."

"A man has *died,* and y'all are making fun of his life's work." He glanced at her sidelong. "Just because they're eccentric and live a different lifestyle doesn't make them less worthy of respect. We are all God's children."

"You're actually defending them? May I remind you: cat food casserole. Taxidermy franken-creations. A fight between two old ladies. The only normal part of that funeral was Super Squirrel."

"You shouldn't mock them in their time of grief."

"No better time to laugh than a funeral."

She fumbled with her seat belt. "Pull over."

"What?"

"I said, pull over. I don't want to ride with you anymore." She managed the latch and flung the heavy buckle toward him. It smacked him satisfyingly hard in the thigh.

"*Ow.* Stop that. We're on the highway. Also, you're wearing slippers. You'd look ridiculous standing on the side of the road."

"Now I'm ridiculous? Then you can laugh at me, too. Oops, my mistake. *You already were.*"

He blew out a breath and coasted to a stop at the side of the highway. "Come on. I'm not laughing at you. I'm stating the obvious. Need I remind you I'm the guy yet again driving your getaway car, so those kids back there don't get any more video? How am I the bad guy?"

She pressed her fingers to her temples. "You're not the bad guy." She dropped her hands. "It's just upsetting. Funerals should bring people together, not tear the family apart even more."

"People hate funerals. They suck. Just a bunch of people going through the motions of what's expected when they're really just bottling everything up inside. Hands down, that's the best funeral I've ever been to."

"Funerals should be celebrations of life."

He made a dismissive noise. "Did you enjoy your mom's *celebration*? Did you? Because by the time mine was dead, I had zero fucks left to give. She sure as hell didn't care anymore, so why should I?"

Helen stared at Jack's profile as the weight of his pain slammed into her. He fell silent, and she bit her lip as she realized she wasn't the only one coming into this situation with baggage.

She thought back to the dog-eared chart the grief counselor had quietly slid across the table in their first session all those years ago. It had felt like the opening salvo of a delicate negotiation. She'd stared at the chart, all soft, calming hues, as if swirls of pastels could soften the intensity of emotion contained in words like *anger* and *denial* and *acceptance* as they orbited the central issue: *GRIEF.* She'd had the urge to bolt. To crumple the chart and hurl it back at the counselor's placid, neutral expression. After her mother's death, she'd felt so many conflicting emotions they'd begun to slam against one another like toddlers fighting over a toy until she'd simply shut down to survive. It wasn't until she'd started baking cupcakes, reaching with every familiar movement toward a normal she knew would never, ever return, that Aunt Iris had booked her an appointment. *So, you don't eat your feelings,* she'd said, as if Helen wanted to fill herself with rage or loneliness. Iris never understood.

But Helen did.

Folks can get stuck at any stage, the counselor had said. *Be patient with yourself.*

Helen watched as Jack's fingers reflexively opened and closed on the wheel.

"You're angry," she murmured. "That's okay. I've been stuck in denial for years."

He scowled and his gaze cut to her, but his expression softened. "It's not anger," he finally said, his voice more gravely than usual. "She could have gotten help, but she refused. She wouldn't listen."

Jack's tendency to give unsolicited advice suddenly began to make a lot more sense.

"I'm sorry. That must have been frustrating."

"Yeah. You can see why I don't think of funerals as celebrations. My mother's was like a family reunion where I didn't know anybody. It sucked." He turned back to the road, letting a long sigh escape him. "But, I'm sure your mother's wasn't like that."

Helen bit her lip and grew still, the memory of her mom's funeral washing over her like magnolias in bloom. Intense and overwhelming and determined. "No. Nothing like that. She planned everything. The flowers. The music. The food. She loved to entertain. Loved to bring people together. It was the last party she ever hosted, and it was beautiful."

Helen fought the swell of emotion heating her chest. She remembered the yellow organza dress her mother had insisted she wear, because it was the color of sunshine, and Mama hated black. She wanted her baby to stand in the sun and eat cupcakes and *smile* every day she could, because she'd be watching from heaven, she'd said, and she'd know if there was any crying going on.

Helen fingered the tiny gold charm at the base of her throat—a small, spiral sun. Her mother had said love is like the sun, people might take it for granted, but it was the source of all life. She'd also told Helen not to mention that part to folks at church, because they wouldn't understand what she'd come to know, being so close to death, that God is love and life and all things all at once and doesn't fit into tiny, human words and ideas and judgments. But, He was definitely there every time someone smiled or ate cupcakes, because God was infinite joy, and she was prepared to share that with Him for all eternity.

It overwhelmed her to think about it—to think about smiling and cupcakes, the enormity of the universe, and the countless decisions she'd made between then and now—when all she felt capable of grasping was the tiny gold charm. She rubbed it between her thumb and index finger and then smoothed it against her chest. "My mother's funeral was every bit a celebration. I'm sorry you didn't get to experience that."

His face slackened, and he shot her a glance before clearing his throat and looking ahead again.

Jack pulled back onto the highway. Helen stared out the window at the passing miles. Thinking about her mother and how the years had unfolded reminded her that she felt less sure of what she was supposed to do with her life than she had as a grieving child by her mother's deathbed. Everyone around her had expected her to behave like the young woman she looked like from the outside, but inside… inside, she'd wanted to run and never stop. Even though she had nowhere to go.

Funny how she still felt that way.

She blew out a slow breath, quietly latching her seatbelt and shifting in her seat. A tractor-trailer barreled by them.

"I still can't believe you made a joke about pigs flying."

"I was trying to lighten the moment. At least I wasn't tearing apart treasured family heirlooms in front of the grieving widow."

"I'm sure a skilled taxidermist could repair it."

"If only they knew one."

She laughed aloud then. They both did. Helen rested her forehead in her hand a moment and then leaned back. "Crashing funerals is exhausting."

He nodded. "It's a first for me."

"Me, too." She glanced at him through her lashes.

His mouth hitched up on one side. "I'm a little ashamed to admit this, but I'm glad you're here. This drive has never been this entertaining." He gave her a look that made her feel unsure and pleased with herself all at once.

"I pity the girl who ends up with you if this was your idea of fun."

"It's one hell of a story," he said.

"That it is."

His blue eyes met hers, warm with suppressed laughter, and something shifted inside her. She blinked, not sure what had changed between them. Her gaze slipped to his hands on the steering wheel. His lean fingers opened and slowly closed as he adjusted his grip, looser than before, as if something had eased inside him as well.

She couldn't say what made her do it, but she reached out to grasp his right hand with her left. He weaved his fingers with hers and squeezed. She faced forward, unable to look him in the eye when she could feel his energy pulsing through his palm.

They eased their hands apart for Jack to drive, but that small connection let them open up in other ways. She told him about her Royally Iced Cupcakery business, and he told her about Lucky's. They chatted about favorite movies (raw, comedic indies and summer popcorn superhero flicks) and baking competition shows (he was a fan), politics (he wasn't) and places they'd like to travel. Then she asked him about his childhood. Jack told her he lived with his mom after his parent's divorced when he was very young, and there wasn't much to say. She died when he was seventeen and then he moved to New Hampshire to live with his dad. After that, he got quiet. Helen knew not to pry.

It felt like progress not to be trading barbs, but the emotional and physical roller coaster of the last twenty-four hours was taking its toll. If only she'd gotten a better night's sleep. And eaten more and guzzled less coffee. She was going to need professional strength whitening strips if she kept this up. She shifted in her seat.

"I need to stretch my legs," she blurted.

Jack blinked. "Now?"

"Soon."

"You've got loads of leg room."

She pursed her lips. "I'm saying, I saw a sign for a rest area, and I'd like to stretch. my. legs."

"You need a pit stop?"

65

Her face grew warm. "If I say I need to wash my hands or stretch my legs that's code for I've had too much of your danged coffee. Now, be a gentleman, and put on your blinker."

He chuckled. "Yes, ma'am."

~ * ~

Jack pulled into an open parking spot in front of a low, brown building. The only other car sat near the far end, the owner pulling a black dog toward a patch of dead grass. Jack tapped his fingers on the steering wheel. Annoyed by the weird looks the woman with the dog kept throwing at him—as if he wanted to watch her dog take a crap—he strode after Helen.

She stopped half-way up the walkway. "I thought you were waiting in the car."

"I thought I'd 'stretch my legs' while we were here." He used air quotes. "Also, I need to walk the dog, see a man about a horse… or as you southerners should learn to say, 'take a whiz.' It's a long drive. If you need a potty break, just raise your hand."

"Why are you being cranky?"

"I'm not—" He stopped himself and shoved his hand through his hair, kneading the stiff muscles at the base of his neck. It ached from too many miles watching for changing road conditions. It hadn't helped that their conversation had dredged up memories and feeling he would rather leave buried.

"Maybe because I'm tired of driving, I'm hungry, and I need caffeine. I'll be out in a minute." He pushed at the door only to stop abruptly. "You've got to be kidding."

Helen read the sign taped to the inside of the glass. "Burst water pipe. Use portable toilet out back." A large arrow pointed to the side of the building.

They walked two abreast to the side of the building before Helen paused and gave him a look. "You go first." He said.

She nodded and disappeared, returning a few minutes later. He found her waiting for him after he'd taken his turn.

"Thank you for stopping," she said, all southern politeness.

"No problem."

"Why don't you let me drive for a while?" She had on that serene, placating expression she used on old people. It annoyed him that she'd use it on him, but that may have been the hunger talking.

Jack strode toward his car. "Um, no."

"Why not? I'm an excellent driver."

"Your arm," he waved toward her shoulder.

"I'm supposed to exercise it."

"You don't have a license."

"Of course, I have a license."

"*With* you?" Satisfied that she'd stopped trying to argue her way into the driver's seat, as if that would ever happen, Jack allowed himself to soften. "I'll grab some take-out coffee and food on the way. I'll be fine. Let's go."

He opened the passenger door and glanced behind him. Helen still stood in the middle of the walkway.

She pointed to the side of the building. "Wasn't that dog with someone when we got here?"

Jack glanced at the mutt sitting in the middle of a brown spot of matted weeds. "Yeah. That woman." He made a vague motion toward the space where the other car had been parked.

"Where is she?"

He frowned at the space where the car had most definitely been parked just a few minutes before. "Out back?"

"Without her car?"

Helen took a few slow steps toward the dog.

"No," Jack said.

"He's not going to bite me," she said. "Look at that sweet face."

"I mean, no, we're not getting involved."

"I'm not getting involved," she said on her way to absolute involvement. "I'm just checking to see if he has tags."

Jack glared at the empty road as if that would make the woman rematerialize. His was the only car at the rest area.

"Oh, you, poor boy," Helen cooed. She crouched in front of the dog, speaking softly, her southern lilt more pronounced than usual as she whispered sweet nothings. The mutt rolled onto her back in surrender. Correction: he. Definitely a 'he.'

Helen smiled, rubbing the mutt's belly and then turned to Jack with a look of triumph. "He's a big softie. Look at him, just wanting some lovin'. Who's a good boy? Oh, who's a good boy?"

"Well?" Jack said, interrupting the love fest. "Any I.D.?"

"No collar."

Jack swore under his breath. He knew what was coming.

Helen patted the dog's exposed belly once more. "Well, we can't leave him here."

"She might come back."

Helen gave Jack the kind of look a mother gives a child when she knows they are lying. "She's not coming back. This dog has been abandoned, and we are not leaving him here next to a busy road."

Jack glanced back at the completely silent roadway. "He'll be fine."

Helen stood, hands on her hips. "I'm not leaving without him."

He strode back to his car.

"Jack!" Helen ran after him, the dog at her heels. "I'm not paying you if you leave me here. That wasn't our deal."

"I said I would take you to Pennsylvania. You are in Pennsylvania. By the terms of our verbal contract, I think I'm in the clear. Also, I'm getting a rope."

He opened the trunk, rummaged, and pulled out a length of cording. He twisted it around, formed a loop and held it toward her.

She audibly gasped. "What do you expect me to do with *that*?"

"Put him on a leash?"

"Oh." She blew out a breath. "I thought you meant for me to do something else with it."

He stared at her, the cording dangling between them. "What, the ever-loving fuck kind of person do you think I am?"

She blanched. "The kind that laughs at funerals?"

He snatched the cord back and strode over to the dog. The dog cowered. Jack willed himself to soften his body language. He hunkered down. "Come on. That's a boy." The dog crawled forward, head bowed. Jack slipped the loop over its head and gave it a slight tug. "Up we go. We'll find you a nice shelter. Don't you worry."

Helen opened the rear door of the car and hurried to lay an old towel from the trunk over the back seat. The dog jumped in.

They got back in the car. Jack started the engine.

Helen turned toward him. "I'm sorry to—"

"We're not discussing it," Jack said. He pulled his cell phone out of his pocket and handed it to her. "Just find the nearest animal shelter. After that, I'm going to get food, and after that, I'm going to crash somewhere with a horizontal surface. Got it?"

She nodded.

"Good."

He pulled back onto the highway. Half an hour later they arrived at a depressing concrete building with a sign imploring patrons to 'spay or neuter.'

"Wait here," Jack said.

"I can come in."

"You're wearing slippers."

She nodded, visibly swallowed, and said, "Thank you."

Jack grunted and opened the back door, coaxing the dog to follow him to the building.

He entered the shelter, the scents of animals and pee and despair hitting him like a wave.

"Dropping off?"

Jack eyed the young kid behind the counter, probably no more than twenty, his hair already thinning. "Yeah."

The kid pushed forward a clipboard with a pen dangling from a string.

"What's this?"

The kid shrugged. "Paperwork. We need to keep track of surrenders."

"He's not mine. He's a stray. Abandoned."

A dog barked from somewhere in the bowels of the building setting off a chain reaction of barking. One of them started howling. It gave Jack the willies. He felt a tug on the rope-leash and glanced down as the mutt shifted behind him. Coward. He'd probably have it way better in here with food and care and shelter. What did Jack know about dogs?

Jack took the pen and started filling out the form. "So, uh. What's your placement rate? How long before this guy is likely to be out of here?"

"Ten days."

"That's not so bad." He turned to the dog behind his leg. "Chin up. The longest you'll be in here is a couple weeks."

"Ten days before they leave… one way or another."

Jack stopped writing. "What?"

"Hey, it used to be eight, but we had a whole adoption thing last month, so we have more capacity."

The kid leaned over. "Bad luck for this guy, though. Black Dog Syndrome and all."

Jack looked at the door marked "Employees Only" and back at the dog at his feet. He dropped the pen and let it swing like a pendulum. "I'm not filling this out."

"We're not supposed to accept surrenders without it."

Jack backed toward the door, palms out. "I guess your hands are tied then."

He tugged the mutt to the car and opened the back door. The dog leapt in.

"What happened?" Helen wanted to know.

"No room," he said. The dog smiled back at him in the rearview mirror. He'd swear to it.

Helen glanced back at the dog. "What do we do now?"

Jack threw the car into gear and pulled onto the main road. "No idea."

He contemplated powering through to Cutler, but he was starved and exhausted and now transporting a rag-tag cast of misfits including a homeless chick and an abandoned dog. If he kept going like this, he'd roll into Cutler like some clown car, which, oddly, wasn't as unappealing as he thought it would be.

"I know I said I wanted to get there today, but we wouldn't get to town until late, and I'm spent. How about we put a few more miles between us and the crazy and find some food and a bed." He winked. He couldn't say why. He never winked. Maybe he was feeling giddy that he'd just single-handedly saved a dog's life.

"Okay."

He schooled his eyelids to behave. "You sure you don't mind another night on the road? Even if it's no better than the place we had this morning?"

"I'd gladly sleep on the floor if it comes to that."

His giddiness lost its glow. "You'd rather sleep on the floor than share a bed?"

"That's not what I said."

"That's exactly what you said."

"I meant, if there were nothing but floor available, I'd sleep there. I'd much prefer a bed, thank you."

"Even with me?"

Her brow creased as she looked at him. "What's gotten into you? We shared a bed this morning, remember? And it was fine. Nothing happened."

No. Nothing had happened, because after several hours of tossing and turning, Jack had given up trying to quiet his mind enough to fall asleep and had gone out in search of caffeine and sugar. Then he'd come back and taken a cold shower.

They could be adults together. Doing adult things. And this did not have to include sex. He was adult enough to know this even though the primal part of his brain helpfully supplied alternative scenarios.

"I'm teasing. This is my teasing face," he said.

"Oh. It looks like your other faces. When you're teasing you should smile more."

"Like this?"

She laughed, recoiling. "Lord, no." Her laughter was sweet like warm honey. His primal brain played with the word honey. Not helpful.

"You're saying I should avoid smiling?"

"Yes, if you smile like a serial killer."

"A serial killer? Okay. Wow."

She squinted and peered at him which made him hyperaware of being examined. "I think it's your eyes. They're too blue. Too intense."

"My apologies."

"They're nice. Very nice, just… you can be intimidating."

"Me? Intimidating?"

"Don't act so surprised. Everything about you is intimidating. You interrogate people. You pin them with your laser eyes… You have a way of making people feel exposed. It's your M.O."

"Do you?"

"Do I what?"

"Feel exposed."

"Of course not." She flitted her hand in the air and straightened the cuff of her sleeve. I'm talking about other people."

He smothered a grin. *Liar.*

"Just to put your mind at ease. I'm punch-drunk tired, so even if I were inclined to abuse my superpowers, I'm too tired to do so." He pinned her with his gaze and smiled. "Even if someone were buck naked."

"Good to know," she wheezed.

He swung his gaze back to the road. "Just to put your mind at ease."

"You do know that this only makes you more creepy? I feel someone should tell you."

He swung his piercing, blue, hypnotic, soul-baring eyes toward her. "It's. A. Joke. We've been driving for miles. I'm tired and hangry with a stray dog and a stray woman. If I were a serial killer, my car would be empty by now."

"I was making a joke," she said.

He ran a hand through his hair. "God, we're so not funny."

"What a shame, for I dearly love to laugh."

He glanced over. Her dark eyes sparkled as her lips fought a smile. She probably wondered if he got the reference. Lord help him, he did.

"And I like to hear it," he said. Then he leaned forward and turned on the radio and pretended he hadn't just admitted he was crushing on the gorgeous woman who was only passing through his life with trouble and chaos in her wake.

~ * ~

71

Helen watched the dog snoozing in the back seat. She couldn't believe how content he seemed with two strangers going who-knew-where. It's like he blindly trusted them to do the right thing by him.

About half an hour after leaving the shelter, they found a pet supply chain store. Jack had run in on account of Helen's lack of proper shoes or a shower. He tossed the bags of food and supplies on the floor of the back seat, tossed her a casual smile and pulled out onto the main road again.

Ever since that strange conversation about beds they'd had, she'd struggled to read his mood. Had he been serious? Joking? What did he even mean? Was he flirting? How did she feel about that?

He'd turned off the radio before heading into the store, mumbling something about reception and too much talk. The silence spun out between them like all the unanswered questions pinging in her brain.

Helen folded her hands in her lap. "Thank you," she blurted. "You're a good person."

Jack seemed surprised she'd spoken. He shrugged. "He's gotta eat."

"Please keep track of the receipt."

"I wish you'd stop doing that."

"What?"

His eyes cut to her. "Acting like I'm poor. I can buy a bag of dog food."

"I know, but I made you take him in. I feel responsible."

"I'm a grown-ass man, Helen. If I didn't want him here, he wouldn't be."

She couldn't argue that. Then it occurred to her. It was true of her, too. If he didn't want her along for the ride, there'd been a thousand opportunities to leave her behind. She wondered why he hadn't ditched her miles ago, even after she'd told him that crazy lie about finding her own way home. She was the very definition of excess baggage.

"You must be getting hungry," she finally said.

His mouth hitched up on one side. "I literally considered buying one of those open-bin dog biscuits and eating it as a snack on the way back to the car."

"We can stop for take-out."

"I'll hit a wall if I stop now." He handed her his phone. "I'd at least like to cross over into Pennsylvania. Can you find a town with food and lodging? Take 84 though. I like that route better."

"Sure." She took the phone and woke it from snooze, accidentally depressing the volume key. It beeped. She stilled, the breath tight in her lungs. Earlier that day, she'd turned off the volume. When had he turned it back on? She snuck a peek at Jack. His expression gave nothing away.

Did he know? Suspect? She slid the volume off again and called up the mapping app. The last thing she wanted was to have Jack's phone blow up with people wondering where the heck she was.

"Did you want to call your family again?" he asked. "Just to check in?"

"The cell service is spotty here. I can do it later when we stop. They know where I am." She smiled serenely, or what she hoped appeared serenely, at Jack. "There looks to be a decent sized town about twenty or thirty minutes from here. Should have everything we need." She gave the town name.

"Great."

"Great."

Jack's phone suddenly flashed an incoming call. Helen reflexively answered it. Better she play interference than have it all blow up in her face.

"Are you answering my phone?" he asked.

"You're driving," she said. "Hello?"

"You!" barked a voice on the other end of the line. "Where in God's green earth are you now? And what in hell were you thinking? Was that a real squirrel? Was it? Don't answer. I don't want to know. Shit on a stick, Helen Walker, if you're going to disappear, at least have the decency to *stay* disappeared. I'm trying to recruit men for you, and then they see you looking like hell warmed over, waving some dead thing, and crying like a… I don't know what, but it is going to be one *hell* of a PR mess."

"Marcia, I'm sorry."

"You should be!" Marcia swore again, a long string of barely decipherable expletives. "You are *so* lucky I'm so friggin' happy right now, or I'd be livid. What the hell?"

She had no answer, because, honestly, what could she say?

"Well?"

"The funeral thing got out of hand, I'll admit."

"Whatever. I don't want to talk about it. Ivy is working on spinning it for the press. I'm in Boston tomorrow for the first casting call. Where are you?"

Helen gave the name of the town. Marcia cursed.

"Do they even have electricity there? Are you in Amish country? Good God. I never pegged you for a runner. But here we are. Tell me you just needed a moment. Tell me you don't plan to leave me high and dry here."

Helen held herself still. "Of course not."

"Good. Whatever happens on your little finding-yourself, eat-and-pray walkabout, I need you ready to roll on schedule. Don't let me down."

"I won't. I promise."

"If your season doesn't start filming on time my neck is in a noose. Understood?"

"Understood."

"Good. Now get your ass to Georgia by the seventeenth or you'll be fined for breach of contract."

Two weeks.

"Alabama," Helen corrected reflexively, because—dammit—there *was* a difference. "I'm from Alabama."

"The seventeenth," Marcia repeated. "I don't care if you have to hire a freaking donkey like the Virgin Blessed Mary. Be there."

"Yes, ma'am."

The line went dead.

Helen's hand shook. *Two weeks.* She had two weeks to gather the courage to see this thing through. She'd made a commitment to the show, and last season hadn't been that bad apart from the repeated rejection thing. Hadn't she mostly balked at the whole Trojan Bus of Love idea anyway? Now that was a non-issue. She wouldn't be riding in it. That was better, right?

She had two weeks to face the fact that she would rather road trip with a random, charmingly cranky stranger than continue down the path she'd been on, but that was tomorrow's worry. Tonight, she wouldn't think about any of it.

"You're not fooling anyone," Jack said.

Helen nearly fumbled the phone onto the floor. "I'm not?"

"No. Anyone can see you're too worried what people will think. Why do you care so much what people think? Just go after what you want."

"I made a commitment."

Also, she'd be out a breathtaking amount of money if she defaulted, but Jack didn't need to hear the gritty details.

"People go back on their word all the time," he said.

"I don't."

He slanted a look at her she couldn't read and didn't care to decipher.

Fine. It wasn't a particularly proud moment to assert that one's word was honorable when you had literally lied to that person just hours before.

Helen's gut roiled from guilt and lack of food. A single powdered doughnut and a handful of baby carrots only lasted so long.

"Sorry," Jack said. "That was a low blow."

"Don't worry about it," she said, flashing him a smile. *And stop being nice to me*, she silently added. "Marcia was just confirming the filming schedule."

"Great."

Great.

CHAPTER 7

The hotel parking lot glistened with puddles, the air damp and chill in his lungs. Jack strode back from the check-in office and opened the back door. He'd half hoped the place wouldn't have a vacancy, at least then he could have blamed his pissy mood on that rather than the fact that the call from the show had only served to remind him he was a stepping-stone in this woman's life.

"Do they take dogs?" Helen asked.

Jack clipped the collar and leash he'd bought at the pet store to the dog and tugged. "I didn't ask."

"What if someone is allergic to dogs?" she said.

Jack grabbed the sack of supplies. "Given the look of this place, allergies are the least of anyone's worries."

She made a face. "Should we keep looking?"

He shut the car door in reply. He was too damn tired to worry about some hypothetical person's allergies, and if that made him a bad person, so be it.

Helen caught up to him outside their unit while Jack waited for the dog to relieve itself.

"He really ought to have a name," she murmured.

The dog sat, scratched behind his ear, then stared dolefully up at them.

"A name implies we're keeping him, which we're not."

"He has a collar and a leash. It looks like you're keeping him."

"I'm not." Jack pushed open the door to their room. Stale air washed over them. He no longer worried about allergies. He shooed the dog into the bathroom and shut the door.

"Zeus," she said. "We could name him Zeus."

"Zeus is for German Shepherds or Pit Bulls. He's neither."

"Leopold."

He gave her side-eye as a reply.

"It's got to be something noble, to boost his spirits and make people want to adopt him. Duke!"

Jack picked up a three-ring binder from the small desk and flipped it open. "More like Doofus. He'd still be sitting there at the rest stop if it weren't for us. And the fact that he signed on with the two of us only proves his poor judgment."

"Duke, it is," she said.

Jack flipped a page. "Looks like our options are pizza or Chinese. I could go either way."

"I'm easy."

She cast him a brief, awkward smile then cleared her throat. His felt thick.

The tip of his tongue touched his lips before retreating. He was dead-ass exhausted and hungry as hell, but he was still a man in the presence of a gorgeous woman, so, yes, he had thoughts. It didn't matter that the day had been a wild ride in every way, or that there were two beds this time, or that she probably hadn't showered in thirty-six hours and would be out of his life and on with hers in a matter of days. Thoughts didn't care. At all. He set the notebook down, flexing his right hand. "I'll decide on the way," he said.

He stepped toward the door and stopped beside her. He wanted to say something. He wanted to tell her that he liked dogs, that he was normally considered funny and a good listener. He wanted to apologize for the way he'd behaved at the diner, explain that it was more than fatigue and surprise that had him lashing out, that his best friend was getting married, and so was his sister, and it made him all too painfully aware that he was stuck in life and hadn't even realized it until a frazzled brunette had dropped into it unannounced and uninvited.

He wanted to say a lot of things, but he caught the uncertainty in her warm, brown eyes and stepped away again, only managing a curt, "I'll be back," before closing the door behind him.

Forty-five minutes had passed by the time he strode up the concrete walkway to their door. His gut warmed with something that felt like anticipation, and he allowed himself a small chuckle as he tapped the door with his toe on account of his hands being full of plastic bags and pizza. He'd had some time to chill as he'd wandered the discount store next to the pizza parlor. He'd decided that ships passing in the night could still, you know, wave to one another. No harm no foul.

The door cracked open. Helen peeked through before shutting it again to release the chain. He strode in like a proud peacock. "I got you some stuff."

She gripped a towel with one hand, her damp hair hanging in a loosely tangled mass down her back. "You did?" She peeked in a bag, her lips pressing together. "I'll be out in a minute."

"Take your time."

A mite deflated from her response, he waited on the edge of the bed, debating whether to dig into the pizza or not.

The dog lay on a towel in the far corner thumping his tail on the carpet, fur glistening. "She cleaned you up, too, huh? Good. No offense, but you stank."

When Helen next emerged, her hair was combed smooth and she had on the leggings and oversized sweatshirt he'd bought her. He didn't dare ask if she was okay with the other items he'd tossed in the cart at the discount store. A three-pack of bikini panties. Tinted lip gloss. Toothbrush and toothpaste. A pair of those white sneakers soccer moms wear. He'd hurried through in the twenty minutes he was told the pizza would take, trying to think what she might need.

"Thank you," she said. "I actually feel human again."

He shrugged one shoulder, pleased. "It was right next to the pizza place. Plus, I was running out of clean clothes to loan you."

"It's all very thoughtful. I can't believe you even found shoes that fit. How did you know my size?"

"You left your others in the car."

Jack took a bite of pizza and pointed his slice toward the dog.

"He smells better," he said by way of thanks. He jumped up, pulled a small bag of store-brand dog food out of one of the plastic bags, tore the lid off the pizza box and tossed some kibble onto it before setting it in front of the dog. "Bon appetit," he said.

"You know that that no-name dog food is full of fillers."

He raised his gaze to meet hers.

The dog chased after the last piece of kibble as it rolled into the corner of the box.

"He seems to like it all right," he said.

"Our vet always recommended grain-free for our Maltipoo. It keeps their coat soft and shiny."

"Noted." Why did it not surprise him the least that she'd have a tiny little designer dog for a pet? The warm fuzzy feeling he'd had cooled. Jack tilted the to-go coffee cup to his lips, drained it, then disappeared into the bathroom. He came back to the doorway, having refilled it with water. "Dork!"

"His name is Duke," she said.

"Doofus it is."

The dog eagerly lapped water from the cup.

"You didn't buy him a bowl?" she asked.

"It must have fallen out of the bag in the car. I'll get it later."

Jack washed up, grabbed another slice of pizza and sat on a bed, his back against the headboard. He stared at the faded print hanging on the wall opposite, digesting his dinner and the day's events. He knew he was overtired, but he couldn't help feeling annoyed.

Helen reached for a slice of pizza.

"Is there a reason you have such a low opinion of me?" he asked.

She froze, her hand in the pizza box, and glanced up. He stared back at her. She did that pageant smile thing that didn't quite reach her eyes and annoyed the shit out of him. "I don't have a low opinion of you."

He ticked off on his fingers. "I'm disrespectful of the dead, think nothing of strangling stray dogs, oh, and I'm apparently cheap. Newsflash: Because of you, I'm already spending two nights in hotels I hadn't planned on, and Wally World only has so many options."

She took a bite of pizza. He waited while she chewed and swallowed. "I'm sorry. I never meant to imply you were cheap."

"But I'm a puppy-killing social boor? Got it. You know what burns my ass? I'm the guy that's taken you in, fed you, even bought clothes for you. I'm not asking for you to fawn all over me with gratitude, but it would be nice if you didn't treat me like crap."

"I know you're not a puppy-killer."

"Thanks. Social boor, it is."

She wiped the corners of her mouth with the back of her hand and managed to make it look classy. "If I'm being brutally honest, you do have a habit of sharing unsolicited opinions."

"I spent the first sixteen years of my life stepping on eggshells. If the truth hurts, deal with it."

"See? That's what I'm talking about. You're sometimes... abrasive."

"Whatever."

"And dismissive."

He swore under his breath, yanked the pizza box toward him then changed his mind and shoved it away again. He stood and rummaged through the grocery bag on the desk and pulled out a brown bottle. "I'd offer you one, but beer probably stains your teeth or has too many calories or something. Whatever. I'm done trying." He grabbed his coat and shrugged into one sleeve, the bottle still in one hand.

"Where are you going?"

"Out."

"Out where? You just go here."

He stood over her, fuming, then took a long pull off his beer. "My car, Princess. I'm going to sit in my car, drink my beer, and try to convince myself I shouldn't just kick your prissy ass to the curb and be done with you."

"Maybe take two beers."

"What?"

"You look almost finished with that one."

He pointedly finished the first, grabbed a second bottle, and slammed the door behind him.

~ * ~

Helen stared at the closed door, expecting Jack to storm back in at any moment, her body tensing in anticipation.

After a few minutes, she realized the tension wasn't about fearing that Jack would come back, but that he wouldn't. She shook herself out of her stupor and turned toward Duke huddled in the corner.

"It's okay, baby," she said. "The yelly man is gone now." She cringed as she said it, because, to be honest, she knew she'd poked the bear. Still, there was a reason folks back home were known for their gentle phrasing and soft manners... it smoothed over the inevitable conflicts in life. It wasn't that she didn't feel emotions, but she knew enough to school herself and *read* a situation for heaven's sake. What would the world come to if everyone just let fly with whatever awful thought sprung into their head? Blurting things out? If he wanted to throw a tantrum and sulk in his car, so be it.

She could teach Jack a few things about social graces, the first of which being that you always offered a lady a drink before you served yourself.

She slid one of the brown bottles out of the carton and stared at the metal top. Jack had used some sort of key ring to open his, which he'd taken with him. She glanced at the edge of the desk, carefully positioned the bottle, and smacked it sharply with her palm. The lid popped off and skittered behind the TV cabinet.

Prissy, indeed.

She sat on the edge of the bed, drank her beer, and ate her pizza and nearly fell on the floor when Jack's phone started vibrating on the coverlet beside her.

She stared at it as if it were an alien egg about to hatch.

It must have fallen out of his pocket. She cast a glance at the door and reached over to pick it up, smoothing her thumb over the screen to wake it up. Yes, she felt guilty, but who didn't have their phone password protected in this day and age? It's like he was inviting her to peek.

She watched as multiple text alerts came through in succession.

And, honestly, it was absolutely an accident that she tapped to open the conversation.

> Jack. It's your dad.
> You haven't picked up calls all day.
> You there? Call me.
> I know you're driving but call me when you get this. K?

Helen scanned the top of the screen. The contact was labeled *Daniel.* As in Daniel Adams? Jack's dad? That'd make sense. Another text popped through.

> Jack come on. You're worrying the moms.

The moms? Guilt swamped Helen like a wave. Great. Now she was worrying mothers.

In retrospect, she would not count her next move as one of her finest moments. Helen started typing.

> Hey, I'm here. Sorry. On the road.

She hit SEND and waited. She didn't have to wait long.

> Finally! So... how are things?

Helen stared at the screen. What would Jack say???

> Fine

She debated whether to add a final period and then finally sent it without one, giving a whole new meaning to the W.W.J.D. catchphrase.

> You know you can tell me if they're not.

Helen licked her lips and quickly typed.

> Not a lot to report. Crap weather. Why? What's up?

They say you've kidnapped that Walker girl.

Helen nearly choked on her own shock.

WHAT??? WHO???

Not me. I'm sure it's a misunderstanding, but... that Marcia Powers is going crazy. Threatened to call the FBI if you don't turn around and bring the Walker girl back ASAP

Helen's fingers typed furiously.

First of all, she's a grown woman, not a girl. And second...
I'm not turning around.

We can work this out. But you can't keep running.

Oh, right, she should probably address that part.

I. Haven't. Kidnapped. Anyone.

She held the camera up, smiled and took a selfie then quickly sent it.

See? She's fine. Here of her own free will.

I'm calling. This is no way to have a conversation.

Suddenly the phone flashed an incoming call. Helen glanced at the motel-room door in panic. What could she do? She answered it.

"Hello?"

"Jack?"

She cleared her throat. "Uh, no. This is Helen. Jack said you'd want to talk to me."

"Yeah, uh, this is Daniel, Jack's dad."

"Yes." She wet her lips. "We've met before. At the wedding? You may not remember. You were quite ill. I hope you're feeling better now." There. She'd chat him up. She could do this. How many awkward dinner parties and church socials had prepared her for this very moment? "That was a delicious meal, by the way. I would love the dressing recipe sometime."

There was a pause. "I'm fine. Thanks. Say, can I talk to Jack for a minute?"

"I'm so sorry, but he's just gone to the car." *See? Not a lie. Tell the truth whenever possible.* "Can I pass along a message?"

"Are you okay? He hasn't done anything he shouldn't, has he?"

"Jack has been a complete gentleman." *If not pleasant.* "I'm sorry if you or anyone was worried, but I just spoke to Marcia Powers not long ago, and it's all worked out. It's a funny story, actually—one I'm sure Jack will want to share when he gets home, but we're on our way to his friend's wedding, so..."

"Both of you?"

"I mean, Jack is. I'm not, of course." *Gah!* "I'm heading home to Alabama. I'm so sorry, but we're, uh, actually on the road, and the reception isn't so good. You're cutting in and out."

"You just said Jack was getting something from the car."

"I meant we were getting in the car. We're on the road now. I may lose you. Thanks so much for checking in!"

She held the phone further and further from her face as she said the last line then pressed END.

Oh, sweet mother of sunshine. What in heaven's name had she just done?

Panicked, that's what.

She looked down at the phone. She should delete the text conversation, because the only thing worse than lying is being caught in a lie. She quickly scrolled through to slide the conversation into oblivion. *There.* Her VBS youth pastor would be so proud.

A knock on the door made her jump. She dropped the phone on the bed like its battery had burst into flames.

"It's me," Jack said through the door. "I forgot the key."

Helen grabbed her beer to appear nonchalant and swung the door wide.

She raised the bottle to her lips and prayed Jack didn't notice her hand shaking. His eyes followed the movement.

"Help yourself," he murmured.

Adrenaline mixed with the alcohol and flooded her with a warmth that had nothing to do with the radiator on the wall. She wanted to tell him he was a decent person, and she didn't think he was a puppy-killer or a kidnapper for that matter, but this was a slippery slope. Jack... Jack was a temporary companion on this detour of hers. She couldn't let herself get attached to him.

"I did," she said. She knew she was being purposefully off-putting, and it felt uncomfortably out of character, but in her defense, he'd been pretty dang blunt at the diner this morning, and he hadn't wanted to get involved until she was practically trailing from his bumper. Also, once he found out she'd impersonated him on his own phone to his own father, he'd thank her for putting emotional distance between them, so really, she was doing both of them a favor here.

She took another sip and watched as he sat to take off his shoes.

Fine. Her actions didn't excuse being ungrateful. He *had* bought her clothes and done other nice things since this morning. She knew she ought to apologize—emotional distance didn't require one to lose all manners—but the words wouldn't form. The dog snored in a heap in the corner, oblivious to the drumming of her pulse in her ears.

"I'm sorry," she finally muttered.

Jack stilled. "For what?"

"For earlier. You know." She waved her fingers vaguely, hoping not to have to rehash it all or blurt out her most recent sins.

He nodded.

She waited.

"This is when you say all is forgiven," she said, hoping he understood how these social niceties worked so they could be done with the whole thing.

"Is it?" he wondered aloud.

She blew out a breath. True, she wanted to put distance between them, but that was mainly for her own benefit, wasn't it? Jack only knew half the story, and while he was rough around the edges, he appeared to have a good heart. "Can we start over?"

"What point do you have in mind? Because if it's all the same to you, this has been a hell of a day." His lips tilted with wry humor. The shadow of stubble darkened his face. He looked utterly spent. And alarmingly adorable.

Helen took another swig of beer to dilute the strange awareness swirling inside her. How odd.

"It has," she said. "And for my part in that, I apologize. Stressful situations can lead to all sorts of uncharacteristic behavior and heightened emotions."

"Meaning?" He skewered her with his gaze. Her skin felt hot where it landed.

"I'm saying, we're not our best selves right now. Either of us." Especially her. She glanced down at his phone on the bed as if it might reanimate and blurt all her secrets. "I know you think I'm some air-headed hot mess of a drama queen, but I'm not. I'm a successful, intelligent, compassionate woman. And you," she continued, ignoring his raised eyebrow, "are clearly a..." *Man? Hottie? Lucky woman's one-night stand?* "...decent person."

"Don't hurt yourself falling all over me."

She pictured herself falling all over him. It didn't hurt one bit.

She bit the corner of her lip. "I know you like to come off as gruff and distant, but don't pretend that Duke and I mean nothing to you. You don't care for things you don't care about."

Jack said nothing.

"So, thank you for the clothes and the food and everything. I *will* pay you back. Not because I think you need the money, but because I'm responsible for my own actions."

"You're welcome," he murmured.

His blue eyes bore into hers, and a flush of something tingly and awkward rose up inside her. It may have had something to do with seeing him as something other than the crusty chauffer of her getaway car. "I mean, at first I thought you were a pompous blow-hard who had an opinion on everything."

"What changed your mind?" He raised an eyebrow which only made her think of pirates and English rogues.

"Who says it's changed?"

She smiled sweetly.

"God, you're difficult," he said, but it didn't sound like a bad thing.

"Thank you. I've never been told that before."

"Seriously?"

"Seriously."

"So, we bring out the worst in each other."

"Or maybe we bring out the fight in each other."

"I don't want to fight," he said. "With you or anybody."

"Me either."

He clicked on the bathroom light and cracked the door, then turned off the overhead lights. "Goodnight."

He stretched out on top of the covers and closed his eyes. She watched him, waiting for him to get under the covers properly, the *tick, tick, tick* of the heating unit on the wall the only sound in the small room.

Except he didn't. After a few minutes it became clear he was well and truly asleep. She tiptoed over to the pizza box and grabbed a second slice, pondering a world where she found herself in a run-down motel somewhere in Pennsylvania with a sleeping man and stray dog, and it felt... weirdly all right.

85

Helen slipped under her own covers and lay her head on her pillow. "You're a strange man, Jack Adams," she whispered.

"Yeah, but you like it," came a low murmur from the next bed. "You totally like it."

CHAPTER 8

The next morning, Jack walked back to the car, a couple of plastic bags fisted in his hand. He wordlessly tossed the bags on the seat beside the snoring dog and got behind the wheel again.

"Thank you." Helen's cheeks went hot. After they'd showered and dressed, she'd asked if he could pick up a few more items for her, like hair ties, mascara and panty liners. If Aunt Iris knew she'd had to disclose her preference between unscented and scented, she'd melt into a discreet puddle of mint julep on the spot. Not that Iris drank mint juleps. She was more of a dirty martini fan.

"I'll put it on your tab," Jack said, casting her a quick sidelong glance.

She nodded and looked out the window as they pulled out of the parking lot. Aside from the panty liner clarification, those were probably the most words Jack had spoken since they'd left the hotel that morning. It was probably for the best. If they made idle chit-chat, Helen would probably blurt out that Jack's father had called or that she found the twist of muscles in his forearm particularly sexy. Then she'd have to figure out how to get further than Cutler without money or an ID. No, talking should be avoided at all costs.

She dozed for a while which must have taken up time, because soon they passed a town limits sign. They rolled through the town of Cutler, its long, industrial-looking brick buildings interspersed with nondescript wood facades. A steeple here. A fast-food restaurant there. It could be Anytown, U.S.A., with its mix of old family businesses and nation-wide chains all commingling and elbowing one another for space.

Helen clasped her hands together in her lap and glanced at Jack's profile. Nerves and hunger swirled in the pit of her stomach. "How long until we're there?"

"Not sure."

"You don't know where your own friend lives?"

"He's moved in together with his fiancé since I last saw him."

"Oh. Do they know I'm coming? That you have a guest?"

"A guest?" Jack asked. "Is that what we're calling you now?" His eyes returned to the road. "Yeah, I texted him. And about Doofus back there." He hooked a thumb toward the back seat. "That dog had better be quiet, because Mike's condo doesn't allow pets."

"He hasn't barked once since we got him."

Jack grunted at the road

"If it's all the same to you, I'd prefer you not mention that it's me who's with you."

"You're the reason I'm not there yet. Literally the reason."

"I think the ice storm could be blamed for that, but that's not what I meant. I mean, that it's me, Helen Walker, from the show. I would appreciate y'all having discretion."

She said it softly as if her presence in his life was naughty gossip she preferred not get out, which is exactly how it felt. As Aunt Iris would say, young ladies don't go spending the night with young men unless there's a ring and a preacher involved.

Iris could dig deep for her Alabama roots when she wanted to for being a suburban widow who used to go to drag shows to get inspiration for pageant gowns.

"I can guarantee he doesn't know who the hell you are even if I said your name."

"You'd be surprised who watches the show."

"I told him I had a friend who'd hitched a ride south with me and might crash for a night or two. He said it was fine. My guess is he's got bigger things to worry about given he's getting married in a week."

She wanted to press further, to ask about sleeping arrangements and more, but then Jack braked, said, "Here's our turn," and they pulled into the parking lot of a small apartment complex.

She wished she'd had time to freshen up or at least put on some of the mascara Jack had gotten her, but he was already out of the car, the driver's door slamming shut and the rear opening. He popped his head in and gave her an impatient look. "Grab your stuff," he said as he led Duke out by his leash and slammed the rear door, too.

Helen scrambled out, gripping her plastic bags from the back seat. She hung back as Jack knocked. The door swung open, and a slim man with dark eyes, wire-rimmed glasses and a broad grin welcomed them.

"Huh." Jack gestured toward the man's glasses. "These are new. Going blind already?"

The man shrugged and patted his thick, black curls. "At least my hair isn't thinning."

Jack laughed, a surprising sound.

The man reached around Jack, his hand extended, eyes curiously taking her in. "I'm Mike. Jack here has told me nothing about you. Also, he implied you were a dude. Which you're obviously not."

"I'm Helen." She fumbled the bags in order to shake hands. "Thank you for your hospitality."

"No problem. Here," he gestured for them to set their things on a bench in the small entryway. "I'll show you around. We're still getting settled, so don't mind the mess.

"So, this is the living room, master bedroom, guest room/office, and downstairs we've set up a gym. It's great for strengthening my knee after the accident."

Jack snorted.

Mike addressed Helen. "I had to cancel our hiking trip last fall on account of a workplace injury."

Jack turned to Helen. "Did I mention he's an accountant?"

"Those old filing cabinets are damn heavy," Mike said.

"Ouch," Helen said.

After the house tour, Mike offered them a drink, and they sat in the living room. Helen wished she could excuse herself and disappear in her own space for a while, but she pasted on her cocktail reception smile and let the men catch up with one another.

Duke's ears perked and he sat up next to Helen's knee. She stroked his head and wondered at the slight tension in Mike's smile.

"So, tell me about this mystery woman you're about to marry." Jack sat back on the sofa, one arm flung wide. "When did this all happen?"

"We moved here last month."

"I meant, how long have you known her?"

"Years, actually, but only as friends. We started dating after my accident. It's what brought us together."

Jack had his back to the entry hall, but Helen watched as a woman silently slipped out of her coat and flashed a questioning look at Mike.

"Good for you," Jack said. "It's good to see you happy. I look forward to meeting her."

"The funny thing is," the woman said, "you already have."

CHAPTER 9

Jack turned toward the woman's voice and then leapt from the sofa to face her. "Jesus Christ."

Helen glanced from Jack to Mike to the mystery woman—who was clearly not our Lord and savior.

"Hi, Jack. It's been a while," the woman waved, her smile guarded.

Mike stepped toward the woman and took her arm. "Jenna, I want you to meet Helen. Helen, this is Jenna."

"Helen?" Jenna cried, her gaze finally leaving Jack. "Helen *W.?* Ohmigod! I can't believe it. It's really you, isn't it? From *Happily Ever After?*"

Helen couldn't help but smile. "Yes."

Jenna turned and smacked Mike on the shoulder. "Why didn't you tell me you had Helen Walker in our apartment? What kind of fiancé are you?"

"Fiancé?" Jack wheezed.

"I didn't know," Mike said.

Jenna squeezed Helen's arm. "I am *such* a fan. Omigod! I'm touching Helen Walker's arm! Wait until I tell Cassie."

"This is your fiancé?*"* Jack interrupted.

They all paused. Jenna let go of Helen's arm and turned to Mike. "I told you we should have warned him ahead of time."

Mike mumbled back. "He wouldn't have come."

"Damn right I wouldn't have come!" Jack bellowed. "Newsflash: I can hear you. We're in the same fucking room together."

"I know this is a shock," Jenna said.

"A shock? A shock is when you stick your finger in an outlet. This is a nuclear bomb. Mike, what the ever-loving hell?"

Helen's spine went rigid. She turned toward her hosts. "Would you please excuse us a moment?"

Jack glared at her like she was the one embarrassing them all instead of the other way around. She gestured for him to lead the way and mumbled something unintelligible about needing Jack for a minute. As if they didn't all recognize he was being led out of the room like a toddler throwing a tantrum.

She found him in the guest room staring out the window, his arms crossed. He didn't speak when she entered the room. She left the lights off.

"Well?" he finally said. "What?"

He didn't turn around. She was grateful for that. "I thought you might appreciate a moment to cool down."

"I'm fine."

She took a tentative step closer. "You were yelling. And swearing. It didn't look fine."

He swore again, low and under his breath.

"Why aren't you happy for Mike? What's wrong with Jenna?"

He cursed yet again, mixing it with a snort. "History," was all he said.

"Do you want to talk about it?"

"I was talking about it when you marched me out of the room."

"That's not what I meant."

"I know what you meant." He shoved his fingers through his hair and mumbled something that was probably best left unarticulated, his back rigid.

She reached a tentative hand to his shoulder. He turned, scowled, and walked past her toward the door.

"Jack…"

He spun on her, pinning her with his gaze. "This doesn't concern you."

"Doesn't it? I'm here. I'm a guest, and everyone else seems to know why you're behaving like a big rude baby except for me. This absolutely concerns me. And you obviously need a moment to collect your thoughts before you say something you'll regret."

"My thoughts are crystal clear. He's making a mistake."

"She seems perfectly nice."

"You only like her because she fawned all over you. Where was your concern about being recognized?"

"I'm in the woman's home. I can't expect to hide from her here."

"If only that were an option."

91

Helen touched Jack's arm. He practically buzzed with adrenaline. "I don't know what's going on, but can we go somewhere else? We don't have to stay here."

"We? This whole trip is so..." He swore again, and Helen's eyebrows raised on their own accord. The man had a serious potty mouth.

"This is what's going to happen. I'm going to go find out where Mike wants to put Duke, get him settled, and then you and I are going to go and make nice with our hosts."

"You can't tell me what to do."

"I can and I will."

She stood a little taller, daring him to disobey her, her pulse thrumming in her veins. Why she felt the need to die on this hill, she couldn't say, but she'd drawn a line in the sand, so there was no way she'd back down. A girl had her pride, and she was sick of people ignoring her.

His tongue touched the space between his teeth and lip for one brief moment before his lips curved into a dark smile. "You're kind of hot when you're bossy."

She blinked. She had not seen that coming. "Don't change the subject."

"Would you rather I yell some more?"

"I'll give you five minutes."

"What happens if I take six?"

She refused to answer. Now, he was just baiting her. Helen retrieved Duke from where he sat, apparently just as unsure of his welcome as she was. "Come on, boy. We'll find you a spot."

Mike suggested they keep Duke in the downstairs rec room. Helen filled a bowl with water, and Mike arranged some old blankets into a make-shift bed.

"I wanted to tell him," Mike said as they climbed the stairs again. Jack stood in the doorway of the guest room, brooding. "It's hard, though, you know?" Mike adjusted his glasses. "But it's been so long since—"

"Years," Jack cut in. "So, it's all water under the bridge. I'm starved. Anyone else starved? I think I'm gonna get some dinner. Who wants to come?"

"I thought we could eat here," Jenna said moving to stand near Mike. "We don't want to make you uncomfortable in public."

"Who's uncomfortable? I'm not uncomfortable. My best friend and my ex-girlfriend are getting married. We should definitely celebrate." Jack's gaze drilled into their joined hands.

"Jack..." Mike shook his head. "It's obvious this has thrown you."

"What? Aside from a friend since—what, fifth grade?—not mentioning he was engaged to my ex? I'm fine. Just *fine.*"

"You always did get hangry," Jenna said with a soft smile.

Jack glanced her way, eyes icy. "Exactly," he said. "Let's go."

Helen's stomach twisted just thinking about spending a meal with the tension pulsing in the room. She faked a yawn. "You know what? Y'all go without me. I'm beat."

Jack glared at her. "You'll be fine once you eat."

"No. I'm quite exhausted."

He grasped her elbow. "Will you excuse us another minute?"

He ushered her into the spare room again and closed the door. "You're coming."

Helen spread her hands. "It's clear y'all have a lot to discuss, and it would only make it more awkward with me there. I'm fine staying. I'll keep Duke company."

"Did it ever occur to you I don't want to discuss it?" he bit out.

"They're your friends. You owe it to them to try and make the best of this situation."

"I owe Mike to try and save him from himself."

"You don't mean that. Jenna seems quite nice. I think she genuinely wants to turn the page."

"You're coming. That's final."

"I can't go out in public. Someone might recognize me."

"You're not that famous," he said for the second time in as many days.

"Jenna knew exactly who I was."

"Get changed. Being a buffer is the least you can do."

"Jack…"

"We leave in three minutes." He shut the door.

"Hangry is right," she muttered before turning to dump the contents of the plastic bags Jack had bought onto the guest bed. Helen quickly changed into fresh underwear (Thank you, Jesus!), a pair of black yoga pants, the white tennies, plain fitted tee, and a soft, heathered-blue open-front cardigan. Yes, she looked like a PTA mom, but she felt more composed at least. She reached for the lip balm she'd requested and paused. It wasn't plain but a soft rose lip tint. Well, that was unexpected. She brushed out her hair again, plaited it in a low braid and decided she was as ready as she'd ever be.

They piled into Mike's car, and Jack took the front passenger seat, ostensibly for leg room. Fine. She'd play the part of buffer. If there was anything she was good at, it was soothing people and bringing them together. Daddy always called her his little Hostess with the Mostest. Thinking about it gave her a small smile of pride. Sure, she didn't know the whole story here, like how long ago Jack and Jenna had dated, how serious it was, or how ugly the breakup, but he and Mike had a strong friendship if it survived all this time and the miles between them. Surely, they could smooth over this rough spot.

Helen sneaked a sidelong glance at Jenna. No doubt, Jack's pride was wounded seeing his ex-girlfriend with his best friend. That had to sting. Jenna was beautiful, too, in a spunky, fit sort of way with her wavy blonde bob and round eyes.

"So," Jenna said, catching Helen staring at her. "How did you...? Why are you...? What's going on here? How are you even here? I'm dying to know."

"She stowed away in my car, and now I can't get rid of her," Jack said from up front.

"It's a bit more nuanced than that," Helen added.

"But pretty much boils down to that."

"This is mind-blowing." Jenna sucked in an audible breath. "My mind is literally blown."

"We should be so lucky."

Helen glared at the back of Jack's head. How was that helpful?

"I just finished watching the finale, and now you're *here*. But... aren't you supposed to be picking men for your season?"

"Yes," Jack said before Helen could respond.

"I'm taking a hiatus before filming starts again," Helen said, hoping that sounded plausible and perfectly sanctioned.

"It must be grueling," Jenna commiserated, as if the average person had any idea what was involved behind the scenes of filming a reality TV show. "But how did you get here... with Jack?" Jenna's eyes slid to Jack, and Helen watched the interplay of emotions over Jenna's unschooled features.

Helen smiled. "I know it's a surprise, just like you are to Jack, but we'll chat over dinner, and you can help him understand how this all came to be."

"What's not to understand? I live in New Hampshire. They both live here. It was bound to happen from sheer proximity alone. I mean, it's not like Cutler has anyone else for either of them to date, right?"

Mike's hands tightened on the steering wheel. "Jenna was my physical therapist. We hadn't seen each other for years before then. Things moved quickly."

"I'll say."

Helen had the urge to smack Jack, which was entirely unlike her. She redoubled her efforts to ease tensions.

She leaned forward. "Would it be too much to ask to choose a place that's not too crowded?"

Jenna's eyes grew round. "Absolutely. Jack told us you were worried about being recognized. We know just the place. Dark with booths. It's great if you don't want to be seen, but the food is good. We go there a lot."

An awkward silence filled the void, only interrupted by the steady beat of the windshield wipers. At the restaurant, Mike asked the hostess for a corner booth in the back. Thankfully, the weather seemed to have discouraged a big dinner rush. They slid in, Helen positioning herself between the men so no one came to blows.

"So," she began, smoothing her paper napkin across her lap out of habit, "are you liking your new apartment?"

Jenna smiled. "My commute is half what it used to be, but I miss having a yard and a garden. I grew up on a farm, so.. Anyway, we plan to look for a house once..." She darted a glance at Mike. "Once summer rolls around. We're just subletting the condo until we find something that suits us."

"A house?" Jack snorted. "That's a big commitment."

Helen watched Jenna bite her lip and dart a speaking glance at Mike.

Mike squeezed Jenna's hand on the table. "It's a commitment I'm happy to make, Jack."

"You've barely moved in together, now a house? You'd think you were..." Jack stopped. Helen held her breath. Mike and Jenna exchanged glances. "Tell me you're not pregnant."

Jenna smiled at Mike. "Not yet."

Helen couldn't help but notice Jack's sharply indrawn breath. *Not yet?* For the love of... could they stop throwing salt in the wound for a single minute and let Jack get his footing?

Jack abruptly stood, his gaze affixed to Mike and Jenna's entwined hands. "I need some air."

Helen watched his long, clipped strides and turned back toward the others. "I'm sure he'll be all right. It's the surprise of it all," she assured them.

Mike pressed Jenna's shoulder. "Let me out. I need to talk to him."

"He has a right to be upset," she said.

"He doesn't have the right to be an ass about it."

Jenna straightened her silverware as Mike went after Jack. "This is so embarrassing. I'm sorry you had to see this. I don't know what we were thinking coming here."

"You were thinking we were in a public place, so he wouldn't make a scene."

"Jack has never been one to worry about making a scene. Trust me on that."

~ * ~

"Jack."

Jack ignored his old friend and pushed open the door to the patio off the back of the restaurant. Empty tables sat with chairs propped against them to shed the rain. Jack leaned against the building and watched as cold water poured from the eaves.

"That's why you didn't tell me her name. Because it was Jenna." He ran a shaky hand through his hair trying to calm the chaos of emotions roiling inside him. He honestly didn't know what he was feeling.

"We knew it would be hard for you."

"We?" Screw it. *Anger. Definitely anger.* "The only hard thing is seeing my best friend get taken in by... that woman."

"That woman is my fiancée whether you're okay with it or not. The history you have is just that—history. I know she broke your heart, but—"

"It was more than that and you know it."

"Yeah, but it was also a long time ago. Not to be harsh, but you're not eighteen anymore. You're a grown man. So, act like one and suck it up."

Jack pushed off the wall and blew out a breath.

"Look," Mike continued, "I was there for you when life went to shit, and now I'm asking you to be there for me."

"But Jenna? You're not even attracted to her. You said so."

"When?"

"Years ago, when she and I started dating."

Mike laughed without humor. "I lied."

"What? We all hung out together. You were just friends."

"What was I supposed to do? Tell you I had a crush on your girlfriend?"

Jack froze.

"Yeah. I was working up the courage to ask her to prom, but you beat me to it."

"You never said anything."

Mike's expression softened. "You were my best friend. You and Jenna seemed happy. Then your mom died…"

"And Jenna and I broke up."

"Believe it or not, it occurred to me it would be a shit move to go after her then. But it's been a while. When I saw her for PT, it was like old friends picking up where we left off. Then it became more."

He shook his head as Jack processed. "Look, I love Jenna. And believe it or not, she still cares about you. It would be our honor to have you there on Friday. If it makes a difference, I planned to ask you to be my best man."

Jack pinched the bridge of his nose. "First of all, I can't believe she feels anything about me, and second of all, what the hell? She can't be okay with that." Hell, *he* wasn't okay with it. Mike liked Jenna? *Back then?* "You must have other friends."

"Yes, I have other friends. But I'm asking you. Just like you once asked me."

"We both know how that turned out."

Mike laughed. "I'm hoping it doesn't end the same way if it's all the same to you. Come on."

"What about your brother? Shouldn't you ask him?"

"You know half my family boycotted his wedding."

"Half your family needs to get over themselves. He and Jamie make each other happy."

"Agreed, but Ben's already said he won't be best man. He wants to be able to bow out if things get tense with my dad."

Jack swiped his palm down his face. His hand shook. "You're asking a hell of a lot of me," he finally said.

"I know."

Jack swallowed. It sucked. The whole thing sucked. Having to face an ex-girlfriend, having to face all the people he'd happily left in the dust all those years ago, having to crush the residual, latent anger and pain he thought he'd long since gotten over in order to stand behind his best— hell, *only*—real friend… it all sucked.

"Don't expect a bachelor party."

Mike's face relaxed into a grin. "No worries." He clapped a hand around Jack's shoulders. "We've got other plans," he said. "All you have to do is show up and play nice. Can you do that?"

Somehow. "Yeah."

They flagged the waiter and ordered drinks on the way back to the table. The women sat already sipping from salt-rimmed glasses the size of their heads. Jack slid in next to Helen.

She peeked up at him through her lashes.

"So," he said, his voice overly loud and brittle even to his own ears, "Mike asked me to be his best man."

Helen's eyes went round.

Jenna stilled. "And?"

"He's agreed," Mike said.

"Oh, Jack. Thank you."

The waiter set down his beer, and Jack took a long, grateful pull. "I'm doing it for Mike." An elbow caught him in the ribs. He scowled. "And, you, of course."

"Do you really mean it?" Jenna asked.

Jack took another drink to avoid answering.

Mike cleared his throat. "Let's not beat a dead horse. He's agreed, and now we should order."

Helen's straw made sucking noises in her bowl of alcohol. "I love weddings. Will it be large?"

Jenna shook her head. "Just close family and friends. We're keeping it simple so we can save for a house. My parents are letting us use their place instead of renting a venue."

Jack closed his menu. "That'll limit the guest list. Their house is tiny."

"The barn isn't." Mike waved for the waiter. "Jenna and Cassie have been cleaning and decorating it. You probably don't remember it well."

Jack stared at Jenna, willing her to look at him instead of keeping her head down, swirling her straw in her glass. He remembered it all right. He'd lost his virginity in that old barn in the bed of her daddy's rusty antique pickup, the worn floorboards sending a splinter into his left knee that'd taken a week to dig out.

"Your dad ever rehab that old truck?" he asked.

Jenna sucked the salt off her lip. "He towed it to the junkyard a few years ago."

"I suppose no sense keeping it around, if no one wants to put the effort into saving it."

She met his gaze then. "Some things don't last," she said, her voice barely audible. "It's no one's fault."

He bit back a reply at a hard look from Mike and raised his beer again.

"A barn wedding sounds charming," Helen said, apparently oblivious to the undercurrents in the conversation. "Rustic and unpretentious and—"

"Friggin' cold," Jack said.

The waiter arrived and took their orders. Helen's elbow jabbed Jack in the ribs, she mumbled an apology and slid her empty glass toward the waiter. He offered a refill.

She didn't refuse.

"Maybe you should take it easy," Jack murmured.

She waved the waiter away with a flick of her hand. "Put it on my tab," she said, and then proceeded to engage Jenna and Mike in painfully boring details about the wedding.

When their food arrived, Jack was well-informed about the color scheme (dove gray and aubergine, whatever the hell that was), the wedding party (one tiny niece, Jack, and Jenna's younger sister, Cassie), and the menu (assorted hot and cold finger food).

"I've never been a girlie-girl," Jenna said, which was a bald-faced lie given the amount of makeup and hairspray Jack remembered from junior prom. "My sister, you'll meet her at the cabin, she's taking charge of all the decorating and such."

"Cabin?" Jack asked.

"Didn't Mike tell you? We're doing a couples' retreat instead of a bachelor or bachelorette party. We thought it'd be fun to get away, you know, have a campfire or two, s'mores, games..."

Mike smiled. "Cassie's been pulling it together. Her boyfriend's parents own a second home upstate they said we could use. Should be fun."

Jack picked at his fries. *Perfect.*

"I mean," Jenna said, "obviously it's not exclusively for couples. Everyone is welcome. You can't help you're not in a couple."

Jack stabbed a fry into a puddle of ketchup.

"You can come and make snarky comments about other people like old times."

"Jenna," Mike warned.

"Oh, come on. I'm sure he hasn't changed that much. Remember how he used to do a running commentary on everyone's choices? Their hair. Their date. You should have seen him at prom. Jack always had something to say."

"Jesus, Jenna. Quit it."

She laughed and ran a shaky finger around the rim of her glass before licking it. "It was all in good fun, right Jack?"

Jack refused to rise to the bait. It seemed fair to say Jenna wasn't any more comfortable coming face-to-face with him as he was with her. He shoved the fry in his mouth.

The waiter returned with refills for the women. Jenna pushed the straw out of the wrapper. "I'm sorry. Wedding stress. Honestly, we'll just be a bunch of old friends hanging out and having a good time. No one will look sideways at you for coming stag."

"He's not." Helen said. "He's with me. We're together. Aren't we, honey?"

Jack forgot to chew. He swallowed his fry whole.

"We're what?"

Helen leaned forward, her braid dangling dangerously close to her drink. "We weren't going to say anything, and you two have got to promise not to tell a single soul, but, yes, Jack and I are together."

"Oh," said Jenna. *"Ohhhhhh."*

"It's not what you think," Jack said. Of course, he didn't know what to think, because Helen had clearly seen the sign for the 'deep end' and taken a flying leap into it.

"What he means is," Helen said. "We can't really say where this is going, but here we are." She leaned into him, eyes wide, and managed to look both doe-eyed and likely to pass out. Or maybe that was him.

"Would you excuse us a moment?" he asked.

Helen slapped her hand on his arm. "Jack, it's okay. You don't have to leave me out to protect my privacy. I'm sure we can trust Mike and Jenna and their friends."

He grabbed her hand and all but hauled her to stand next to him. "Give us a minute, will you? Don't let the waiter take my food. I'm not done."

"Or my drink," Helen said over her shoulder. "I'm still working on it."

~ * ~

Jack's hand gripped Helen's in delicious warmth. She decided to let him take the lead, as he tugged her in a winding path through the tables and around a corner. It felt a bit like he was pulling her through tables toward a dance floor. She missed dancing. And dances. Jack stopped just inside an exit door near the other corner of the restaurant. The rain drummed rhythmically outside the door like the beat of distant music. Her pulse thumped in her chest.

"What the hell was that?" he whispered at her. "You're not coming."

She planted her hands on her hips. "You're going to let her get away with that?"

"With what?"

"Did you not hear her? With all the digs? Nuh-uh." She waggled her index finger at him. "She can just walk that right back."

He screwed his face up in confusion. "If this is you trying to extend your stay and put off the inevitable, that ship has sailed."

"Don't be insulting. If I'm trying to extend anything it's time with Duke." She lifted her chin and concentrated on holding her head steady. *Wow.* That drink packed a punch. What was it called? Rum Ramblings? Rum Rambler? Raspberry Rumbler? Delicious.

"If I go on this camping thing, I'll go alone," Jack said.

"And listen to that woman lord it over you how you're still single? Y'all need to have some pride."

"I'm fine."

"That's a lie. You were burning with resentment back there. I could literally feel your body heat rise."

"Could you now?"

"Don't look at me like that. I'm saying, I could tell it bothered you."

"Everything about this bothers me."

"Of course, it does. Coupled up folks can be harsh even without trying, and Jenna is definitely trying. I'm doing you a favor here."

"By lying about us? We're not together."

"Technically, we are."

He stared at her for one long moment. "You're going to regret this when you're sober."

"Excuse me? I am not drunk. I'm tipsy, and those are two very different things. What I am is riled. And a little hungry to be honest."

"I don't need you to protect me. I'll handle this."

She sucked in a breath. "Wait. Are you planning to sabotage the wedding?" He didn't confirm nor deny, so she ignored his flabbergasted expression. "Because I would totally understand. I wouldn't approve, but I would understand." She patted his arm. "Friends stick together."

"So, we're friends now, are we?"

"I don't fake-date strangers."

He blinked at her, his mouth tipping into the first, full genuine smile she'd seen from him. "Except if it's on TV to help your business interests."

"That's not the same thing at all. Anyway, we'd better get back."

They slid back into their seats. Jack cleared his throat. "Sorry. Just needed a moment."

"It's fine," Mike said.

"I was just reminding Helen that as excited as she is about joining us, she doesn't even have clothes aside from what she has on."

"You can borrow something from me," Jenna said. "Or we can pick some things up while the guys are getting fitted for their tuxes. We'll be in the middle of the woods anyway. No one will care what you wear."

Helen smiled and slurped up the last of her drink through her straw. She turned and pretended to pluck a dog hair off the back of Jack's collar, then leaned close to his ear. "Told you I was going."

~ * ~

They managed to finish dinner without anyone else stalking off and rode home in relative silence. Back at the apartment, Jack volunteered to walk the dog as an excuse to avoid everyone, and he wasn't ashamed to admit it. When he got back, he shrugged out of his jacket and set it on a hook by the door. It took him a moment of staring at his jacket inches away from the denim one Jenna had worn earlier before he felt ready to step into the living room again.

It wasn't as if he still had feelings for her. The years in between and the way they'd parted, though, didn't leave him with the whole warm-fuzzy, bygones-be-bygones mentality everyone expected of him.

The woman had left him in his lowest hour. He might forgive her, but he was unlikely to forget.

He sucked in a deep breath, unclipped the dog's leash, and stepped down the entry hall to the living room. Jenna shot up from the couch and fake yawned. "Busy day tomorrow. I'm going to bed."

Mike's eyes went a little round behind his glasses. "It's only 8:30."

She shrugged. "We've got final fittings for the tuxes tomorrow, and then we pack for the trip." She gave a little wave and shut the bedroom door behind her.

Mike gave the dog a friendly pat then turned to Jack. "That's the woman I'm going to marry," he said. "Don't make me regret wanting to include you." And with that, he followed Jenna into the bedroom and shut the door.

Jack blew out a puff of air and headed for the guest room. He could sense Helen trailing behind him.

"Well that was quite the meal," she said.

Jack grabbed his backpack and stuffed in the few clothes he'd taken out.

"What are you doing?"

"I should think it was obvious."

"We don't leave for the couples retreat until the day after tomorrow."

"Correction. I don't."

"I don't understand what's going on here."

Jack paused, his T-shirt fisted in his hand, "I need to clear my head."

"What does that mean?"

"It means, get a good night's sleep, Princess, because tomorrow is a big day."

He hoisted his pack onto his shoulder and headed for the bedroom door.

"Jack, wait. I can see you're upset…"

"I'm not upset. I came here to hike and that's what I intend to do."

"Your best friend is getting married in a week. He wants you there as his best man. When will you be back?"

In the entry, he pulled his coat off its hook. "You'll want to put the dog downstairs overnight in case he isn't house-trained."

Her hands found their way to her hips. "You mean to tell me y'all are walking out on your best friend over a relationship that ended, how long ago? Years? I can't believe you'd be that immature."

Something snapped inside him, sparking a fire that made him want to lash out. "Says the woman who stowed away in my car."

"That was an accident. I never intended to end up with you, trust me."

"And yet here we are."

He swung his backpack onto his shoulder again and tugged the apartment door open. Helen slid her shoes onto her feet.

"Are you going to leave me here? With them?" she hissed. "I can't impose like that the week of their wedding."

"Then make yourself useful."

"Jack."

He stopped just inside the threshold.

"What do you want me to tell them?" she finally asked.

He ran a hand through his hair. "You'll come up with something."

"You'll be back for the wedding, though, right?"

He refused to look at her.

"Jack, you promised."

He yanked the door open fully, huffing out a breath. "What do you want me to say?"

"This isn't about what I want."

"Isn't it? Isn't that why you're butting in where you're not wanted?"

"Oh, I see. It's fine for you to give unsolicited advice, but heaven forbid you listen to reason."

"Reason? *Reason?* Who are you to give me advice about anything? Why are you even still here? And don't give me that bull crap about the show being just fine with all this. I'm not stupid."

The blood pooled in her gut, hot and unsettling. "I don't know what you mean."

"Now who's avoiding the truth? Forget it. Your problems aren't my problems anymore."

Then he stepped out and shut the door in her face.

~ * ~

The air grew thick in Helen's lungs and she forced herself to concentrate on breathing in and out as slowly as possible. He left. Just like that. Gone. It shouldn't feel like abandonment, because, honestly, what were they to each other but unwilling companions? She should be relieved he was gone, cutting the tenuous thread that bound them, and yet it felt like grief, so familiar she almost welcomed it.

Grief deadened it all, the lows and highs eventually weighed down by the nothingness that remained when all the emotion had burned itself out.

She'd thought that going on the show would help her ignite that spark she only vaguely remembered. She hadn't felt it again until she'd come face to face with a man in a diner parking lot challenging her very existence. Then that spark, that spark had jumped to life, fighting to be seen and heard and...

She threw open the apartment door and dashed down the sidewalk toward his car as he backed out, thumping on the hood with the palm of her hand.

"Hey!" he yelled through the windshield. "Knock it off!"

"Stop," she said. "Don't you dare drive this car away." She skirted the hood and yanked the passenger door open, practically hurling herself inside. "Not without me."

He stared at her, his blue eyes bright with astonishment and fury. She honestly wasn't sure if she cared. His lips pressed together, and he threw the car into drive and skidded out with a squeal of tires.

They drove through the dark streets for what felt like miles, the tension between them thick as cold grits.

They'd left the confines of Cutler, the passing countryside a smattering of groves of trees and wide, open fields. Abruptly he pulled off the main road and skidded to a halt in a patch of dirt and weeds.

He closed his eyes and leaned his head back. "Why are you here?" he finally said, his voice thick with exasperation.

"We're not done."

He rolled his head toward her and opened his eyes. "I should have left you with the dog."

"Duke!"

"He's fine. Jenna will look out for him. She loves dogs."

Jack lifted his head and squinted into the distance, the faintest breath of twilight on the distant horizon. She watched his breath raise and lower his chest. His Adam's apple shifted as he swallowed.

"Jack, I want to help."

He snorted at that. "No offense, but you bring me more trouble than peace. I'm good."

He opened the door and stepped out. Helen scrambled out her side. "You don't seem good. Wait. What are you doing?"

He slammed the trunk closed and hoisted his backpack onto his shoulders. "I'd think that'd be obvious.

"You're hiking now? It's after dark. And we're in the middle of nowhere."

He pulled something out of his pocket, settled it on his head and flicked a switch. A beam of light blinded Helen for a moment before illuminating the edge of the road. "If you leave the car, don't lock the doors."

"Don't—?" Of all the things she expected him to say, that wasn't one of them.

"If somebody tries to steal it, I don't want them gouging the paint."

"Won't that make it easier to steal?"

He looked at the car. "It wouldn't be the first time." Then he turned and started down a narrow dirt path that disappeared into a copse of trees.

Helen glanced up and down the deserted road and at Jack's rapidly fading light in the forest. She scrambled over the guard rail, tripping over some unknown toe hazard. Water still dripped from the trees. "Jack, wait."

No reply.

She puffed out a sigh of relief when his tall form came into view. He didn't turn around, just kept walking.

"Jack, please. We'll get lost out here."

"I know exactly where I am."

Her heart hammered a bit in her chest as he took an abrupt turn and left the relative safety of the path they'd been on. She reluctantly pushed through the trees after him, wet limbs smacking her. "Where are we going?"

"I don't know where you're going, but I'm unsuccessfully trying to be alone."

She paused, hands on hips before she realized he hadn't stopped and wasn't even looking. "You don't really want to be alone."

He did stop then, the beam of his headlamp raking over her before turning away again. "You have no idea what I want."

"Then tell me."

He did stop then, she knew it, because she plowed into the back of him. He was surprisingly solid for such a lanky guy. She stepped back with a mumbled apology, expecting him to keep going or swear at her or... something.

Instead he stood rock still, the beam of light facing ahead.

"I want..." He paused and his breath came so slow and even she instinctively knew he was measuring each breath. "I want for once in my fucking life, to not be collateral damage in other people's lives."

He spoke as if there was no one to hear him, his voice low and harsh and pained. It was the kind of admission you spoke to yourself when you're feeling crushed and grieving and so, so alone—like when you're sitting in your dorm room with the Pottery Barn furnishings and all the creature comforts you could ever want, and you feel so... lost... you curl up, knees to your chest, so numb you fear you can't even cry.

The light of his headlamp spun toward her. "I don't even know why I'm bothering to explain, because if you were really listening, you wouldn't be here."

She knew it was a defense mechanism, the snark. She also knew that sympathy would only push him further away. "Don't be insulting. And take that off. You're blinding me."

He turned and started walking again. She trailed behind.

"Maybe if you didn't isolate yourself, people would take your feelings into account more."

Oof. Okay, she really needed to pay attention to his momentum. She stepped back again as the beam of light swung back toward her.

"Isolate myself? That's rich coming from a woman who's so desperate to escape her life she's literally chasing a strange man into the woods at night. One who has made it *abundantly* clear he does *not* want company."

"This isn't about me."

"So, you don't deny it."

"Stop deflecting."

"Deflecting? You don't want to talk about your own problems any more than I do."

"*A-ha!* You admit you have problems you're not talking about." She shouldn't feel so triumphant, but it felt like a victory.

"Doesn't take a rocket scientist to see Jenna and I have history."

"What did she do to you that's so awful you can't forgive her?"

"I'm not discussing this. You invited yourself on this hike. I don't have to participate in group counseling activities.

"Here's the deal," he said. "I've agreed to be your ride until we can get you on your way home, but this is where it ends. As soon as possible, I drive you to the bus station, get you a ticket, and you can leave me, and Mike and everyone else to sort this out like the grown-ups we are. This… situation… and my history don't concern you. Got it?"

She took a slow breath in and out, her expression neutral. "I'm not leaving you."

"You don't have a choice."

She squared her shoulders. "I can help."

"Are you deaf? I don't want your help."

"She still has feelings for you, you know."

He jerked as if sucker punched. "What?"

Helen waved her hand. "I'm not saying she's still in love with you, but whatever happened between you still tugs at her. That's why she kept digging at you at dinner. You owe it to both of you to resolve this so you can move on with your lives. Preferably before the wedding."

"Oh, for the love of… Why would I take your advice about anything? You're a cupcake maker for Christ's sake. A cupcake maker who's been dumped twice by the same guy on reality TV."

She stood, her pulse kicking up a notch. How dare he swing at her when she was only trying to help? "I was a communications major, for your information, and I'm also the successful owner of multiple bakeries. You're a… a… line cook stuck in the same job you've had for probably a decade."

His eyes went dark, and she stepped back as if she'd just accidentally sliced him with the truth.

"Touché," he finally said.

"I'm sorry. I don't mean to be harsh," she said. He grunted in reply. "But your best friend and your ex are getting married in less than a week, and I think you could use someone on your side."

"And that someone is you?"

"Yes."

"Jack? Helen?"

They stared at one another as if the other had just called out both their names. Jack ripped his headlamp off and clicked off the light. "Don't. Say. A. Word," he ground out.

"Jack? Helen?"

"We're over here!" Helen called, more than a little relieved to have company.

Jack elbowed her, or maybe it was his pack swinging toward her as he maneuvered for an escape route.

A bright flashlight beam rippled off the nearby tree trunks. A stick snapped and tree branches rustled. Jenna and Mike came into view. Mike sighed, "I told you this is where he'd be."

"What the hell?" Jack growled. "Can't a guy be alone?"

"You know you should never hike alone," Mike said.

"I'm not alone. I'm with Helen. Sort of. Why do you have a pack on?"

Mike shrugged. "I had an idea this might happen."

"What?"

"You running away," Jenna said.

Helen had never seen an expression turn so dark. "I wasn't running. I was hiking. That thing I came to do. That thing I said I'd do, but I suppose if you you're the kind of person that doesn't have any qualms about going back on their word—"

"Oh, grow up," Mike spat. "Look around you. If you hadn't noticed, we're not teenagers anymore. We should be able to be honest with one another."

"Don't," Jack warned, and in that moment, Helen wanted Mike to stop, too. Jack had a look in his eyes like a cornered animal.

But, Mike wasn't done. He tossed his pack on the ground. "Don't what? Challenge you for a change? Ask you to step up? Or is that not allowed? *Jesus.* We're asking you to be a part of our wedding, and you're throwing a friggin' tantrum."

"A tantrum? Fuck you. Fuck all of you. You know what she put me through. How it ended. Am I supposed to just forgive and forget because you've decided you want to screw her now?"

Mike went rigid. Jenna stepped forward, bracing her arm across her fiancé. Helen's mouth went slack with shock. There was lashing out and then there was *lashing out.*

"How dare you," Helen breathed. "How dare you say something so reprehensible to your best friend and his fiancée? *To me?* Apologize immediately. Go on. Apologize. I don't care how angry or hurt you are, that's no way to talk."

Jack's face screwed up as if he'd swallowed something dry and unpleasant. "I've got nothing to apologize for."

Helen looked from Mike to Jack and back again, their expressions rigid with anger and hurt. She caught Jenna's eye. "Jenna, may I have a word?"

She pulled Jenna aside and whispered in her ear.

Jenna nodded and tapped her fiancé's shoulder. "I need the keys."

Mike scowled. "Now?"

"Now. It's a girl thing."

Mike rolled his eyes, fished in his pocket, and handed over the keys, never breaking eye contact with Jack.

Jenna gave Mike's arm a squeeze. "Try not to kill him."

Jack grunted. "As if."

Helen nodded, and she and Jenna hurried back down the path toward the road.

Jenna glanced behind them, the beam of her cellphone's flashlight jumping in front of them as they walked. "How long until they figure out we're not coming back?"

Helen shrugged. "Time enough."

"Mike will be pissed, but Jack will be livid if he feels trapped here. I hope you know that."

"I don't care. He should have apologized. You don't deserve what he said."

Jenna screwed her face up. "You've only heard the highlights. I really hurt him."

"That's not an excuse. We've all been hurt."

"Yeah, well I sent my father out to break up for me, and then the cops arrived, so…"

They'd reached the road. Helen stepped over the guardrail, opened the door to Jack's car and retrieved his keys. "I still can't believe the man leaves his keys in his car. That's asinine."

Jenna laughed, a nervous chuckle, and they stared at each other, clutching the car keys. "Now what?"

Helen leaned against Jack's car and shrugged. "We wait. They need some alone time to work this out. And if they don't, we leave them until they do."

Jenna leaned back against the car next to Helen and stared at the path into the woods. A firefly winked at them, dancing in the treetops.

Jenna sighed. "He asked my dad for permission to marry me," she whispered. "He wanted to do it right. Even asked Mike to be a witness.

He'd turned eighteen after his move to New Hampshire, but I was still underage. He refused to do *it* unless we were married and legal."

Helen nodded in the dark, processing this information.

"I thought you should know. What you're seeing now? It's not the Jack I remember. I mean it is in a lot of ways, but... he's a standup guy at heart. I know he's feeling blindsided, but he means the world to Mike, and there was a time..." Her words trailed off.

Helen didn't have a chance to respond. The agitated leap of a flashlight beam swiped across them as the sound of heavy footsteps announced the men's return.

"They're still here," Mike said.

Jack simply glared at the women as he stepped over the guardrail. He held his palm out. "Hand them over."

Helen's fingers flexed, Jack's keys hot against her palm. She dangled them in the air a moment, then turned and handed them to Jenna. Jenna promptly dropped them down her cleavage. Jack growled. "Mike, we're taking your car."

Jenna turned to Helen and handed over Mike's keys. Jack stepped closer. "If you drop them down your shirt, I warn you now. I'll fish them out. No qualms whatsoever."

Emotion and exertion made Jack's chest pulse with every breath. *In. Out. In. Out.* Helen stared at his chest, not daring to meet his eyes knowing they were pinned on her, willing her to hand over Mike's keys.

She thought about dropping the keys down her shirt, but Jack had no qualms, and his hand was large, and as much as this was neither the time nor the place, it made her flush thinking about his hand inside her shirt.

Jack took another step closer, and now it was her breath that came in short bursts of awareness. "We both know," he murmured, "that you're not wearing a bra and they'd fall to the ground. Game over, Princess. Hand me the keys."

Princess.

She went rigid at the word, her gaze rising to meet his as she grasped her waistband and shoved the keys into her pants. *Sorry, Mike.*

Jack's jawline tightened. His eye twitched. His lips pressed together, and his gaze slowly descended to the awkward bulge in the front of her pants. Finally, he spoke. "That can't be comfortable."

She refused to be amused. And, no, for the record, it was not. They were cold. And bulky. And one of them jabbed her in a way that made her afraid to move, but she would not be minimized or dismissed.

"You are not going to ruin your best friend's wedding. We aren't leaving until you and Mike work this out. No more running. No more yelling. Mike is your lifelong friend and he deserves better than this."

Jack's fingers flexed between them, and then he fisted them and dropped his arm to his side. He leaned in, his mouth a hair's breadth from her ear. "I'm really not thinking about Mike right now," he murmured.

Helen didn't know how to answer that. She wasn't thinking about Mike now either which felt kind of awkward with him being only a few feet away.

Mike stepped over to Jenna, either oblivious or ignoring the undercurrents between Helen and Jack. "Give Jack his keys," he demanded.

"No. Helen's right. I'm not leaving until we talk things through, and neither are you."

Jack hadn't moved, but Helen would swear he was closer. "I won't be blackmailed," he said.

Jenna pushed past her fiancé. "I get it, Jack. You have every right to be angry, but I didn't mean to hurt you, and I never intended for you to go to jail, but now you're punishing me *and* Mike for something I did when I was seventeen, and that's not fair."

Helen could feel her eyes popping wide. "Wait. You went to jail?"

"I wouldn't have if her father hadn't called the friggin' cops."

Jenna shook her head. "He didn't call anybody. Leo was on patrol when he saw you arguing with my father. It was an unfortunate coincidence."

"Which wouldn't have happened if you'd had the guts to break up with me personally. I asked you to marry me and make a life with me, and you couldn't even be bothered to turn me down to my face?"

"You didn't ask me to make a life with you."

"To hell I didn't."

"No, Jack, you didn't. You asked me to be an accomplice in committing a felony. You asked me to leave my family, forever, because I'd be a wanted criminal, *married* to a wanted criminal, and you asked me to do it all without even saying goodbye."

His mouth hardened. "That's not the point. The point is you bailed. We had a plan. That's why I drove all the way here."

"In a car you *stole* from your father! Jack, why can't you see how crazy that was? You did something impulsive and illegal, and I nearly did, too, but we were kids, just stupid kids. By some grace from God, we ended up not going to jail and not abandoning our families. I don't know about you, but I feel lucky."

"Lucky." Jack's mouth hitched up on one side without humor. "So lucky. My mother killed herself slowly, I got sent to live with a father I barely knew, and when I finally took charge of my life, the woman who promised to love me forever left me in the street pleading for her to come out of her friggin' house and stand by me."

"I was scared. I didn't know what would happen next."

"Me, either." Jack muttered those two words, as if torn from some hardened part of his soul. His eyes burned across Helen as he hitched his pack onto his shoulders. "Good talk," he said. He snapped on his headlamp, turned around and started walking.

Helen shoved her hand in her pants, fished out Mike's keys and handed them over. "Sweet mother of sunshine," she breathed. "Someone could have clued me in."

"It's been years," Mike said. "We thought he'd be over it."

"You never get over heartbreak," said Helen. "You just get used to living with the pain. You two go home. I'll handle this."

"What will you do?" Jenna asked.

Helen looked at Jenna. She wanted to be a forgiving person. She wanted to be mature and understanding and kind, but she wasn't there yet. Not after what she'd just heard. "I'm sure as hell not going to leave him crying on the street all alone, I can tell you that much. Watch Duke until we get back. Please." Then she turned and started toward Jack and didn't look back until she heard Mike's car drive away.

She followed Jack down the road, not close enough for him to hear her breathe but not so far that he wouldn't know she was still there. She shivered despite her sweater.

A couple of minutes went by before his steps slowed and then stopped altogether.

"Why are you following me?" he asked. His voice sounded rough. It tethered itself to an answering sadness in her own chest. Tugged.

"Because you've been left alone too often."

"I promise not to harm myself."

"That's not what I meant. I meant, I know how you feel."

"Do you?" He turned then, the beam of his headlamp momentarily blinding her before he yanked it off his head, the light zig-zagging like lightning across the pavement. "I doubt it."

"You're hurt and feeling abandoned because you were just a boy grieving for his mother and the one person you thought you could count on let you down."

"Wrong."

"Wrong?"

"She left me blubbering like a newborn baby on the sidewalk and watched me from her window while I got dragged off by a dipshit cop happy for some excitement on a random Tuesday. She yanked the bottom out from under me and then *watched it happen* like I was some sideshow."

"You were embarrassed," she said.

"Ya think?"

"And angry."

He didn't speak.

"I don't blame you either way, but it doesn't help you get over it. You need to be the better man, Jack. You need to show Jenna she made a colossal mistake instead of proving her right for not sticking up for you. Make her see you're no longer that teenaged boy."

Thinking about young, hot Jack crying out for his first love while Jenna watched, unmoved, from the sidelines lit a fire of injustice in Helen's belly. What would she do to have a man love her half that intensely? Heaven help her, barring the illegal components, it sounded seriously romantic.

"I'm sorry. What?"

His confusion focused her thoughts. There was no way Jack's story ended on a note of rejection. She knew too damn well how that felt. "I'm just saying. We are going to that couples retreat."

"After all that," he waved his arm down the road, "why would you even want to?"

"I'm from the South. We may hate your guts, but if we've made a promise, we will stick by our word to the grave—even if we spit in your breakfast every morning before we serve it. It's called being loyal. We southerners are very big on loyalty."

"That's a horrifying visual."

"I'm just saying, you need to show Jenna and Mike you're living your best life. You don't have time for their pity. My pageant coach, Mrs. Greenbow, refused to let any of her girls wear waterproof mascara. Do you know why? To train us to keep our cool. 'Never give them the satisfaction of seeing your mascara run,' she said."

"I have no idea what that means."

"It means, no matter what, you have to follow through, hold your head high, walk that stage, and smile like you've won even if you're dead last."

He raised one eyebrow. "I'm literally a line cook in my father's pub and sleeping in Mike's spare bedroom because I'm too poor to keep paying for hotels. I have a gas-guzzling car that's more of a magnet for

113

teen girls and paunchy old guys than women my age, and I'm standing on the side of the road talking my troubles out with *you*."

"You make that sound like a bad thing. I clean up surprisingly well."

"I'll give you that." He said, and his eyes held a hint of something else now. Something warm and vulnerable.

"Chin up. By the end of the wedding, everyone will wish they were you. I promise," she said.

He side-eyed her. "I'd say that's pretty much a given if I'm with you."

He smiled, a slight uplift to the corner of his mouth, and she felt an answering tug within. She swiped away an errant wisp of hair as it blew across her face, and when she looked up again, the slight smile had grown.

"For someone whose life is kind of a shambles, you give surprisingly good advice. Thank you." She warmed under his praise. "Although you're kind of pushy about it. But in a well-intentioned way."

"It takes one to know one," she said.

He nodded, and his tongue darted out to wet his lips as they formed a half smile. "I'll take you to Alabama," he said.

"What?"

"We're most of the way there, right? What's a couple more days on the road?"

"Why would you do that?"

He shrugged. "Maybe it will confuse Jenna and piss her off a little. Or maybe, I'm beginning to like your company after all."

She should say something, she was sure, but her thoughts jumbled up like a swirl of cotton candy at the county fair, all light and airy and sweet. Something had changed between them, and she struggled to understand how they'd gone from snapping at one another to… this.

"I'd be most appreciative," she murmured.

There was that smile again, and she realized what had changed now. Jack wasn't looking at her like he wanted to slam the door in her face. He was looking at her like he wanted to invite her in.

He nodded, curtly, "Good."

They stood there, unmoving, the soft sounds of night humming around them.

"I'm sorry about Jenna and Mike. I shouldn't have pushed. I get it now."

"It's done."

He glanced down to where she'd rested her hand on his forearm out of habit. "I'm sorry," she said. "I know we've talked about the touching thing." She pulled her hand away. "Someday you might actually get used to people getting close to you."

He nodded and his bottom teeth flashed as he nipped his bottom lip.

"If we're going to be spending the next few days together," he said, "we're going to have to come up with some ground rules. Number one: stop overthinking everything. Number two: stop trying to fix me. I'm not broken. And number three…"

"Yes?"

"I want it clear from the outset that if I kiss you, it won't be because I'm trying to get back at Jenna or trying to distract you from talking. It's because you're hot, and I'm alive, and I want to."

The air sucked out of her lungs with each word that passed over his lips, and she stood there, her feet glued to the pavement, winded and light-headed and incandescently hopeful.

"Oh?" she said, her body leaning toward his of its own accord.

His gaze dropped to her mouth which flooded with anticipation.

"Just so we're clear," he said.

"Got it." Her mouth parted as the air grew light and fast in her lungs. "Are you gonna kiss me now?"

His teeth nipped at his bottom lip again, and she nearly combusted despite the cool, night air. "I was thinking about it."

He smiled, a slow grin that drew her closer by some invisible thread.

She slanted her lips toward his ear. "Rule number one," she murmured. "Stop overthinking everything."

She didn't have time to pull back as his head turned and his mouth claimed hers. It wasn't graceful as first kisses go—him shifting to gain better access, her tugging her hair out of the way—but what it lacked in finesse, it made up for in enthusiasm.

Sweet mother of sunshine, how this man could kiss!

His right hand came up to tangle in her hair and cup the back of her neck as his left rested on her lower back, his fingers sliding up under her sweater in search of heat. Her whole body sighed into his arms as his forearms flexed, drawing her upward and into the kiss. Nothing about the kiss was hard or coarse. Instead, it drew her toward him, as if he were breathing her in, his touch like a spark to the dry, combustible places inside her.

Helen moaned—in a ladylike way, *thankyouverymuch*—and touched the tip of her tongue to his.

He stumbled backward. Probably because his answering response was so hot, she leaned all her weight up and into the kiss, gripping his shirtfront with her fists as she did so. In her defense, it had been a while, and she'd never experienced a kiss so unexpected and *hot.*

He laughed under her lips, steadying her, and she pulled back to give him an indignant glare.

No one laughed while kissing Helen Walker.

But when his eyes opened and she saw the unfocused heat there, she could do nothing but grin up at him. "Knocked you off your feet, did I?"

His tongue touched his lips. "In more ways than one, Princess. In more ways than one."

He blew out a long, slow breath, shaking his head as if to clear it, and she found for once she didn't mind the nickname. "I'm thinking we should head back," he said.

She nodded—it's not as if they could make out on the side of the road forever—and started toward the car. "So, we're staying with Mike and Jenna?"

"Yeah," he said.

She slanted a look up at him. His jawline in profile scrambled her thoughts in indecent ways. "There's only one bed."

He smiled without looking at her. "I'm well aware."

"But your ex-girlfriend will be sleeping in the next room."

He paused. "I'm violating the hell out of rule number one right now. Just so you know."

A flush of heat coursed through her. "You and me both, mister. You and me both."

"This would be easier if you'd stop looking at my lips."

"Take your eyes off my chest and we're good to go."

"My eyes aren't..." His gaze dropped to her chest.

"You were saying?"

"You are nothing but trouble, Princess."

"Don't demote me. I'm the Cupcake *Queen.*"

"That you are," he said. "Lord help me, you are." And he pressed her forward with his palm on the small of her back. They stretched the distance home with shy, knowing looks, fingers grazing, and the occasional shoulder bump.

CHAPTER 10

Well, that took a turn.

Jack pretended to check the time on his phone while Helen prepared for bed, rebraiding her long dark hair like in some old movie.

He'd not understood how incredibly sexy it was to watch a woman braid her hair before bed until he thought about *unbraiding* it. Yup. It was going to be a long night.

She flashed him a soft, shy smile, peeled back the sheets and slid those long legs in. He regretted now the choice to buy her a T-shirt style nightshirt instead of those long-ass flannel pajamas that covered everything. He'd thought nothing could be less attractive when he'd pulled it from the rack in the store, but the flash of her legs, darker than the white sheets, had him abruptly turning away to "find something" in his pack.

You'd think he was a sixteen-year-old again for all the control he had over his own body. He backed up to the bed, sat, and turned out the bedside lamp before she could see the tent in his shorts.

He lay in the dark and stared toward the ceiling willing himself to think of anything but the soft rustling of covers beside him as Helen turned to get comfortable. Her leg brushed his, smooth and cool, and he jumped with surprise.

"Sorry," she mumbled.

"No problem."

He concentrated on breathing, exhaling slowly in a long breath. Inhaling...

"Are you all right?" came a voice from the dark.

"Fine."

"You sure?" More covers rustling. "You sound agitated."

Oh, good Lord.

"I'm fine." The rain, back again, drummed the roof of the condo.

"You don't sound it." The bed jostled as Helen pushed to a sitting position. "Are you thinking about Jenna?"

"No." At least he hadn't been. Now he stilled, waiting for the knife of Jenna's betrayal to pull itself from the old wound. How many times had he felt that particular pain, that flood of emotion pouring out since the night she'd sliced out his heart and walked away?

He waited for the pain, resentfully, begrudgingly, closing his eyes in anticipation of the inevitable.

Instead, he felt a soft hand slide over his shoulder to cup his cheek. "It's understandable if you are."

"Rule number two," he murmured, his voice strained.

Soft lips pressed against his forehead. "I don't play by the rules," she said.

Jack trapped her wrist in his hand. "This isn't a game."

She stilled. "I know."

"Then what are you doing?"

She blew out a breath. "Trying to distract you."

"From what?"

"The fact that your ex and best friend are having sex in the next room."

"They're not—" Except his denial was cut short by the distinct sound of rhythmic squeaking coming through the wall. *"Are you kidding me?"*

He let go of her wrist, grabbed his pillow, and crushed it to his face. Helen clicked her light on.

She tugged at the pillow. "Stop. You'll suffocate."

"Tell me when it's over."

"I think they only just started."

He tossed the pillow at the foot of the bed and sat upright. At least the tent in his shorts was no longer a problem. "Fuck my life."

"It could be worse."

He stared at her, incredulous. "How?"

"They could be moaning?"

"I can't believe you find this funny."

"What else are we going to do? Make more noise than them?"

He blinked. Surely, she wasn't suggesting this was some sort of Sex Olympics.

"I mean, not make more noise having sex, because obviously we're not doing that."

"Obviously," he said, even though he thought the idea had merit.

"Maybe there's a fan or a radio we could turn on until they're done?"

He threw back the covers. "I'm not staying here listening to that." He skirted the bed.

"You're leaving me here to listen on my own? I'm coming with you."

He cracked the door, and they tip-toed out. The sound of squeaking bedsprings became more urgent.

"I seriously want to impale myself with the nearest object," he muttered. "Is it echoing out here more than through the wall? How is that possible?"

"The rec room," Helen said, a little desperately.

Jack opened the basement door, turned on the stairwell light, and they made their way down to an excited Doofus. "Hey, boy. Want some company?"

Doof wagged his body and trailed after them to a beat-up couch with hideous gold flowers. The springs creaked as Jack sank onto a cushion. He swiped a hand over his face and stared at the few pieces of random gym equipment, ironically the very reasons his ex and best friend were right this moment upstairs bumping uglies. "How long do you think we need to hide down here?" he asked.

"You're asking me? They're your friends. How long does sex take?"

He stared at her.

"I mean, I know how long sex takes, obviously. But, is it, um, good sex or, ah, faster sex?"

"Those are not mutually exclusive." *Aaaaaaand,* just like that, the tent thing became a problem again. Jack grabbed a ratty afghan off the back of the couch and tossed it over his lap.

It was Helen's turn to stare at him.

He wet his lips.

"We could discuss what happened earlier," she said. "You know, the kissing."

"I'd rather not." He grimaced and shifted to get comfortable. "Rule number one."

She puffed out an impatient breath and patted the dog's head. "So, we're going to pretend it never happened." She made it a statement.

"I didn't say that."

"Don't you think it confuses things between us? The kissing?"

"There is no 'us.'"

"We're two people sharing a car across the country. It's you in the car and me in the car, and together we are an 'us.'"

Jack fluffed the afghan. "This feels like talking about it."

She slumped against the back of the sofa. "Was it just two people with high emotions letting things get out of hand?"

"If things had gotten out of hand, Jenna and Mike wouldn't be the only one's getting it on right now. It was just a kiss."

"Technically, several."

He stretched his arm out along the back of the sofa, trying to appear at ease, and nodded. "Fine. Several."

"We probably shouldn't let it happen again."

His gaze dropped to her mouth. "True."

"Not that I didn't enjoy it." She smiled up at him through her lashes, an invitation if he'd ever seen one. "Because I did."

He trailed his fingertips along her shoulder and traced lazy circles there. "Am I going to have to reference rule number three?"

"What was that one again?"

"Me proving that when I kiss you, it's not because I have an ulterior motive. It's just two people kissing. Because we're alive. And we want to."

She nodded. He leaned toward her.

Her palm planted itself on his chest. "No ulterior motives. No expectations. Just two people passing the time. Kissing."

"If that's all you want."

"We're both adults," she murmured.

"Last I checked." He pressed his lips to her jaw, inhaling the soft, sweet scent of her, then cupped her cheek with his hand and leaned forward. He grazed his lips against hers. The couch creaked as his body sank toward hers on the sofa, and the irony wasn't lost on him. He skimmed his lips across hers again, a jolt of heat running through him as she rose up to meet him. Her lips parted, and he took advantage of that, too. She might be a hot mess, but—*day-um*—she was still hot, and he didn't mind blotting out all the memories, past and present, in a satisfying and mutually enjoyable way.

"This doesn't have to *mean* anything," she said, her breath shallow as he shifted closer to trail the tip of his tongue up to her earlobe.

"Rule number one," he whispered, forgetting which rule he was invoking. They all led to kissing.

She grabbed his face between her palms, muttered, "You and your rules," and dragged his mouth to her own.

Lust shot through him like a lightning bolt, and he forgot about the damned afghan or rules, because Helen had somehow shifted so that he was now lying on top of her, between her legs, her hands cupping his back and—hell, yes!—his ass, as they cruised past first base, whistled through second, and charged exuberantly toward third.

His brain shorted out as she arched underneath him, one hand tangling in the hair at the back of his head, the other clenching his ass-cheek. He pulled back, his breath ragged as he tugged the hair tie out of her hair with one hand, his fingers shaking the strands loose. "I've been wanting to do this all night."

Her dark eyes went black, and she pulled his lips against hers again for several intense minutes before they both came up for air.

Her hand slid under his shirt, sliding over his bare skin. He nipped his way down her neck, his left hand simultaneously smoothing up one heavenly thigh. She sucked in a breath and hummed with appreciation. He lowered his mouth over the fabric covering one breast and sucked until he felt her nipple grow hard in his mouth.

"We're just kissing," she reminded him between gasps, her hands at his shoulders.

He paused and looked up at her flushed face. "Just kissing," he promised.

She hadn't said *where*.

Her head lolled back on a satisfied moan and her hands slid behind his shoulders to tug him closer, so he took that as confirmation that this kind of kissing was still okay.

He shifted lower, pressing his open mouth on the fabric below her breasts until it grew damp, his hands sliding up both thighs. He waited for her to open her eyes. "I want to kiss your skin," he said.

He didn't recognize his voice, strained and low as it was. He wasn't even sure she'd heard him. But then, her tongue darted out to wet her lips, her eyes locked with his, and without saying a word, she tugged her nightshirt higher.

He'd never been so turned on by a pair of plain cotton underwear in his whole entire life.

His heart slammed against his ribcage as he bent to press his lips against the inside of her thigh. He breathed in the warm scent of her. Her hands tangled in his hair and squeezed.

His erection throbbed against the sofa cushion.

He darted his tongue against the sliver of heaven where fabric met skin, and she bucked under his hands.

Blind heat exploded in his body as he thought about burying himself in her in more ways than one, and he blew out a breath to steady himself. If he didn't slow down, this would be over before they got started.

"Do that again," she whispered, and he realized she thought he'd blown on her on purpose.

This was way more than kissing.

He pulled back to say something, to check in, to be sure this flirty, over-the-clothes "kissing" wasn't crossing boundaries they couldn't pull back from even though he was pretty certain they'd whizzed by that point about ten hot minutes ago.

"Whoa. Wow. I am *so* sorry, guys."

Jack froze at Mike's voice, and Helen rocketed off into the far corner of the sofa like she'd been shot from a canon. She yanked her nightshirt down to her knees and hauled the afghan over herself for good measure.

"Hey, Mike," Jack said, slowly rising to a seated position. He'd never been more disappointed in fast sex.

Mike's hand covered his face. "I saw the light and thought there was a problem with the dog. I thought you guys were asleep in your room."

"Yeah, not sleeping," Jack said.

"Right," Mike backed toward the door, feeling his way with his other hand. "I'm gonna go now."

"We'd appreciate that."

Jack waited until he heard the door at the top of the stairs click closed.

Doof sat and stared.

"Well, that was poor timing," Jack said.

Helen jumped to her feet, smoothing the nightie with a shaking hand. "Did he see anything?"

"Naw. If anything, he saw my back. You were covered."

She nodded, her face a lovely shade of crimson. Her hair fell over her shoulders loose and wild, and her lips looked thoroughly kissed. He wasn't gonna lie. He liked her this way. He reached out a hand and tugged her toward him.

She let out a sigh that said she wanted to pick up where they'd left off. "Jack…"

"Come here. He won't be back. Guaranteed."

"We don't have protection."

He smiled. He could think of lots of ways to work around that.

She couldn't seem to drag her gaze away from his mouth. Apparently, she was thinking about those things, too.

But did he really want to have cheap sex on Mike's used sofa?

Helen deserved better than that. She also deserved to be a conscious choice and not a distraction.

"You should go to bed," he said.

"Now?"

"Yeah." He could not believe the words coming out of his mouth.

"But I thought… we were still kissing."

"That could take a while," he said. "It's late."

"It doesn't have to take long."

He sighed and met her confused gaze. "I'm trying to be a gentleman."

"I'm tired of being a lady."

He shoved his hand through his hair. "Oh, God."

"Don't take the Lord's name in vain."

"It's not all I want to take. But not tonight. Go to bed, Princess."

But instead of saying it like a slur, it came out as an endearment.

She pressed her lips together and nodded. "Okay. It's just as well." He raised an eyebrow in question. "I need time to violate rule number one in peace."

He laughed, which was a release of its own though not nearly as satisfying as some things he could think of. "We're terrible at following rules."

She walked toward the stairs her hips swaying like she was crossing a stage. "Hey, don't complain to me. I don't make the rules."

And then the light went out and Jack was alone in the dark with a big dumb dog and his very messy thoughts.

~ * ~

Helen woke the next morning alone.

She glanced toward the other side of the bed where Jack would have been had things not gotten wildly out of hand last night.

She flushed warm thinking about Jack's kisses, his lean form poised between her thighs, those intense eyes looking up at her from hooded lids. Lord have mercy, these thoughts weren't helping anyone. How did she even find herself here in a virtual stranger's spare bedroom having sexy thoughts about someone she'd known for less than three days?

You bribed a man with imaginary money, her mind helpfully provided.

She flopped to her back. *Well, that wasn't precisely true.* She *had* money, and Jack hadn't been forced to agree to the plan. He was also getting some distractionary—*was that even a word?*—heavy petting and a stand-in partner for the couples' retreat. *(It should totally be a word.)* So, it wasn't like "bribe" really applied in this instance.

She pushed her tangled hair from her face and wondered whether it was safe to leave the bedroom. After they'd arrived back at the apartment last night, Jenna and Mike had pled exhaustion and gone to bed (and we all know how that went.) Jack had given Helen a long, tired look, and mumbled something about the dog not walking himself, and she'd been left to prepare for bed on her own. By the time she'd finished her shower and dressed in the only nightie, such as it was, Jack had bought her, he was in their bedroom puttering around in nothing but a pair of knit shorts and a tee.

Lord help her, those shorts hadn't hidden a thing.

She flushed so hot she threw off the covers, and even though it made her think about Aunt Iris complaining about "the change of life," it didn't stop her thinking about last night. She hoped Mike and Jenna were awake, because facing two people who you've heard having sex was probably easier than pretending that Jack didn't make her all kinds of old-fashioned horny which she was in no way prepared to parse out this morning.

What had she been thinking inviting herself on this couples' retreat thing? Jack had plainly stated he didn't want her coming, and when she replayed last night in her mind, Jenna's comments felt less cutting and more defensive. Sure, their history was messy, but was it going to help everyone move on to see Helen and Jack together or was she inserting herself in a situation where she didn't belong just to avoid the inevitable?

In short: yes.

She hated having these talks with herself. She shoved herself upright, ran her fingers through her hair, and smoothed her sleep-wrinkled nightie.

Squaring her shoulders, she opened the bedroom door. Jack stood in the kitchen cradling a mug.

Oh, have mercy, they were alone.

"Good morning," she said.

He nodded and took a sip from the mug.

She glanced around. "Jenna and Mike not up yet?"

"Out for a run."

"I thought Mike injured his knee. Is running safe?"

He blinked at her. "Do I look like an orthopedist?"

Point taken. "Any coffee left?"

"I didn't think you drank coffee."

"Someone once told me that's what whitening strips are for."

His lips curved appealingly as he eyed her over his coffee cup, then he pulled another mug from the cupboard and filled it for her. "Cream is in the fridge."

"Thank you."

She prepared her coffee, her back to him, acutely aware he was still leaning against the counter behind her, his thin sweats loosely tied, his plain tee sleep-rumpled like her own. She wondered when he'd come into the room to retrieve the sweats.

When she turned back around, he was holding a spoon toward her.

"Thanks, by the way," he said.

"For what?"

"Offering to be my wing-man for this couples thing. You're right. It'll probably be less awkward not being the odd man out."

"Oh, yeah. About that…"

"If you want to back out, I won't blame you. No harm no foul. I'll bring a book or something."

She stared down into her mug and stirred. *Jack wanted her to come?* Her chest grew warm, and she smiled into her mug. *Rule number one, Helen.* "No backing out. It sounds like fun."

"You don't have to pretend anything though. We can tell them we're just friends."

Her chest glow dimmed a bit. "If that's what you think is best."

"Although you already told them we were a couple, which last night probably only reinforced."

She sipped the hot coffee as a delaying tactic. "True." She sucked up the courage to ask the hard question. "Which would you prefer?"

He shrugged, a surprisingly boyish movement. "I wouldn't mind the company."

Which wasn't an answer at all, of course, but then Jenna and Mike burst through the front door, so any further discussion was overshadowed with breakfast making and discussions about who got to shower first.

The important thing here is that *he wanted her with him.*

It felt good to be wanted for a change, even for just a little while.

~ * ~

Jenna loaned Helen a powder-blue baseball cap and dark sunglasses as a disguise, and they slipped into a large second-hand shop after dropping the men off to get fitted for their tuxes.

Jenna paused, her hand hovering over a rack of women's clothing. "I can't believe I'm shopping for used clothing with you. You could probably buy my entire wardrobe for the cost of one of your dresses on the show."

Helen slid the hangers along and pulled out a couple items to try. "I'll tell you a secret. Most of the gowns are rentals or loans from designers, the sportswear and swimsuits are promos from the manufacturers, and everything else is mail order, because I'm usually too busy to shop for myself. I also tend to wear the same things every day when I'm home, because it's easier. *Oooh.* How cute is this top?"

"Only someone with your coloring could wear that. I'd be washed out."

"I need to focus. How cold will it get at the cabin? I probably just need a sweater and another pair of pants. And proper boots for hiking if we're doing any of that."

"Don't forget pajamas, and... OMG. *This.* You have to try this on." Jenna went on tiptoe to unhook the dress from its hook. "It's beyond gorgeous."

"And a bit impractical."

"Not for the wedding."

"I..."

"You're invited, of course. You can't do the pre-wedding trip and not come to the wedding."

"I don't know. That's very sweet of you, but I don't want to be a distraction."

"Try the dress anyway. I want to see it."

Forty-five minutes later, they dropped the dress at the dry cleaner against Helen's objections "just in case" and continued on to the rental shop to meet the men.

Jenna slowed her steps. "So, this is really awkward, but Mike told me about last night."

Helen schooled herself to keep her face neutral. "Oh?"

"Yeah, and, I know it's none of my business, and you and Jack are both adults, and I don't want details, because *Happily Ever After* is my guilty pleasure fantasy, and I don't want to know it's not real, but... Jack's a good guy. If you're going on the show in a couple of weeks, don't lead him on. Make sure you're on the same page."

Well, bless her heart. Coming from the woman who'd left Jack weeping into a sewer grate, Helen didn't feel she owed anyone an explanation. But, Jenna had a point. "I won't. Last night was... We got carried away. It won't happen again."

"What are you two whispering about?"

Helen jumped at the sound of Jack's voice.

"Nothing. Just girl talk," Jenna said.

But the look on Jack's face made Helen wonder if he'd overheard more than he was letting on.

CHAPTER 11

The next day, Mike and Jenna left to run errands and buy groceries on the way to the cabin, so Jack and Helen were on their own. It was mid-morning by the time they left the condo. A light breeze and parting clouds promised a change in weather from the cold rain they'd had on and off for days. Helen glanced back at Duke, lolling on the back seat. He'd fallen asleep some time ago.

"You don't think we should take him with us?"

Jack didn't even look at her. "We've been through this. It's too much to keep track of him at the couples' retreat," he scrunched his face up as if it was unpleasant to force the words out. "And Mike's folks have missed having a dog around since theirs died last year. I promise, they're thrilled."

"Their son is getting married in days. I can't believe they want to add watching Duke to their to-do list."

He did glance at her this time, his eyes conveying his impatience. "He's a dog. They live in the country. He's so low-maintenance he doesn't even bark. All they have to do is remember to set out food and water a couple of times a day. It's more of an imposition to keep wiping dog prints off my back seat."

She reached over to pet Duke's silky head, then pulled back to massage her shoulder. Stupid injury. She could generally ignore it unless she moved wrong or overused it. "I hope he doesn't miss us, that's all."

"He's hardly known us long enough to miss us. He'd have formed as much attachment to a roomba trailing hotdogs."

"That's a strange visual."

"I think I'm getting hungry. Anyway, we're here."

A crisp American flag waved from the small porch. A wooded area nearby cast dappled shade onto a bright spring lawn, and wide fields and a farm spread out beyond like a Norman Rockwell painting.

Jack cut the engine and turned to her. "It's dog paradise out here. He'll be fine."

Just then, the front door swung open, and a small woman with a large smile hurried toward the car. "Jack! Oh, it's been too long. Good to see you." She insisted on a hug from Jack, pressing her smiling face into his chest before pushing him back to offer Helen similar treatment. "I'm Ruth. Nice to meet you." They completed introductions and exclaimed about the weather before Ruth turned back to Jack. "Can you believe my baby is getting married?"

"Not at all," he said.

Her face softened and she patted his arm. "Just goes to show God's plans aren't always what we think they should be. But here you are with this lovely girl and Mike has his Jenna, and it all works out in the end, right? Did'ya eat yet? I can make you some dippy eggs and toast. You still like that? Or if you want some lunch..."

"We should get back on the road. I'll take a rain check, though."

"You bet you will." She grinned again and eyed the car. "Where is he?"

Jack let Duke out, who made a beeline for Ruth's crotch.

She pushed his snout away and let it morph into a scratch behind the ear. "Mister, you've got to learn some manners. Now, sit!"

Amazingly, Duke obeyed, plonking his fluffy butt on the drive and looking up adoringly for guidance on his next trick. "Well done." She scruffled his head again and smiled up at Jack and Helen.

Jack threw Helen a look that could only be construed as "I told you so" and popped the trunk of the car to retrieve the bag of dog food.

Helen let her gaze wander over wide open fields and reached for happy subjects for small talk. "So, you must be excited about the wedding."

"Very. Jenna went to school with both boys, don't you know. Comes from good family."

"Do her parents live far from here?"

"Just a few miles."

"I'm sure it will be a beautiful wedding if their property looks anything like this."

Ruth's face pinched. "I'd prefer a church wedding, but at least it's a proper wedding this time."

Jack handed over the bag of food. "Jamie had a proper wedding, too."

"A Justice of the Peace isn't the same, but I understand they do things differently in the city."

Jack pressed his lips together and let his eyes skim over the fields as if searching for something.

"We'll take good care of Duke here," Ruth said.

"I know." Jack nodded, his posture tense. "Well, we should go."

"Already?" Ruth asked.

"Why don't you let her make you something. You said you were hungry," Helen added.

"We're burning daylight."

Helen said her goodbyes and waited until they were back in the car, the gravel road scrunching under the tires before she spoke. "What was that all about?"

"I don't know what you mean."

"You got all weird all of a sudden. Is she a bad cook?"

"She's an excellent cook. I just wanted to get going."

He was lying. She could tell by the way his fingers opened and closed on the steering wheel as if he were internally debating whether to discuss it with her or not.

His fingers closed again and stayed that way.

Fine. He could keep whatever it was bottled up inside. It made no difference to her. She wasn't the one headed for an early grave from all the angst hardening her insides. But, heavens, he was an unpleasant companion when he went tense and silent.

She sucked a breath into her lungs and let it out long and slow.

"For God's sake, cut it out," he muttered.

"I'm not doing anything but breathing," she insisted.

"You're overthinking and judging me," he said.

"I was not."

He glanced at her.

"Fine," she said. "I was."

"I know. You purse your lips when you're feeling judge-y."

"I do—" She was about to deny it and then noticed her lips were feeling tight. She pressed them together instead.

"The night of the finale, it was like you were sloshing a cough drop around your mouth."

"You watched the show?"

"Lucky's had a viewing party every week on the big screen. Hard to miss it. Larger than life-size."

"No."

He chuckled. "Yeah. It was pretty funny." He mimed her pursed lips.

"I was nervous."

"Don't lie. You were pissed." He glanced at her. "I don't blame you. You were forced to stand there while your ex proposed to his new girlfriend on live TV. I'd be pissed, too."

"I was freezing."

"You must hate that producer for putting you through that."

Helen folded her hands carefully in her lap. "I don't hate her. I find her heavy-handed and coarse… and sometimes I dream about her tripping over a fire ant nest, but I don't hate her."

He laughed aloud at that, his eyes crinkling wickedly. Her insides fluttered, and she wondered when she'd made the shift to thinking about his eyes crinkling. In bed. When he was in bed, she bet his eyes crinkled like that a lot.

Had his eyes crinkled like that when they'd kissed last night?

She suddenly felt very warm.

She rolled down the window and hoped her face didn't look as hot as it felt.

"You all right?"

No. No, she was not all right. She was feeling very, extremely *not* all right.

"I'm just warm." And thinking impure thoughts about a man I barely know and barely like.

That wasn't entirely true. She didn't dislike him. Mostly he made her feel unsettled and *seen* in a way she couldn't quite control. And very, very warm.

His eyes crinkled again, a light tension at the outside corners, and she fisted her hand instead of giving in to the urge to run her fingertips over the fine lines there. "Don't tell me you're finally acclimating to the cold."

"I'll be fine in a minute. It's this shirt you got me. The fabric doesn't breathe."

"Sorry. Wally World didn't have anything more upscale."

She pulled at the neckline, and one of the tiny white buttons danced across the dashboard.

"Settle down over there. You'll put an eye out."

"It wasn't sewn on well."

Flames. Her face flashed with heat like someone had lit her hair on fire. "I'm just going to grab something lighter."

She leaned over the seat to grab one of her plastic bags, knocking into Jack in the process. The car weaved on the road.

"Sit down before you get us arrested."

"Relax. I'm not—"

A quick bleep of a siren and the flash of lights behind them cut her off.

Jack swore under his breath and glared at her.

"Whoops," she said, choking back nervous laughter.

He went silent as he coasted to a stop.

She scrambled to pull her sleeve back over her shoulder as the cruiser's door shut behind them.

"I didn't mean—" Helen began, resting an apologetic hand on Jack's arm.

He shook her hand off, but not before she detected how tightly he held himself.

"Relax. I'll talk to them," she said. "It was my fault."

"You've done enough," Jack said. Helen bristled. He didn't have to take that kind of tone with her.

An officer peered in the window. Jack rolled it down with jerky movements.

"Everything all right?" The officer's voice rumbled low and even.

"Fine. We're fine," Jack said. "Everything's fine."

"'Cause you were driving a bit unsteady there." The officer paused a beat. "I'd like to take a look at y'all's license and registration if you don't mind."

Jack leaned across Helen's knees as he fumbled with the latch to the glovebox.

"I'll get it," she said, gently taking over for him. She shuffled through the stack of crumpled fast food napkins and paperwork before finding the registration. She handed it over.

Jack avoided looking at her as he passed it out the window.

"License, too," the officer repeated.

"Right." Jack shifted and tensed to pull out his wallet.

The officer turned and walked back to his cruiser. Minutes ticked by.

Jack ran a hand through his hair and blew out a shaky breath. "What the hell is taking so long?"

"Relax," she said. "We weren't doing anything."

"*I* wasn't," he snapped.

"I'm sorry I bumped into you, but who buys polyester these days? It doesn't breathe."

"Maybe you should have been more selective about whose car you ran away in. Choose a Lexus or a Porsche next time if you want breathable fabrics. Or—I don't know—pack your own damn clothes!"

"No need to bark at me. It was an honest mistake."

"It always is with you."

She bit her lip and remained silent as the officer gave Jack a warning to watch the road, then returned to his cruiser.

"You're stressed about being stopped. And seeing Jenna for the next few days. I get it. Maybe if you—"

He closed his eyes. "Don't."

"Oh. Right. Rule number two. 'Jack's not broken.'" She knew she sounded petulant, but it was his fault she'd felt hot. She wasn't the only one to blame. He clearly had his issues.

"Just get your shirt so we can go."

"I'm not hot anymore."

"Your face is flushed. Get the damn shirt," he said, but it didn't have any heat in it.

She flopped over the seat to retrieve the shirt. Jack's jawline tensed as the cruiser made a U-turn in the opposite direction.

She sighed and looked at his profile. "Why are we bickering?"

He pulled out onto the road again. "Apparently, because I didn't buy cotton."

"For real. It's not about the shirt."

"Maybe we don't like each other."

"I didn't get that feeling last night."

A reluctant grin creased his cheeks. His face flushed. "I like you. All right?"

"I like you, too," she admitted. "So why are we snipping at each other?"

"Because we don't know what we are to each other."

"I'd like to think we're friends," she said.

He smirked without humor. "With benefits?"

"Not all-inclusive benefits, let's put it that way."

"Not yet."

She nodded and asked him to look away while she slipped into her tee. She tossed the long-sleeved shirt in the back.

The cautious side of her counseled her to rein it in. She was feeling *feelings* because running away (yes, she said it) and being in an us-against-the-world sort of situation felt electrifying. But, none of it was sustainable. In just a few short days, her season would begin, and everything that happened here, out of the eye of the public, had to remain hidden.

A romance grown in the dark had no more future than a flower asked to bloom without sunshine.

"What we have isn't sustainable. I mean, after the wedding…" She sobered and clasped her hands in her lap. "I think if we continue being intimate, we'll only cause each other hurt feelings."

"I can separate the two."

"I can't."

He went silent.

"So, I think we should just rein it in, ya know?"

He nailed her with his gaze. "Don't need to beat a dead horse."

"Right." She glanced at the road then back at his profile. "I just wanted to be clear."

"Friends with limited benefits. Got it."

He turned on the radio to a hard rock station and ignored her the rest of the ride.

CHAPTER 12

"Turn here," Helen said.

Jack frowned at the iron gates on either side of the drive. "Are you sure you typed the address right?"

"They said fifty-nine. This is number fifty-nine." Helen pointed to the shiny brass numbers reflecting the sunlight on the right-hand side of the massive wrought-iron gate.

Jack eased through the entrance. "Forgive me if I'm skeptical. You've already tried to get me arrested once today."

He'd been cool toward her ever since she'd told him they shouldn't have any hanky-panky. Just like a man, wasn't it? It only proved that if she wasn't there for the "benefits" piece, he wasn't interested in being "friends." Fine.

She shrugged and didn't take the bait as the tree-lined drive brought a long, low-slung home into view. Hills painted with the soft browns and fresh greens of spring rolled into the distance. "Wow."

Jack slammed on the brakes. "This can't be it. They said it was a cabin."

"I think Jenna's exact words were 'log cabin.'"

Jack glanced to her and then back at the building. He put the car into gear and glided to a stop next to someone's compact, high-end SUV. "Jesus."

"Stop complaining and taking the Lord's name in vain. It's gorgeous."

"I'm not complaining." He visibly twitched. "We should probably wait for Mike and Jenna, though."

Helen opened her door. A cool, but pleasant breeze pushed puffy clouds across blue skies above. "Don't be ridiculous. Who knows how long it'll take to buy groceries? I'm tired of being cooped up."

She headed to the wide, covered entry.

"You could give me hand," Jack said.

"I want to introduce myself first. We can get our things later."

She knocked twice, the heavy brass knocker surprisingly satisfying to whack. She'd like to do that to a certain someone's noggin.

The door swung open, and a small, blonde woman screamed. "Omigod! It's true! *Sam!* Sam, get down here!" The woman grabbed Helen's elbow and yanked her into the tiled foyer. Wide, floor-to-ceiling windows on the far wall flooded the room with light. Helen had a brief glimpse of artfully arranged cream-colored sofas, muted accessories and a massive stone fireplace before a man the size of a linebacker blocked her view. "Sam, this is *Helen Walker*, the Alabama Cupcake Queen." The woman nudged him with her elbow which hit him approximately at hip level. "I'm Cassie, Jenna's sister. I'm such a fan."

Sam shook Helen's hand and flashed an easy, generous grin. "Glad you could come. Cassie can't stop talking about you. She and Jenna watched your whole season. She's promised to contain herself."

Cassie swatted Sam. "It wasn't her season. It was Ian's. Hers is coming next." Her face clouded as Jack stepped into the foyer, luggage bulging from his arms. "Hi, Jack. It's been a while."

"Hey, Cassie. Last time I saw you, you were—"

"Twelve."

"Right."

Jack cleared his throat.

Helen glanced around at everyone's suddenly tight expressions. "Sam, have you met Jack?" she asked. "Jack is Mike's friend from high school. He's going to be the best man at the wedding." Helen smiled guilelessly, proud that she didn't snort over the words 'best man.'

Sam nodded. "Good to meet you. Hey, let me show you your room so you can set that all down."

"Are we the first one's here?" Sam and Cassie led the way toward what could only be characterized as the East Wing.

"No, the rest of us are hanging out in the game room until Mike and Jenna get here." Cassie waved her hand above her head. "It's on the lower level."

Jack turned to Helen. "Does that mean basement?" he whispered. "Who doesn't say basement?"

She shushed him with a finger to her lips and scurried to catch up with their hosts.

Sam opened one of several dark, paneled doors at the end of the hallway. "Once you're settled, come on downstairs."

Sam and Cassie disappeared through an opposing door.

Helen peered over Jack's shoulder. "Is that a king-sized bed? I've died and gone to heaven." She pushed past him and tested the mattress with her palms. "Oh, wow. It's one of those foam mattresses, and this comforter is light as a feather."

He shrugged. "Looks comfortable enough." He dropped their things in a heap by the wall.

"Come on. Don't tell me you expected this."

"I don't think anybody expected *this*." He dutifully walked over, nonetheless, and pushed on the mattress. "Nice. So big you won't even know I'm in the room with you."

"Perfect," she said. Yes, she was still salty. He could grow up any minute.

Jack peeked around a door to their right. "Jesus. There's a rain shower."

And he could stop swearing, too.

"If this is all too much creature comfort for you, you can pretend you're camping. Just walk in fully clothed and drown yourself."

He laughed, a low rumble that had Helen darting a look at the massive pillow of a bed. Even though she was annoyed with him and knew distancing herself was the right choice, his low laugh still had the power to make her *think thoughts*.

"Well, we should be comfortable at any rate. Makes spending four days with my ex almost worth it."

He left unspoken the fact that he'd also be spending that time with a woman who'd, rightly, shut down any hopes of further sexy times.

He grimaced and faced her. "Listen. I'm sorry about before. Being around cops isn't my favorite thing."

Oh. *Oh.* "That makes sense."

"And you're right. We should cool it." He tilted a wry smile her way that didn't quite reach his eyes. "I get it."

Helen expected an angry, quickly veiled flash of bruised ego, but in that moment, all she sensed was something almost akin to regret.

Here she was thinking about how all this felt to her. Of course, Jack was preoccupied with having to make nice with his ex. To top it all off, Helen had just shut him down, too. Looking at it that way made her soften toward him despite herself. "At least this place gives you plenty of places to hide," she said.

"True."

"Come on. Let's go be social. Jenna's not even here yet."

~ * ~

Jack paused on the last step and took in his surroundings. Dark wood trim, soft lighting. The space sprawled ahead of him like the fairway at a carnival, a pair of pinball machines on one side, a pool table on the other. A fireplace and leather couches flanked large glass doors leading out to what looked to be a hot tub and patio. This place was next-level man cave. He couldn't help but think it was the type of room a woman like Helen would be used to—all tricked out with high-priced casual décor. It was the kind of room you used for Super Bowl viewing parties and magazine spreads.

It couldn't have made him feel more out of place.

Jack made a beeline for the bar on the far end.

A man and woman paused their game of pool and waved in greeting. "Jack and Helen," Sam made introductions from behind the bar, "this is Connor and his wife, Lori. College friends." Sam didn't specify of whom, but it didn't seem to matter.

The woman, Lori, bent low, her dark, chin-length hair swinging forward as the crack of the balls echoed throughout the space. "Ha! I win again. This never gets old." She grinned and approached the bar. "Sam, I'd like a celebratory tonic and lime."

"I'll have one, too," Helen said. "It seems too early for alcohol."

Jack was trapped in a house with strangers, his ex, and an uptight beauty queen. "I'll have a beer if you've got it."

"Coming up." Sam opened a mini fridge behind him.

"Make that two." Connor, short and stocky with a close-cropped beard and faded Steelers ballcap sank onto a barstool. "To console myself. My wife is highly competitive. That's three games in a row now she's won."

His wife slid onto the stool next to him. "There's nothing wrong with being a winner. I happen to enjoy it."

"A lot."

"I would think you'd want the mother of your children to be of superior DNA."

"And humble. I think we should add humble."

Lori accepted her drink. "Too late now."

"Wait." Cassie, just arriving, stopped inside the doorway of the nearby stairwell. She held a bag of chips in each hand. "Are you not-so-subtly saying what I think you're saying?"

Lori's cheeks grew pink. "This is a whole lot more awkward than I thought it would be, but, yes. My husband knocked me up on our honeymoon. Surprise!"

Cassie dropped the chips on the bar and rushed in for a hug, as women do. "Congratulations! I'm so excited for you."

Helen turned to look at Jack, and his pulse leapt with adrenaline. Fight or flight. He turned to retrieve the bags of chips, because... good God. *Three days to go.*

"Does Jenna know?" Cassie practically levitated with excitement. "She's gonna flip that you beat her to baby-making."

Lori grimaced. "It was an accident. I mean, we're thrilled, but it wasn't as if we were trying. But," she shrugged, "these things happen."

"Nothing makes a single guy more uncomfortable than hearing that phrase in this context." Sam pried off the cap to his own beer. "Congratulations to both of you. And Cassie? Belt and suspenders from here on out."

Cassie grinned. "Whatever you're into, babe."

Jack cleared his throat, loudly ripped open a bag of chips, and contemplated how quickly he could feign a stomach issue. Helen was deep into smiling, hugging, congratulatory mode.

Footsteps echoed in the stairwell. Jack braced himself for seeing Jenna.

"Ben!" Cassie called out. "Where have you been hiding?"

Jack waved to Mike's little brother. Finally, a familiar face.

"Our room. Jamie's catching up on some work stuff. I'm supposed to send apologies and bring back a Diet Coke, but I may stay. You all look like you're having way more fun down here."

"Lori's pregnant," Cassie blurted.

"Babe, it's not our news to share," Sam said.

"It's okay," Lori said.

Ben pressed his lips together. "Congratulations?"

"Thank you," Connor puffed his chest. Jack wasn't sure if it was for real or for show. "It was tough going, but I got the job done."

Lori swatted her husband and laughed.

This was going to be a long week.

Jack took a swig and pointed his bottle toward Helen and Ben. "Helen, meet Ben. Mike's little brother. Ben, this is Helen."

Ben gave Jack a long, probing look before greeting Helen. Jack kept his expression impassive. What was there to say? *Here's the woman who made out with me once on your brother's sofa, but now doesn't want anything to do with me, so we'll be sharing a room—and a bed— for the next few days, because FML.*

"Everyone!" Cassie called out. "I just got a text from Jenna. Go get changed into comfy clothes you can move in. They'll be here any second. We start the first activity in twenty minutes!"

Oh, goody.

~ * ~

Jack retreated to the bathroom to change clothes. He had less than zero interest in "activities" involving any of these people. From the happily married and pregnant Lori and Connor to the saccharine-sweet Cassie and Sam, Jack already regretted agreeing to be a party to this. The only thing moving him to pull on a pair of shorts and a fake grin was the fact that he didn't want to be the one to make his best friend miserable. Life with Jenna would do that soon enough.

He paused and stared at his reflection in the mirror.

Stop it, he told himself. *You're better than this.*

Was he, though? He'd come on this trip intending to use the time to take a good, long, hard look at himself. It was no secret he'd landed in Sugar Falls as a grief-stricken, angry teen, but that didn't excuse why he'd let himself get stuck in that place for more than a decade.

Hearing that Mike was getting married had rocked him. Seeing his younger half-sister get engaged had only added to the sense that he was, for lack of a kinder phrasing, wasting his life.

The kicker was, how often had he judged his own mother for being stuck in the past? For clinging to a vision of herself or former self that didn't allow her to move forward?

It stung to realize he was no better.

Seeing Jenna again, as hard as it was, only forced Jack to face the hard truths he could no longer ignore. He was a thirty-three-year-old cook in his father's pub with no family, no future, and a handful of friends he held at arm's length. The image of a cynical teen who'd seen too much and didn't give a damn living out of a sleek black classic car with the windows perpetually rolled down had worn thin over the years. It was only so long before cutting and cynical became grumpy old man.

Quite the catch, he was. No wonder Helen had pumped the brakes.

"It'll be fun," she said, as he finally pushed open the bathroom door. She stood in a ray of literal sunshine all fresh-faced and smiling in yoga pants, T-shirt and high ponytail like she was ready for Saturday brunch and the farmer's market.

He grunted his reply.

She made a face. "That's what you're wearing?"

"What's wrong with it?"

"Cargo shorts when out in the nineties."

It stung, but he played it casual. "Which makes no sense. Where do you carry your snacks?" He paused. "Or your car keys?"

She smoothed her hands down her hips in a self-conscious manner. He could see the moment she caught on that he was referring to her stuffing Mike's keys down those very pants on a dark roadside right before they'd first kissed. He knew the moment she remembered the kiss, because her tongue snuck out to touch her lips before retreating again.

"We should go," she said.

"Relax. They're not going to start without us. And if they do, there's a hot tub I've had my eye on. Win-win."

A pert swing of her ponytail told him all she thought about that suggestion. He followed her down the hall toward the sound of voices.

Let the games begin.

~ * ~

After a rousing and R-rated game of *Pass the Orange/Sex Positions*, Cassie announced everyone could take a break for a few hours before dinner. This gave Jack and Helen far too much time to bump into one another without anything specific to distract them.

"So," Jack said, sliding Helen a look she could only define as lurid, "you know a lot of sex poses."

She refused to be daunted. She might be southern, but she wasn't a prude. Sex was a natural act between two people who cared about one another.

And, also, two people who were alive and found each other "hot."

"I taught yoga for a while," she said by way of explanation.

"Right."

So, what if she'd done a bit of outside research to see how she might spice things up and make things in the bedroom with Travis more... interesting? Let Jack think what he wanted. It hadn't worked anyway. Travis had deemed her initial ideas too "inappropriate." Helen had muttered something about "flexibility" and dropped any further suggestions.

They hadn't even gotten to the Flying Crane, so his loss.

Jack scrubbed the back of his neck with his palm. "You're a lot more competitive than I thought."

"I don't like coming in in second place."

"I suppose not." He rummaged in his pack even though there were empty dressers all around them. "I think I'm going to hit the hot tub."

She rubbed her aching shoulder. Contorting herself for the game had not done it any favors. "Sounds heavenly." She paused. "But, I don't have a swimsuit, so you're safe."

"I didn't say anything."

"I know."

He didn't have to. It had been written all over his face.

"I'm sorry if I made you uncomfortable," she said. "It was all in good fun."

"I'm fine. It's you I wouldn't have expected to be okay with it. Didn't you object to the Trojan Bus of Love thing?"

"That was different."

"How?"

Yes, how? Her brain demanded. "That was public. This was... private."

"Right. So, do you often mimic sex positions in front of your family and friends?"

"I refuse to be shamed for being sex-positive. But there's a difference between enjoying sex and selling it as if that's all you're good for. I'm worth more than that."

His expression grew thoughtful, and his smirk dimmed. "Good point."

"Thank you."

He fisted his swim trunks in his hand, murmured something about seeing her around, and left.

Helen blew out a breath, hands on hips. Now what?

She pushed open the bedroom door and wandered down the hall in search of distraction.

"There you are," Cassie waved to Helen from one of the couches in the living room. She and Sam snuggled, hands and bodies intertwined. "Congratulations, you challenge winners!"

"Thank you."

"Where's your co-winner?"

"Headed to the hot tub. I didn't bring a suit, so... is there a library somewhere?"

"I have suits you can borrow."

Helen looked at Cassie's teeny form. "I doubt they'd—"

"They're stretchy. Besides, who's going to object? Jack?" She laughed and pushed off Sam's chest. "I could use a soak before we start dinner, anyway. Limber me up for later."

Sam turned beet red.

"I've got ideas," Cassie chortled, and she grabbed Helen's hand and practically dragged her down the hall.

Of course, the largest suit Cassie owned which actually, you know, covered Helen's assets and wasn't more suited to the French Riviera was a two-piece red number with gold ring accents at the hip and center chest. One false move and it would be showtime. Helen wrapped herself in an oversized towel and trailed Cassie to the hot tub.

"Mind if we crash your peace and quiet?" Cassie didn't wait for a reply but stepped over the edge of the tub and slid into the bubbling water.

Jack avoided Helen's gaze as he shifted to the other side of the tub. His hair was damp, curling slightly with the heat, and she couldn't stop staring at his chest.

"Sammy!" Cassie called back into the house. "Can you bring me something fruity?"

Sam backed his way out of the house, two tall glasses in hand. He handed one to Helen. "One step ahead of you. Frozen strawberry daiquiri," he said. "Cassie's favorite."

"I don't know how I got so lucky, but here I am," Cassie cooed, popping up to give her beau a quick kiss before taking her drink and sinking into the tub. "He anticipates my every desire."

Helen took a tentative sip from the straw sticking out of her glass.

Whoa. Apparently, Cassie's desire was to make dinner while soused.

"Thanks," she said. "It's delicious."

"So," Cassie said, waving Sam in to sit beside her. "You two seemed to be having fun with the *Sex Positions* ice breaker. I modeled this whole week around games from dating shows, so it's kind of ironic that Helen's here."

"This is how they expect you to find your future fiancé?" Jack murmured to Helen. "By grinding up against him?"

"That isn't like any challenge from *Happily Ever After*, I assure you."

"Right. Your show is classier." He winked. "Got it."

Helen's blood began a slow simmer. How dare he mock the show? Granted, there had been that moment when Marcia had let her brainstorming run off the deep end, but Helen would never have agreed to go on it if she'd thought it in bad taste overall.

"You can learn a lot about a person by how they react to you grinding up against them," she said.

"*Ooooh,*" Cassie laughed. "This sounds interesting."

Jack's eyes flashed as he braced one arm along the side of the tub. "Or maybe Helen's the type of woman who's all smoke and no fire."

Oh, no he didn't.

Helen let go of her towel and slowly closed her lips over her straw, all the while holding Jack's gaze. His pupils dilated satisfyingly.

Sam cleared his throat. "You know what?" he said. "I think we should get a start on dinner."

"I just got in!" Cassie said.

Sam waggled his eyebrows.

"But, we should get started before this goes to my head," Cassie said.

After they were gone, Jack spread his other arm out. Water droplets clung to his skin.

"So," he said. "Did I scare you off?"

"Of course not." Helen stepped up onto the platform surrounding the tub. Just to prove her point, she reached her glass toward Jack. "Hold this for me?"

Their fingers grazed as she transferred the glass to him, sending an electric current up her arm.

She slid into the hot water and accepted her drink back. She sipped it, trying to stop just sort of brain freeze. Sue her, she liked sweet and fruity drinks.

"Nice suit," he drawled, his eyes hooded. "Thought you didn't bring one."

"It's Cassie's," she said.

His gaze slid across her collar bone like a caress. "Surprised it fits."

"You and me both."

His mouth curved with humor. Not quite a smile.

"What are you doing?" he asked.

"I'm just sitting here, enjoying a soak, sipping a very alcoholic drink."

"You know what I mean."

"I know you want to be alone, but it was Cassie's idea, and now that I'm here, it feels really good on my shoulder. Can we just call it a truce for a few minutes?"

He held his palms to face her. "Hey, I'm not here to fight. You go ahead."

"Thank you. It's not my aim to make things more awkward between us, believe it or not."

His snort said he didn't quite believe that.

"What? You're the one making snarky comments about grinding and sex position games and whatnot." She sucked on the straw again. "For your information, I wasn't grinding. I was playing the game. That's it. They are our hosts. I'm not going to tell them their sex game is in poor taste. This has nothing to do with you. Smoke without fire," she muttered, taking another sip.

He laughed without humor. "All for fun, is it?"

"When in Rome," she said. Which wasn't a particularly outlandish comparison given what her history books had to say about Ancient Rome. "Anyway, no reason we can't sit here and relax without getting all hot and bothered over it."

"Easy for you to say. You've got the iced drink in your hand."

She sipped her drink. True.

They sat in silence for a couple of minutes, the steam making Jack's face flush. Not that she was looking.

His eyes closed.

Helen slurped the last of her drink and set the empty glass on the decking by the tub. She sank lower.

"Don't fall asleep on me." Jack spoke without opening his eyes. "I don't want you to drown or anything."

"I'm not going to drown."

"Good. It would ruin hot tubs for me forever."

She glanced up. He was half-smiling, his lids heavy.

"We wouldn't want that," she said.

"Nope."

Blast the man. She was trying to keep her distance. For both their sakes.

"You're impossible," she said.

"You're not the first person to say so."

"But you're not the worst," she said, jumping to clarify. "I mean, you have your qualities."

"Keep going. I think part of the wound doesn't have salt in it yet."

"Why did you take me?" she blurted.

He suddenly looked like he'd swallowed a golf ball. "Take you?"

"Back in New York? Why did you agree to take me with you?"

"Oh. That." He shifted, his face finding some semblance of normal again. He shrugged.

She watched his face shadow. She didn't think he'd answer.

"I know what it feels like to be out of options," he said.

"But you had a choice. You could have refused."

"Maybe I liked doing something impulsive again. It's been a while. The last time didn't end well."

The last time.

Helen fell silent. Would this time, this choice, end any better for him?

"I think I'm done cooking for now." Jack rose to his feet, droplets sluicing off his body as he hauled himself in a flood of water onto the decking.

"Jack…"

"Good talk," he said. "The suit's your color."

He picked up her empty drink glass, a ghost of something she couldn't define in his eyes, and left her wondering whether he regretted this impulsive decision, too.

~ * ~

Helen woke early and crept to the kitchen.

She'd slept poorly, Jack's proximity and these strange feelings of compassion for him making it difficult to center on her own problems. She started the coffee maker and slumped against the counter to wait.

"You're an early riser."

Helen turned to see Jamie, Ben's husband, pad in. He wore a bright red flannel robe that clashed adorably with his strawberry blonde hair. "Good morning. Trouble sleeping. I figured I'd start the day."

He nodded and pulled mugs down from a cupboard saving Helen the task of searching for them. "Same here."

"Why couldn't you sleep?"

"Could have something to do with anxiety over spending time with Ben's homophobic relatives. Or I could be constipated. It's a toss-up."

"Sorry."

"Either way, it'll pass, right? Sorry." He must have caught her grimace. "Ben always tells me I have a twelve-year-old's humor and a seventy-year-old's filter."

She laughed and opened the refrigerator to get the carton of cream. "I'm sorry about the relatives. Hopefully the humor will get you through."

"Oh, I'm fine," he said with a curt wave. "They can all go to hell for all I care."

"It matters to Ben," she said.

"Way too much." He heaved a sigh and splashed some cream into a mug before sliding it toward her. "But, that's what makes him the sentimental, sensitive fool I fell in love with."

"How long have you been together?"

"We'll be married two years this September. Together for eleven. Dating for seven." At her quizzical expression, he elaborated. "Ben didn't

145

know we were dating for a few years on account of him thinking he was straight."

She hid a smile as she poured the coffee. "But you convinced him."

"No. I just waited on the sidelines like a sad puppy until he stopped beating himself up for not liking any of the girls throwing themselves in his path."

"I'm sorry for the girls."

"Don't be. He was an excellent boyfriend. Every bit the gentleman. What girl turns down dinner, a movie, and a chaste peck on the cheek?" He laughed and sipped his coffee.

"Are you pulling my leg?"

"I'll behave with more caffeine."

They drank their coffee in silence a few moments.

Jamie waved his mug toward the empty doorway. "So, what's the deal with you and Mr. McHottie?"

"Just friends."

"You couldn't keep your hands off each other yesterday."

"You mean the game?"

"Is that what you two call it?"

Helen felt the heat of a blush creep into her cheeks. "It was nothing. Just having fun."

"You might be having fun, but he was into it."

"I assure you, he's not."

Jamie raised an eyebrow. "Believe what you want, but there are some things a man can't hide." Her fame flamed. "I meant feelings. Get your mind out of the gutter."

Helen grabbed a third mug from the cupboard, filled it, and mumbling something about Jack being a bear without his morning coffee.

She hurried out of there like her hair was on fire.

As if! Jack might lust after her, but there was a Grand Canyon divide between lust and "feelings"—and neither would make parting at the end of this any easier.

She transferred the mugs to one hand and inched the bedroom door open. Clear, blue eyes met hers.

"You're awake," she said, kicking the door shut.

Jack pushed himself up against the headboard, the sheet sliding down to pool at his waistband. He ran a hand through his sleep-tousled hair. "Is one of those for me or are you double-fisting again today?"

"One is for you." She handed him a mug and stood by the window to sip hers.

"I won't bite if you wanted to relax."

"I am relaxing," she said.

"On the bed," he said. "You're making me tense standing there like that."

"It's a beautiful morning. I'm enjoying looking out at it."

"We managed to sleep here without being all over each other, so I think we'll be fine."

He should speak for himself. She'd barely slept a wink.

"Thanks for the coffee." He set the already empty mug on the nightstand. "I'm gonna shower."

"Jack…"

He paused, his hand on the bathroom door. "Yeah?"

She'd been about to ask him if Jamie was right, if Jack felt more than lust for her. If he had feelings. But then she realized she was talking about the man who doubted people could fall in love over the course of an intense eight weeks of reality dating. To admit he had feelings for her in a matter of days? Who was she kidding?

"Nothing. You go ahead. I'll shower after," she said.

"Sure."

~ * ~

Jack rested his head against the shower wall and let the fake rain wash over him.

Lord help him, he was an idiot.

How the hell was he going to spend another week with this woman when he could barely spend one night without reaching out to finish what they'd started, "friendship" be damned? Why in hell had he promised to take her all the way to Alabama? Was he some sort of masochist?

It was bad enough he'd committed to stand by and smile while the ex he'd spent years vilifying in his memories married his best friend. He had to go and add "unattainable goddess" to round out the misery.

He'd slept fitfully right up until early this morning when he'd had a bizarre dream of piping frosting onto a conveyer belt of cupcakes only to have a naked Helen slide out on the conveyer belt, so he'd piped frosting onto her. Then the dream fast-forwarded to Helen lying, frosting-covered, as the centerpiece of a buffet table like some freaky Henry VIII banquet. Jack had grabbed Helen's hand, and they'd run out of the mansion into his waiting car to speed away.

Yeah. It didn't take Freud to decode that one.

Then he'd woken up to the latch of the bedroom door clicking and Helen sliding into the room bearing coffee and looking all lush and sleep-rumpled.

After an evening of competitive board gaming, Cassie had promised another day of "flirty fun" as she'd called it.

Jack emitted an audible groan. Any more flirty fun, and he'd be embarrassing himself.

A soft knock interrupted his thoughts.

"Jack? Are you almost done? Cassie just came by and said we're starting at nine, sharp."

Oh, goody.

~ * ~

Helen grinned and relaxed into the sofa. Another twenty-four hours had come and gone, but for an intimate retreat with complete strangers, Helen was having a surprisingly good time. Aside from the residual tension between Jack and the bride and groom, Helen found everyone to be relaxed, friendly, and good-natured. They'd played more games, done couples' yoga, and had a campfire the night before, and this morning enjoyed a half an hour of guided meditation followed by a leisurely hike. After an hour strolling through open fields and along tumbled stone walls and winding country lanes, they'd returned for brunch. Cassie asked them all to meet back at one o'clock in the living room for the afternoon activity.

All the diversions and good food almost allowed Helen to forget that this was only a temporary getaway at a venture capitalist's second home planned by their son's terminally exuberant girlfriend and wasn't any more real life than reality TV.

Helen slanted a look to her right where Jack scowled at the proceedings. It would have been easier if he'd choose a mood for the day. Since this morning, he'd swung between easy-going laughter on the hike to brooding and monosyllabic replies like a thirteen-year-old about to get her period. She was getting whiplash trying to keep up with it.

Cassie introduced the next activity as *The Dating Game* (a twist on *The Newlywed Game*) where they earned points for correctly answering questions to show how well they knew one another.

Most folks were on target with their answers. Lori "forgot" a particular girlfriend in Connor's past, and Helen was shocked to learn that Ben had only ever had one partner, the sweet romantic. They moved through middle names, body counts, celebrity crushes, and whether they'd kiss on the first date.

"Next question," Cassie said. "What is the most unusual place you've had sex?"

Helen froze, her pen hovering over the blank sheet of paper. She peeked up at Jack. She scribbled her guess on the paper and waited.

Apparently, vehicles of various sorts were popular with this crowd. Including one tandem bike which she was still trying not to picture.

They got to Helen. She turned her notepad around.

"Outside?" Jack said.

"I'm afraid you're going to have to be more specific," Cassie laughed. Helen's face grew hot. "*Where* outside?"

Helen blinked. She'd only ever had sex in a bed. Once in a shower, but—no—they finished in the bed, so did that even count? Standing sex was definitely, er, sexy. She tried not to picture shower sex with Jack. She wondered if he'd complain about the size of the shower stall the way Travis had, bump his elbow on the corner caddy, and then swear about it.

Yeah. Standing sex was hot only if you didn't have things smacking your elbows.

"Against a tree?" Helen blurted.

Jack sucked in a breath.

"Wait. Am I right?"

His lips tilted, his face flushed, and he nodded.

"That can't have been comfortable," Connor mumbled.

"It was in a snowstorm, the middle of winter, so we were well-padded," Jack said, "and that's all I'm going to say about it."

They did a few more rounds where Jack and Helen managed to score a few more points.

"Final question," Cassie announced. "Both of you will answer this one, revealing your own answer and guessing your partner's. Ready? Who was your last sex dream about?"

Helen's pulse kicked into overdrive. She glanced up, but Jack was staring hard at his notepad, his pen fisted in his hand. No doubt he was dreading hearing what his ex was dreaming about, and she couldn't blame him.

"This feels very personal," Helen murmured. "I don't know what to write."

Cassie grinned. "No worries. This final round is just for you to share with your partner. Ben and Jamie are our high scorers and get uninterrupted hot tub time until dinner and no after-dinner chores. The rest of us get free time until dinner prep at five. Great job, you guys!"

149

Lori made a beeline to the bathroom, Ben and Jamie left to put on their swimsuits, and the others dispersed for the rec room and "nap time."

Jack looked at Helen's notepad. She'd written the name of a celebrity chef known for his BBQ.

Jack chuckled. "I need details."

"I'd just watched an episode on smoked meats. I can't help what my subconscious does. Stop laughing."

Jack swiped at a tear with his knuckle. "Nope."

"What did you write?"

She pulled down the notepad he had held to his chest. Blank.

"That's not fair. You didn't even guess at mine."

"I was just about to write the name of a man famous for his barbecue sauces."

"Very funny."

"You didn't guess mine, either" he pointed out.

"How am I supposed to know what goes on in that twisted mind of yours?"

"It's not *that* twisted."

"You have sex against trees. In snowstorms. Who does that?" Helen sobered. "I hope it wasn't Jenna, because that would be awkward." She collected the discarded notepads and pens and stacked them on the coffee table. "Wait," she whispered. "*Is* that who your sex dream was about?"

"Hell, no. I'm not that conflicted."

"Is it someone you think I could guess?"

He shook his head and started up the shallow steps toward the entry hall.

She trailed after him. "I told you my name. It's only fair you tell me yours."

"Helen," he said, his back to her.

"What?"

Then his blue eyes slid to hers and held for one speaking moment, and he shrugged. "You asked."

Helen.

He'd dreamed about *her?* No. He must be pulling her leg.

She caught up with him at the end of the hall.

"We're in a five-thousand-foot house. Is it really necessary for you to hover over me?" he asked, his palm splayed on the closed door to their room.

"I know what you're doing," she said, resting her hand on his arm. "You're trying to shock me and keep me at arm's length. I get it. But it was just a game."

150

He pushed into the room and grabbed a new towel from the stack on the dresser.

"I didn't sleep well last night, so I'm going to take a hot shower and probably a nap."

"Fine. I'm going to read this book." She grabbed a random book out of the shelves by the dresser. *Adventures in Ornithology.*

"Looks riveting," he said.

"I like," she fanned the pages, "nature." Then she dropped onto the bed, crossed her legs at the ankles, opened the book and pointedly ignored him.

CHAPTER 13

Helen re-read the word *swallow* several more times before deciding she didn't enjoy birds nearly as much as she thought she did.

"I need your help."

She carefully closed the book and set it on her lap, before deigning to give Jack her attention. "With?"

He swallowed, his Adam's apple bobbing heavily in his throat. Her gaze lingered there a moment before sliding down. He wore nothing but a towel held taut with one fist at his right hip. Or was it his left? Helen's eyes focused on that fist, simultaneously willing it to remain closed and praying it let go.

She forgot about birds.

"I have… that is, I think I have a tick."

"I see." She did not.

"On my ass."

Her gaze flashed to his. "*Oh.*"

"I was hoping you'd remove it."

"Me?"

"That's why I'm standing here asking."

"Can't Mike do it?"

"He and Jenna are napping."

"Wake him up."

Jack's head cocked, and he gave her a look. "Sweetheart, I doubt they're sleeping, and as unpleasant as it is to have a tick on my ass and have to ask you to deal with it, it'd be more so to have to knock on a door when your best friend and your ex are in the middle of sexy times."

She could not stop blinking. Where was she supposed to look? At his chest with its smooth muscles? At the smattering of hair? Or, at the fine but distinctive happy trail running down to the taut edge of that towel?

"Fine."

His face registered relief, and he strode forward, handing her a little orange scooper tool. "This should make it easier. I'm glad I threw one in my pack."

She accepted the tool, their hands brushing briefly. An electric spark shot up her arm as if recognizing this was both an inconvenient time for sexy thoughts and just the moment to make her hyperaware she was about to see this man's naked ass. And she wasn't the least bit sorry, heaven help her. Her pulse pounded thick and heavy in her veins as she scrambled off the bed.

Jack avoided her gaze and turned away. His grip on the towel loosened.

"Wait," she said, grabbing his hand, despite the risk of further shocks of awareness. "Put something on. I may have to look at your," she cocked her chin toward his backside, "but you can keep your other bits covered, please and thank you."

She could smell the soap on his skin, feel the heat radiating from his body. She fought the urge to fan herself. Yes, he definitely needed to keep things covered.

He turned his head to stare at her, and the tip of his tongue danced out to touch his upper lip. "I'm not sure you're grasping exactly what needs to happen here."

Heat flooded her face. "I'm asking for a limited view, so to speak. For modesty's sake."

"I have a blood-sucking parasite latched to my ass and you're worried about modesty? Do you need a sterile surgical field or something?"

"Don't be ridiculous."

Yes. A limited field of view as opposed to wide swathes of manly backside would definitely help. "Just... put a sock on it or something?" *Yes! A sock.* She pulled her bag of clothes closer and hurriedly scrounged, pulling out a short pink-striped sock. "Will this fit?"

He snatched it from her hand. "Less and less the more we discuss it," he muttered as he turned to the bed and fiddled with the sock. She watched as his skin blotched red on the back of his neck, grateful he wasn't observing her own heated cheeks. "There." He lay face down and waited.

Hoo boy.

She stepped closer.

She was about to see Jack's naked ass. And, yes, she was calling it that. Because... *day-um*... he hit all her sweet spots. Despite his brusque personality, she might have flung herself in his path any number of times over the last couple of days except for that pesky duo of self-control and self-respect.

She paused for composure and then peeled the towel to the side, exposing two smooth, muscled buttocks. Her self-respect high-fived her self-control and flew out the window.

"So, how's it look?"

Her gaze skittered over Jack's backside. *Like two firm melons.* She sent up a silent prayer of thanks for the exquisite male form and then followed it with a prayer for forgiveness for impure thoughts. *So. Many. Impure. Thoughts.* "How's what look?" she wheezed.

"The tick."

Right. Her gaze paused its general appreciation for a more clinical inspection. *Ah. Ew.* It was attached at the juncture of his thigh and left butt cheek. Coming face to face with it, she was definitely having second thoughts about whether she was the right woman for the job.

"So..." she said. "I just, kind of, scoop it?"

"Slowly, from back to front. Don't rip it out, or you could leave part of it."

She shivered. And not in a good way. *Just slide the scoop up.* She tried again, swallowing her disgust. "Maybe I could ask Mike."

Jack twisted to speak to her. "Just try again."

"I think I need to... maybe..." She tilted her head, squinted. Internally debated optimal scooping angles while not being distracted by this man's glorious hamstrings.

"Any chance you could get on with it?"

"Right." She took in another breath and tried to think about other things.

Hamstrings. Ham. Smoked meats...

Her brain danced around with the words, making a mockery of her focus. She nearly snorted with uncomfortable laughter.

"Not gonna lie," he said. "This is not how I pictured the first time you saw my ass."

"Not how I pictured it either." She froze. Had she said that out loud? *Yes. Yes, sweet heavens*, she had.

He twisted to look over his shoulder. "Did you just admit to picturing my ass?"

She shoved his head into the pillow. It was oddly satisfying. "Are you actually coming on to me while I'm performing a medical procedure?"

He said something, but it was muffled by the pillow. It sounded like, "Maybe." His body shook with laughter, tensing in ways that made her aware of muscles she probably ought not to be aware of, being a casual acquaintance and all who'd nixed further intimacy as a Bad Idea with capital letters.

"You're going to have to hold still. I can't focus on your ass. I mean..."

His body shook harder.

"Relax your butt," she said. "No. That's not helping. Maybe tighten it?"

He swung his face to the side and gulped air, his face red with laughter or embarrassment she wasn't sure. "Just do it already."

She sucked in a calming breath and tried again, stifling her squeamishness. "Got it!"

Jack flung himself upright to look, knocking into Helen's arm and launching the contents of the scoop into the air. He grasped her wrist and looked at the empty scoop. "You lost it."

"I didn't lose it. You bumped me." The pink sock waved in her peripheral vision. "*Ack!* Lay down. You're naked!"

He flumped to his front again. "Right. Sorry." His ass cheeks tightened as he twisted his torso to speak to her. "Did you get a look at what kind it was?"

Seriously? "Not before you flung it across the room, no."

He pulled the towel closed over his lower half, her sock tossed to the side and looking like it craved a cigarette. "We should look for it."

"You want to look for it," she parroted.

"If it's a deer tick, I'll want you to monitor the bite to see if it develops a rash."

She blinked as her brain processed. So, if they *didn't* find it, she'd have to look at his naked ass every day? Oh, the horror.

Jack squatted to search the carpet, his quads flexing as the towel split open. He jumped up. "Got it!"

Pity that.

He motioned for her to bring him the scoop. His shoulders sagged with relief. "Good. Looks like a dog tick. They don't carry Lyme. Doesn't look like it was on for long, either."

They proceeded to have an intense entomology lesson while Jack explained all he knew about ticks and disease. She'd never been so interested in bugs in her life. Much more interesting than birds. "Interesting," she murmured, so he'd keep talking. He smelled *good*. Something undefinable and delicious. She inhaled.

"Better put some antibiotic ointment on it, just in case," he said.

"The tick?"

Jack frowned. "No, the bite."

Okay, maybe she hadn't been listening all that closely.

She retrieved the first-aid kid from the bathroom counter and pulled out the tube of antibiotic. "Bottom's up," she said.

"I think I can manage."

"Right." She passed him the tube, and he disappeared behind the bathroom door again.

He reemerged a few minutes later in a pair of longer knit shorts and a T-shirt. The shorts clung to his body like a lover's caress, and now Helen couldn't stop picturing what lay under the thin, dark fabric.

"Thanks," he said.

"You're welcome. I'd say anytime, but…"

"I'd just as soon this be a one-time thing."

They nodded awkwardly at one another.

"So…" She glanced down at his bare feet. Suddenly everything about his exposed skin seemed energized. "We should probably see if we can get a head start prepping dinner."

It was only two o'clock.

"Good idea."

They reached for the doorknob at the same time as if this were a scripted meet-cute in a movie, each pulling their hand back after contact like they'd touched an exposed wire. She needed to move away for her own sanity.

Her feet glued themselves to the floor.

"About this," he said. "This stays between us, right?"

Her tongue slid over her lips, and she forced herself to meet his gaze. Sweet mother of sunshine, but his eyes were blue. Why were they so dang blue?

"Who would I tell?"

He smiled in what must have been relief. "Thanks."

"No worries." *No worries? Since when was she Australian?* "I was glad to help. I mean, it was no trouble. You'd do it for me if our roles were reversed." It wasn't sexual at all. Just one friend helping another in his time of need.

His pupils dilated, and his mouth hitched up in one corner. "You bet."

He's picturing my ass, she thought. Right in this moment. She could tell. The thought made her abort a nervous laugh which came out as a cough-snort.

"You okay?"

"Fine. I'm fine. Just… dry throat."

She reached for the door handle again.

"Just so you know," he murmured to her backside, "I was."

She didn't have the nerve to ask what he was talking about as she hurried to the kitchen without looking back.

~ * ~

After dinner they played romantic movie charades until things took a dark turn with Connor acting out *Footloose* in a way no one could have predicted. Then Sam admitted he'd never seen *Princess Bride* and it was decided that had to be immediately remedied.

The rec room smelled of buttered microwave popcorn as Jack stretched and announced he was calling it a night.

"Me, too," Helen said, uncurling from her spot on the floor.

After seeing her sitting like a pretzel for two hours, Jack no longer doubted she'd been an excellent yoga instructor.

He made a hurried exit.

"Are you that tired?"

Jack slowed his steps. "Big day tomorrow. Scavenger hunt and all. Don't want to be too tired for the fun."

A light hand on his shoulder stopped him in the darkened hallway.

"I'll leave as soon as we get back to Cutler," Helen said.

He swung around. "Why? I told you'd I'd drive you home."

"It's obvious this is hard for you. I shouldn't have worried about Jenna. She and Mike seem happy together. You don't need me hanging around making you and everyone else uncomfortable."

"You don't make me uncomfortable."

"You can't stand to be in the same room with me."

If she only knew.

A screech from downstairs curtailed further discussion.

A string of curses followed.

Multiple footsteps tromped up the stairwell and the door to the basement burst open. "Are they freaking *kidding* me?" Jenna cried.

"I'm sure we'll work it out in the morning," Mike soothed, although his eyes looked panicked in the low light coming from the rec room.

"What's going on?" Helen asked.

Jenna held out her phone. "The caterer just emailed and asked for the final head count for our wedding on the twelfth. The *twelfth*. Our wedding is the fifth!"

"I'm sure she just mis-typed," Mike said. "We'll call in the morning to confirm."

"Absolutely," Helen reiterated.

Jenna blew out a long, slow breath. "I'm texting her. There." She pressed *SEND* and pocketed her phone. "You're right. I'm sure it's a mistake."

Her phone pinged moments later, and she pulled it from her pocket.

Her face drained of color.

"It's a mistake, right?" Mike asked. "Just a typo?"

Jenna slid her phone back in her pocket with a shaking hand. "I need a drink."

Mike trailed after his fiancée toward the kitchen.

"Oh, no," Helen murmured.

"Well, that stinks," Jack commiserated. "Maybe it's a sign."

Helen gave him a quelling look.

"Too soon to joke about it?"

"This isn't a joke. This is a disaster."

"Inconvenient, sure, but not the end of the world."

"This is your friend's wedding, too," she said. "Have some sympathy for him and the stress this will cause if you can't at least summon the decency to feel sorry for Jenna."

"It's not like they don't know anyone who cooks. We've already done a funeral. I think we can handle a wedding."

Helen's eyes grew bright and she threw her arms around him. "You're right. We *can* cater the wedding. I might even have time to make a cake."

"They already have a cake on order."

"But if the baker were to bail on them, I *could*."

"Let's start with the main meal and let somebody else pipe the frosting."

She grinned and dashed off to the kitchen, oblivious to the fact that Jack was heading for his third shower of the day.

A cold one this time.

~ * ~

Jenna and Mike were beyond grateful for the offer of help for their caterer woes and pleased with Helen's suggestion of going with simple, comfort foods served buffet-style. Helen spent the next couple of hours running menu options and technical details by them and then scribbled notes and grocery lists until well past midnight.

By the time she made it back to their room, Jack was fast asleep.

She crawled under the covers.

158

"Hey," he murmured, rolling toward her.

"Hey. Sorry to wake you."

"You didn't."

She could've sworn she'd heard him lightly snoring when she first came in, but no matter.

"Thanks," he said.

She lay on her back, staring in the dark toward the ceiling. Delicious warmth called to her from his side of the bed. "For what?"

"You know." His voice was low and groggy, and she leaned toward him to hear better.

At least that's what she told herself.

"It makes me happy to make other people happy," she said. "You only get married once."

"Hopefully," he said.

She slanted a look at him even though it was too dark to see.

"That might be the most romantic sentiment I've ever heard you speak," she said.

She could hear his smile. Don't ask her how. He shifted, the bed sinking her toward him a little more. "No one gets married hoping for it not to work," he said. He sounded more awake now given the complete sentences.

She didn't want to keep him up, but curiosity and hope got the better of her. "Does this mean you'll give Mike your blessing?"

"I'm helping, aren't I? If memory serves, there's an Elks Club or a Masonic Hall or something down the road from Jenna's parents' house. If we can get permission to use their kitchen, it'd make life easier. I'll make a few calls in the morning."

"That's a really good idea."

"I know."

She chuckled and reached out to give him a playful smack for being cheeky.

He wasn't wearing a shirt.

Her fingers lingered, absorbing the warmth of his skin. She became aware of her breath. Of his. The bed slowly shifted as Jack moved, giving her all the time in the world to move to the cold side of the bed.

Instead, she instinctively turned and lifted to meet Jack's kiss.

Soft. If she didn't know he was there, she might have mistaken the first grazing brush of his lips across hers for a breeze through the window. *Again.* This time she took in the warmth and pressure before they lifted. The heat of his body soaked through her T-shirt, and she stopped pretending this wasn't real, stopped pretending she didn't want it to happen, and let her fingers slide into his silky hair so he wouldn't lift away this time.

He smiled against her mouth just as slowly as he'd kissed, and she couldn't resist the urge to smile back. One of them made a soft *mmm* noise. She wasn't sure who. It didn't matter.

"I thought you were nearly asleep," she said between kisses.

"I was thinking about you."

His palm cupped her cheek as he pressed another lazy kiss to her lips.

Have mercy.

A slow-burning heat began to coil deep inside her, and she didn't have the energy or will to tamp it out.

He pressed another kiss to her lips, his tongue teasing them, asking her to open for him. "I'll stop if you want me to," he murmured.

Well, sure, stopping would be the *prudent* thing to do. The thing they'd agreed to do.

She should definitely not slide her bare leg up between his knees, fitting her body to his, if she wanted to cool things down. And she most certainly shouldn't open her mouth and touch her tongue to his or arch her back in unspoken invitation if she wanted to keep things uncomplicated between them.

No. If she really wanted him to stop, she wouldn't let his words die out, unanswered, except for the occasional moan as they deepened the contact.

His palm, splayed, slid down her side to her hip before pulling her toward him.

The slow-burn of before ignited in a flash, and Helen pressed her hips to his in a movement as old as time.

He murmured something that sounded like a cross between a curse and an exclamation, and it made her smile in satisfaction against his mouth. She moved her hips again, with more purpose. More pressure.

He let out a low, hungry groan.

"Helen?" said a third voice in the dark.

Helen froze, her panties in a literal twist, one of Jack's palms splayed across her ass cheek. "Yes?" she whispered, hoping she hadn't heard a voice.

"You awake?"

Jack stilled. "That's not you talking, is it?" he whispered against her earlobe.

160

The door creaked open to allow a sliver of distant light shine onto the bedroom carpet. "I had an idea to contact the community center down the road from my parents. To use their kitchen. Should I do that?"

Helen breathed out to steady her voice. "Can this wait until the morning?"

"I was going to email now, just to get a head start."

Jack's chest shook under her palm. "Yeah. Go ahead. Great idea."

"Okay. I will. And, Helen?"

Jack's whole body vibrated with suppressed laughter.

"Yes?"

"Thank you. I really appreciate your help."

"No worries. Y'all sleep well."

"I will."

The door clicked shut. Jack snorted.

"Remind me again why I'm helping my ex get married?" he asked.

"Because it's the right thing to do."

His tongue touched his lips. She was surprised at what she could see now in the light from the moon shining through the window now that her eyes had adjusted. "Not to sound like a bad porn flick, but where were we?"

Where. Indeed.

"Getting ahead of ourselves," she said. "I mean. I'm not prepared. You're not prepared. It's not like we can go door to door here and beg for a condom."

"Just say the word."

She laughed and pushed him to his back. He landed with an *oof.*

"Stop. You steal my better sense right outta my head."

"You're welcome."

Lordy, the man was impossible. Impossibly challenging. Impossibly sexy. She stared into the dark and pondered how she ended up all hot and bothered and lying next to a man she barely knew. It was every which way wrong.

"Don't take this the wrong way," she said. "But you're the last man I should be doing this with."

He stayed silent.

"I mean, you're tempting as hot buttered cornbread on a cold morning, but I start filming in a couple weeks. I can't be gallivanting around like I don't have a care in the world."

"You know your southern comes out when you're tired?"

"Stop changing the subject. I'm serious. I can't just be a number in your body count."

"I'm not asking you to be. I thought this was mutual."

She sighed. "I have responsibilities."

"And I don't?" She felt him shift away to a sitting position.

"You know what I mean."

"Maybe you should spell it out."

"I didn't go on the show on a lark. I have a business to grow. Employees that depend on me. You have… yourself. Heck, you didn't even want to take on the responsibility of a dog."

"Who bought that mutt food and supplies and saved it from being killed?"

"That's not the point. The point is you don't want any of that, and I respect that. I do. But that's not my life right now. I can't forget that."

"It doesn't make me a bad person to set limits."

"No, it doesn't. But it does make you lonely."

"I work in a literal pub. We serve hundreds of meals a week. I'm not lonely."

"Right," she said, even though that only proved her point. Hundreds of meals, but did he sit down with those folks? Eat *with* them? Share their triumphs and sorrows? Share his?

"Tell me something," she said. "If I weren't with you on this trip, would you be here right now? On this retreat?"

He didn't answer.

"I thought so."

She blew out a quiet breath as she thought about the days that led to this moment: her sitting in the dark in a bed in the Pennsylvania countryside with this man. "I like you, Jack," she whispered. "I know you have a good heart. But if we're going to be intimate, I don't want it to come from a place of loneliness. Yours or mine. I want it to come from a place of hope."

She waited, her breath held in her lungs, for him to speak, for him to tell her he wanted to get in his car with her and keep driving and having adventures, because she made him feel alive and giddy and lucky like he didn't know what would come next but was excited to find out. With her.

The bed moved as he shifted down under the covers again. "It's late," he said. "We should get to sleep."

Which wasn't the answer she hoped for at all.

CHAPTER 14

The next morning, they gathered in the covered entry after breakfast. All signs of the rain of the past week had given way to bright spring leaves, dappled sunshine, and balmy temps.

Helen inhaled the cool air and glanced over at Jack. He leaned against the porch column a few feet away, hands deep in his cargo shorts pockets. Well, at least they'd have a place to stash things.

Cassie stood out front with the energy of an Activities Director at summer camp. "Now that we're all here, let's get this started." She pulled bright pink paper off a clipboard and handed one folded sheet to each couple.

"Today's activity is a romantic scavenger hunt. Now, no peeking yet, let me tell you the game first."

"We are so winning this one," Lori said.

Connor patted her back. "Easy, honey. It's just for fun. There aren't prizes."

"Actually, there are prizes," Cassie announced. "I've got a bottle of champagne for whichever couple comes in first." Lori moaned. "As well as chocolates and other goodies.

"Ground rules are simple," she said. "No interfering with other couples. Anyone caught tampering with game play will be immediately disqualified. Whichever couple completes the challenge first, wins.

"Any last questions? Oh, stay on the grounds. There's pretty obvious fencing around the property, so you can't get lost. Now, go!"

Everyone unfolded their paper. Helen glanced over Jack's forearm.

Collect the following items:
- *Something from nature that represents you as a couple. Explain.*
- *A pair of underwear.*
- *Something that can hold liquid. (A tsp. or more.)*

- *Water from a mountain stream.*
- *A smooth pebble. Name it.*
- *Retrieve one of the balloons hidden somewhere on the property. Tie it to your partner's left arm.*
- *Memorize this list. Exchange your list for one of the tools on the porch. Choose wisely.*
- *Be the first couple to complete the tasks and return to the porch to win. Good luck!*

Jack handed her the paper. "There's a stream down the hill over there. A pebble can be found anywhere."

"We should figure out how to carry water and get that last."

"You think?"

She ignored his bad mood as Lori and Connor snatched up the single water bottle from the 'tools' pile and dashed off down the drive. Jenna and Mike grabbed a small coil of twine.

"Quick," Jack said, "Give me the list."

"I'm still memorizing."

He waggled his fingers. "Hurry up or we'll be stuck with the—"

Ben and Jamie snatched the scissors and ran away laughing.

"Rubber band," he finished. "So helpful."

Helen held up a finger as she finished reading, committing the words to memory. "I think I've got it." She handed over the paper and picked up their 'tool.' She passed it to Jack.

"What good is this?"

"Just put it in your pocket," she said. "We can't head in the same direction as everyone else. They'll find the balloons first."

The started down the hill behind the house. Morning dew from the grass dampened Helen's pantlegs.

They stepped over a tumbled stone wall into the woods beyond where the grass of the field gave way to forest where walking was, if not easier, at least dryer.

Jack bent to sweep his hands down his legs.

"What are you doing?"

"Feeling paranoid, wishing I'd thought to spray my legs with insect repellent, and wondering what the hell I'm doing in life."

He only looked like he was half joking.

"I don't see any ticks," she said.

"They're tiny."

She bent and peered at his calves. She flicked at a spot with her fingernail. It was a freckle. "All clear," she announced.

He was frowning at her when she stood up again. "Let's get this over with. Hand over your underwear."

"I'm not giving you my underwear."

"Well you won't want mine after I've been hiking all over and sweating in it."

"You're not that hot."

"That's not what you said last night."

She pursed her lips. "I vote we table this discussion until later. What first?"

He glanced around and started walking.

"Do you know where you're going?"

"Does it matter? The balloons could be anywhere, we're likely to be last, and I can buy my own alcohol and snack food. I'm going for a hike, then heading back for a nap."

She pushed a branch aside to follow him and let her thoughts wander.

"I need to know,' she asked his back. "Was the sex in the snowstorm planned or unplanned?"

He didn't turn around. The muscles in his shoulder flexed as he lifted a branch to slide under. "What do you think?"

"I'm going to say unplanned." She ducked under the branch. "But sex requires certain parts to be exposed. I just can't quite figure out how you—"

"We managed."

"Well, it couldn't have been easy."

He paused and flashed a sly smile. "But worth it."

She swallowed over the lump of awareness that clogged her throat. "Why a snowstorm? I don't get it."

"Why not a snowstorm?"

"Didn't you have a bed?"

He stopped. "What's with the intense interest in my sex life?"

"I'm just curious."

"Okay. Fine. You want to know? She was wearing a long skirt. It was scratchy, but I didn't mind, because it was red plaid and, sue me, I think that's sexy. It wasn't snowing when we started out on our little walk, but then it started to squall. More of a short-lived thing, so I may have exaggerated the 'storm' part. It was a logging road near her apartment. She was on the pill and had a perfectly nice full-sized bed, but her roommates were home. I was twenty-five or six. I can't remember now, and she had blonde hair. I did get snow in places that prefer to be ice-free, but it was good, and it was hot, and it was spontaneous, and I don't regret a minute of it. Any other questions?" The tendons in his neck drew tight as he tilted his head, one eyebrow raised in challenge.

Her breath felt shallow in her lungs as she imagined having hot, spontaneous sex with young Jack against a tree.

She shook her head.

"Good."

"I was just curious," she murmured, "what kind of girl has sex against a tree."

He slanted her a look. "One who likes having sex."

"Right."

They walked a little further.

"Don't worry," he said. "You're clearly not that kind of woman."

"I like sex," she said.

"Sure. But in a bed. It's fine. Snowstorm tree sex isn't for everybody."

She'd never so desperately wanted snowstorm tree sex in her life.

"Why did you break up?" she asked.

He shrugged. "She moved. Not enough snow in Houston to make it work long distance."

He stopped to wiggle his foot. Kept walking.

"Was it a serious relationship?" she asked.

He stopped again, his shoulders heaving with a sigh. "Why?"

"I'm still trying to figure you out. You're a decent looking guy. Seemingly intelligent. Heck, you even know how to cook."

"Your point?"

"What's wrong with you?" He turned and stared at her. "I mean, why are you still single?"

"I might ask you the same thing. Sometimes life just works out that way. Why are you?"

The problem was, she wasn't. Not entirely. Not the way people thought of single. She'd felt the weight of expectation to settle down with the perfectly appropriate Travis since she'd been old enough to think he had cooties. Heck, after casually dating through college, she'd come home and let that same expectation pressure her into going into business with him.

Her dad had blessed the endeavor with a bakery.

In any other time or place it would have been a cow and a dozen chickens.

When they'd moved in together, she told herself it made sense to commute together—as if time efficiency and a low carbon footprint were valid reasons to progress a relationship.

166

"I was in a relationship," she hedged. "But it didn't work out."

She omitted the part about the casting director of *Happily Ever After* contacting her about appearing on the show and going home that very night to announce she needed some time to plan out her next steps.

Travis had begrudgingly agreed it would be good exposure for the business. She said she should move back in with her father. It wouldn't look good that she was living with someone before going on a show that purported to find a person's love match.

They hadn't spoken about the engagement ring he had hidden in his sock drawer.

"Whose fault?"

"What?" she asked.

"That things didn't work out?"

"It was no one's fault."

"It's always somebody's fault," he said.

"What about you and Jenna? It wasn't her fault or yours. It just wasn't right. She wasn't your person."

He was silent. She knew she was right.

"After Jenna, it took a while to do more than casual stuff."

She nodded.

"You know what I mean," he said.

She did.

"A few years later, I met a grad student, Leslie. We were together for nearly a year. She's in Antarctica now."

"That didn't end well."

He laughed. "Research."

"Where'd Gloria come in?" she said, mentioning the other name she'd heard during *The Dating Game* they'd played the day before.

"She was a couple years later. We met at the pub. One thing led to another. Then she finished grad school and took a job in Houston." He kicked a pinecone, and it skittered along the ground. "There were a couple others, but they were short-lived for one reason or another."

"And here you are."

"Here I am."

He looked thoughtful. She wondered what he was thinking.

"One day you're eighteen, stealing a car, running away to get married and conquer the world, and the next day you've passed thirty, still standing at the same grill you tried to leave at eighteen."

"You must have had things you wanted to do."

"If I'd gone to college, I would have been 'undeclared.' Jenna was right to dump me." He glanced over. "Never tell her I said that."

She mimed zipping her lips.

"What about now? You seem to have settled into things at the pub. You make a mean beef barley soup."

"Settled is a good word. I've thought once or twice about running a place of my own, but I'd need start-up capital, and a place the size of Sugar Falls can only support so many restaurants." He shrugged, a surprisingly vulnerable gesture. "I had hoped this week would be time for me to figure that out."

"And?"

"Haven't had a lot of mental space."

"Sorry about that."

"It's all right."

But she knew it wasn't.

The air felt cool on her cheeks. It was nice to talk. She didn't feel quite so lost and alone knowing she wasn't the only one trying to figure out her next step.

She paused. "I wish I knew where we were headed."

He sighed. "I don't know, but if it's all the same to you, I'm done talking about it. I just what to get through the next few days without having to analyze everything to death."

"No. I meant, where are we?"

He glanced behind her, turned slightly. "The house is... that way." He pointed to her right.

"I'm pretty sure it's that way," she pointed the opposite direction.

"No... Wait a minute." He took a few steps in the direction he'd pointed, stopped. "There. There's the rock wall."

"That's a different one. The first one was by the fields. We left it ages ago. This is in the middle of the woods."

He swore.

"We're lost, aren't we?" she said.

"We'll just follow the wall until it connects with something familiar, so we don't keep going in circles."

She plucked something off the ground and held it up. "It's an acorn."

Jack stared at her.

"A *giant* acorn. I bet it could hold water, don't you?"

Jack silently stuffed the acorn into one of his many pockets and kept walking.

"You could use the GPS on your phone," Helen said.

"That's not exactly sporting of you." He looked back. "Also, it's plugged into the charger back at the house."

"Oh."

They hiked in silence for a while.

Helen pointed through the trees. "Look. Our field."

Jack frowned. "That's not our field."

"Of course, it's our field. What field would it be?"

She pushed through the underbrush and stopped short.

Jack came to stop beside her. "A different field with a fence."

Helen pointed beyond a copse of trees and another pasture to a roof in the distance. "Is that the house? Have we really gone this far?"

He sighed. "Looks like it."

She reached forward to part the fence and crawl through, but Jack stopped her. "Wouldn't it be easier to use the gate?"

A dozen yards down the fence line he unlocked the gate and ushered her ahead of him.

"This is how folks back home get shot," she said. "Wandering around private property without permission."

"Don't worry, they'll shoot you here, too."

She stopped and glanced behind her. "Is that a real danger?" she asked.

"Only if you get caught. Come on. I'm tired of wandering aimlessly. Lori and Connor have probably already popped their champagne."

They set out toward the house again. The field dipping and rolling, an occasional boulder popping up from the grass for variety.

"You suppose they have horses?"

Jack shrugged. "Maybe."

"I used to ride," she said.

"Not anymore, I take it."

"Gave it up when my mom got sick. It worried her."

"We didn't have enough money for it to be an issue."

Helen glanced at Jack's profile. His thick hair flopped across his forehead, a few wisps dark with sweat.

She turned her attention back to the fence ahead. She should focus on getting through the day. By tomorrow, they'd be back in Cutler and diving into food prep for the wedding. There was literally no time for detours—mental or otherwise.

"I hope there's a gate soon," she said. "I'd rather not have to walk back where we came from."

"As if that's even an option."

They were nearly at the fence now, walking diagonally uphill toward the house in the far, far distance.

A warm hand grasped hers. "Watch your step," Jack said, tugging her toward him so she'd avoid a gopher hole she hadn't noticed.

He dropped her hand. Pity that.

"Hold on. I've got something in my shoe." Jack sat on the ground then bounced to his feet again. "This grass is soaking my ass. Hang on." He balanced himself with one hand on her shoulder, pulled off his shoe and sock, then turned the sock inside out to remove a clump of fuzz.

"Are you almost done?" she asked.

"Don't move."

Jack's voice sounded strange. She scowled. "Now wha—?" But he clamped a hand over her mouth to stifle the last bit of sound. She yanked at his palm. "Your hand smells like feet."

Jack ignored her and pointed. "Bull. Behind you."

"Ha. Ha," she said.

"I'm not joking," he whispered.

Helen turned. About fifty yards away, his coat a burnished, ruddy brown against the green spring grass, grazed a very, very large bull. She knew this because it had horns.

Jack bent to grab his shoe and sock. "I don't think he's seen us, but I vote for getting the hell out of here."

"He's between us and the gate."

"Screw the gate. I'm taking the nearest exit."

A moment later Jack's body jerked and slammed face-first onto the ground beside her. He cursed, groaned, then cursed again, the words muffled by the grass under his face.

"Stop swearing. What's wrong with you? Now he's looking at us, and he does not look happy." Helen sank to her knees beside him. Really. This was *not* a time to be joking around.

"The fence..." he said. "Electric." He slid his face sideways and rested his cheek on the ground. "Who electrifies their fences?"

"Everyone?"

"Jesus. My ass is burning."

She glanced down at the ass in question. She could concur it looked hot despite the cargo shorts. "Electric fences don't flatten people. Get up."

"I need a minute," he said. "My left leg is going numb. Wait. That's my right leg. Jesus, I don't know my left from my right."

She stood up, shading her eyes from the sun, and scanned the fence line for a gate. "Stop being such a baby and for heaven's sake, be quiet." She grasped his arm. "Shock or no shock, we have to get out of here."

He cursed in reply but stumbled to his feet.

"Ever play limbo?" she asked.

His palm rubbed his butt in response.

"We're going to go under the fence."

"You're insane," he said.

"Just lie on the ground and shimmy under. There's a spot right over there with a space wide enough."

He followed the direction of her gaze. "We'll never make it."

"He's moving closer," she said, tugging him over to the fence. "Just lie on your back and make like a snake. And don't kick up with your knees."

"Considering I can barely feel my legs, piece of cake."

The grass dampened her shirt as she lay on her back and began to vibrate herself toward the other side. Small stones reminded her it had been years since she'd done this particular maneuver... before she'd developed into a C-cup. She narrated to calm her nerves, because being electrocuted under a fence in the middle of Nowhere, Pennsylvania, was not how she wanted to meet her maker. "Don't lift your head whatever you do. Tommy Hanson did that once and he's never been the same."

Jack cursed again.

"That was a joke," she said wriggling her way sideways. "Although, he did knock himself out for a second or two. How much further do I have to go?"

Jack swung his head from her toward the direction of the bull and back again. "You're half-way there."

She sucked in her breath, willing her body sideways, wincing as her shoulder tensed and released. When Jack declared her past the wire, she rolled away, sucking in a breath of relief. "There. Easy. Now you do it." She stood to check on what the bull was doing. He lifted his head and sniffed the air. She dropped to her knees. "But *hurry*. He's snorting. I'm pretty sure that's bad."

"Ya think?" Jack sank from his knees to the ground and stretched himself out. The man would be toast if he didn't pick up the pace.

She stood to see over the rise. The bull stared back at her. She slowly sank down out of his sightline. "Okay. You're good. Unless he charges, you have plenty of time. Now move sideways toward me."

"Does he look like he's going to charge?"

"Do you want me to keep jumping into view to figure that out?"

"No." Jack lay his head back on the ground and shifted his shoulder exactly one millimeter closer to her. "If I die, give my car to my sister. She's always wanted it anyway."

"You're not going to die. *Come on.*"

His body lurched alarmingly.

"Move more gently, but quickly, and be *quiet*."

He grunted and his body jiggled a dozen times. He gained an inch.

"That's it. Keep that up. You're doing great," she whispered, making a mental note about the car. "Flatten your feet sideways. How big of a shoe do you wear anyway?"

He glared and tilted his feet to the side. He shimmied some more, this time more effectively.

"You're half-way there. Just don't rush it," she said.

"Hurry up. Don't rush. Make up your mind, woman."

He jiggled and shimmied and cursed and grunted. She heard hoofbeats. Adrenaline flooded her body as she grabbed Jack's free arm and hauled on it will all her strength. Her shoulder screamed, her feet slipped on the damp grass, and she fell to her butt as Jack, finally free, rolled toward her, his face planted against the side of her right boob.

Her lungs sucked in hard breaths as her heart slammed in her chest. She shoved at his shoulders. "Get up," she urged.

"Relax. We're on the other side."

"I don't care. When there's an angry bull looking my way, I get the hell out of Dodge."

He grunted in agreement, Helen supported his elbow, and they hurried to a copse of trees further up the rise.

~ * ~

They made it about a hundred yards before Jack tripped, cursed, and laughed all at the same time. "Save yourself," he said. "I'm stopping here."

Helen looked down the hill at the field. The bull had wandered off in the opposite direction, indifferent to two foolish humans.

Jack crawled the two feet to a large oak tree and sat with his back against it.

"Does it still hurt?"

His blue eyes sliced to hers in answer.

"I'll take that as a 'yes.'" She sank down to sit beside him. Sunshine filtered down through the canopy above dancing light on the forest floor. "That wasn't so bad," she said.

He wet his lips with his tongue. "Speak for yourself."

"Electric fences aren't that strong. Birds sit on them. You'll be fine."

"Birds don't complete the circuit. I did."

She glanced down at his unshod foot. "Do you think it had something to do with your bare foot and the wet grass?"

He gave her a long, hooded look. "I'm going to go with 'yes' on that one."

He leaned forward to pull on his shoe.

"Where's your sock?"

"A necessary casualty," he said. "I don't know. I dropped it somewhere between the bull and here. I'm good."

"Can I get you anything?"

He blinked at her.

"Right. We're kind of limited on supplies."

"Just some quiet would be nice."

"Sure."

She leaned back against the tree next to him and waited for her heartrate to slow to normal again.

"I'm gonna be honest," he said after a while, "I'm a little afraid of what's gonna happen next."

"This isn't my fault," she said. "You're the one that took off your shoe."

"I'm not the one that started talking about snowstorm sex."

"I hardly see how that contributed to your being sockless and chased by a bull."

"It got us lost."

"How?"

His eyebrow did that thing again as he looked at her mouth. "Because I had to concentrate not to think about it being you."

Oh.

"It would've been helpful," he said, "if you'd at least been paying attention."

"That would assume I wasn't imaging tree sex with you," she admitted, the heat of a blush warming her cheeks.

"Tell me why we haven't jumped each other yet?"

"We're trying to remain friends. It's less messy."

"Being your friend has left me sockless in a forest recovering from near electrocution and narrowly avoiding being gored by a bull. If we weren't friends, we'd be sated and happy against a tree somewhere in sight of the house."

"You make a good point."

"Being friends has left us frustrated and cranky. I'm convinced we'd be less grumpy if we spent a little time making each another happy."

"But this can't last. Soon we'll be going our separate ways. Better to think well of each other."

"Better to be happy until then, I say."

His lips curved and the hair fell over his eyes a little, and she'd never felt less concerned about the future than this moment.

He mumbled a curse.

"What now?" she asked.

"I see a balloon," he said. "And what appears to be a search party."

CHAPTER 15

When they finally returned to the house, Helen and Jack showered, then ate a late lunch. Sam suggested everyone might enjoy free time after the morning's adventures.

Helen was grateful for the chance to plan logistics and food for the wedding with suggestions from Jack. That is, until his latest idea.

"I'm not serving chicken nuggets at a wedding," she said. "I have an excellent buttermilk batter recipe."

"It's the same thing," Jack said. "And you can buy it bulk, frozen at the warehouse store. It's worth the hour's drive. You're slathering it with gravy anyway."

"The gravy is being served *on the side.*"

"It's still boneless, breaded chicken breasts. Sounds like chicken fingers to me. I'm not talking dinosaur nuggets."

"It's not my decision," she'd hedged, knowing Jenna would hate the idea.

"I love it," Jenna declared a few minutes later when they presented her with the idea. "If there's enough food for everyone, and it tastes good, they won't care if it's fancy."

"Can I still serve garlic mashed new potatoes and gravy? And a fresh vegetable medley"

"Have at it."

Helen walked past Jack, her notepad in hand. "Not a word," she muttered.

He laughed.

She found she didn't mind.

They ate frozen lasagna for dinner, tossed salad, and toasted slices of buttered baguette, the boxed wine and laughter flowing freely.

Helen held it all tight, the serendipity of this moment of finding friends and Jack and a space to breathe and not having to think about what came next.

Jenna grinned, "I can't believe by Monday I'll be a married woman."

"This time next year, this little one will be here," Lori said, pointing to her belly.

And just like that, thoughts of Duke and home and the grueling commitments of a reality TV show came crashing back, because moments like this were fleeting. None of them would be in the same place next year. Next week. Especially Helen.

"Group photo!" Cassie announced, raising her phone and snapping a selfie.

She jumped from her seat and scurried around the table, sloshing her wineglass on the table next to Helen before leaning down to whisper loudly in her ear. "I've been meaning to ask. Can I enter twice?"

Helen glanced around for guidance. "Enter?"

"The contest," Cassie said, as if that made it clearer. "For tickets to the finale? Can I post a selfie with you or can I just nominate a bachelor for the show or do both?"

Go home, Cassie, you're drunk. That's what Helen wanted to say, instead she said, "I am not following you."

Cassie punched some buttons on her phone. Helen struggled to focus on the words in front of her and then felt the blood rush from her face.

"Tag the show with a picture of Helen W. or nominate an eligible bachelor over eighteen to be on the show with the hashtag 'runawaycupcakequeen' to be entered to win tickets for two to the HEA finale?" She spoke the words with increasing alarm. "Is this for real?"

"You were trending for a little while a few days back, but that's when you were dressed as a homeless person waving a dead animal. It was hysterical!"

Helen set her glass down, half-finished. "I should start clearing," she said, picking up her plate and Connor's next to her. She stacked them, looked around a bit, and turned toward the kitchen.

"Wait. You didn't answer me. Can I enter twice?"

Helen stared at Cassie. "Sure."

Jack followed Helen into the kitchen and set a stack of plates in the sink for rinsing. "You okay?" he asked.

"The Runaway Cupcake Queen? Now Marcia's got everyone everywhere trying to take my picture? It wasn't bad enough it was the paparazzi that started this whole fiasco to begin with?"

"Can you blame her? It's pretty brilliant, if you ask me."

"So now you're on her side? Thanks."

"It's this or a giant gold bus." He lifted his hands like a balancing scale. "Your choice."

"The bus was a horrible idea."

"Right? So, have fun with it. At least you've been warned this time. We can make you a paper crown."

"You're right. I'm just stressed thinking about tomorrow. Logistics. It's a lot to prep in one day without facilities or suppliers, and now I have to dodge random people wanting to take selfies?"

"We'll be fine. Cutler is basically the middle of nowhere. I'll be nearby, and—"

"I know. I know. I'm not that famous."

"I was going to say, you'll handle it like a pro, but okay."

Ben and Jamie carried in more dishes. "Are we talking wedding prep again?" Jamie asked. "Because I worked at Dairy Queen in high school. I'm not just a pretty face."

"Thanks," Helen laughed. "I'm sure we'll need extra hands one way or another."

"Just say the word."

Ben's cellphone rang. He glanced up apologetically. "I should get this."

Helen turned to Jamie. "Is everything all right? You two have been quiet tonight."

Jamie waved away her concern. "We're just waiting on some news."

Lori and Connor hurried through the door. "Strawberries. Are there strawberries in here?" Lori swung the fridge door wide. "Or kiwi. I could go either way."

Cassie, Sam, Mike and Jenna arrived in a burst of laughter. "Board games in ten minutes," Cassie announced. "If you're late, it's going to be *Naked Pictionary!*"

Sam tugged the wine bottle out of Cassie's grip and set it on the counter. "Nobody wants *Naked Pictionary*," he said. "That's drunk Cassie talking."

Cassie laughed and looped her arms around Sam's neck. "Drunk Cassie has the best ideas. Didn't you say so earlier?"

"That's between me and drunk Cassie," Sam murmured, his face flushing red. "And now everyone is staring at me, so we're both switching to lemonade."

"I'm up for some games," Jenna said. "Jamie?"

Ben pushed open the door again and crossed the room to take Jamie's hand. He squeezed.

Jamie closed his eyes a moment and then smiled brightly. "Ben and I are going to have alone time. Raincheck on the games."

Jenna pouted. "It'll be fun."

"Thanks, anyway," Ben said.

"Come on," Cassie said. "Or, *Naked Pictionary...*"

"Score! Kiwi!" Lori called from the bowels of the fridge.

Helen set down the dishtowel she'd been holding. "We'll all go. It'll be fun."

Ben kept shaking his head repeatedly, tiny short movements. Jamie gave Ben a kiss on the forehead and squeezed his wrist.

Helen grimaced. Couldn't they have couple time later? It was his own brother's bachelor couples retreat. This was a time for family to celebrate together.

"Stop it." The words burst out of Jamie's lips.

Helen looked around. "Who?"

"*You.* You're making your awkward face again."

"I'm not making an awkward face."

"Just now you did. When I kissed Ben."

"I swear I didn't make a face. I have no problem with your lifestyle."

Ben shook his head. "Jamie," he warned. "This isn't about her."

"Lifestyle?" Jamie made a frustrated sound. "Being vegan is a lifestyle. Off-the-grid living is a lifestyle. But when will you people understand being gay isn't a *choice?*"

"Don't throw vegans under the bus. It's a perfectly healthy way to eat." Lori glanced around, a spoon stuck in a half of a kiwi. "It is."

Connor elbowed his wife.

Jamie rolled his eyes. "You were eating cheese an hour ago."

"Well, I'm not strictly vegan during the pregnancy. My doctor said—"

Jamie threw his hands up. "Who cares what your doctor said? I'm surprised you're even asking him. It's not like you planned to get pregnant."

"No, but we're still happ—"

"This isn't about you, Karen!"

"Excuse me?"

Ben laid a hand on Jamie's rigid shoulder only to have it shrugged off. He watched his husband storm out. The front door slammed. Ben swiped his palm over his face.

"I am so sorry," Helen said. "I didn't mean…"

Ben let the air out of his lungs like an invisible weight had descended, crushing him. "We shouldn't have come," he said.

"Of course, you should've," Jenna said. "You're Mike's only brother. You belong here and at our wedding as much as anyone. Your father will just have to deal with that."

"I know I belong," Ben said, eyes flashing. "Would everyone stop assuming everything in our lives revolves around being gay? Jamie's angry and disappointed and frustrated, and so am I, because we thought we'd found a surrogate, but... she told us this afternoon she was having second thoughts. And she just called to confirm she's made her decision."

Ice cubes tumbled loudly into the bin in the fridge as everyone waited for someone to break the silence.

Mike spoke. "I'm sorry."

Jenna reached out and let her hand fall. "Me, too. I had no idea you were hoping to get pregnant."

"That's the thing, isn't it?" Ben said, his voice raw. "For us, it doesn't happen by accident. We've got to jump through all the hoops and do all the legwork and interviews and pray we're found worthy." His face contorted as he fought to keep his emotions in check. "But we are worthy.

"We've been together longer than any of you. We have a six-figure income and a baby-proofed home... and a *yard*. we're good people... but it's not enough. It's *never enough*. We're always, no matter how hard we try, not enough."

"Don't say that," Jenna said. "You know you are."

He held a palm toward her. His hand shook. "*Don't*. Don't tell me I can't feel what I'm feeling. Don't tell me I can't even have *that*."

"I didn't mean--"

"I want a family," he said, his voice barely audible. "A family of my own. A family where we can just be us without all the expectations and pressures and prejudices. I just want to be a dad who pours cereal and worries about retirement and teaches his kid how to change a tire. I want to be the dad I deserved."

"We had the same dad," Mike said.

Ben shook his head, a bone-deep weariness overcoming his features. "No. We didn't." Then he turned on his heel and strode out.

Jenna stepped forward as if to follow him, but Mike stopped her. "Let him go," he said.

Her eyes pooled with tears as she swung to face her husband. "He's right," she said. "He shouldn't have come."

"Don't say that."

"Knowing how your dad feels about Ben and Jamie, Mike... you have to choose. They can't both be there. It's not fair to Ben to subject him to more rejection. Either tell your father he can't come or let Ben bow out."

Mike opened the fridge and retrieved a beer. The sound of the front door slamming echoed down the hallway.

Sam, Cassie, Lori and Connor mumbled excuses and quickly exited. Jack raised his eyebrows at Helen.

"I am so, so sorry," she breathed. "If I'd known..."

Mike pried the lid off his beer and tossed the opener on the counter with a clatter. "How could you? Hell, I didn't know, and I'm his brother."

"I wish he would have said something earlier," Jenna said. "And here we've been going on and on about Lori's pregnancy this whole time."

Jack picked up the opener and slid it back in the drawer. "They were probably hoping for better news."

"First the caterer and now this. It all well and truly sucks," Jenna said.

No one could argue that.

"We can still elope," Mike said.

Jenna shook her head. "Running away won't solve this. It was going to be hard enough before. How are they going to face coming to the wedding now?"

"By living our best life. Like we always do." All eyes turned toward Ben. He and Jamie stood in the doorway, side by side. "Don't worry. We're adults. We won't let this ruin your day. I've avoided Dad since I came out. I can do it another couple of days."

"We'd understand, though, if you chose not to," Mike said.

Ben shook his head. "You didn't miss my wedding. I'll be damned if I'll miss yours."

"I can ask him not to come," Mike said.

"I won't ask you to do that."

"I know, but it's my wedding, and you're my brother. It shouldn't be this complicated."

Jenna stepped forward to grip Ben's arms. "It isn't. You're coming. It's my wedding, too. Now, give me a hug, and let's get some sleep. Tomorrow is a busy day for all of us."

Helen stood to the side, wishing she'd had the good sense to make excuses like everyone else. Instead, she was stuck behind the island waiting for a natural break in the conversation in order not to interrupt.

They said their goodnights, leaving Jack and Helen alone. Jack opened the fridge and held up a bottle of lemonade. Helen nodded.

He filled two glasses and handed her one. She took a long gulp, all her classes in etiquette be damned. She wished it were whiskey.

"I'm heading to bed," Jack said. "You coming?"

Helen hesitated. "You go ahead. I think I'll watch some TV or something."

"You didn't cause this," he said.

"I didn't help it, either."

She watched him leave and glanced around the kitchen that up until ten minutes earlier had felt full of fellowship and fun. It just showed how you never knew the pain others kept hidden. Or how well they were dealing with it.

She turned off the light.

She made her way to the empty game room. Her gut clenched as she passed the pool table where they'd all laughed about Connor's lack of skills in getting a ball in a pocket and all the double entendres that had generated; the moment during romantic movie charades that Jack had winked at her which, no doubt, meant nothing, but caught her off guard and yearning for something she couldn't define.

She found a spot on the sofa and tucked the throw laying on the arm around her. A flick of the remote, and the gas fire sprang to life.

She sat, swirling her lemonade in its tumbler until it grew warm.

She wondered what would happen to Jack after she was gone. She wondered whether in ten years he'd still be in Sugar Falls, enjoying the occasional fling, but never taking a chance on adventure or love. She wondered if her life would be just as quiet back in Heaven. Just warmer. She wondered if, when she had children, she'd take them to work with her, or would she stay home, disappearing behind the front door only to come out styled and fragrant for church and special occasions.

"I didn't think anyone was still up." *Jamie.*

Helen swung her feet to the floor. "Just thinking," she said. "But I don't have to do that here."

He shook his head and headed to the bar area. The dark wood and brass made her think of cryptic barkeeps with sage but brutal advice. She could probably use a little of both right now.

"Don't leave on my account." He selected a bottle from a high shelf and poured into a glass. He took a sip and faced her.

She stood. "I should get to bed."

"Sit," he commanded. "Keeps me from drinking alone."

She perched on the edge of the sofa. "I'm sorry for earlier. Truly."

He shrugged and finally met her gaze. "I usually do a better job of ignoring the irritating things straight people say."

She nodded, knowing she deserved the jab, and sipped her lemonade. "How's Ben?"

"Angry. Hurt. He's drafting an email to the surrogate."

181

"Do you think she'll change her mind?"

"Doubtful. But I'm the cynical one." He glanced over. "And usually much less confrontational." He raised his glass. "Hence the alcohol. We Irish tend to drown our troubles."

"We Southerners tend to eat ours."

He made a sound that might have been laughter if it hadn't carried the sharp, ragged edges of weariness. "You don't appear to have suffered all that much."

"Eating one's feelings isn't particularly ladylike. Or so I've been told."

"A rather odd sentiment coming from a baker."

"I'm nothing if not thoroughly conflicted."

His laugh was genuine this time. He slid back to rest against the cushions. "Aren't we all." His gaze met hers and held.

"I'm *so* sorry about earlier." She wouldn't defend herself or tell him that that's just how folks back home talked about being gay, that she didn't have the language to get it right. She knew better.

"Normally I would've let it slide. Not every battle is worth fighting."

"Still, I never meant to upset you."

"I'm not upset. Just exhausted. Okay, yes. I'm upset, too." He took another long sip. "It's been a helluva day. And we still have the wedding to look forward to. Fun times."

"I'm sorry."

"You apologize a lot."

"There's a lot to be sorry for." He raised one quizzical eyebrow. "Aside from putting my foot in my mouth, I've disappointed—or will soon disappoint—a lot of people in the coming days. I'm just getting my practice in."

He smiled darkly. "I'm in the mood to celebrate someone else's misery. Feel free to elaborate."

She looked into her drink. "You know the show, *Happily Ever After?* This," she waved her glass in a circle, "wasn't planned. I don't think they even know where I am right now."

His eyebrows disappeared into his hairline. "You've run away for real," he said. "That's a plot twist. And?"

"And," she dragged it out, because she hadn't even fully committed to it in her own mind, "I intend to break things off for good with my partner when I get home again. Go our separate ways."

"Because of Jack," he said. "Because you two are a thing."

"Jack and I aren't a thing," she denied, even though it felt like a betrayal to do so.

His eyebrows hit his hairline again. "Please. I thought we were in true confessions territory. I might as well be drinking on my own. You and Jack are *definitely* a thing. Everyone can see it. My dog could see it and she's half-blind."

"Everyone?"

"That first night, Ben said, 'Those are friends with a hell of a benefits package.'"

"He did not."

"I swear, he did."

"We've never had sex!"

"Not for a lack of wanting. I saw you in the *Orange/Sex Positions* game." He slanted her a look. "The way you play with your hair every time Jack comes in the room and those 'want to eat you up with a spoon' looks he gives you? Get a room."

"It's not that simple. Half the time I think he barely tolerates me."

"He's sexually frustrated. Trust me. It's the same look Ben gave me our entire freshman and sophomore years of college. All hunger and resentment seething with sexual tension." He chuckled and shrugged. "What can I say? I was a gay Catholic boy from Boston, and he hadn't even come out to himself much less his family. So. Many. hurdles."

"Mike mentioned you ran track."

Jamie grinned. "Yes. Yes, I did. Quite successfully."

She laughed and thought about how confusing and overwhelming love and attraction could be.

Did Jack really look at her like that? Did he think about her the way she, inevitably, seemed to find herself thinking about him? Did he wonder, too, if the stars aligned, and they both left their jobs and families and homes, and she didn't have the show… Oh, who was she kidding? There was no scenario that would make things work between them. There were, in Jamie's words, too many hurdles.

"Even if you're right, it doesn't matter. I have to go back eventually whether I want to or not. I'm under contract."

Jamie made a disparaging noise. "I'm sure they could find a way to break it if they weren't feeling it. Do they know you want out?"

"Considering I'm here and not picking up men in a golden tour bus? They have to know I have doubts."

"Doubts is looking over your shoulder while you do the thing anyway. You've gone and run for the hills. There's a big difference there."

"Why will no one believe it was an honest mistake? I was being chased then fell asleep," Jamie made a *mm-hmm* noise, "and by the time I realized it, we were across state lines." Yes, it sounded fishy even to her own ears.

"Why didn't they just send a car to get you?"

Helen sipped her drink. Her hand shook.

Jamie chuckled and sucked in an excited breath. *"They did."*

She wet her lips. "I told Jack they told me to find my own way home."

"And he bought that?"

"Briefly. He was sleep deprived, and I may have mentioned worrying about paparazzi. He was heading in the right direction at the right time. Things kind of escalated, and now we're here."

"You've suddenly become a whole lot more interesting."

"Thanks?"

"So, spill the tea. Why is Cinderella running away from all her Prince Charmings to hide out in a cabin in the woods?"

"Doing the show... it's intense. It's not at all what I expected. I'm used to being photographed, being on stage... I did pageants way back when. But the show? It exposes you in ways you don't expect."

"They took your makeup kit away."

"Now you're making fun of me."

"A little." He sipped his drink and leaned forward. "I'm still trying to get over how dozens of men and exotic locations is something a person would run away from."

"The challenges aren't a cake-walk. They expose your vulnerabilities and fears. They narrow down who's compatible and who's not. Sometimes the show helps you find the right person. In my case, it confirmed who wasn't."

"Are we talking about someone in particular?"

"Yeah. I just hope he can move on."

"Well, this is awkward, isn't it?" A third voice spoke from behind them.

Jack stood in the shadow beyond the light of the fire, but Helen could feel the tension radiating toward them.

Jamie stood. "I'm gonna head upstairs. You two," he gestured vaguely between them, "should talk."

~ * ~

Jack waited for Jamie to be out of earshot before continuing to the bar. He tilted the bottle Jamie had left there to read the label, hoping a random bottle of liquor would tell him where to start.

"You probably have questions," Helen murmured.

So. Many. Questions.

"I just had a very confusing conversation with my dad," he said, stuffing his hands into his pockets. "Should we start there?"

Her face went pale then flushed pink.

"About that…" She let her words trail off, as if the universe would conveniently fill in a logical explanation. It didn't.

"I honestly don't know whether to be mad you invaded my privacy and pretended to be me or grateful that when my own father thought I was capable of kidnapping a stranger you stood up for me."

"I did," she said. "Stand up for you."

He nodded and took a thoughtful step forward.

"I apologize for invading your privacy. That was wrong of me. I shouldn't have, obviously, but I panicked."

He blew out a long, steadying breath and rocked onto his heels. "So, who's the schmuck you're kicking to the curb?" His gut grew heavy as he waited for her to speak.

"Travis," she finally admitted.

"Your business partner?"

She nodded.

He wanted to be elated she wasn't talking about him, but then realized he was the side-guy. He was the distraction occupying her time until she figured out what came next in her life.

"Huh," he said. "So, you were dating your business partner—a classic move, by the way—and then decided things weren't awkward enough, so you decided to break up with him by going on a dating show? Why didn't you just send him a cold-hearted text out of the blue like a normal person? Props to you, though. This is next level harsh."

He wasn't proud of his biting, sarcastic tone, but he hadn't lied to her, either. He could feel superior about that.

"Travis knew I was having doubts."

"I would think going on a dating show would be a clue." Jack sank his fingers into his hair and clenched. It did nothing to help him understand the labyrinth of twisted rationalizations that brought this woman into his life. "Does the show know? That you've got a little side hustle going? A guy back home. Me. Just a whole string of us between Canada and the Gulf Coast to keep you company in case Marcia the Matchmaker strikes out?"

"That's not how things are, and you know it."

"I'm not sure I do. Were you at least straight with Ian, or did you pretend to be in love with him right up until he dumped you?"

"I didn't pretend anything with Ian."

He made a dismissive noise. "Right. Who cares if you find a husband if you can hit a million Instagram followers?"

"It wasn't love, but I did genuinely care for Ian. You get caught up in your feelings when you're away from home and your usual support system. It changes the way you look at someone. I thought I could love him, given time, but then it was clear we weren't a good fit."

"Ah. Another guy that doesn't fit your life. This seems to be a pattern. Did it ever occur to you that you're the common denominator in all this? That maybe it's not Travis's or Ian's or my fault you're not happy, but yours? Stop running away and blaming other people for the fact that you don't know what the hell you want."

Okay. Yes, he was lashing out, because it was becoming abundantly clear that he was no one special. He was just one in a long line of men who didn't 'fit.' Whatever the hell that meant.

She raised her chin, her dark eyes flashing. "You have no idea what I want."

"That makes two of us, then."

She jumped to her feet. "I don't owe you an explanation."

"You're right," he said, and she made to move past him, "But, you'll have to stop running eventually."

"I'm. Not. Running," she enunciated.

"Could have fooled me."

She cursed at him then, a long, colorful string of words that envisioned him flayed and flambéd for not leaving her in peace when she'd already had a rough night and a long day ahead and now had to worry about dodging amateur paparazzi hoping to score a seat at the finale. "What does it matter? In a few days, I'll be home, you'll be home. It'll all be over."

What if I don't want it to be?

He nearly said the words, nearly blurted them out like so much emotional vomit that would have, no doubt, had her recoiling and him wishing he could fade into the woodwork. But, she was right. In a few days, they'd be parting ways. Mike and Jenna would be married. Helen would go back to her life, and he'd be no closer to figuring out what the hell he wanted to do than he was before he met her.

Because, clearly, his murky future life didn't include her.

"Why," he finally managed to ask. "Why did you do it? Why did you have to involve me?"

Her head told him 'no' in short shaky movements. "I was overwhelmed, okay? I thought the show would be my way out. I thought

I'd get opportunities and see things, but... it's exhausting to be on TV 24/7. I haven't sworn in months. I haven't been without a full face of makeup. I'm afraid to drink coffee or eat beans or a thousand other things that might look bad on camera or reflect badly on my family." She paused for breath.

"You haven't answered my question."

"Once my season begins, I'll have eight weeks before I'm right back where I started. Right back in Heaven where everybody remembers me as that Walker girl who lost her mom and was always so pretty and should just settle down already, because what's she waiting for? Surely, she'll come to her senses and marry that Travis boy, because they always say it's the one just under your nose who's your true love. Bless them, won't they make beautiful babies?

"*Yes*, I'm running. I'm running toward something, someplace, *anywhere* that isn't where I've been, because I can't *breathe* there. I can't have my own thoughts. I'm not allowed my own dreams or my own mistakes." She threw her hand in the air. Her eyes grew bright with unshed tears, and her accent heavier. "I can't just up and decide I want to go to a concert and be a sixteen-year-old because my mother is sick and she could *die*, and how would I feel then?"

"You want to know why I fell asleep in your stupid car? Because I've been running ever since I was sixteen. I've been searching for something that isn't predetermined by my family or as meaningless as a cupcake. I'm been praying for a glimmer of hope that my life had something unexpected in store for me. Something exciting and daring that maybe I don't have answers for, but it was still okay. Because it's never been okay not to know what came next. No one ever let it be okay."

She paused for breath.

"Hey, it's all right," he soothed.

"No, it's not all right. It's not all right for you to pretend you have control over people like you're God or a senator or something. It's not all right for you to ask the hard questions but not be prepared to hear the truth. I don't have the answers. There. I said it. I may have issues. I may be confused and struggling not to hurt the people I love because I can't bring myself to be who they want me to be, but you... you're no better. I may be running, but at least I'm not treading water, lashing out at everyone who makes the mistake of getting too close, because I'm still angry about crap that happened fifteen years ago. Grow up. See a therapist."

"I'm not treading water."

She practically spit her reply. "Are you kidding? You're a line cook in a pub. You haven't had a lasting relationship since you were dumped for committing a felony in the name of love. You don't own a pet or a home, and you drive an incredibly impractical car. You are literally a seventeen-year-old trapped in a man's body, and if you can't explain why you can't move on, then why should I listen to anything you have to say?"

Numb.

No other word could describe the impact of her words. It was as if every cell in his body stopped moving, stopped dividing. Stopped. And the only thing left in his awareness was the heavy, hard thudding of his own heart as it began moving again as though it had been frozen and was only in this moment beginning to beat again.

She stared at him with a look of alarm.

She should be alarmed. She had no idea the overwhelming flood of emotion slamming into him like a sucker punch.

"I was at prom," he finally said, the words low and halting. "I was at prom when my mom died. I didn't know until later, until after I'd danced and gotten drunk and screwed my girlfriend. I was still drunk when I found her, so you can imagine how that went, huh? I stopped myself from calling 9-1-1 because I was underaged and drunk, so I sat, alone, with my mother's dead body waiting for the buzz to wear off so I could call somebody to take her away."

"Oh, Jack..."

"Is that what you wanted to hear? Is that the explanation you were dying for? Because I have more. Like the fact that I learned at my mother's funeral I had grandparents living half an hour away whom I'd never met. Who'd allowed their only daughter and grandson to struggle on their own while she spiraled. Who watched as the father I'd only met a few times became my legal guardian and then didn't even have the guts to speak to me before I was taken from the only home I remembered.

"Yeah, I'm a line cook in a pub, because that's the only out I had after throwing the last shred of my dignity into a backpack and driving my father's car nine hours to propose to my girlfriend only to be left bawling in a jail cell." He swore then, his voice catching. "So, forgive me if I don't come off as all rainbows and unicorns."

She stared at him, mouth open. "How... how did she die?"

He'd expected her to back down, not dig deeper.

"She had a history of eating disorders. It got worse after I was born. Things fell apart with my parents, they divorced, and she moved back to Cutler. She managed to pull it together for a long time, but it got harder

188

for her when I started dating. The night she died, she'd taken diet pills she'd bought on-line. They triggered an underlying heart condition."

Helen clasped a shocked hand over her mouth. "I'm so sorry." She dropped her hand. "I saw a lot of that in my pageant days. It's one of the reasons I quit."

"And started a bakery. Because a cupcake will solve all life's problems."

She seemed aware of the irony. "It seemed a good idea at the time," she said with a wry smile, "not that I can eat any of it now. I'm contractually obligated to maintain my weight, or I have to pay for alterations."

"That makes sense." He snorted, not quite a laugh. "I cook food ten years too late to save my mother, and you cook sweets you can't eat."

They stood like that, a few feet apart, thinking about the vagaries of life.

She tilted her head on a half-laugh. "We make quite the pair, don't we? I guess it's true what they say that like attracts like."

"I thought it was opposites."

"That, too."

He wet his lips and cocked his head. "Is it worth putting yourself through a full season just for the money and PR?"

"I signed a contract. If I back out, I'd face some hefty financial penalties. There's no running from that."

"I suppose not."

"I never meant to drag you into this. If it's any consolation, I'll always remember the hot guy in the cool car I ran away and had crazy adventures with. If only for a little while."

He allowed himself a bittersweet grin. "I am hot," he said.

"So hot." She smiled, a warm, wide grin that crinkled her big, beautiful, dark eyes.

"And we have had some crazy adventures."

She laughed, one of her dimples caving in. "I wish there could be more."

The way she looked at his mouth told him what kind of adventures she was thinking about having.

"Me, too," he said.

She stepped forward and laid a featherlight palm on his chest. "Really? Because, the more I think about it, the more that sounds like a plan I could get behind."

"You don't know how much I'd like to jump on that plan," he said, covering her hand with his. He let out a frustrated groan. "But not in the same house as my ex-girlfriend."

She sighed, her tongue wetting her lips as she looked up at him, frustrating him in all the best ways. "I have a confession," she said. "I thought your ex was okay at first, but she's really beginning to annoy me."

"You're only a few feet away from a couch and a billiards table. Be very careful what you say."

She moved closer. "You're really going to let the fact that your ex is upstairs stop you?"

"I'm not going to have our first time together marred by my looking over my shoulder. Trust me, it's something I will give my full attention to when the time comes."

"Promise?"

He groaned and pressed a kiss to her forehead, not daring to go any lower. "You're just like your favorite drink."

"How so?"

"A sweet tease. Now get upstairs and wear something ugly, because we have a long day tomorrow, and I just remembered there's a hot tub through those doors."

She smiled wide, grabbed his hand, and he let himself follow.

For as long as he could.

CHAPTER 16

Thursday passed in a blur of warehouse store grocery runs, checking on Duke, picking up wedding attire and, of course, massive amounts of food prep. The manager of the hall down the road took pity on them and agreed to let them use the kitchen through Friday morning so long as they cleared out in time for an evening event already booked.

Sweet potatoes roasted alongside sheets of baking cornbread. Helen stirred the roux for the baked mac and cheese.

The door adjoining the parking lot creaked shut behind Jack as he hauled in another bag of potatoes and dropped it by the counter. Sweat dampened the mop of hair at his brow, and he impatiently swiped it out of the way with his forearm.

Helen's pulse rocketed, her mouth going dry. "Thank you," she said, reaching for decorum and the container of salt.

"That's the last of the potatoes," he announced. "If you can spare me for an hour, I've got to run into town. Is there anything else you need? Ingredients for succotash?"

"Haha. Lima beans are gross. We've discussed this. Pick up my dress at the dry cleaners?"

"Got it." He winked. "See you in a bit."

She grinned like a schoolgirl with her first crush as Jack pulled out of the parking lot, then gave herself a mental shake. There was too much to do to get sidetracked and doe-eyed. She checked her list. She needed to prep the vegetables, mash the sweet potatoes, and make gravy. She would've liked to make biscuits, but those were best fresh, and tomorrow she'd have no time. Cornbread was a solid substitute. She planned to add to that a fresh tomato salad, a hot vegetable medley, and garlic mashed potatoes. None of it would win any nouveau cuisine cooking awards, but it was good, honest, comfort food, and she knew how to make it well. The key to success was to not skimp on butter or salt. Let everyone's arteries and diets recover some other day.

The sun hung low by the time Jack's car pulled back into the lot. Helen heard the door slam and his shoes on the gravel drive. He dropped a plastic bag on the center island.

"I know you've been cooking all day, so I thought you'd want something to eat."

She nodded and pulled the pot of gravy she'd been stirring off the heat. "You… you got a haircut," she said inanely.

Gone was the mop of tangled hair that had habitually fallen into his eyes.

His fingers ruffled the shorter strands as if he missed tugging at them. "Yeah. I was overdue."

"It looks good." As in, *have mercy* good.

"I'm sorry it took so long. I had to wait to get in."

"Very handsome."

He pulled his hand away, and his hair fell perfectly back into place like he was a model posing in front of a fan. "Glad you like it."

"I do." She grinned, knowing she was flushed from the heat of the kitchen, her own hair pulled into a hurried ponytail that had begun to slump hours ago, but she didn't care. His expression told her he found her just as desirable.

They ate, and talked, planned logistics for the next day and finished food prep.

By nine o'clock they were locking up for the night.

"Are you sure we shouldn't pick up Duke?" Helen asked for the fifth time.

"He's fine. I stopped in on my way into town. He learned three commands while we were away, had no accidents, and had his first vet appointment. Mike's mom is so grateful we're doing the food, she's happy to watch the dog through the honeymoon. Besides, he has to go right back to their house during the wedding. They're the only ones with a fenced yard."

She knew he was right. Duke was in excellent hands, and she was grateful Jack didn't pressure her to decide what to do with him next. She didn't want to decide. She didn't want to give him up. It felt like Duke had been put in her care for a reason. What that reason was, however, was as unclear as everything else she'd moved into the category of Tomorrow's Problems.

It was a large category.

They drove the rest of the way to Mike's condo in companionable, exhausted silence.

Jenna, Cassie, and Sam were staying at Jenna's parents' house for the night. Mike had waved an exhausted goodnight to Jack and Helen an hour ago and retreated to his bedroom. They'd made a couple mugs of herbal tea and reviewed the day, discussing plans for the next.

It felt different now, Helen thought, as they moved about the small guest room. Just a few days ago, she'd been anxious and confused, an outsider looking in. But now… now she and Jack shared knowing, soft smiles and little inside jokes as they readied for bed. She checked the finger he'd nicked while slicing vegetables earlier that day and couldn't stop admiring how his new haircut highlighted the slice of his cheekbones and the sliver of close-trimmed sideburn begging for her touch.

"In case you had any ideas," she said, as his hand grazed her body in another casual and totally unnecessary way, "these walls are thin, and I want to be able to face Mike in the morning. So, no hanky-panky."

Jack's eyes crinkled with a mischievous grin. "What if I promise to be quiet?"

Helen's heart thumped in her breast. She bit her lip as Jack's hot gaze dropped to her mouth. "We have to get up early," she said. "And, I have to shower."

He closed the space between them, his body so close she could close the distance if she inhaled too deeply. "Is that an invitation?" he asked.

She felt her body sway toward him. "Have you seen their tiny shower?"

His eyes danced. He nipped her earlobe. "I have."

She allowed herself a moment to imagine how she and Jack could make use of the tiny shower down the hall and then splayed her palm on his chest. "It's gonna be a long night if we keep this up."

He chuckled, and it vibrated through her hand, up her arm and into her heart.

For the umpteenth time, it amazed her that this was the same man who'd she'd once thought was grumpy and gruff and, dare she say it, forgettable.

She'd never forget him.

For however long they had to enjoy, she'd be grateful for the crazy, mixed-up, emotional rollercoaster ride, because for the first time in a long time, she felt she could be herself. Her heart swelled as she thought about Jack swallowing his pride and hurt and accepting that Mike and Jenna hadn't set out to wound him. They'd simply followed their hearts.

Jack bopped the tip of her nose with his fingertip. "You've gone awfully quiet."

"Just thinking. I'm glad things are working out for you and Mike and Jenna. I know it's not easy."

"It's damned awkward is what it is."

"I know, but it's important. It's nice you've made an effort. They're like family to you, and family is important."

"Not all family."

She knew who he was talking about. "Do you ever think about visiting them? Your grandparents?"

He shook his head. "No. They're just strangers who send me an obligatory birthday card every year."

"Do you ever reply?"

"No. I figure they'll eventually get tired and drop it."

"Jack, they're reaching out to you."

"Too little. Too late."

"Is it?"

"Look, we're not going to go down to the athletic fields and toss a baseball and go for ice cream. Those days are long gone. It's done."

"But it still hurts that you didn't get to share those things."

Jack ran an agitated hand through his hair. "Can we not talk about this now?"

"Maybe it would help to visit. For closure. Clear the air and help you work through your resentment so you can let go."

"I'm fine."

"You practically spit every time they're mentioned. You're not fine. And we're going or I won't leave town with you."

"So, stay."

"Jack…"

"Stop trying to fix things that aren't broken." He flicked off the light and rolled away from her.

"We'll discuss it later," she said.

Because the thing about Jack was, she knew he wasn't broken. He was just unfinished.

~ * ~

Helen woke before sunrise, the tasks of the day swirling in her mind, the warmth of Jack beside her calling her back to sleep. She held the feeling of peace and contentment and belonging close. Too soon this last day would be over. Too soon, she'd have no more excuses to pretend that she and Jack were anything more than sexually attracted roommates in a youth hostel about to go on their separate adventures in life. This was a vacation fling, not real life.

She blew out a breath, closed her eyes, and willed herself not to wake from the dream.

Sometime later, Jack stretched beside her, yawned, and pressed a kiss to the tangle of hair on the side of her head. Apparently, he'd chosen to forgive and forget—emphasis on forget—their conversation from the night before.

"Time for coffee," he murmured as he slid out and away from her.

She shielded her own yawn and swiped the hair from her face. "What time is it?"

When he told her, she'd stumbled to a more or less vertical position. "I can't believe how late you kept me up."

"You weren't complaining last night."

"That's because you're very good at goodnight kisses. And other stuff." She waved vaguely in the air and stifled another yawn. Blinked. "I need clothes. And breakfast."

"And coffee," he said, steering her toward the door.

Jack prepared coffee as Helen rummaged for actual food. The doorbell sounded. Mike stood in the doorway to his room, yawning. "Holy shit. I'm getting married today."

The doorbell sounded again, and Jack went to answer it. Helen overhead a mumbled conversation, heard a thump, then another, and then Jack thanked the person.

"Hey, Princess, your fairy god luggage has arrived."

Helen dropped the container of oatmeal on the counter, her jaw dropping as Jack wheeled two giant baby-blue suitcases into the living room. "Is that mine?" Helen asked, recognizing the show's signature luggage but still not believing her eyes.

"It's not mine."

"But… why? How?"

Jack peeled off a manila envelope taped to the side and handed it to her.

Helen –
Clean yourself up. See you soon.
—Marcia
#runawaycupcakequeen

"What does she say?" Jack asked.

"That I better not have broccoli in my teeth." As if she needed more pressure on this day, Marcia had to go and remind her that the eyes of the world—and every *Happily Ever After* fan—were going to be on her today. "I need another shower."

"You just took one last night."

Yes, and now she had to shave her legs.

"Are you almost done? We've got to get to the hall."

Forty minutes later, Jack's voice rattled through the door. Helen nearly poked her eye with a mascara wand.

"Five minutes," she said. She recapped the mascara and considered her reflection. Large, delicately lined eyes with impossibly long, thick lashes (thank you, falsies) looked back at her. Two carefully curled tendrils framed her face with the rest of her hair pinned into a strategically neat chignon. She had no time to fuss with flyaway hair today.

Marcia had sent everything from a full makeup kit to underwear, push-up bras and an at-home waxing kit (as if she had time!) None of the half a dozen gowns and dresses suited a barn wedding in rural Pennsylvania, so Helen pulled the thrift store dress off its hanger. She slid it on and smiled at the cornflower-blue fabric dotted with tiny white and lemon-yellow rosebuds. It had a fluttery hem and vee neckline and small cap sleeves, and she'd probably freeze to death in it, but so be it. She slid her feet into a pair of wedge sandals from the luggage, grabbed a white lace wrap and cracked the door open.

"If you could zip me, I'd be forever grateful."

Jack nodded. He wore dark gray trousers, his crisp white shirt open at the collar and looked good enough to serve as appetizer, dinner, and dessert.

"You clean up nice," she said.

His eyes flashed his appreciation. "So do you."

They didn't have time to linger. Helen gathered some just-in-case items for makeup or clothing mishaps, Jack grabbed his suitcoat still in its plastic wrapper, and they hurried themselves and one slightly frazzled groom out the door.

Jack dropped Helen at the hall to begin final prep and the heating of hot dishes.

"Are you going to be all right?" he asked. "I need to bring Mike to the farm."

"Under control," Helen assured him.

A couple of hours later, Helen could hear tires in the parking lot. She scanned the platters, bowls, and pans of prepared food, neatly lined up on the counter, waiting for Jack, Connor, and Jamie to load and drive to the farm. More pans covered in foil were tucked into the still warm ovens and would be transferred to chafing dishes on the other end. Helen turned the burner under the gravy off. Anything that needed last minute re-heating could go in the oven at Jenna's parents' house while the wedding party took pictures.

"Well done," Jack said, and Helen felt herself puff with pride. She swiped a rag over the counters as they emptied them of food, checked to be sure they'd left nothing behind, and hurried to catch her ride.

The day was cool but bright, and Helen kept herself busy under the reception tent transferring the last of the hot food to chafing dishes and rechecking that everything was as ready as it could be. Guests had begun to arrive, and she could see clusters of relatives here and there, ladies carefully navigating the uneven ground in their heels, men looking vaguely uncomfortable in their dress clothes.

Helen slipped off her apron and tucked it behind one of the serving tables for later and went in search of Jack to let him know all was well.

She frowned at the sound of terse voices coming from the back door to the house.

"What do you mean you want to cancel the minister?" Jack whisper-yelled standing on the back steps and facing the open field. "Don't you want to get married?"

"Would you keep your voice down?" Jenna's exasperated reply came through the window from inside the house. "*Of course,* I want to get married."

Jack turned and rattled the locked screen door and swung a frustrated look toward Helen, as if she were somehow to blame for whatever was happening. "Let me in, Jenna, and explain yourself."

"I don't want anyone to see my dress. Just get Mike."

Cassie's face appeared at the screen door. "And Ben."

"Not until you tell me what the hell's going on," he replied.

Helen set a hand on Jack's arm. Tension radiated off him in waves. "The ceremony starts in twenty minutes," she said.

Jack stalked off and returned a couple minutes later with Mike, Ben, and Jamie in tow.

"Jenna?" Mike called through the window.

"Mike," she said. "I want to cancel the minister."

Mike's face went ashen. "Are you breaking up with me?"

"No!" Jenna's face appeared at the screen door now, her eyes awash with unshed tears as her mother awkwardly held a multi-hued afghan in from of her. "No. I want to marry you more than anything, and I want our wedding to be perfect. But it won't be perfect without Ben."

Mike turned to his brother. "He's right here."

"I know," she said, smiling through tears. "But he's more than just a guest, Mike. He's your brother. He's a Justice of the Peace. He's done other weddings for his friends. *He* should marry us, not some minister we've met once."

"It's a little late to ask him. Isn't it?" Mike turned to his brother with a hopeful expression.

Jenna clasped her hands.

"It would be an honor to officiate," Ben said. "But I can't. I'm not legal here."

Jenna's face fell.

"You meant well," Mike said. "I would have loved for Ben to officiate."

"Come with me." Helen tugged Jack toward the minister stepping out of his car. "I have an idea."

CHAPTER 17

Jack greeted the minister and explained the situation.

The minister smoothed a hand over his thinning hair. "If that's what the bride and groom want, I don't see why we can't make it work."

Jack glanced at the windows of the house where he could hear Jenna's mother and sister fussing and smiled to himself. Finally, he felt he'd earned the title of Best Man.

Jenna had made mistakes, but today wasn't one of them. Today she'd marry the man currently striding toward Jack looking nervous and relieved and excited all at one time. Maybe, had things been different, he and Jenna would have been happy. More than likely, things would have eventually crashed and burned, their relationship crushed under the weight of unrealistic teenage fantasy.

Her heart was in the right place. She wanted to make her future husband happy. On that, they'd always agree.

Something eased in his chest, maybe it was relief or release, he couldn't say which. He looked toward the barn. Helen waved and gave a questioning thumbs-up as she stood just outside the entrance, most of the guests already seated and waiting inside. The skirt of her dress billowed, the color of spring flowers, and he knew the sense of rightness he felt was more than gratitude that nothing had derailed Mike's wedding. The past week had been a rollercoaster of crazy, hard, frustrating, exhilarating, wonderful adventures filled with flying squirrels and sleepless nights and a delightfully caring and obstinate beauty queen in a sequined gown and a bathrobe who looked just as elegant with one false eyelash stuck to her cheek or shimmying under an electric fence as she did standing in the sunlight in a summer dress.

He'd done more living in the last week than he had in the last ten years.

He'd be forever grateful for the runaway cupcake queen long after her crazy life and dumb dog and soft southern drawl faded into memory.

"Don't get all sappy on me," Mike said, slapping Jack out of his thoughts with a palm to the shoulder. "I'm getting married in a few minutes. You're supposed to be happy for me."

"I am," Jack assured him.

"I'm happy for you, too," Ben said, catching Mike's elbow. "But it's your wedding. It's okay if you change your mind about this."

Mike smiled. "I know."

"Dad might walk out on you."

"Leaving would be his choice. Including you is mine. We're doing this."

"Great," Jack said. "Let's get this show on the road."

They climbed the short rise to the barn. Jack escorted Helen to her seat and took his place beside Mike.

Everyone grew quiet as Jenna's cousin lifted her bow into position and eased into the first quiet notes on her cello. They waited for a glimpse of the bride, sunlight streaming through the open doorway onto the weathered barn floor.

The air smelled of old barn and springtime, and Jack's chest grew tight and heavy with anticipation. He heard Mike's breath catch.

Jenna, flanked by her father and mother, appeared. Everyone stood and murmured with awe and appreciation, but Jack couldn't keep his gaze from sliding to the woman biting her lip in the back row, her eyes glistening, her baby-blue dress fluttering in the breeze. He couldn't help but wonder how it would feel to have *her* walking toward him. Choosing *him*.

Jenna's parents embraced their daughter and found their seats. Her father avoided Jack's gaze. Jack didn't blame him. Today wasn't about the past.

The reverend welcomed and thanked them all for coming and encouraged everyone to take a moment to ponder the meaning of marriage. "A wedding is not only the sacred union of two people, but the joining of two families. Two families called to put aside the past, put aside differences, put aside doubts in order to support this man and this woman in love." He paused. "In that spirit, I call forward, the groom's brother, Benjamin, who will assist me in officiating today's service."

Jenna turned to Mike with surprise, but Mike simply grinned as Ben took the reverend's place and the reverend took a seat in the front row.

Ben sucked in a nervous breath. He clasped his hands in front of him, then dropped them.

Mike reached out to hold Ben's hand and mouthed, "I love you."

Ben nodded. "That's why I'm doing this." He addressed the congregation. "Like most of you, I never expected to be standing here. Not until about five minutes ago. But life is like that, isn't it? You're humming along, thinking you know how things will go, what the future has in store, and *BAM!* Detour. Or, in Jenna and Mike's case, a filing cabinet." A few people chuckled. "Love is especially like that. It's almost as if it's all around us, waiting for us to notice it's there. *It's right there.* Just waiting for the right moment to shake us out of what we expected, what we thought we wanted, to see what's waiting for us if we'd only open our eyes."

Ben couldn't seem to help looking toward his father. Mr. Weber's gaze remained fixed on the floor. Ben continued.

"We're here today—you and me—because of a mistake. Because of a freak accident. Because my lazy brother couldn't bother to shut one drawer before opening another. But that mistake changed everything, didn't it? It led Mike to rekindle his friendship with Jenna, and the next thing you know, it's nine months later, and we're all standing in a barn." More laughter filled the rafters.

Jack watched the play of emotions on Mike's face. *Humor. Surprise. Love. Joy.*

And it hit him. His friend was truly happy.

It also hit him he was happy, too.

He'd thought once, long ago, that Jenna was his future. His true love. But he looked at her now and saw someone else's bride, not his.

His gaze sought out Helen in the back row. The soft smile he received in return had him bracing for an impact he couldn't comprehend.

"But seriously," Ben continued. "You can plan all you want to build a career or get married or start a family, and it doesn't mean any of it will happen on your timeline or even at all. The best things in life aren't always planned. And that's okay. Be ready to change course. Be open to the possibility that love doesn't care if you're ready. It's simply waiting for the right moment to drop a filing cabinet on you. So, brace yourselves."

Ben reached out to grasp hands with Jenna and Mike. "I love you guys."

Jamie sniffed and flashed a thumbs-up from his seat in the front row, eyes glistening.

Mike smiled at his brother. "Let's do this."

And they did.

~ * ~

The next few hours flew by in a blur of vows and wedding photos, cake cutting, and dancing. Helen and a few aunts and cousins busied themselves restocking the buffet, bringing plates to elderly relatives, and corralling the random child running between the tables.

Jack frowned as another pimpled teen sidled up to Helen for a selfie. The kid couldn't possibly be a fan of the show. He probably only wanted to press his raging hormones up against a gorgeous woman so he could brag about it on social media. Jack didn't blame the kid, but he didn't have to like it, either.

Not that he had any personal claim on Helen. She'd made it perfectly clear the couple times during the reception when he'd gotten close to her that "they shouldn't be seen together."

Because he was only good enough for her in private?

"What's got you sulking in the corner?" Jamie flopped into the folding chair next to Jack, his brow glistening from yet more dancing. "You're looking positively broody."

"I'm relaxing. There's a difference."

Jamie followed Jack's traitorous gaze. "So, what happens next?"

"Next?"

Jamie slid Jack an impatient look. "After tonight. Is she still doing the show?"

"I haven't heard otherwise."

"Does she want to?"

"What day are we asking?" Jack pick up his flute of champagne only to realize it was already empty. "It doesn't matter. She's under contract. There's no way out."

"There's always a way out," Jamie said. "I'm a lawyer. Trust me when I tell you there is always a way out."

"She'd have to pay big bucks if she backed out. I don't see that happening."

Jamie sighed. "Now you're bringing me down. Go dance with a beautiful woman."

"I don't see that happening either."

"Then I feel sorry for Helen, because she's coming this way."

Jack turned to see Helen winding her way between tables to where they sat. "The aunts shooed me away. Mind if I join you?"

"Why don't you get this guy onto the dance floor? He's moping."

"I'm tired, that's all. So are Helen's feet."

"These wedges are surprisingly comfortable," she said. "But I think I'll sit."

Jamie excused himself to join the flower girl on the dance floor.

Helen's face couldn't hide her longing to join them.

"Go dance," Jack said, not giving a flying duck anymore.

"I'd rather sit with you."

"I thought we weren't supposed to be seen together." He struggled to keep the petulant tone out of his voice. Failed.

"We can be seen next to each other, as friends, but there are a hundred cell phones here plus a photographer. If pictures of us looking like a couple hit the internet, Marcia will have a fit, and I'll be in breach of contract."

Oh. Right. The damned contract again. So, he was supposed to sit here and smile as his ass grew numb on a stupid folding chair, pretending they were just friends?

"People might begin to put two and two together when we leave in the same car."

"About that," she said. "Mike and Jenna aren't leaving for their flight until tomorrow. They can't possibly want us in their spare room tonight, so Jamie and Ben said you could claim the extra bed in their hotel room, and I'm going to bunk with Jenna's parents tonight."

Perfect.

"You can pick me and Duke up in the morning. Jamie said check-out is eleven."

"Great."

She reached a hand out to touch his thigh and just as quickly pulled it back again as a furtive smile curved her lips. "Save me a dance? After all this?"

He hated dancing, was a horrible dancer, but he found himself looking forward to stumbling in circles with Helen in his arms for as long as she'd let him. "Sure."

CHAPTER 18

The next morning, before the newlyweds fled to a Caribbean beach, Jack stopped by Jenna and Mike's to collect Helen's luggage. He didn't linger picking her up at Jenna's parents' house. She didn't blame him, given the history there.

Jack held her car door, murmured something about needing coffee and having to collect the dog, and waited for her to buckle before pulling out of the drive.

"Have you had breakfast?" he asked.

"A cup of tea."

"Maybe we can grab a bite on our way out of town."

She nodded and smoothed the folds of her skirt. It felt odd to be in her own clothes again. She shifted to look at Jack. "I was thinking, before we leave town, you might want to call your grandparents."

He let out an exasperated sound and shot her a hard look. "Not this again."

"Just a quick visit. You can use me and Duke as an excuse not to stay long. I just think you'll regret not taking this opportunity to reach out—"

"Drop it."

She pursed her lips. "I know you're a grown man and you can make your own choices, but I think you're making a mistake."

"I have nothing to say to them."

"Thank them for all the birthday cards."

"I don't know their number."

She handed him a folded piece of notebook paper. "Cassie helped me look it up."

He ignored the paper. "Why is this so important to you?"

"Because I want you to be happy, and you'll never be happy if you believe they didn't want a relationship with their only grandson."

"Maybe they didn't."

"You don't believe that." She held the paper out. "Call them."

He snatched the paper from her hand and pulled the car to a stop on the side of the highway. "They get *one* chance."

~ * ~

Idiocy. Wasn't that the definition of trying the same thing expecting a different result? He'd left himself open for how many years, waiting for more than a discount greeting card with the words "Happy Birthday! Love, John and Marie." They'd always added a phone number, but that was it. The same message, different year. What had he been expected to do with that number, anyway? And why didn't they call *him?* Why was it up to him to reach out first?

"There," Helen pointed. "The blue house, right? We're here."

Jack rolled to a stop at the edge of the lawn and cut the engine. He wasn't ready to commit to the driveway.

Helen cracked the window for the dog and was out of the car by the time Jack had taken one last deep breath and opened his door. She smiled up at him and took his elbow. "Don't be nervous," she said.

"If they're assholes, I'm leaving. With or without you."

She squeezed his arm in reply.

The door opened before they'd made it halfway up the walk, his grandparents waiting on the threshold with an air of hope and trepidation. Jack hung back, his hand on the small of Helen's back as if he were ushering her ahead of him instead of using her as a shield. If anyone could navigate uncharted social waters, it was a woman who'd practiced speaking on the fly in front of judges and whose voice was liquid honey.

He wasn't sure what he'd expected. His grandfather stood tall, shoulders slightly hunched, silvery gray hair thinning. Even though Jack had only seen the man once at his mother's funeral, it robbed him of his breath to come face to face with him again. But, it wasn't the moment that affected him, but the familiarity. Jack looked just like his grandfather, and the knowledge that they were very much family, if only through biology, slammed into him.

Marie—his grandmother—stepped forward first, and Jack's attention swung toward her.

He'd pictured someone like his mother only older, but this woman… where his mom had been all angles and brittle brightness…. this woman was soft, round. She smoothed her shirt over her hip and gave a tentative smile. "Welcome," she said. "You're earlier than we expected. Come in."

They stood, awkwardly staring at each other like the strangers they were, his grandmother doing a poor job of disguising her obvious curiosity about Helen, until Helen smiled and stepped forward.

"Thankfully there was very little traffic between Cutler and here. I'm Helen. Jack's friend."

"Marie," she said, shaking Helen's hand before pulling her forward into a hug.

As soon as Helen was released, she was swept into a second hug by his grandfather. "I'm John."

Helen was still smiling as she pulled away. "A pleasure to meet you both."

Jack nodded. He hoped they'd head inside soon. He wasn't the type to hug strangers, blood relatives or no.

His grandmother bit her bottom lip. "Please call us Marie and John. I suppose anything else would feel awkward."

Jack nodded and forced a smile. It was a small thing, but he appreciated the fact that they were sensitive enough to realize he was here for closure, not to start something with them. He'd spent three decades of life living without them. The time to bounce on grandpa's knee or eat grandma's cookies was long past.

"Marie made some sandwiches if you're hungry," said his grandfather.

"I'm not—" Jack said.

"How lovely," Helen interrupted.

They entered the living room and Helen excused herself to help Marie in the kitchen.

He stood in the archway to the living room, his hands buried in his pockets, feeling too big for the space.

"Please. Have a seat."

His grandfather stood near the fireplace, mirroring Jack's posture. "I hear you're a cook like your dad. You enjoy that?"

Jack shrugged and picked up a framed photo of a blonde-haired girl off a table by the window. It didn't take a rocket scientist to guess who it was. "It pays the bills."

She wore her hair in pigtails, eyes sparkling, her face flushed, shirt covered in flour as she patted dough out on a cluttered table. He guessed it was Christmas given the cookie cutters and bottles of colored sugar nearby. It surprised him to see his mother so comfortable in front of a camera, before she knew enough to worry about the pounds the lens added.

He set the photo down again.

"She was six in that photo," his grandfather said from behind him.

Jack nodded. He stuffed his hand back into his pocket before he gave in to the urge to reach for the others. It didn't feel right to handle them. They belonged to someone else. They weren't his memories. These weren't his mother. These were the daughter John and Marie had known.

Their girl in a soccer uniform, posing with a ball.

Again, as a cheerleader at the top of a pyramid.

Then in her cap and gown.

But like a book where the pages had been ripped from the binding, he knew there was more to his mother's story, more that had happened in the later years when she'd stopped smiling for the camera. She'd met his dad while on vacation, then instead of going back to college, she'd eloped, and the bright future, the scholarship money, the expectations of marrying a doctor, or a lawyer, or someone better were dashed on the shores of forbidden love.

They'd told her it was a summer fling.

They'd told her to give the baby up.

They'd told her he—Jack—was something they'd pay to have... discarded.

"She was a beautiful girl," John said, as if this fact made everything clear.

"Yeah." What was he supposed to say? It was his mother. And they'd turned her away because of him. They didn't get to ask for a do-over.

"Please, sit down."

"I'd rather stand."

John's features pinched, and he stepped toward Jack, a light sigh his only answer.

"I don't suppose we appear the most sympathetic people in your mind," he said.

"No."

"I am curious what she told you about us."

"Enough." Jack blew out a breath. What was the point getting into any of it? "Seems to me it's sometimes better to leave the past where it belongs."

"I doubt Marie will agree with that."

Jack shrugged. It wasn't up to him to make his grandmother happy. Or anybody. He'd spent most of his life trying to make his mom happy only to watch her disappear into herself, slowly fading before his eyes until she'd become the ghost she'd longed to be. Wishing for a different outcome hadn't changed the crap that had already hit the fan, as it were.

Jack looked longingly toward the front door. "I'm going to need to get some water for my dog."

"You have a dog? Why didn't you say so? Bring it in."

Jack looked dubiously at the cream-colored living room furniture. "He's a big dog. And black."

"Bring him out back, then. We have a fenced yard he can stretch his legs in."

Grateful for a purpose other than rehashing the past, Jack went to fetch Doof. His grandfather followed him down the front walk.

"Nice wheels."

Jack hid his groan. He liked the car and all, but it wasn't like he was a super car buff. It was transportation. "It was my dad's."

He wasn't sure why he'd said that, but it slipped out like a gauntlet thrown down to see how John would react.

"I recognized it," John said, that slight pinching between his eyebrows returning.

Jack opened the car door, and the dog bounded out to sniff inappropriately at John's crotch. Jack didn't stop him.

John patted Doof's head. "Hey, buddy. Good boy."

They made their way via the side yard to the back of the house. John opened a gate in the carefully maintained wooden fence that separated their yard from their neighbors. It was well-tended if not fancy, neatly tended beds softening the harsh lines. A wall of golden yellow forsythia lined the fence. It had been his mother's favorite flower.

Which is why he always made plans to leave New Hampshire and hike with Mike before it dared to bloom. By the time he reached Cutler, the blooms had mostly passed.

He unclipped Doofus's lead and watched him bound beneath the trees at the back of the yard.

"There you are!" Marie crossed the deck behind them, a rigid, bright smile on her face and a tray laden with food in hand. "Let's sit in the screen porch," she said.

Helen sidled up to Jack holding a pitcher of something with random chunks of fruit bobbing in it. "How's it going?"

"Fine." They hadn't come to blows or anything.

Jack stared at the stack of white sandwiches on Marie's platter, their mashed-up contents disguised in copious amounts of mayonnaise.

"I have tuna salad, chicken salad and egg salad sandwiches. In case you were vegetarian," she added.

"They look delicious. Thank you, Marie." Helen poured Jack a glass of the fruit water, a chunk of peach or nectarine plopping into his cup like a random, out of place foreign object.

Not unlike him.

John swirled his water, a lone grape swimming in his cup. They all stared at the neat pyramid of crustless sandwiches.

"So," Jack said, "you mentioned there was something you wanted me to have. Something that belonged to my mother?"

John cleared his throat. "Yes. I don't suppose there's any reason to wait."

Jack nodded. "That'd be great. I have to get Helen back home."

"There's no hurry," Helen insisted. "We're in no hurry."

John pushed his chair back to pull an envelope from his back pocket. He held it out.

"What's this?" Jack asked.

"It's yours," Marie said, reaching over to grasp his hands. "We want you to have it."

Jack slid his hands out from under Marie's. His fingers grasped the smooth parchment from the stranger who called himself grandfather. It wasn't just any envelope. No. This envelope had fancy little flecks in it. "What is it?" Jack repeated.

"Your college fund," Marie said.

Jack stared at the envelope and then back up and tried for a half-smile. He probably failed. "You're a little late."

"What Marie means is, it was your mother's college fund. We'd intended to save it for you, but seeing as you never attended..." John trailed off.

Jack dropped the envelope on the table. He might have gone to college had he known there was money for it. He scrubbed a hand through his hair.

"We brought it to the funeral, but the timing wasn't right," said Marie. He couldn't bring himself to call her grandmother yet. She tentatively pushed the envelope closer. "Please. Take it."

"What am I supposed to do with it?" That probably sounded ungrateful, but it felt a bit like a stranger handing you a wad of cash saying, "take it." There had to be strings even if he couldn't see them yet.

"Start a business. Go to school. Whatever you want."

He didn't know what he wanted.

He wanted a do-over, but that wasn't an option.

Jack pushed his chair back. "Thanks so much, Marie, for the sandwiches. We should probably go."

"Jack…" Helen called, but he was already half-way across the lawn to collect Doof by the time she caught up to him.

"Jack. These people have waited years to meet you. We can't leave yet."

He patted his leg. "Doof get the hell over here."

"Jack," Helen hissed. "They want to know their only grandchild."

"Do they?" he shot back. "They didn't even want me born."

He heard her gasp, but he wasn't looking at her. He cursed at the damn, stubborn dog.

"What did you say?" she asked.

"You heard me. When my mother got knocked up, they offered to pay to get rid of me. I'm not all that interested in what they 'want' now."

"It's true," John said from behind them. "We did. We didn't know what else to do."

Jack swung an 'I told you so' look at Helen before facing his grandfather. "Is that envelope really her college fund or just you trying to ease a guilty conscience."

"Jack," Helen warned.

"I didn't have to admit it," John said. He swallowed, his face twisting. "She was so bright. So much potential. We wanted what was best for her."

The blood pounded in Jack's ears. He didn't want to hear this man waxing nostalgic over his mother.

"The truth is, Ann—your mother—had already dropped out of school and married your father. They'd had problems from the beginning, and we could see… she was spiraling. Offering to take the baby, give it up, or… whatever she needed. She wasn't ready to be a mother. We wanted her to know she had options. No matter what. That we'd be there for her."

"The way you were there for me?" Jack's gut felt hot.

"We offered to raise you," Marie said, her big round eyes glassy with tears. "You were our baby's baby. Of course, we wanted you."

His body shook as he finally got the damned dog to come close enough to clip the leash on his collar. He waved away Helen's restraining hand. Some things needed to be said. "Seeing as I was born against your wishes and never saw you until I was standing over your daughter's grave, you'll forgive me for finding that hard to believe."

If he'd had help, if he'd had support, hell, if he'd *known they existed*, he might have been able to save her. Then, they wouldn't all be standing here eating stupid crustless sandwiches and pretending they were at some goddamned tea party.

"You're right," Marie said, stepping closer. "We did abandon you, but not on purpose. Not willingly. We wanted more than anything to be a part of your lives, but your mother wouldn't allow it. So, we kept our distance. We didn't know what else to do."

So, his mother was a liar. Jack tried to process everything he was hearing and realized it didn't matter. They'd lived thirty minutes away, but it might as well have been a thousand miles.

He could feel his head shaking, his body instinctively rejecting the truth. It didn't make sense, because it was so different than the narrative he'd been fed all these long years, and yet it made perfect sense. "I can't do this." He nodded and tugged on Doof's leash. "Thanks for... letting me stop by."

Helen caught up with him as he wrestled with the gate latch. "Jack, wait." He swore, grabbing the gate with one hand and rattling it so violently it sprang loose and let him out. "Don't leave them like this. Jack, they're hurting, too."

He swung toward her then, the bark of humorless laughter rising like vomit in his throat. "*They're* hurting?"

Helen just looked at him, those wide, dark eyes dripping sympathy, and he wanted to lash out at anything. Anyone.

But, then she stepped into his space, smoothed his forehead with her cool fingertips and wrapped her arms around him.

He stood, rigid, in the circle of her arms, breathing in the scent of her hair.

"Shh," she soothed. "*Shh.*"

He didn't want to be soothed. He had every right to have said the things he'd said. Feel the things he was feeling. This wasn't a scraped knee.

He pushed her away. "Stop. I'm not a child."

His breath felt heavy in his lungs as he reached the driveway, emotion *this close* to shooting out of him like a firework without a rocket to guide it.

She caught up again. "I know you're angry. And hurt. But this is the only family you have left aside from your father. You've waited your whole life to meet them. Why would you throw that away so easily?"

"Not my whole life," he shot back. "She told me they were dead."

"Who?" And then she stopped. "Oh my God," because now she knew, too. Now she could see how incredibly dysfunctional his childhood had been. That he'd lied about not being broken.

"My mother. She told me they were dead. I didn't even know John and Marie *existed* until the funeral. So, process that, Princess."

Helen stared at him, her eyes swimming with an empathy he wasn't ready to receive. "Don't you see? The only reason you're lashing out is because your mom isn't here to take the blame she deserves. She cut them out of your life. And them out of yours. You all paid the price. It's no one's fault."

"Don't you think I know that?" He slumped against the side of his car and stared at the sky as his vision grew blurry. Swore. "I know that."

"Oh, Jack…"

"Don't hug me, woman."

He glanced over at her as she stood, stricken, tears streaming down her face as a dog's snout butted his hand.

He stared at her, his heartbeat heavy in his chest. "Fine," he said.

She ran into his arms. He told himself he was comforting her as she clung to him, squeezing him tight.

"Jack?" she said into his shoulder.

He squeezed her back. "I'm not taking the damn check."

CHAPTER 19

After looking at the routes, Helen recommended they take I-79 south rather than heading over to Interstates 71 and 65. They could avoid the big cities, she'd said. Jack had agreed, but the truth was, now that they were well and truly on the way home, Helen wanted to drag her feet like nobody's business.

She'd helped smooth things over with Jack's grandparents, promising they'd keep in touch, and giving everyone a tender hug whether they were ready for it or not. She wondered what would happen once she was no longer there to urge them toward one another. Maybe she could stay in contact, just to check in with him from time to time. Would he allow that?

They rode for a while, the windows down, Jack's music blaring from the radio. She pushed her sleeves to her elbows and sighed, the vinyl seat sticking to the backs of her thighs.

"Holy mother of sunshine," she muttered, "It's hotter than a… oh, never mind. Does this thing not have A/C?"

Jack gave her a half smile, although she noticed that even though he wore only a tee, his brow glistened with sweat. "It's your neck o' the woods, not mine. I guarantee it's cool and breezy back home."

"How hot was it supposed to get again?" He told her. It did not make her feel better to know.

"Once the rain moves through, things should cool down," he said.

"When will that be?"

"Sometime tomorrow."

She grimaced and looked out the window wishing she'd eaten something.

Jack turned off the radio. His fingers flexed on the steering wheel. "Thanks," he said.

"For what?"

He glanced at her and held her gaze a moment before turning back to the road. "You know."

Her chest felt light. "You're welcome."

"For somebody who has a reputation for being all kind and nurturing, you're awful bossy."

"I know."

"I like it."

She turned and smiled at him. "I know."

He reached across the seat and squeezed her hand, his knuckles grazing her thigh. She let him ride like that for as long as he wanted.

He finally stretched his fingers, mumbled an apology, and glanced around.

"Where are we?" he asked.

"Besides West Virginia?"

"You mean the middle of nowhere." He took the next exit. "I'm starved and on the verge of hangry."

"You should have taken the sandwiches your grandmother offered." He slanted her a look, but it wasn't sharp, more the kind you use when you have an inside joke. "It would have been polite," she said.

"She called them three different flavors, but they all looked identical."

"That's the fun of it," she said.

A few miles later, they pulled into a low, roadside store advertising discount cigarettes, lottery tickets, and farm-fresh eggs.

Helen needed to freshen up, so she took a couple twenties from Jack to buy food while Jack walked Duke. She murmured a greeting to the man lolling behind the register, asked for directions to the ladies' room, and picked up a basket once she'd freshened up and blotted her body with paper towels.

Helen wandered the aisles. Fruit. Cheese. A loaf of bread. Candy? She wondered what kind of candy Jack liked.

"Go with the nubby ones, they're my boyfriend's favorite."

A voice in Helen's ear had her nearly jumping out of her skin. She glanced up to a girl with several piercings lining her left earlobe. Helen couldn't tell you anything more than that one detail, because just beyond the girl's earlobe was a large display of condoms. Right next the candy. Clearly it was a high-class establishment.

"Oh, I'm not..." she said. But, honestly, she didn't know how to finish that sentence.

I'm not thinking about having sex. Well, I am, but...

I'm not having sex with Jack. Oh, you want the truth this time?

I'm not not thinking about having sex with Jack.

I'm not thinking about having sex with Jack without a condom, that's for dang sure!

"I'm not familiar with this brand," she finally said, her face igniting in actual flames if sensation were any indication.

"It's the only brand I use. Haven't been knocked up once." The girl winked. Light green eyes. Or one green eye. Helen couldn't say as her attention crept back to the condom display and the girl paid for her purchases and left.

Drinks. Helen, thought. She should get drinks. And these gummy things. And a jug of water for Duke. And a package of moist towelettes. She quickly filled her basket, paid while avoiding all eye contact, and hurried to meet Jack at the car.

"Hey, good news," he said, oblivious to the fact that her face was melting off her cheekbones as she set their purchases on the floor of the back seat. "Some girl just told me there's a great trailhead or scenic spot down the road that can't be missed. How about we eat there?"

She held up a finger, unscrewed the cap of one of the jugs, and tilted it to her lips.

"Whoa. Unsanitary," Jack said.

She guzzled, not caring one whit about sanitation. She hadn't had sweet tea in so long, it felt like coming home again. Finally, she took a breath. "What?"

"What if I wanted some."

"You'd hate it. Plus, I know where your mouth has been."

He laughed, and her face flamed hotter as if plasma-hot blushes were an actual thing.

He didn't say a word, but took the jug from her hand, and took a long, slow drink, his throat muscles working deliciously as he swallowed. Helen looked away. He wiped his mouth. "Jesus. That stuff is liquid sugar."

"Pure heaven is what it is. Pure heaven." She pulled the jug back. "I got you and Duke water."

"We're using separate cups."

She didn't argue.

Several miles down the road, Jack pulled off the highway and cut the engine.

"Is this it?" she asked.

"Beats the hell out of me. Maybe we should have taken that turn a mile back."

"You could ask for directions."

"From whom? We're in the middle of nowhere."

"We can go back."

"Nah. Let's eat. We can backtrack later."

"I'm not sitting on these vinyl seats another second. I need shade."

"Come on, Duke." Helen paused as Jack called the dog out of the car. It was the first time she recalled hearing him call the dog anything other than Doof or Doofus. She grabbed the bag of food and jug of tea and followed Jack across the road and a small grassy field to a stand of trees on the other side.

The trees formed a thick canopy high overhead, the area underneath clear enough for an impromptu picnic once Jack spread out the old blanket he kept in his car. The leaves on the trees danced in a hot gust of wind. Helen set down the groceries and peeled off her thin overshirt and dropped it to the ground, half-tempted to do the same with the tank top she still wore underneath.

"I'm surprised you didn't do that miles ago," Jack said.

"I've been warned not change while you're driving."

He blew out a slow breath through pursed lips. "Tell me what you've got in that bag."

She opened the top and pulled things out as she listed them. "Bread. Cheese. Some peaches. Candy. A chocolate bar. These pepperoni things." Her hand found the box of condoms. She stuffed it under the towelettes. "Nacho pretzel things… This and that."

"We'll start with the bread, cheese, pepperoni and," he reached into the bag before she could stop him, "these nacho things." He grinned and tore open the pretzel bag as her pulse skittered to an even pace again.

Jack crunched some pretzel nuggets while she filled a collapsible bowl with water for Duke.

They made sandwiches, such as they were, and ate in silence for a little while.

Helen took another long, slow drink of tea. The branches above swirled in another gust of wind. "I wouldn't be surprised if those clouds meant business."

Jack swiped his brow with the back of his hand. "We should be so lucky. How is it so damn hot here?"

Helen shrugged. There were all levels of hot, and this didn't even come close to Alabama's drenching humidity—the kind of weather that slowed everything down, including words, as if even speech was too weighted down to carry through the air.

"This is nothing."

"It must be well over eighty degrees."

She laughed then, because eighty was nothing. Try one hundred degrees with ninety-nine percent humidity. The kind of humidity where you pray for rain, knowing full well it'll just move the wet from the sky to the ground, drenching everything in between and not satisfying anything but your longing for a sense of movement. "You'll get used to it."

He picked up one of the peaches and sank his teeth into it. "Wow. This is delicious." He held it toward her, twisting it so she could continue where he left off.

"Oh," she said, staring at his teeth marks on the soft flesh. "I can have one of my own."

He gave her a look, saying they'd already shared cooties drinking from the same jug of tea, which was perfectly true. She held his hand steady as she brought the fruit to her mouth, acutely aware that his lips, his teeth, had been in this same spot moments before. She took a small bite.

He watched her do it.

It shouldn't have been sensual, eating a simple peach, but with nothing but the sound of the leaves rustling overhead, it became the focus of her senses. The tangy flavor of it, the slight resistance as she chewed. She swallowed, her eyes still locked with his, painfully aware she was happily and willingly taking part in a cliché. She took another bite before releasing his hand and knew why sharing fruit with a man was a forbidden act as old as time. He smiled into her eyes, took another bite, and her heart skittered in her breast. Another cliché.

She didn't want to be a cliché. Not with Jack. Not here.

What was she even doing here?

Like that bite of apple in the garden, this peach would lead to *truth* and *knowing*, and, if the Bible were any indication, the cursing of all humanity.

She closed her eyes. She was a fool. Jack was giving her a ride. Then he would go back to New Hampshire and find some sassy northern girl who liked flannel shirts and watching hockey and they'd have beautiful sandy-blonde-haired babies together.

Helen and Jack? They weren't a match. They came from different families, backgrounds, were settled in different parts of the country for crying out loud. They were the quintessential definition of opposites attract.

Which sounded good and all but only meant there was chemistry between them but no future.

"Hey. Do you want some chocolate or not?"

"What?" Helen blinked up at Jack, surprised to see him holding a piece of chocolate bar toward her. "It'll melt if we don't eat it."

"Sure. Thanks."

"Where'd you go?"

"Just daydreaming."

"About air-conditioning, I'm guessing."

She laughed then. "No." She looked up at him. "About you and me, actually."

He rolled the square of chocolate in his mouth. "What about us?"

She shrugged and stared at the piece of chocolate melting between her fingers. "Mostly how we're very unlike each other." She popped the chocolate into her mouth.

"How so?"

His blue eyes followed her movements as she sucked chocolate off her finger. She grew self-conscious. Swallowed. She waved her hand vaguely. "Lots of ways. North/South. Parents who loved each other/divorced parents. Family expectations/No family expectations."

"Sweetened and unsweetened tea."

"Exactly."

"Those seem like pretty superficial differences." He bit into another peach, juice running down his chin before he swiped it with the back of his hand and held the fruit toward her. "We both like peaches."

She leaned toward the fruit. It smelled divine. She wanted to taste its flesh very, very badly. "Everyone likes peaches," she said.

"Not everyone." His lips twisted in that half-smile half-smirk she'd come to recognize was Jack about to challenge her.

She avoided replying by taking another bite. Sweet juice exploded in her mouth. Jack pulled the fruit away and wordlessly leaned toward her, his gaze holding hers.

"We do have one other thing in common," he said, his voice a low, gorgeous rumble that made her body hum in anticipation.

"What's that?" she breathed. But she knew.

"We both want to kiss each other right now."

"Speak for yourself," she said.

He was gentleman enough to pause. "You *don't* want to kiss me now?"

"No." She smiled, slow and sweet. "I wanted to kiss you before."

His eyes sparked, a bright heat before he closed the gap between them, his lips pressing to hers.

He tasted of peaches and sunshine and the kind of sweet temptation that's been allowed to ripen over millennia. She grinned against his mouth, and his free hand snaked around her neck to bunch in her hair and draw her closer. As if she needed the encouragement.

His mouth slid over hers like a lazy summer breeze.

"You taste like sass and sweet tea," he said.

She leaned into the kiss. "This is a bad idea, isn't it?"

His lips teased her with slow, easy kisses. "Yes," he said. "Probably."

But sweet temptation tugged him against her, or maybe that was her fingers fisted in the damp fabric of his shirt. She heard the thud of the half-eaten peach hitting the ground. It seemed laying her down beneath him was more important than finishing their meal.

His lips hovered over hers again. "You are so damn hot," he whispered.

"That's the weather talking," she said.

He paused, a chuckle vibrating against her breast and making heat pool in all the right places. "No, sweetheart. It's you. Trust me. It's you."

She didn't know what to say to that, and thankfully he didn't wait for an answer before teasing her lips open with another sizzling kiss that had her hands sliding around him to tug impatiently at the hem of his shirt.

He laughed and blocked her hand. "I'm drenched. You don't want that against you."

She nipped his ear. "Don't tell me what I want."

He let out a low, hard laugh and ripped his shirt off, tossing it aside. "You're gonna kill me here."

"That's not where I thought this was headed," she said, "but either way, you'll die happy."

She deepened the kiss, earning a groan from Jack. His hand smoothed, hot and demanding, down her back to pull her against him.

She wasn't naïve enough to believe the fabric of his jeans was bunched. There was definite tenting going on. She pressed her hips closer, telling herself it wasn't a sin to appreciate the good things God and the universe had done in creating this man. Very good things, indeed. And she meant to celebrate every last one of them.

Helen tilted her pelvis, frustrated with the lack of steady contact. She grabbed his ass and pulled him against her. Hard.

He tore his lips—and hips, sadly—from hers and rested his forehead against hers. "Just give me a second."

"What's wrong?"

He blew a shaky breath out. It tickled her ear and caused a shot of heat to jet back to her happy places. "Just trying to remember there's a time and place for everything, and this is neither of those things."

"I see." Her happy places began to cool.

He rested on his elbow beside her and brushed her hair from her cheek. "It's not that I don't want to keep going. It's that I want to keep going, if you know what I mean."

Her thighs felt heavy as she grinned at him. "Check the bag," she said.

"What?"

"I brought dessert."

Jack frowned but did as she instructed. He pulled the box out, his eyes going hot and dark as he looked over at her. "You bought condoms?"

Heat left her happy places to flush her cheeks. "That seems like a rhetorical question."

He dropped to his hands and knees and crawled up her body, the box in hand. He hovered over her. "Now what would a sweet southern girl want with a box of condoms?"

"No idea, but this sassy southern woman was thinking about sex."

"If it weren't so blasted hot here, I'd think I'd died and gone to heaven."

He glanced at the box, his pelvis rocking against hers as he started to laugh. "Were you hungry when you bought these?" he asked.

"Yes, why?"

He showed her the box. The words *Fun Fruit Flavors!* called out in bold print.

"Well," she said, her tongue licking her lips as she struggled to contain her own laughter, "you do like peaches."

"I don't know how you think this goes, but in my experience, it won't matter to me what flavor they are."

She grinned wide and knowing. "Honey, if you take your time and do it right. We'll both taste peaches."

He caught his breath as he took her meaning and kissed her hard and long, his hand pushing up and under her skirt to the places that waited for his touch. Her body felt heavy and impatient all at once. She rolled him to his back.

He winced, then his body heaved with deep rumbling laughter.

"What's so funny?"

"You're squashing my peaches."

She looked at his crotch. "I'm so sorry." She fumbled with the fastenings on his jeans and tried tugging them off to relieve the pressure on them.

He laughed harder.

"What now?"

"When I said," he wheezed, "that you were squashing my peaches," he choked with laughter, "I meant *my peaches.*" He sat up, despite being hobbled by jeans half-way down his legs.

She looked behind him. Two mashed peaches stuck to the ground and to the space between his shoulder blades. "Whoops," she said.

"Peaches have pits," he said.

Her eyes pooled with laughter. "I could have Duke lick it off for you."

Jack's eyes went dark. "That's not the kind of licking I had in mind."

Her breath caught as he leaned toward her. "A gentleman doesn't say things like that."

He pressed her to the ground with his body and slid his hand under her tank, his fingers teasing the flesh at the edge of her bra. One finger slid underneath it. "Good thing I'm not a gentleman," he murmured.

Another hot gust blew the leaves above with whirling, chaotic possibilities. To think that a week ago this man had been a stranger. Now it felt like the most natural thing in the world to lay in the sunshine, tracing her fingertips over his bare torso.

She pulled him in for a kiss. "Your back is sticky," she said.

He rose up to finish kicking off his jeans. "Frankly, Scarlet, I don't give a damn."

A rumble, low and distant rolled down the valley as another gust of wind blew through. He asked her what flavor she wanted.

"Enough foreplay," she said. "We'll get rained on."

He released the clasp of her bra and her breath caught as he lowered his mouth. "Do you care?"

Oh, sweet mother of sunshine.

She did not.

~ * ~

Helen lay, boneless and spent, staring up at the swirling leaves above. She traced lazy circles on Jack's shoulder as it was the only part of his body she had the energy to reach. "I think the rain is coming," she said.

The distant thunder had grown closer, but Helen resisted the impulse to move.

"I think you're right," Jack said, apparently equally uninterested in movement.

Duke lumbered up from where he'd flopped during lunch and sniffed at Jack's back. His tongue swiped up it, catching Helen's fingers on the way. They both jumped.

"Go away, dog. You're killing the mood."

"That's not the only thing killing the mood," Helen said, as the rustle of wind became the patter of rain on the canopy overhead.

Drops of water sprinkled down around them, the light growing dim.

"We should pack up," she said.

Jack blinked, looked around, then down at her lips again. "It's just a passing sprinkle."

He bent to kiss her when lightning flashed followed quickly by a loud clap of thunder that echoed down the valley.

"That's not just a sprinkle," she said.

"We won't melt," he said.

She stuffed her arms into her tank top and yanked on her skirt. The underwear and bra could wait. "We should get to the car."

Jack tugged on his pants. "We're probably safer here than running across an open field. We'll wait it out."

"We'll get soaked."

"I think it's too late to worry about that."

They were standing now, the rain growing heavier, droplets sliding down the bare skin of Jack's torso to the waistband of his jeans.

Helen's chest felt tight. "Trees are tall."

"Fine. There's a grove of younger trees over there."

"How do you know they're younger?"

He grabbed her hand. "They're smaller around."

Right.

The rain started falling so hard water droplets bounced back into the air on impact. Helen called for Duke who grabbed the leftover cheese in his mouth before charging ahead as they hurried toward the relative safety of the shorter trees.

Water sluiced down her hair, soaking her scalp, plastering her tank top to her skin. She ran, as much to escape the rain as to escape the darker emotion threatening to crash in on her. She strove to ignore the flashes of memory that mirrored the lightning in the sky.

Jack hunkered down as he ran toward a copse of trees. "There," he said, pointing, and he pulled her under a natural stone outcropping. "This is as good as we'll get." He sat on the ground, tugging her onto his lap.

Adrenaline buzzed through her. She recognized the swell of something else, too, and swiped a hand down Jack's back, touching his bare skin to ground herself here. In this place.

His muscles bunched under her touch. "It's washed the peach juice off," she said.

He nodded, his eyes darkening like the sky as he looked at her. Water soaked his hair, and he pushed his hand through it in a habitual gesture. Thunder boomed overhead. She jumped.

"Relax, Princess."

She arched an eyebrow at him, grasping at the distraction of their usual banter. "You called me Princess again."

"It's not an insult."

"Then what is it?"

He blinked against the rain, water droplets clinging to his thick lashes. He didn't reply, just shook his head as if trying to order his thoughts before dipping his head to kiss her.

The rain fell, cool and refreshing, but his lips were warm against hers, and she clung to his heat and urgency, hoping, this time, the memories would stay at bay.

More thunder rumbled and emotion exploded inside her. Something dark, powerful, overwhelming, and raw.

She tensed under Jack's hands, his chest suddenly seeming too wide, his mouth too close, the water pouring over them pushing her into sensory overload.

Another flash of lightning had her seeing a window, a heavy rain pounding against the glass, and the weight of a different emotion, thick and choking, made it difficult to speak. Not that she had words. Her thoughts jumbled in her head like dancing hail, and she shook her head side to side praying the rain would stop and the oppressive grief could float up and out of her to follow her mother's spirit once and for all.

But she was sixteen again, stepping into the front hall, the rain pouring off her coat onto the tiled floor. Her father's voice like she'd never heard it before, pleading, in a distant room upstairs.

She was rushing up the stairwell, her footsteps loud and echoing in the empty hall until she found herself at the doorway to her mother's room.

She stopped, unable to cross the threshold, knowing that doing so meant crossing into a space of knowing, that of all the scenarios she'd imagined of how her mother died that this was the moment it happened.

Here.

Now.

Like this.

Her father bent over his wife's still, small form, begging her not to leave him. Not to go. His words were a jumble of desperate pleas against the inevitable. Anyone looking on could see that death wasn't a door but a journey they'd all been walking for so many, weary months.

Let her go, Helen found herself praying. *Just let her go.*

She didn't think she'd said the words aloud, but her father clung to her mother's pale, pale hand and said over and over…

I'm not ready.

I'm not ready.

I'm not ready…

When he finally let his gaze rise to notice Helen standing there, she gingerly stepped forward, sliding down to kneel at her mother's side as if she might jostle her into the afterlife.

But no matter how fiercely she clutched her mother against her own frantically beating heart, her mother's heart stayed silent.

She finally pulled away, her soundless wail of grief rising toward heaven with her mother, and even nature seemed to fight the loss, as the winds blew the branches of the magnolia against the window along with sheets of rain. And the day mourned the death of her beloved light.

CHAPTER 20

Just as quickly as the skies opened up, the rain slowed to a trickle. Jack held Helen close and kissed her cheek.

The rain on her skin tasted salty, and it took him a moment to realize it wasn't just rain. "You all right?"

She swiped her hand over her hair and crossed her arms in a self-protective gesture. "Just thinking about something else for a moment."

"Something not good."

She shook her head and gave him a forced smile. "I'm okay. Honestly. Where were we?"

He laughed then, which maybe wasn't the most empathetic thing to do. "Forgive me for saying, but I'm not really the kind of guy that's turned on by weeping females."

"I wasn't weeping."

"I could taste tears."

He hated calling her bluff, but having your woman cry in the middle of things was a definite mood killer.

A long breath rattled out of her. "I'm sorry," she said.

"It's okay." It wasn't okay. It was crappy timing considering he was on full-scale, adrenaline-rushing, blood-pumping alert for this woman, but he'd triggered something, somehow, and the playful mood of a few minutes ago wasn't coming back.

He reached out to cup her shoulder, urging her to lean into him, on him. "We don't have to talk about it."

He held her there, just held her, stroking his palm down her back, not knowing what else to do.

"I can hear your heart beating," she said. Her voice whispered up to him.

"Probably pounding like a freight train."

"I like it."

He smiled, his chin resting lightly on her head, as the rain mellowed to a soft spattering around them. Thunder sounded, but at a distance, rumbling down the valley.

She let out a long, silent exhale, stepped out of his arms and wiped her face. "Thank you."

He stood, easing the cramps out of his legs. His jeans plastered themselves to his thighs. "No problem."

"I'm sorry about the timing. It's just... the day my mother died... it was raining like this. It... I get flashbacks."

"Sorry."

"Not your fault. It's easier being with someone, so thank you."

"Do you want to talk now?"

"Not really."

Okay.

"It's just... I've talked about it so much over the years. There's nothing left to say."

He told himself it was fine. She didn't need to confide in him. That he was still, despite having sex by a field in some unknown town in rural West Virginia, virtually a stranger to her.

He started walking back to where they'd left his shirt and shoes, his rain-soaked skin already feeling hot again.

Helen let out a long breath beside him. "It was a Saturday evening. Aunt Iris had gone home. My mother told her to go, because she was tired and didn't want her fussing. I... had gone out for the night."

He stopped, and she stood there in her wet clothes, looking down at her hands as she worried the small band on her little finger. "Storms were predicted. My mom had asked me where I wanted to go so badly in weather like that. I told her Bible Study. She said I was a good girl." Her voice caught. "And then she died. While I was gone, she died."

Her eyes, wide and dry, sliced to his. "But it was a lie," she said. "The last thing I told my mother was a lie."

"Where did you go?"

"A concert," she said. "And it wasn't even very good."

He couldn't help it, that made him smile, even though he knew it was horrible timing.

"The storms hit just as I got home. A tree took out the power and phone. My dad had to walk out to one of the neighbor's nearer town to call the coroner. I stayed behind."

He nodded again, letting her speak. She said they had nothing in common, but he knew what it was like to have to wait for the coroner.

After he finally made the call, they told him to hold the line, but what for? Holding the line meant there was still hope help would come.

Yeah. He knew what it felt like.

"I'm sorry to burden you with this," she said. "Especially now."

"No burden. You're sad. It's okay to be sad."

She nodded, but it didn't seem that she believed him.

He draped his arm over her shoulders and tugged her close to drop a kiss on the top of her head before letting her go again. He wanted to hold her tight, but he didn't know if that was a good idea. He was getting attached, could feel himself sliding toward her, leaning on her, and he didn't have a track record of letting go gracefully.

"I get it," he said. "Losing people sucks."

She gave him a wry smile. "It sure does."

They collected their things and headed back to the car.

The rain had only served to make the air more humid, and clouds gathered again in the west, high and foreboding.

"I'm going to go out on a limb and suggest we find a place to stay for the night," he said.

"Somewhere dry would be good."

"With food."

"And hot showers."

"Don't go all high-maintenance on me, Princess."

She pursed her lips, but for the first time she didn't call him on it.

"I'll bow to your highness later. Maybe I'll feed you grapes," he said.

A faint hint of color stained her cheeks. "We'll see."

He liked her soft smile.

Jack opened the trunk, and they dropped their wet things in a heap, the sodden package of condoms on top. He looked at the box.

One more night. One more night together and then Helen would be home, and there'd be no more excuses, no more detours.

He wondered if she'd let him keep the dog.

CHAPTER 21

The light was low in the sky, the air blessedly cooling by the time they found a hotel. Helen opened the car door, grateful she'd finally have a chance to shower and change. Sex in the woods and getting caught in the rain sounded romantic and all, but the truth was, she had dirt and bug bites in places she didn't want to mention, her hair had dried in a tangled, matted mess, and her underwear still felt damp.

Jack rounded the back of the car. "I'll be back in a minute."

"You're caked in mud."

His eyes crinkled. "I'm pretty sure you'll want to stay on the down low until you've freshened up or the Runaway Cupcake Queen hashtag is going to trend in a whole new direction."

Less than ten minutes later he was back. "We're good to go, but fair warning, looks like it's prom night."

Just then, three cars and a pickup sped into the lot, music blaring, teens in satin and tuxes spilling out, laughing and hollering to one another as they made their way to the entrance.

"Are you kidding me?" she asked.

He shrugged.

"Well, I can't walk through the lobby looking like this. With Duke. What about Duke?" Another car drove into the lot, its occupants looking their way curiously. Helen ducked. "And why do you have to have such a conspicuous car? Who drives something like this as their regular car?"

Jack didn't answer. He pulled one of her suitcases out of the trunk and slung his pack onto his shoulder.

"What are you doing?" she hissed from her crouched position beside his car.

"Bringing clean clothes to the room. Do you need the other one?"

"No, the big one is good, but hide it. Those cases are easily recognized."

He blinked at her. "You're worried about the cases now?"

"What grown man has baby-blue luggage?"

"Can you get Duke?" he asked in reply.

"I'm not walking in there like this."

"Stop panicking. I have a plan."

Fine. It was a decent plan, considering, but it still left Helen loitering at the back door of a hotel fearing paparazzi which wasn't a fun flashback for her.

The rear exit creaked open, and Jack's face appeared. "The coast is clear."

Helen tugged Duke's leash, and they entered the dimly lit stairwell. The door swung shut. "Is it okay to bring him in?" she asked as she followed Jack up the stairs.

"Pet-friendly room." He rounded the corner and kept climbing.

"What floor are we on?"

"Third."

"The third? Who puts a pet-friendly room on the third floor?"

"Do I look like management?"

He held a hand out to pause her as he checked the hallway. "Okay. We're safe."

Carpet in a mottled pattern of brown, gray and green muffled their footsteps. The hall sconces flickered annoyingly as they passed the ice machine.

Jack paused to work the room key.

"Hurry up," Helen mumbled. "I hear voices."

"*Ohmigod!* Is that a..." The door swung open, and Jack all but shoved Helen into the room. "...puppy?"

Helen could hear Jack responding.

Yes, Duke was a rescue. Yes, it was horrible that someone would abandon a dog like that. Yes, he'd been caught in the rain. Thanks, but he'd probably pass on joining their after-party.

Finally, the door cracked open, and Jack and Duke spilled through.

"Make some friends?" Helen laughed.

Jack pulled off his shoes and dropped them in a heap on the floor. "I forgot how much teenage girls like to talk."

"And dogs."

"Yes, and dogs."

"And good-looking men."

He rolled his eyes. "They are literally half my age."

"Where I'm from, that's not always a deterrent." She slid off her own shoes. "So, who gets to shower first?"

"Who says either of us has to be first?"

229

She knew that look. It made her melt like butter left on the counter, but the truth was: a.) she felt disgusting, and b.) the closer they got to home, the more she wondered how she would cope with having to walk away from all this.

"Why don't you go," she said. "Then you can find us some dinner while I clean up."

Jack's eyes flashed another look, but he quickly hid it.

Helen knew that look, too. Disappointment.

"Sure."

By the time she'd pulled out her toiletries and some clothes to wear, Jack was already walking around with a towel around his waist.

"I'm gonna get dressed if you want the bathroom."

Right. She didn't move.

"Go get cleaned up. We can do that later," he said.

"Do what?" She shook herself out of her stupor and picked up her clean clothes. "I don't know what you're talking about."

She closed the door on his low, knowing laughter.

By the time she was done showering, dressing, drying her hair and generally making herself feel human again, Jack was long gone.

She sat on the edge of the bed and turned on the television. She scrolled through twenty channels, and finally clicked it off again. Duke sat by the door and whined.

"He'll be back any minute," she said.

The minutes ticked by, and Duke nudged her with his snout, then whined again.

"Do you have to go out?"

At the word 'out' Duke began to hop excitedly by the door.

Helen checked her reflection. All right. She no longer looked like something trapped in a sewer drain, so it was probably safe to take Duke out for a potty break. She clipped his leash on, blocked the latch with a "we're resting, come back later" sign, and crept out, hurrying toward the stairs.

She'd never done so much sneaking around in her life.

She hurried down the stairs and out the back door, clinging to the handle as Duke yanked hard on the other end of the leash. "Oh, no you don't. I've been burned this way before. Let me find a rock or something."

Duke pulled on the leash. Helen wedged her foot in the door and reached down to pick up a rock. She hauled the dog back toward her, set the rock in the door, and carefully released it to prop the door open.

"There." She let go of the handle. "Now we can sniff that grass."

She took three steps away. The rock slid. The door slammed shut.

Helen blinked. "You have *got* to be kidding me."

Duke peed on every piece of vegetation within a ten-foot radius then proceeded to squat.

Helen stared at the pile. A sign on a disposal baggie dispenser cheerfully depicted the words, "No pooping without scooping!" It was empty, because *of course* it was.

Helen looked around. She peered into the trash bin next to the dispenser. Several rain-soaked bags of poop lay at the bottom along with an empty pizza box.

She picked out the pizza box with a mental note to wash hands immediately upon returning to the room.

She looked at the back door. There was nothing to be done but use the lobby. She held Duke's leash short as she walked up and around to the front double doors. *Walk with purpose* she counseled herself. Just then, a group of teen boys moved through the lobby. Helen skirted by the front desk by walking on the other side of them toward the elevators, then turned and entered the stairwell.

Excellent! They'd hardly batted an eye. She counted the landings and exited on the third. Duke trotted along happily, and she offered him 'good boy' looks. "Almost there," she whispered, like he could understand. "We're right after the ice machine."

She paused, pleased with herself for making it back undetected and went to open the door.

It was locked.

"Jack, open up," she whispered. "It's me."

No answer.

"*Jack,*" she whispered more loudly. "Open up." She knocked. She knocked again.

The door swung open.

It was *not* Jack.

"*You GUYS!!!*" a girl in lime green taffeta squealed, assaulting Helen's sensibilities in more ways than one. "You won't *believe* who's at the door!"

~ * ~

Jack searched the lobby, back lot and his car. He called up and down the stairwell and waited for a reply. The pizza he'd brought back was long cold, but it was the least of his worries. Where the *hell* was she? And with the dog? Surely, if she were kidnapped, they wouldn't take the dog, too?

He approached the front desk. "Excuse me. Have you seen a woman? With a dog?"

The clerk pointed behind him. "You mean her?"

Jack turned. The doors to the downstairs ballroom were propped open, loud music pumping from within, clusters of teens dancing and talking. And there were Helen and Duke right in the middle of it.

"Thanks." Jack strode toward the door. An adult usher stopped him.

"I'm sorry, only students and chaperones allowed."

"I'm with her," he said, pointing.

"Sorry."

"But, that's my dog."

"Duke? Why didn't you say so?"

The chaperone let him pass, as if Duke was some sort of celebrity and Jack was trying to crash his private party.

Helen sat to the side of a cluster of kneeling girls in brightly colored dresses all cooing at and ruffling Duke's fur. He rolled to his back for tummy rubs and a squeal of approval lifted above them like a balloon.

"...it's true, yes. I like to be charitable, because we can't know what her circumstances were. Maybe she couldn't keep him, and the only shelters weren't safe, and she felt leaving him was his best hope." Helen glanced up and saw Jack. "Ah! Here's the man who saved him. Everybody, this is Jack."

A dozen pair of eyes swung toward him.

"You are such a hero!"

"Why can't more men be like that?"

"He's adorable!"

Jack wasn't sure if that last comment was meant for him or the dog. He gave a short little awkward wave. "Hi."

The girls swooned. Jack didn't know swooning was an actual sound before that moment.

Helen stood. "Well, I should probably go."

"No!"

"Stay!"

"Look how happy Duke is!"

Helen laughed and tugged on Duke's leash who looked mildly put out to leave his adoring fans. "Come on, boy. Time for dinner. You all enjoy your night."

The teens waved, said their goodbyes to the dog, and someone shouted, "We love you, Cupcake Queen!"

Jack took Helen's elbow as they got on the elevator.

"I thought we were avoiding that sort of thing," he laughed as they got on the elevator.

"I knocked on the wrong door," she said.

He slanted her a look.

"It was an honest mistake," she said. "Then I had to wash my hands because of the poo, and by then it was all over chat that I was in the building, and the next thing you know, one of the chaperones asked if I'd be willing to come to the ballroom so they could keep things under control."

Jack pulled out his cellphone. He held it toward Helen. "Marcia will be happy. You're trending again."

"Already?"

"There's also a new hashtag."

"What?"

He held up his phone again.

At prom with #runawaycupcakequeen, but #whosthehottie ?!?!?

Feeling like a princess partying w Duke + #runawaycupcakequeen... Can't help but wonder tho #whosthehottie?

Came for #runawaycupcakequeen. Staying for #whosthehottie

Who else is hard stanning for #runawaycupcakequeen and #whosthehottie?

Who gets Duke if #runawaycupcakequeen & #whosthehottie split?

Helen clicked on the reply.

You can keep the dog. Dibs on #whosthehottie ☐ #thirsty

She handed Jack back the phone. "We have to get separate rooms now."

"What? Why?"

"Because it's out there that we're together. As in *together* together."

"We are together. We're the very definition of together."

"Jack." She said his name like he should know better. And he did. Which, frankly, sucked. "You and I both know... what we have... It's not a forever thing."

The elevator dinged.

Yeah, he knew that. He knew it would end. He just hadn't realized it would end this soon and with so little fanfare.

The doors opened, and Jack held out the room key. "I'll talk to the front desk."

CHAPTER 22

The next morning Helen woke and glanced over at the unmoving lump on the other side of the bed. No, it wasn't Jack. Duke lifted his head and let it flop again, as exhausted by the laughing, footsteps and door-banging that had continued into the wee hours as she was.

She stared at the popcorn ceiling. One tiny, hairline crack by the wall drew her gaze. She wondered why it was there. Felt irrationally angry that it stood out as it did, marring the perfection of an otherwise pristine surface.

And, yes, she realized she was projecting her own frustrations at having a perfectly lovely whirlwind romance marred by having to go home today.

Today.

She threw back the covers and padded to the bathroom to splash her face with cool water and brush her teeth.

Welp. Today was the day she accepted that she couldn't run from her responsibilities forever. She had to suck it up, head home, and get on with being the next Mrs. Right.

Never let them see your mascara run.

She spit, rinsed, and spit again, dried her teeth with a towel and pressed the 'express whitening' strips into place.

A knock sounded on the outer door. She padded over and cracked it open. "Oh," she said. "I thought we were waiting until nine to check out."

Jack stood in the hall wearing those same soft shorts, a faded tee for some indie rock band and carrying a pizza box doing double-duty as a tray. "Thought you might want something to eat."

Helen backed away from the door to let him through. "I can't right now." She fake-grinned at him. "Whitening."

"I guess that means you don't want the coffee."

"Probably not."

Jack set the small bakery bag on the desk and paused. He seemed to be wondering what came next. He wouldn't be the only one wondering that.

"So…" He still held the makeshift tray.

Her heart constricted in her chest. What else was there to say?

"Before we go back…" She tried to put into words what the last week—had it been only a week?—meant to her. "I just want to say, I'm really glad I chose your car."

Everything unspoken between them seemed to hang in the air, waiting to find voice. All the truths that left her raw and scared but knowing she was alive and breathing and able to feel hovered on her lips. It was as if the darkness of the last fifteen years had suddenly, in the span of a week, been filled with light.

He pressed his lips together and set one of the coffees on the desk anyway, just in case she changed her mind.

"Me, too," he said.

Her heart beat like a drum in her chest, slow and thudding like time that refuses to stand still.

"Don't go back to the show," he said.

"Jack… I'm under contract. I can't just walk away."

"Have you tried?" he asked. "In your whole life, have you tried?"

She thought of the night her mother had died. She thought of the humidity thick in the air. She thought of the way death could slide into your life when you were looking the other way, and she wanted more than anything to stay here, present, with Jack and never look away. "Yeah. I've tried."

"No, you haven't. You took one step off the beaten path, got your wrist slapped, and haven't ventured sideways since. The worst part is, you're doing it to yourself."

She ripped off her whitening strips and threw them in the trash. "Where is this coming from? I've ventured off the path."

"Not really."

"What do you call the last week?"

He looked at her, emotions raw. "Everything."

She couldn't swallow. Couldn't process.

"The last week has been ridiculous and frustrating and amazing and eye-opening and painful and glorious," he said. "I want more."

Her head jerked in denial. "It's not sustainable. What we have… what do we even have?"

He laughed without humor. A short chuckle cut short with the blade of cynicism. "Nothing, I guess."

"Jack."

"It's ironic, isn't it? I've thrown myself at two women in my life, and both times, it ended badly. I should learn."

"This isn't the end, Jack."

"Isn't it?"

She wanted to say "no." She wanted to claw back to that field and those feelings and reassure him that, no, this was only the beginning of something, but surely that was a lie.

"I'll be ready in half an hour," she said instead.

He looked like he wanted to argue, but then he turned and left without another word.

They exited from the rear stairwell. It seemed prudent to keep a low profile. To Helen, it felt like a fitting bookend, beginning and ending her time with Jack.

The back door to the hotel *snicked* closed behind her. Jack wordlessly loaded her luggage in the trunk. She waited for Duke to do his business and got in the car.

Jack pulled onto the main road.

"You paid, right?" she asked after a few minutes. The silence seemed fragile, like one wrong word, and they'd both shatter.

Jack nodded. He hadn't made eye contact since bringing her breakfast. "When I bought our muffins."

"Great."

They drove for a little while longer. "The muffin was delicious," she said. "Thank you."

"Glad you liked it."

She looked out the window and fought back tears. *Grief.* She knew that's what this feeling was, this fragile feeling like too sudden a movement, a sharp word, could make you shatter. Even though they were still here, still riding along, still looking for all the world like the same two people that couldn't wait to run into a field with hope and laughter and fruit-flavored condoms... They were twenty-four hours closer to the end.

She knew this kind of grief, too. The anticipatory kind of grief. She knew this kind of grief was almost worse, because it didn't know how things would play out, so you grieved every scenario in your mind.

It was almost a relief to pass over the state line into Alabama.

Almost.

CHAPTER 23

She made Jack stop for gas, delaying the inevitable, but as they rolled through the cluster of familiar streets and buildings that comprised downtown Heaven, she felt the walls of her life closing in again like humidity on a hot July day. It felt more crowded than she remembered, the streets and shops bustling with traffic and people, but when you've spent an epic road trip just you and someone else, three felt like a crowd.

She distracted herself with the mundane. She'd check in with Shawna, the assistant manager, at the Birmingham location. She'd phone her dad, of course, and Travis would want to know she'd arrived, but it felt safer easing her way toward the tougher conversations.

She'd need to get her car back from Spence, her cousin, who had promised it would be fully detailed and running like a top upon her return.

She'd want to pick up almond milk and lip balm and…

"I hope you'll tell me when I need to turn."

Helen glanced up, the intertwining canopies of the Southern Live Oak trees lining Main Street blurring in her vision. "It's not for another few miles."

"Okay."

She watched the familiar landmarks and lush scenery slide by, feeling oddly detached from it all. "It feels like I've been gone a lot longer than I have," she said.

"I'm sure your family will be happy to see you."

She nodded. "Don't be surprised if they ask you to stay."

His hands gripped the wheel a little tighter. "Stay?"

"For a day or two. It's a southern thing. If they don't get a chance to feed you, they'll be insulted."

I'm not ready to let go.

Her heart pounded in her chest.

"I don't want to intrude," he said.

"For a day or two," she said. "Before you hit the road again. I can show you around."

"Sure," he said, meeting her eyes. His look said he could see right through her. She didn't care. "For a day or two."

She attempted a carefree smile, but her heart pounded in her chest. Postponing the inevitable wouldn't change the outcome.

Either way, her heart would break.

He couldn't know that, though. He had no way of knowing she'd recklessly tumble so easily from carefree flirtation to something deeper in such a short time. She didn't dare call it love. It was too soon for that. Still. Her feelings for him had become anything but carefree.

"Take the next left," she said.

The trees opened up, the houses growing sparser, and then there were the open fields, a few horses quietly dipping their heads to graze. It really was heaven here. Beautiful and gracious with the outside, busy world feeling a million miles away.

It seemed ironic that she'd leapt at the first chance to leave.

Maybe her heart had known she'd have to leave Heaven to find a man like Jack Adams.

"What the...?" Jack slowed the car to ease between the vehicles parked on both sides of the roadway. They passed trucks with trailers. Vans. Then were stopped altogether by a barricade across the road.

"Oh, no," Helen whispered, reality crashing in and making it hard to breathe.

"I take it we're here."

"Yes," she said. "I mean, my house is... I wasn't expecting..."

She craned her neck, trying to see beyond the sprawling detritus of a production crew. She unbuckled, her hand shaking with nerves. "I should go. Prepare them."

"Prepare them? For what?"

"I don't know." She got out of the car, automatically opening the back door to let Duke out to pee. "You. Duke..."

Jack got out now, too, his eyes sparking in the sunlight. "You mean *me*. You're preparing them for me."

"I didn't say that."

"That's exactly what you said."

"Jack." She didn't need this now. She felt over-warm and anxious and exhausted, like she'd just stepped off a fourteen-hour flight and didn't know what time zone it was. She lowered her voice and side-eyed the security guard. "Don't make this difficult."

"So sorry," he said, all but hurling her luggage onto a neighbor's lawn. "So sorry I'm making *your* life difficult."

"That's not what I meant. I'm grateful for all you've done, but—"

"I don't want your gratitude," he all but bit off.

She took a deep breath and stepped closer. "I get it. Emotions are running high for both of us. I just need a few minutes. Can you give me that?"

He bit his lip and shook his head. "Fine." He turned away.

Her heart lurched. "You're not leaving *now*, are you?"

He stopped, his back to her, his body rigid, hand grasping the door handle. "Not before I get paid."

His words were like a field-hockey stick to the gut. Illegal and intended to wound. She knew he was lashing out. She wanted to, too, but they'd known this was coming. They'd been pushing against time ever since they'd left Sugar Falls.

"My checkbook is at the house," she said.

He blew out a frustrated breath but didn't look back.

"I'll park the car," he said, and he slammed the door and threw the car in reverse.

Helen watched Jack wind his boat of a car back down the road until he was out of view and Duke nudged her palm with his snout.

She gave herself a mental shake, remembered Mrs. Greenbow's training, and smiled at the security guard.

Helen side-stepped scurrying crew members. The sounds of shouted directions and construction assaulted her as she approached her childhood home. Production for *Happily Ever After* looked like some high-tech, sprawling refugee camp had sprung up overnight with food service tents and RV-style campers, delivery vans, and more. They'd re-landscaped, put a fresh coat of paint on the trim, added a small, gurgling fountain, scattered charming stone benches, and erected a pergola by the trees in the side yard. The changes disoriented her. She wouldn't be surprised if, behind the freshly painted front door, the house beyond was empty. She paused, half-wondering if she should knock.

She eased the door open, Duke at her heels.

Aunt Iris stood in the center of the living room, looking, thankfully, unchanged. She wore the soft but steely demeanor of a woman perpetually displeased with something but still smiling through it, because she has *manners*.

"Well, bless your heart," she said, all blinking smiles, "I know you mean well, but that's just not going to work. If Helen's going to be on TV again, she'll at least need a proper facial, and her skin will need time to recover, or she'll be red as a beet."

Marcia Powers wore her signature, off-camera outfit of black skinny jeans, white, oversized blouse and black booties. She adopted the same steely expression as Iris but without the smile. "We film Wednesday."

"So soon?" Helen gasped, pushing into the room.

Marcia turned. "It's about time you got your ass down here."

"Helen! You're home!" Iris looked Helen up and down. She turned back to Marcia. "See? *This* is why we need more time."

"Your family likes to play fast and loose with schedules. I'm locking Helen down before she bolts on me again."

"I'm not enjoying your attitude."

Marcia rolled her eyes. "You sure seemed to enjoy the check we wrote you to film here."

"That check was for my brother, a widow, I might remind you. He doesn't have anyone to manage the house as it should be managed. I can't run two households."

Helen's head spun. Filming wasn't supposed to begin this soon. She was promised more time. She put a hand up. "Iris, enough about the facial."

Iris sucked in an agitated breath. "*I can see your pores.* The entire nation will see them. You're not little Helen Walker at the county fair. Oh, dear heavens, what is *that.*" Iris pointed a pale-pink lacquered nail at the dog.

"Duke," Helen said. "He's a stray we picked up at a rest stop."

"Lovely. Now we have a *dog* to add to all this?" Iris made a sweeping motion with her arm.

Helen ignored her aunt. There were bigger fish to fry here. "Filming isn't supposed to start until the seventeenth."

Marcia shrugged. "Some actor got his pet project blown up by a sex scandal—his own fault, the perv—so the network was scrambling to fill the time slot. I offered a teaser for the upcoming season. We're doing a live special event. Wednesday."

"*Live?*" No wonder Iris was freaking out.

"We agreed to host the show here," Iris said, addressing Marcia. "Not to parade our panties on the line for all the neighbors, to see. You can't possibly have everything ready by Wednesday."

"This isn't my first—"

Iris had the nerve to cut Marcia off. "I know you do this for a living, you've already said as much." She bent to the clear glass pitcher sweating on the marble coffee table and poured a glass, turning to Helen with a centering breath. "Now, I know you're an adult, and you make your own choices, but the fact of the matter is, you made a choice to throw this family into the spotlight, and if we aren't all going suffer embarrassment, things can't just be thrown together, they have to be *managed*." She smoothed a shaky hand over her pencil skirt. "Have some sweet tea."

Helen ignored the proffered glass. Iris wasn't in charge here. "There's nothing to manage. I'm home. I didn't break a nail or have sex on television, so your worst fears were unfounded. That, at least, should make you happy."

Iris looked wounded. "What could make me happy about seeing you strung along for ten weeks only to be rejected for another woman? A mechanic no less? *On national television?* It was painful to watch."

"You mean it was painful to see me come in second again."

"Don't be ridiculous. If you'd really wanted to settle down, you could have had any number of men."

She said the words, but they were less a comfort as a critique. They were too close to what Iris had said right after Helen had come in as first runner up in the Miss Alabama pageant all those years ago. *If you'd really wanted it, you could have won.*

The implication being that Helen *hadn't* wanted it—or hadn't wanted it enough—to will it into being.

Aunt Iris's disappointment hadn't started with Helen's lack of marriage or the pageant loss. That particular look had first marred Iris's otherwise perfect features the night Iris had burst into Helen's parents' bedroom, shot a look across the bed at Helen and demanded, "How could this happen?" As if Helen had somehow been careless in letting her mother slip away when Iris was out of the room.

But that was years ago now. Helen knew, now, it had only been Iris's shock and grief speaking. She didn't blame Helen. She blamed herself for not having been there and had spent the ensuing years throwing herself into the role of surrogate parent like her life depended upon it.

She'd fussed over Helen's quiet despair, fretted over Helen's manic baking, and cried over their beloved Maltipoo like the dog had never peed on her favorite Italian leather pumps.

Helen knew Iris's involvement came from a good place, but as she'd said: Helen was an adult now, making her own choices.

She was an adult that had learned well to stand on a stage in front of hundreds of onlookers and smile and shake hands and pretend she wasn't fracturing into a million brittle little pieces inside.

Because the truth was, she had wanted it. Not at first. Not as she'd been forced to let Iris primp and tease and, God help her, pluck eyebrow hairs until tears came to her eyes. It was better than hearing Iris fret about how fat Helen would get spending so much time in the kitchen, which was all well and good *later* when she was married, but she was only sixteen, and was it healthy to spend so much time alone?

Helen would be lying to say she hadn't eventually come to like the attention, and it seemed to make Daddy proud, and in those years after their small household had grown smaller, she would have done anything to make his eyes spark with delight again.

Even become someone she wasn't.

But, of course, that ended, too. Aunt Iris's hopes of shepherding her niece to national competitions went down in flames when Helen was declared runner up.

Helen walked to the front window and stared down the driveway wishing she hadn't been so quick to turn on Jack.

Apparently, she was very bad at handling endings.

She sucked in a breath and turned to face them. "I've had a long drive today, and I'm tired. I know I've signed a contract and I've made my bed and all the other metaphors you two are likely to carry on about, but I want to be clear, to both of you. *If* I continue with the show, it will be on *my* terms."

~ * ~

Jack re-positioned his backpack on his shoulder as he reached the security barricade. The security guard gave Jack the hairy eyeball, mumbled into his headset, clipped a clearance badge to Jack's shirt, and waved him through. Helen's baggage bounced over the uneven ground behind him.

Jack ignored the occasional hurried but curious glance as he turned at the gate at the edge of the street. Two urns filled with green spikey plants and flowers flanked the entrance to a straight, white walkway leading to a perfectly proper, perfectly presented, perfectly pristine southern home.

Sweat trickled down the center of his back as he hauled Helen's bags onto the porch. He caught the tail-end of conversation through the door.

"...cast and crew have pulled together a mini-miracle out there. And hashtag runaway cupcake queen is the gift that keeps on giving. You should be thanking *me*. Your likeability ratings are sky-high."

The door flew open, and Marcia, the show's host and producer, burst out. "Thank God, you're here," she said. "Take those upstairs and then find me some aspirin and an iced coffee. I'll be in my trailer."

Jack watched her charge down the walkway without a backward glance, her footfalls like gunshots.

Helen stood just inside next to a woman wearing the expression of someone who has just witnessed a dry heave.

He stepped inside and extended a hand. "You must be Iris."

Helen made introductions, Iris half-heartedly greeted him, then murmured something to Helen and shot off in the other direction like a pastel version of Marcia.

Helen did that deep breathing thing she did in tense moments. Jack waited for her to finish and open her eyes.

There had been no gracious invitation extended his way. He supposed he shouldn't be surprised.

"So," he said, hands in pockets, "how's it going?"

"How does it look like it's going?" A short bubble of what tried to be humor puffed out of her lungs. "Hide your keys, because I'm this close to stealing your car and heading for the hills."

"That bad?"

"We don't start filming next week," she said. "We start Wednesday."

Well. No sense putting off the inevitable.

They stared at one another, the tense exchange at the car and whatever had happened since, a mess of unspoken words and emotions between them. She spun and poured something from a pitcher into a glass. She held it out. "Here. You look… thirsty."

He bit his tongue and took the glass, downing the contents in one long gulp. He winced. There was only so much sweet he could swallow. He held the glass out. "I can see you're busy, so just tell me where you want your bags."

"Jack, you're not my bellhop." Her tongue flicked over her bottom lip. He looked away. It was no longer his place to notice that kind of thing.

"There's a guestroom. You're welcome to use it."

He wanted to. More than anything. "I—"

"Welcome home." Jack stilled as a third voice entered the conversation. "Iris said I'd find you here."

Helen's panicked gaze flickered from Jack's to a guy in tan khakis, and navy polo striding toward them like he owned the place.

"Travis." Helen swallowed and exchanged a stiff hug and kiss on the cheek with the newcomer. Her gaze bounced off of Jack's. "What are you doing here?"

"Spence was done with your car. I offered to drop it off. Save you the trip."

"That was thoughtful of you."

Travis rolled back on his heels and stared at Jack. Helen shook her head. "I'm so sorry. Travis, I want you to meet Jack. Jack, this is my—"

"Partner," Travis cut in, holding his hand out. "Helen and I go way back." They shook hands, Travis's gaze traveling up Jack's jeans and sweat-soaked tee. "So, you're the guy who—"

"Saved me," Helen said. "From the paparazzi. He's been amazing. My port in a storm. He literally gave me the shirt off his back."

"And then she doused it in lasagna," Jack said to stop her babbling.

"And cat food," she added.

"But that's another story." Jack caught Helen's eye and bit his lip, remembering the moment he'd had to tear her gown off her. He wondered what Travis would have to say about that.

"Sounds like quite the adventure," Travis said. "Anyway. I have to get back to work. You'll stop in later? There are things we need to discuss."

Helen rubbed her temple. "I'll try. Tomorrow at the latest." His hand was on the front door when for some unknown reason, she stopped him. "And, Travis?" He paused. "Thank you."

CHAPTER 24

"Business partner," said Helen. "He only meant business partner."

"That's not the way it sounded."

Helen stopped fussing with the bedding and held out the matching pillowcases. Jack could stuff his own pillows if he was going to continue to poke at this. He'd only agreed to stay once she'd pointed out it was a place to rest before heading home again, and likely as not, the show and crew would have all the local hotels booked solid.

She was beginning to regret it, though, as she'd hoped Jack would be a reprieve from the chaos, not an added source of stress.

"I can't help the way it sounded. I'm telling you, we broke up and I moved out before the show."

"You were living together?"

"Don't sound so shocked. It's the twenty-first century. People live together even in Alabama."

"I knew you'd broken up, but I didn't know you were living with him. *Him? That guy?"*

"Yes, *that guy*. And he has a name."

"I know. He was all too proud to tell me while standing over me like some puffed up peacock."

Helen set her hands on her hips. "Are you jealous? Is that what this is about?"

"Doesn't he have a job? How does he have time to 'swing by' with your car?" He used air-quotes.

Helen bristled. "He was doing me a favor."

Jack pried back the curtain at the window to peer outside. The view was blocked by the back of a pop-up tent. He dropped the curtain back into place.

"This place is a zoo," he said, stating the obvious.

He looked utterly miserable.

She couldn't blame him. She had no right dragging him through this, too. "I know. And I know that I signed up for it, but you didn't. If you want to leave, I understand."

"Is that what you want?"

The distance across the bed might as well have been the span between Sugar Falls and Heaven. "No. I want you to stay," she said.

He paused his forceful stuffing of the pillow and set it on the bed. "Okay. Then I'll stay."

"You will?"

"Yeah."

"How long?"

"As long as you need me to. Hell, I've come this far."

"Thank you." Relief flooded her. She'd been certain he was ready to bolt as much as she was. "I'm completely blindsided by this special event Marcia has planned, I have a million details that need my attention, and I need an ally. Someone I can count on to keep me sane."

He shook his head but opened his arms as if he were fighting his better judgment. "Come here," he said. "You know you can always count on me."

She let him fold her in his arms, resting her head on his shoulder for one, sweet, long exhale. He squeezed tight.

She stepped away. It was late. They were tired, and she needed to be at the bakery by seven-thirty and back here and in hair and makeup by ten.

She paused, her hand on the door. "Oh, one more thing."

"What?"

"I'll need you to watch the dog."

~ * ~

Late the next day, Jack pulled back the curtain to the spare bedroom only to be met by the wall of white canvas again. It irked him that he couldn't even see out the windows in this place.

He dropped the curtain and glanced at the half-read mystery laying open on the bed. He was bored, frustrated, and done, but he'd made Helen a promise he'd at least stay through the start of filming. After that, there wasn't anything to stay for. She'd be gone for good.

He'd been out of his room a handful of times, but only to walk Duke in the "designated area." There was an actual sign for it, erected by one of the *Happily Ever After* crew. Apparently, Marcia's new vision involved taking over Helen's house, transforming it into some teenage girl's

247

fantasy romantic backdrop and keeping Jack locked away. Out of sight, out of mind.

He would have gladly loaded Duke into his car and driven somewhere far, far away, but there was an actual castle blocking his exit and no one anywhere seemed capable of or willing to move it.

Iris had been running around, her beige heels clicking like tap shoes on the wood floors, blessing Marcia's heart so hard and so often Jack was sure one of them would burst into flames.

"I need space for the canapés," Iris insisted, her voice rising in pitch. "We're having friends and family here for the premier, and I intend to serve something other than that cafeteria food you all eat."

"Ma'am, I need to keep the flowers somewhere…"

And so it went.

"Hey." Helen's face peeked around the guest room door later that afternoon. Jack had left it ajar to feel less like a prisoner. "Aren't you a sight for sore eyes. Can I come in?"

She had on a silky lemon-yellow dress and beige heels and wore her hair in a high, smooth ponytail fastened in a gold clip. Every day she was home, she looked more southern, polished, and contained. It was hard to imagine she'd just spent hours catching up with her bakery staff and not sipping tea somewhere.

"Have you brought entertainment? I'm bored out of my mind."

"You could take Duke for another walk."

"Done that. Did you know you have alligators?"

"Did you see one?"

"No, but I saw a sign for one."

She waved a hand. "They're rare. Don't go near the creek."

"Which way is the creek?"

"Right," she laughed, kicking off her heels with a sigh. "I forget that. Just past food service."

She flopped into the small, upholstered chair in the corner. "I will be so glad when this is all over." She caught his eye. "I mean, not because I want to see you leave, but because Aunt Iris and Marcia do *not* play well together."

"I knew what you meant."

Helen pushed out of the chair and padded over to him and laid her hands on his chest. He could feel the warmth of her palms through his shirt. "I know this sounds crazy, but I'm looking forward to introducing you to people, you know, at the cocktail reception before the premier."

"I don't know why." He said. "According to your aunt, I'm sarcastic, I talk too fast, I eat too fast, and I need to find God."

"Aunt Iris has a lot of opinions."

"I'm also leaving soon."

She leaned her forehead to his chest and sighed. "Don't remind me. I know." She raised her head and pressed a single kiss to his mouth. He clung to her, sipping from her lips, like she was his last drink of water before he entered the desert.

She eased back onto her heels. "I know," she repeated, her voice shaky. "But I wish you weren't."

His hand slid down her back and lingered. Sue him, but if he had to give this up tomorrow, he'd take all he could today. "I'm not going to hang around and watch you date thirty other guys."

"I'm not asking you to." Her eyes widened. "*Wait*. Maybe I am. Jack, *what if you go on the show?*"

"I might end up not liking the lead."

"I'm serious. You could be one of my bachelors. Marcia won't care so long as she gets her happy ending."

"She'll never go for it. I'm #*whosthehottie*, not a random stranger. People will accuse the show of being rigged."

"We'll say we were only friends, but you always thought there was a spark of something between us. You'll see me as the one that got away, and you're going on the show to see if you can ignite that spark into something more." Her voice rose with excitement.

"You've been watching too many of these shows."

"I know it sounds crazy, but I think it could work. I'll fulfill my contract. We'll give Marcia her happy ending. I'll get the money to expand the business for Travis. Everybody's happy!"

Excitement radiated off her. She looked so hopeful that his own pulse kicked up a notch. What if he did go on the show? His own sister had done it. Ian had done it, And, if Jack said 'yes,' then whatever was between them wasn't over after all. They could see this thing through.

Helen went on tiptoe to kiss him again.

He paused, her lips a breath away from his.

"Wait," he said, easing away. "I can't just join the show—for *two months* of filming. I have a job. Commitments."

"Anybody can fill in for you," she said. "I'll talk to Marcia."

Helen waved excitedly before clicking the door shut. He stared at it, waiting for her excitement to infect him, too. Instead, he stood, with his feet rooted to the floor, unable to believe he wouldn't be left standing alone at the end of it all.

CHAPTER 25

By the time Helen lay her head on her pillow that night, it was already the next day.

Her alarm sounded, and she threw an arm out to whack it into silence. As if she'd been able to sleep, what with her mind swirling with all the things she was committed to do for the show, Iris's increasingly strident comments, and hoping against hope that Marcia would agree to letting Jack be cast for her season. It was the only way out that didn't have she and Jack riding off into separate sunsets at the end of this.

She blew out a long breath. *In. Hold. Out. Hold. In. Hold....*

Helen flung back the covers. Ivy had slid the day's itinerary under the door at about five minutes to midnight. Helen was due for her mani-pedi, waxing, and a trim at six o'clock sharp. Promotional photos would be taken at nine. She needed to choose a gown in time for wardrobe to make any last-minute adjustments for the premier, and somewhere in there, she needed to track Marcia down to see if she could convince her to cast Jack as one of her bachelors. Yes, it felt like juggling with knives, but if everything worked out as planned, they'd make it through this week, have eight weeks of fun on a reality TV show, and move on with their lives. Hopefully—if she didn't julienne herself in the meantime—together.

Helen rolled out of bed and dashed for the shower.

Three hours later, tweezed, plucked, shaped, and pampered to within an inch of her life, then stuffed into a powder-blue chiffon gown, she hurried behind Ivy through the patio doors and to the side yard.

"We need a variety of backdrops, so we're going to start here by the fountain, then wardrobe change, then over to the patio for some 'poolside fun' and then back to the pergola for 'wining and dining' shots.'" Ivy lifted her gaze from her clipboard. "Any questions?"

Helen eyed the row of buff men in sleek black tuxes, Zorro-like masks over their eyes. "I'm assuming I shouldn't talk to the men."

Ivy's frowned. "Why ever not?"

"Isn't that why they're wearing masks? Because I shouldn't meet them until the premier?"

Ivy laughed. "Oh, honey, these aren't your bachelors. These are paid models. They're just here for promo shots. You," she pointed to a particularly large, dark specimen before walking toward him purposefully. "How much can you bench press?"

Good heavens. Ivy was turning into a Mini-Me of Marcia.

Ninety grueling minutes and some questionable poses later, Nick, their cameraman, called for a wardrobe and set change. Helen heaved a sigh of relief at the chance to rest her cheek muscles.

"Ten-minute break," Ivy hollered. "I need the bachelors ready, dressed, teeth clean, and poolside in ten minutes. And *no oil yet.*" She mumbled some more instructions into her headset then ushered Helen back inside. "You're doing great. We're going to switch things up out there, get you into something fresh and fun, and keep this energy rolling."

Helen slumped into the chair in their makeshift dressing room. "I'm starving."

Ivy called for a protein shake into her headset. She waved the girls from wardrobe over. "Nick says, the red dress. The color will pop against the water."

"Water?" Helen asked, automatically pressing her lips together so she didn't get lipstick on the delicate chiffon as wardrobe pulled it over her head.

"Yup."

"Then why am I in a dress and not a bathing suit?"

"Not in the promo shots. We'd have to blur your butt and boobs."

The protein shake arrived. Helen leaned over to sip from the straw. "Any chance I could have a word with Marcia during the break?" Ivy frowned. "I promise to make it quick."

Ivy tapped her pen against her clipboard. "Ten extra minutes, but no more. She's in her trailer."

"Thank you." Helen grabbed a white robe off a hook and booked it for Marcia's trailer.

~ * ~

Marcia stared at Helen and slowly blinked. "Could you repeat that?"

Helen rushed through her thoughts for a second time including all the reasons why it made sense for everyone that Jack be allowed to join the cast.

"So, you're telling me you want to quit the show?" Marcia's voice was uncharacteristically level.

"No. I'm saying I *want* to, but this is a way I don't have to."

"Could you give us a minute?" Her stylist seemed only too happy to exit Marcia's trailer. Marcia motioned to Helen. "Have a seat."

Helen scanned the padded bench where various items of clothing had been laid out for selection. She scooted over an ivory pantsuit and perched on the edge of the bench.

Marcia sat on a swivel chair, her back to a three-sided mirror. Another staffer had already gone to fetch something refreshing, chilled and sugar-free. Marcia breathed in and out with measured breaths.

"I know this is unexpected…" Helen began.

Marcia cocked her head as if she were addressing a simple child. "No. I saw this coming a mile away. You know what your problem is?" Helen shook her head. "You don't trust the process. Even though I have a *perfect* record. Even though every other dating show has couples dropping like flies or spoiler sites dredging up secret girlfriends… Even though *my* couples keep getting married and having babies… you still don't trust me.

"I've selected thirty men for you, Helen—*for you*—and one of those men *will* be your future husband. Count on it. Now run along. I don't need you second-guessing me."

"Thirty men I've never met," Helen pointed out. "The other shows do the same thing. It's like throwing thirty men at a wall to see if one of them sticks," she said this in a rush, knowing she was parroting the very arguments Jack had made to her. "Jack… Jack is someone I've met and *like*. He's already… sticky."

Memories of peach juice and Jack clouded her focus for a moment.

"He's another guy you've dated," said Marcia. "Do you know how many men I've dated? Do you? Too many, that's how many. And not one of them ended up being my fiancé. You can't trust your own judgment in these things."

"What if we're meant for each another?" Helen asked, getting a little desperate. "What if we're soulmates?"

Marcia burst out laughing. "Soulmates? There's no such thing as soulmates. If every person waited for their One True Love, like some magical unicorn, humanity would die out. Except for all the perverts having sex. The truth is, any number of men in this world could make you perfectly happy. I'm not trying to find you a unicorn. I'm trying to find you one, solid, reliable, photogenic horse to ride off into the sunset on. If he's a goddamn stallion and you want to ride him hard, so much the better. *Soulmates…*" She laughed again, carefully wiping a tear from her eye so as not to smear her eyeliner.

Helen stood, defeated. "Will you at least consider it?"

Marcia shrugged one shoulder. "Tell Ivy to have wardrobe fit him with a suit. I'll make my final decision before the premier." Helen turned to go. "And Helen?"

She paused, hopeful.

"Have makeup take care of that zit."

CHAPTER 26

Helen slumped into the makeup chair again, defeated. She'd tried, at least.

Maybe if Jack approached Marcia as well, wore her down a little, it would sway her. "Has anyone seen Jack today?"

Lily zipped the delicate chiffon dress back into its protective bag. "Is he that cute guy with the dog?"

"Yes."

"Yeah, he got angry about his car being blocked in, told a gaffer to walk his dog, and said he was going to town to get some peace and quiet."

"Without his car?" Helen asked.

Lily shrugged. "He said he'd walk."

Oh, for Pete's sake. "Thanks."

Eight minutes later she was trussed in a scarlet mermaid gown, mincing herself poolside.

Apparently, the extra ten minutes mattered. The gaffers had to do virtual gymnastics to block and reflect and arrange the lighting just so, so Nick didn't stick his tongue in his cheek and shake his head, saying, "No good," which was basically Nick throwing in the towel.

One of the gaffers called over during a shot. "Where do I put the dog?"

The model holding her—Adam? Wayne?—struggled to keep her from falling on her backside as he did a "dip" toward the pool. Helen squinted, the sun in her eye. "Put him in the bedroom," she said. "Upstairs."

"You're squinting," Nick said. He waved to someone to lift the blocking apparatus higher. "Perfect. Beautiful. Lift her. Lift her. She's like a feather in your arms. Gorgeous. Okay. Group two now."

"Group two!" Ivy hollered. "I need group two guys now."

Nick lined up a new set of bachelors, rearranging them until he was satisfied their chest sizes and heights and skin tones were all aesthetically pleasing, before instructing them to lift Helen as she lay stretched out, her head cradled in her hand, the other hand on hip.

Because that was simple.

They fumbled her the first couple of times, and she narrowly escaped scraping her bare arm stem to stern on the cement.

"She's got to hold herself stiffer," complained the guy on the end. Helen didn't even bother remembering his name. She nicknamed him 'Flaccid' in her mind. He had her *feet* for crying out loud. How hard could that be?

She heard whining. Helen sighed. Duke had wormed his way onto her father's bedroom balcony above the pool.

"Somebody move the dog!" Ivy barked into her headset.

"He's fine," said Helen. "He's just worried about me. I'm fine, baby!" she called up.

Duke whined and clawed at the railing.

"Just take the shot," Ivy said, "and we can take another break, deal with the dog, and oil everybody up."

The men arranged themselves and hefted Helen into position. An assistant arranged her skirt, positioned her arm and fluffed her hair. The men wobbled and recovered.

"I need everyone, eyes on me, and *smiles!*" Nick called from behind the camera. He clicked dozens of shots, waving his arm to indicate they should keep going.

Flaccid dropped her feet. "Guys…" he said.

Duke barked from above. Helen broke eye contact with the camera and looked up as Duke's body hung over the railing, his back feet pinwheeling. He barked again.

"Duke, no!"

He jumped.

Apparently sixty pounds of animal falling at your feet will startle a person. Or several.

No sooner had Duke landed on the cement at her feet, but the men holding her leaped out of the way, falling backward into the pool. The problem was, they were still holding her.

She went under, gasping, chlorine stinging her eyes. The water around her roiled with five other bodies trying to right themselves.

"Stand up! Stand up! Get out! Get out!"

Helen flailed until her feet were under her again—no small feat given the narrow skirt opening—and stood in the three-foot water.

Correction, four other bodies were in the pool. Flaccid, was still standing poolside flailing his arms, screaming, and dry as a bone.

"Get out!" he said. "Alligator!"

And that, Helen would see in hindsight, was the moment all hell broke loose.

Giant reflective screens dropped atop staffers as they tripped over electrical cords and dove behind equipment. The model bachelors in the pool, God bless them, hauled Helen to the deck as her sodden skirt hobbled her ankles. How mermaids were supposed to swim like this was beyond her.

"Jesus, it's huge…" this from one of the men.

Helen swiped the mascara and chlorine from her vision. "I've seen bigger," she said, aiming for bravado. A long, fat gator watched them from the other side of the pool. *In. Hold. Out Hold.* Helen breathed through the panic to clear her thoughts. Panic wouldn't help anyone, certainly not Duke who lay on the cement, whimpering.

"Oh, baby," she said.

Ivy tried to tug Helen toward the house. "Everybody inside," she called. "We're calling animal control. Nobody panic."

Helen didn't intend to panic, but she sure as hell wasn't going to leave Duke a sitting duck. She knelt down to scoop him up from behind. Sweet mother of sunshine, he weighed a ton. She tried to stand up. Couldn't. "A little help?" she wheezed. If she couldn't stand up again, they'd both be alligator food.

Two of the buffer models lifted her, dog and all, to her feet. One of them took Duke from her arms.

"He's hurt," she said. "He needs a vet."

Ivy looked them all over. "Somebody else can take him. You guys need to get to wardrobe."

Helen looked at the gator walking around the pool toward the house. "I'm taking my break," she said, and ushered the man carrying Duke out the front door. The driveway, yard, and road were like some accident scene littered with clusters of people talking excitedly and hugging one another, grateful to be alive since they'd just escaped the jaws of death.

What she didn't see was a car.

Duke whimpered again and swung his big brown eyes toward her. Helen fought back tears and ran to the road in time to see someone backing Jack's car onto the neighbor's lawn.

She hurried over just as the staffer closed the door. "There. It's not blocked," he said.

"Give me the keys," Helen demanded. "It's an emergency." She instructed the model carrying Duke to lay him on the seat beside her and assured him she'd be fine. She could feel ugly sobs rising in her throat, and she preferred, if she had to lose it on the way to the vet, to do so in private.

She spun deep troughs in the neighbor's lawn before careening down the road toward the vet's office, hot tears sliding down her face. Duke lay his head on the seat beside her and closed his eyes. She panicked. She could see he probably had a broken leg the way he'd been holding it, but internal injuries were invisible. And he'd landed on cement.

She'd only had him a short while, but he was *hers*. She'd committed to take him in. No matter what anyone said, it would break her heart to let him go. Sometimes when you know, you know.

She rolled through the stop sign at the end of the road, turning toward town, and realized it wasn't just a dog she'd fallen for in such a short time.

It was Jack.

As soon as she got to the vet, as soon as—God willing—Duke was all right, she'd find Jack and tell him. And Marcia and the show and everything else could figure their own selves out.

She reached Main Street and sped through town. Past Spence's Auto. Past Lou's Pizza. The light turned yellow; Helen gunned it. It turned red just before she yanked the wheel to the right to make the turn. *Good Lord, this car was a boat*, she thought.

Edie Johnson stepped off the curb at the crosswalk.

Helen cursed. She swerved hard to the left, to avoid the old witch of a woman. Her shoe tangling in the fabric at her ankles, and she punched her foot down.

On the accelerator.

The car jumped the curb and slammed into a tree. Helen's head bounced off the steering wheel. She blinked, not sure if whatever she felt sliding down her cheek was tears, blood, or pool water.

"Helen? Lord have mercy, Helen? Are you all right?"

Edie, bless her, jiggled and tugged until the driver's door popped open.

"I'm fine," Helen lied. She stumbled into the sunshine, blinking, shaking off the shock of the impact and swiping at her face.

She staggered toward the back of the car, kicking off her blasted shoes on the way. A familiar figure jogged around the corner then ran to grab her by the arms.

"Jack," she said. "I'm so sorry. Your car…"

"I don't care about the damn car. Are you hurt?"

He was shaking her or maybe that was the adrenaline coursing through her, the pounding of blood in her ears.

"No. I'm okay, but Duke. He's hurt." She stifled a sob, because now that Jack was here to help, she felt that much closer to falling apart. "He fell from the balcony. He's in the front seat."

Jack flung open the passenger door. Duke had fallen to the floor in the accident.

Helen gasped. "Is he…?"

Jack eased out of the car and stood, the dog in his arms. "Heavy? Yes."

"Alive?" she asked.

"He's breathing," but that's all he'd promise as his eyes reflected the worry she knew were in her own.

Helen ushered them across the street to the vet's office and prayed they were in time.

CHAPTER 27

Jack had barely spoken since the doctor took Duke into a back room. Helen had tried again to apologize for crashing his car, assured him she'd have it fixed good as new, but he'd grown impatient with her. Somehow it didn't seem the right time to announce she'd discovered feelings for him.

So, she sat on one of the plastic chairs in the waiting area, a puddle of pool water slowly drying beneath her, hands clasped in her lap to keep them from shaking.

Jack stood at the front window, his hands shoved deep in his pockets. He only turned around when the door from the back room finally opened and the vet waved for them to come back into the examination room again.

Helen held her breath, Jack at her side.

The vet absently pet Duke's fur. "The good news is, he has a broken leg, but it's only a hairline fracture. We'll put him in a cast, immobilize it, and it should heal without surgery. The bad news is, in a fall like that, we always worry about internal injuries. Generally, by this point, if the injuries were severe, he would have started exhibiting symptoms, labored breathing, coughing or vomiting blood..." Helen looked up in horror. "But so far things look good, so I'm cautiously optimistic. If you don't mind us keeping him for a day or two, we can manage any pain and let you know if anything changes."

Helen leaned toward Duke and kissed his cheek. He didn't respond.

She left her number at the front desk and let Jack usher her back outside.

He handed her a paper towel he'd pulled from the wall in the vet's office. "To clean up," he'd said.

She swiped at her face. The towel came away streaked with mascara. "Oh, that's lovely." She swiped a couple more times and then gave up. Mrs. Greenbow would be so disappointed.

Jack took her chin and examined her face. "Better." He brushed her hair back and frowned at her hairline.

"Jack, about your car…"

"For the last time, I don't care about the stupid car. I'm just glad you're all right."

She didn't feel all right.

She felt everything slipping away. If they lost Duke, too, it would feel like one more fragile thread tethering them together will have broken.

By the time they made it back to Jack's car it seemed half the town had arrived to gawk at the fancy car from out-of-state somebody drove into a tree.

Helen had to make a statement. Spence came to tow the car back to his garage. Edie Johnson insisted she needed someone to calm her frazzled nerves until her husband could come and take over.

Spence gave them a loaner, so they could get back to the house. Apparently animal control had come for the alligator, and Ivy wanted them back ASAP.

Helen blew out a long, steadying breath. She reached across to squeeze Jack's thigh. "Thank you."

"For what?"

"For not flipping out on me. For taking care of Duke. And me."

"It's my job," he said, the smile not reaching his eyes. "Remember? Not a big deal."

"It is to me." She had mascara streaks down her face, a bruise on her browbone, her hair hung in dried, tangled ropes, and her dress was wet and ruined, but she didn't care. None of that mattered, because she finally knew what she wanted.

She wanted Jack.

She wanted him no matter whether Marcia was on board with the idea.

And, she planned to tell him all of that just as soon as she was presentable.

CHAPTER 28

Helen resisted the urge to stamp her foot with impatience. She'd not had a moment to call her own since coming back to the house yesterday afternoon. They'd continued promo shoots through the dinner hour, and by the time she'd torn herself away to seek Jack out, he'd claimed he had a headache and was going to bed. She'd told him Marcia was thinking of casting him and he should see wardrobe for a suit.

Then he'd thanked her and shut the door.

She didn't blame him. Since returning home after the accident, she felt suspended in the space between what was and what could be. And now, having slept on the knowledge that she had feelings for Jack, she knew it wasn't fair to ask him to wait for her until she knew for sure she was free and able to pursue something with him.

That is, if he wanted that, too.

She pasted a neutral smile onto her face, squared her shoulders, and stepped out of the bathroom. And ran straight into Jack.

"Jack!" She righted herself and drank him in like it was Margarita Monday and drinks were half price. "Wow. You look… Wardrobe likes you."

"Thanks."

She smiled. His didn't quite reach his eyes.

"You're coming to the reception at the friends and family tent, right? Iris said they'd start serving at four-thirty. The premier is at eight, but Marcia wants audience seated by seven."

She didn't know why she was babbling about the schedule. Surely, he already knew, as Ivy had taken to sliding the day's itinerary under everyone's door like the night staff in a hotel.

"I have to get to hair and makeup. Any special requests?" she asked.

His gaze held hers as if he were trying to articulate everything unspoken between them but couldn't form the words. "I know this will come off as incredibly sexist, but…" He leaned forward and whispered in her ear.

If he'd worn a cocky grin or knowing leer, she might have been offended, but, instead, he looked… wistful. "You got it," she said.

He nodded, hands in pockets, and walked, head bowed, down the hall to his room.

~ * ~

Jack swirled the whiskey in the bottom of the heavy on-the-rocks glass Helen's father had given him and tried not to fidget. The suit wardrobe had given him made him feel like a kid going to prom, but he'd liked the way Helen's eyes had lit up when she'd seen him in it, so he swallowed his pride and kept it on. He hadn't packed for standing in an overstuffed parlor with the lord of the manor grilling him about his history and intentions.

Jack tried to answer as best he could how he'd come to find himself on a spur-of-the-moment thousand-mile road trip. He made sure to gloss over key details and definitely left out the fact that he'd lain naked in a field in rural West Virginia with this man's only daughter.

He cleared his throat. "No, sir," he replied to whether he'd ever been to Alabama before. He'd never uttered the word 'sir' before in his life, but something about the time or place demanded it.

Helen and Jack had barely spoken two words since she'd been whisked away upon her return yesterday, Ivy muttering about 'low lighting' and 'wardrobe' and 'Marcia having a conniption.' Apparently, the alligator had been carted off to greener pastures, some poor staffer had been promoted to alligator patrol, and Jack was free to not get in the way.

Mr. Walker turned and smiled as Helen finally descended the stairs. "There's my girl," he said. "You look beautiful, honey. But you always do."

Helen caught Jack's eye over her father's shoulder as her dad hugged and released her. Her dad held her at arm's length. "Let me see that smile." She dutifully grinned. "Gorgeous. Have you ever seen teeth so perfect? You're my best advertisement, sweetheart." Her father turned to Jack. "I made those teeth."

Helen rolled her eyes. "He means, he straightened them. Dad's an orthodontist if he hasn't already mentioned it."

"Ah, here's a man with a perfect smile." He clapped Travis on the back. "I made his, too," he said, conspiratorially.

Helen rolled her eyes and took her father's arm. "Stop bragging about people's teeth. There's such a thing as patient confidentiality."

"Travis doesn't mind, do you? He's practically family."

Her father squinted at Jack. "Smile."

Helen cocked her head. Jack complied.

"Not bad. Braces?"

Jack shook his head. "No."

"It wouldn't take much to fix them. We see a lot of adults nowadays."

"There's nothing wrong with Jack's teeth," Helen said.

"Orthodontia isn't just for cosmetics. Do they ever bother you? Any pain? Sensitivity? Excessive or uneven wear?"

Jack shook his head.

"I like his teeth." Helen insisted. All this talk made him feel like a prospective horse found wanting after inspection.

"Sure. Sure." Mr. Walker shrugged and topped off his drink. "Men can get away with an imperfect smile. Gives 'em character."

The hum of guests arriving and mingling came through from the rear patio where Iris had gotten permission to host selected friends and family before the live premier. She'd run around like a headless chicken in a twinset and heels for the last three hours, ordering around *Happily Ever After* lackeys as if they were her own personal army. Jack had no idea what unholy union Iris and Marcia had come to for that to happen, but someone made a pact with the devil. Or so Helen had said.

His gaze slipped down over the strappy, slinky white dress Helen had on, her hair falling in loose, artful waves over her shoulders. "You look amazing," he said. "But you already knew that."

"It's still nice to hear."

The noise of multiple conversations grew louder as they approached the patio doors, the party, apparently, well on its way.

Helen paused to look up at him, waiting for him to say more, and under the cool, serene confidence she always seemed to project, he saw a moment of uncertainty.

"It's true," he said, allowing himself to touch her, his fingers weaving themselves into the silky strands of one of her curls. "You look sexy as hell," he said, flashing a grin. "That dress even matches your teeth."

She laughed, her eyes dancing with delight and surprise, and then someone tugged her through the doors, and the curl he'd been holding slipped through his fingers.

~ * ~

By the time she'd made it to the other side of all the friends and family who'd turned out to welcome her home and attend her premier, Helen's cheeks hurt from smiling.

She'd been so eager to leave, but, *oh,* how she'd missed them all. Her cousins and their little ones, the ladies from church, employees, even some friends from her pageant days had come to welcome her home, spilling off the patio into the back lawn, laughing and chatting and hugging under the fairy lights strung in the trees like angel dust from the heavens.

It even *smelled* like home, like the earth and things blooming and something sweet you wanted to stick your tongue out to taste. Someone handed her a champagne flute, and Helen took a sip, the bubbles dancing on her tongue like fireflies in the night.

After seeing Jack in his suit, she'd let herself believe that Marcia had come around. She wouldn't have bothered unless she planned to have Jack cast, would she?

"Hello? Hello? Is this on?" Iris tapped a microphone.

Helen took another swig as Iris appeared on a lighted dais near the pool. She prayed Iris kept it short and sweet. Iris scanned the crowd. "Helen? Helen come on up here. This is your party, after all. I'd like to make a toast."

People laughed and herded Helen toward her aunt. She could walk, *thankyouverymuch.*

"Can I also get Travis up here, too?"

What the heck did she want with Travis?

"As most of you know, Travis is Helen's right-hand man. There you are." Iris waved Travis onto the platform with her. "He's held down the fort while Helen's been gone, and we're so blessed to know him. Let's everyone give him a hand!"

Iris covered the mic and hissed for Helen to get her fanny up there already, folks were waiting.

"Anyway," Iris swirled her champagne to the point where it was at risk of actual sloshing. "Thank you all, so much, for coming to celebrate Helen's special night. I know, if my dear, sweet sister-in-law were still alive—bless her soul—she'd be weeping tears of joy right along with me." She waved her glass in the air.

Oh, sweet mother of sunshine.

"As you know, Helen and Travis grew up together, went to university together—Roll Tide!—and built the highly successful Royally

Iced Cupcakery business together." *Wrap it up, Iris.* "They make a good team. But our Helen… she always was apt to run off in one direction or another. And now that she's nearly thirty…" Iris paused on a hushed whisper for dramatic effect and cast a knowing look at her audience. "Well, I'm just going to say, Helen," Iris reached an arm out to hug Helen again as if she'd run away, then smoothed her sweater again—a lady never left herself unsmoothed—turning back to the hushed crowd. "Helen, I know Marcia Powers takes pride in always bringing her leads a happy ending, but if by chance she doesn't come through this time, we would gladly give our blessing—"

Helen's jaw practically hit the dais as she realized where Iris was headed. She grabbed the mic and yanked it away from her aunt. "What are you doing?"

"I'm giving a toast," Iris said, yanking the mic back, her smile tight.

Helen tugged it back and held her hand over it. "You're practically announcing my engagement."

"He's not going to wait forever," Iris hissed through her teeth.

"Iris, I broke up with *him.*" Helen watched with dismay as Travis stood on the other side of her aunt and mouthed, "we need to talk." She pulled the mic to her own mouth. "Iris," she laughed, forcing herself into jovial mode, "always trying to play matchmaker. Looks like Marcia Powers might have some competition, huh?

"Anyway, thank you all for coming tonight!" Helen switched off the mic, unplugged it from the cord, and gave Iris the evil eye as she rushed from the dais.

Travis made his way through the milling guests, nodding and grinning at those who stopped to rib him about Iris's 'joke.' Somehow, he'd managed to get to the other side, while Helen was trapped between a great aunt with a walker and her cousin's one-year-old taking its first steps.

Then she saw Jack.

~ * ~

"The crab cakes are empty."

Jack looked down at the small woman with stiff blue hair poking him with a party pick. He was still processing what had just happened on stage.

The sound of dozens of southern drawls speaking at once hit him like stepping off a plane in a foreign country. He watched Helen weave her way through the crowd, people turning to ask her questions about the

265

show, her relationship with Travis, her plans. It hit him as Helen hugged and teased them with her smile, that this was her home. These were her people. This is where she belonged, among the verbal twangs and southern-fried everything... a world where everything screamed red, white and blue.

He hadn't realized how much of a Yankee he'd become since moving to New Hampshire until he'd been dropped like a fish out of water in the center of Helen Walker's backyard.

Iris was pushing Helen toward Travis because it made sense.

Pushing on the end of the string... pushing out their time together by even eight weeks... didn't.

"Jack," Helen reached his side, smoothing her dress in a habitual motion, as if the fabric could possibly do anything but glide over her. "I'm going to kill Iris for this. What was she thinking?"

"That you and Travis should get back together."

"Well, that ship has sailed. She needs to get over it."

"I said, the crab cakes are empty."

Helen hugged the dour woman with the stiff hair. "Edie, Jack doesn't work here."

"Well, what good is he? What does he do?"

"He's a chef," Helen said, patiently.

Jack cocked his head and looked at her. "I'm a cook," he said.

"The same thing," Helen waved her hand. "But he's not in charge of the crab cakes."

Edie rolled her eyes and wandered off muttering.

"Why did you do that?" he asked.

"What?"

"Call me a chef. You've never called me a chef."

"It's the same thing," she said.

"*Helen*," Ivy appeared out of nowhere, tapping her clipboard at double-speed. "They want you in hair and makeup."

Helen nodded. She reached back her hand. "Come with me?"

Jack knew he'd be shut out once they reached the door of the office they'd converted to a dressing room, but he let Helen twine her fingers with his. "Sure." And, he trailed behind her like he had a right to chase after Helen Walker of Heaven, Alabama.

CHAPTER 29

Helen asked what time it was. The stylist, carefully pinning Helen's hair back into an elaborate updo, paused. "Six-thirty-seven," she said.

Helen's nerves stretched so tight she feared she might snap and put an eye out. Marcia was nowhere to be seen and still hadn't given Helen a final answer about Jack.

Wardrobe *tsk tsked* about having to re-use the blue chiffon gown seeing as they'd never been given time to do a final fitting on anything else. Helen impatiently stepped into the dress and stood for them to fasten it.

The door swung open and Helen felt the string holding her last nerve stretch tighter. "Well?" she asked, without preamble.

Marcia frowned. "Where's your sling?"

"I don't need it. My shoulder is healing." Helen rotated her arm, only wincing a little.

"I'll have Ivy get one for you."

"I don't need it," Helen insisted. It hadn't passed her notice that Marcia was avoiding her question. "You gave Jack a suit," she said.

Marcia shrugged and listened to someone speaking into her headset. "He earned it."

Helen gave her a pointed look. "Well? Is he on the show or not?"

Marcia paused. The wardrobe girls looked up. "Not."

The air sucked out of the room. "What? Why?"

Marcia shooed the attendants into the hall and shut the door.

"The higher ups don't want him." she paused. "They don't want you, either."

Helen sank into the chair. "I'm sorry? Did you just say, they don't want me, either?"

"Apparently they aren't thrilled our competition beat us to the punch with a beauty queen from Alabama. They're ready to go in a new direction."

"I don't understand."

Marcia looked impatient. "Do you want out of your contract or not?"

"I do."

"Then wear the damn sling and stop asking me questions." She rolled her eyes and smiled which she seldom did. "Would you trust me for once?"

Helen braced her hands on her hips. "I have four words for you: Trojan Bus of Love."

"Well, this is a *good* plan. Lord, you people make it difficult to make you happy. It's like you *want* to stay miserable and alone." Then she smiled like a beautiful, frightening, avenging angel, threw open the door, barked for Ivy to bring Helen a sling ASAP, and dashed off to 'give them a premier like no one's seen.'

Once hair and makeup finished, Helen promised to remain pristine and hurried down the hall to Jack's room. She had no clue what Marcia had planned, but if it meant she wouldn't have to continue with the show, and that Jack wouldn't have to put his life on hold for the foreseeable future, she was all for it. It wasn't as if she *needed* the cash the lead position paid, and the bakeries were doing a fine business as they were.

This might, against all odds, work out after all.

What was the line from that movie again?

When you finally realize you love somebody you want that future to start right away.

No, that wasn't right. But it was the gist of it, and that's all she had time for. Helen practically flew down the stairs and around the corner. It felt as if Lily and the crew had fussed forever to get her ready, but here she was, and not a minute to spare. It was ten minutes to seven, and the lightweight, blue chiffon made her feel like Cinderella gliding through fireflies on her way to the ball.

Helen blew out a breath and knocked on the guestroom door.

CHAPTER 30

The fabric of Helen's dress fluttered around her legs as she danced with nervous anticipation. Her heart beat like it wanted to spring free.

The guestroom door cracked open, then swung wide.

Jack sucked in a breath. *"Wow,"* he said. "You look amazing."

She floated through the doorway, arms lifted so he could appreciate the full effect. This was so much better than soggy mermaid dresses. "Thank you."

She returned his assessment, letting her gaze linger. Nothing about Jack's crisp white shirt, navy suit, or classic tie screamed 'look at me,' yet she couldn't tear her eyes away. "You look amazing, too," she said.

"Thanks."

She smiled and grasped his arms to pull him in, but he didn't yield like she'd expected. She hesitated. The duvet lay smoothed on the bed. The book he'd been reading was back on the shelf. His backpack sat on a chair.

It was full. And clasped tight.

The air stilled as Jack walked past her to shut the door with a quiet *click.* She watched his shoulders rise and fall, taut under the dark suit.

Jack faced the door. "I want you to know, I'll be insulted if you try to pay me now. So, don't."

Helen's lungs tightened, and her pulse grew sluggish.

He hung his head and turned, the blue of his eyes brilliant with unshed tears. "Let me at least have my pride."

"What are you doing?" she whispered. But she knew, even though every cell in her body rebelled at his words.

"I'm going home," he said.

"But you don't have to. I mean, you don't have to do the show. I don't either. Marcia…"

He looked at her, hands in his pockets, his perfectly imperfect teeth worrying his lip as he chose his words. "Do you remember when you suggested I go on the show? Be one of the men vying for you?"

"Yes, but—"

"Do you remember what you told me when I said I couldn't? That I had a job and commitments?"

"Of course. I said somebody could fill in for you. And they could have."

He shook his head. "No. No, you didn't. You said *anybody.* Anybody could fill in for me. Anybody could do what I do, because I'm just a line cook in a pub."

"I misspoke. That's not what I meant. You know that."

"But you didn't. Earlier, you said I was a chef."

"You are. I've had your soup. You said yourself that was your recipe. I don't even know why we're discussing this. Didn't you—?"

"*Stop.*" He cut her off, his voice hard and broken all at once. "Stop acting like you don't wish I were something or someone else. I—*we*— need to face the truth. We've had a great time. Epic. But, we're not meant to be together. No matter how hard we try to shove a square peg into a round hole, we just. don't. fit."

"We *do* fit," she said. In all the ways that mattered, they fit so tightly, there were times she felt they were the same person, with the same experiences, the same needs...

"You can't leave yet," she said. "Your car fixed. And Duke!"

He blew out a breath and pulled her close. "I've already decided." He set her away from him. "It's better for both of us."

"Don't I get a say in this? A chance to defend myself?"

"I'm not mad. What you said... It's all true. I've been stuck for a long time. I need to go home and figure out what comes next for me."

"What if I'm what's next?"

It'd be easier if he seemed angry. She could handle the Jack who poked you, challenged you to the point of retaliation. She didn't know what to do with this Jack. His thumb swiped a tear from under her eye and she nearly lost it.

He shook his head. "We're not even headed in the same direction." He held up a hand to keep her from interrupting. "It's been... great. But, we owe ourselves the chance to figure out what'll make us happy instead of leaping headlong into a crazy TV show or a long-distance relationship or whatever other scenario is a convenient excuse not to face the hard truths holding us back."

"What if this was our chance to do that?" she asked. "What if, like Ben said at the wedding, this is our moment to snatch our happiness? To forget that it sounds crazy, that we're different people, that we've only known each other a couple of weeks... What if we're meant to leap into the unknown right this moment or we'll miss our chance?" She waited for his answer, her words like a soap bubble floating higher with each passing second.

"Then we're not ready."

She opened her mouth to insist she was.

"*I'm* not ready," he clarified.

And that bubble burst.

He leaned forward and pressed a single, soul-searing kiss to her brow. She could feel the tremors of his own grief as his lips lingered against her skin an extra heartbeat too long before he set her away again. "I took a leap like that once. I paid the price for fifteen years. Don't ask me to do it again."

In. Out. In. Out.

Like treading water in an endless ocean, Helen knew she had to keep going, she had to keep breathing. But for how long? How long before she found the one who would save her?

Jack's mouth hitched up on one side. "You don't need me where you're headed. You're not the same woman that left Heaven a few months ago. Go find yourself, Helen. Go be that queen you were meant to be."

In. Out. In. Out.

She nodded. She might not need him wherever she was headed, but, oh, how she *wanted* him.

He just didn't want her.

She held back tears. She was so tired of being everyone's second choice.

A knock at the door startled them, and they stumbled another step apart.

"Seven o'clock!" someone shouted.

Helen smoothed her dress. Her hands shook. She clasped them in front of her. "So, I take it this is goodbye?"

"I'm headed to the airport," he said in answer.

"I hope you have a safe flight. And a happy life. I really do."

He nodded, his gaze holding hers hostage. *"Helen..."* he said, but emotion seemed to rob him of the ability to say anything more, because he shook his head, grabbed his pack and walked out.

She held her breath until she heard the front door close.

271

In. Hold. Out. Hold. In. Hold....

She measured her breaths until she could feel her heartbeat again, until the urge to flee and scream and act out in myriad socially unacceptable ways finally passed.

She could do this.

Hadn't she held it together on that stage when she'd clapped for the new, reigning Miss Alabama that *wasn't* her? Hadn't she been dumped on national television not once but twice and still held her head high? She could damn well fake it through a live premier with a broken heart without losing it. Hell, she'd been holding it together most of her adult life.

She could do it for the next few hours.

CHAPTER 31

A woman introduced herself as Helen's new handler. No doubt, the one from the season before had been fired for letting Helen lock herself out of an inn in the middle of the night in a small town in New Hampshire.

It all seemed a lifetime ago.

Helen requested some earbuds and music 'to keep her calm.' In reality, it was an excuse not to have to speak to anyone. Ivy brought her a sling, which she dutifully put on even though Lily *tsk tsked* how it messed with the lines of the gown. Somehow, she made it through until the premier.

Marcia ascended a platform erected near stadium seating the crew had erected between Helen's house and the neighbor's, an enormous faux castle backdrop managing to look charming and not cheesy. How the *Happily Ever After* crew accomplished it all was one of the true miracles of the show—and they'd done it all amid photoshoots, an alligator capture mission, and the lead racing away in a stolen car with an injured dog.

Helen stifled a bark of laughter as they called for quiet on the set.

The handler at her elbow motioned for Helen to step forward. "She wants you to stand on the X until she calls you over. Remember. Don't look at the camera. Look at the audience." Helen glanced over to where a large sign above three tiers of seating spelled out *AUDIENCE* in capital letters. Dozens of women in the target age demographic for the show, as well as many familiar faces, all excitedly cheering on command, filled the seats.

Helen moved to the designated X and waited for her cue.

"And we're *live* in 3… 2…!"

The light went on indicating they were broadcasting, and Marcia turned to face the camera. Helen watched through a staffer's live feed.

"Good evening and welcome to the *live* premier of this season's *Happily Ever After!*" Applause sounded from the audience. "This season we'll have tears and heartbreak, love and laughter and our guaranteed *happily ever after*. But first," Marcia paused for dramatic effect, her expression growing serious. "I have an important announcement. As many fans of the show already know, our dear southern belle, Helen W., suffered rejection and heartache and, unfortunately, injury while filming last season." Marcia gestured toward Helen. "Helen, come on out here."

Marcia gave Helen an uncharacteristic hug for the benefit of the viewing audience as they applauded her appearance on the stage. "We'd hoped that limiting her commitments in the days leading up to tonight—some R and R if you will—would give her time to heal, but, as you see, we've had a setback. There was a *second* incident during filming just yesterday—a harrowing fall and close call involving an alligator—only in Alabama, right? Roll Tide!"

The audience dutifully hollered, "*Roll!*"

"But after serious consultation with our medical team, we've decided it's not fair to ask Helen to serve as the lead this season given how physically demanding our challenges can be. Now, now..." She smiled and patted the air reassuringly. "We have Helen's assurance she'll look for love in her own time, and we wish our Cupcake Queen her very own Prince Charming. Let's give her a round of applause."

The cue for audience applause flashed. Helen waved with her free hand.

"Later tonight," Marcia continued, "we'll announce the winners of our runaway cupcake queen social media contest, but first, you may be wondering what's next? Well, let me tell you.

"We have an epic season in store for you. A first in reality television. Please welcome... the beautiful... the charming... not one, but *two* pageant queens... the *twins*... the former Miss Georgia Peach *and* Miss South Carolina, Ashley and Emily Robins!!!

"That's right—we have twin leads for a can't-miss, double the trouble season of *Happily Ever After!*"

CHAPTER 32

Empty.

That was this feeling—this feeling of nothing. Nothing to look forward to. Nothing to show for all the tears, and leaps of faith, and hard work.

Helen had expected heartbreak would feel more like *something*. Instead she didn't feel anything.

She pulled the mystery Jack had been reading from the shelf. She wondered if he knew how it ended. A burble of dark humor rose up inside her. *They die, of course. And then everyone else in the story tries to pick up the pieces and move on.*

"There you are."

Helen jumped then closed her eyes. She owed Travis a lot of things, an explanation for her aunt's behavior earlier among them, but now was so not the time.

"Hey," she said, schooling her expression and turning toward him. She faked a smile. She knew the motions. "Quite a night, huh?"

He nodded. "Can we talk?"

Like she wanted *one more talk* today. She was so done talking. Had said all the words and then some. "Sure," she said. Might as well get it over with. "We can go wherever you want."

He grimaced and pulled the door shut. "It's a madhouse out there. It's quiet here."

Perfect.

"About earlier," she started, "I'm sorry. My aunt's heart is in the right place, but—"

"It was humiliating," Travis finished for her, his jaw tight. "Humiliating to have her carry on as if I'd be lucky to have you."

Okay. That was harsh.

"Because," he held up a hand to halt her from interrupting, "you don't want me. You want that guy you dragged home like some stray."

His look kept her from protesting. "It's true. We built a business together. We moved *in* together. I waited for you to finally see that you don't have to run away from Heaven to find happiness. Then you ditched everything to go on that show—"

"You told me I could," she broke in. "No, you said I *should!* To get exposure for the business. You wanted to explore other markets. Franchise opportunities…"

"What else was I supposed to say? No? Don't do it? I want you here? How much did you want me to grovel?"

"We broke up," she whispered, her heart tight. "We fell out of love."

"No. You did."

"Oh, Trav…" She moved toward him, but he stopped her with a look.

"Don't," he said. "I'm over it, believe it or not. Over you."

"I see." She didn't. But, she did see that she'd blindsided him the day she'd announced she was moving out. What he didn't realize was that she'd been as shocked by the overwhelming and urgent need to get out as he had been—like that single call from the casting director had poked a hole in a dam she hadn't known was at its breaking point.

Travis worried his lip with his perfect teeth. "Do you even like this guy?"

This guy. As if Jack and her feelings could be reduced to a generic, impersonal phrase. Jack was so much more than *this guy.* He was a confidante. A rescuer. A challenger. A lover. The holder of her heart and keeper of her secrets.

This guy had somehow made her fall in love, imagine a future of her own making, and grow more as a person in two short weeks than Travis had managed in two long years.

"Yes," she said.

He shook his head, processing. "I know I'm probably supposed to be gracious and tell you to go for it, but I'm not feeling gracious. I'm pissed. You know why Iris thought we'd get back together? Because I thought it, too. You always left one foot in the door. You always went along for the ride no matter whether you were miserable inside. You were never brave enough to make a stand, cut your losses, and go after what you really wanted."

"Not true. I broke up with you, didn't I?"

"You said it wasn't working for you *right now.* That sounds like maybe, someday, we would work, doesn't it? Because, why wouldn't we? We're still in business together. Our families are still neighbors…"

"I was trying be kind and let you down easy."

He blew out a long breath. "I know, but it's not kind to linger in someone's life after you've told them you want to cut them out of yours. I deserve to be something other than your back-up plan. I deserve more than being the one the great and beautiful Helen Walker *settled for*. I deserve my own chance to go after the love of my life."

"You're right," she said, knowing exactly what he meant. "You do."

"Don't agree with me. I'm not looking for agreement."

"Then what do you want?"

"I want you to follow through for once. I want you to dry your tears, suck it up, get in your car and drive away and never look back."

"What?"

"I want you to get out. Get out now, because if you don't while you have this opportunity, we're both stuck here, and we'll be stuck together. And I deserve a chance to move on, too."

She really needed to use waterproof mascara if she was going to cry on the regular like this. Helen swiped at a tear. "I so want you to be happy," she said. "I really do."

"I know. I want that for you, too."

She nodded, swallowing the wave of emotion crashing over her. "It looks like I'll have to wait for mine," she said, "seeing as Jack broke up with me. He's decided we're too different. He's already left."

Travis heaved a sigh. "When are you going to stop letting other people make decisions for you?"

"What am I supposed to do? Chase him down at the airport?"

"Why not? I don't know much about what's between you, but no guy drives someone a thousand miles out of his way unless he wants to be with them. A lot. That's a hell of a road trip."

It was. Epic, in fact. Life-changing. Jack had said so.

"What would I even say to him?" She couldn't believe she was entertaining the idea.

"What do you want to say to him?"

"That I'm in love with him," she whispered.

Travis rolled his eyes. "I'll drive."

"I don't know which flight he's on. He may already be gone."

"Do you want to stand here dithering or figure it out on the way?"

"On the way," she said, struggling to undo the straps of her sling. If she were going to chase down her man and declare her love for him, she wanted to be able to embrace properly. When she was finally free, she raced to the door and flung it open. Marcia stood outside.

"No time to talk," Helen gasped. "I'm going after Jack."

"I thought someone brought him to the airport."

"Yes. I'm going after him."

Marcia looked at Helen then Travis then Helen again. She huffed out a breath through her nose like a bull about to charge. "Not without me, you don't. You're still under contract through midnight, and if you get your HEA in an airport, I'm getting that shit on tape. Nick!"

They piled into one of the show's SUVs, as it was the only vehicle large enough to accommodate everyone. "To the airport, and step on it!" Marcia commanded the driver.

"Ivy, figure out what flight he's on. I don't care how. Helen, find a mirror and a tissue and clean that face, but not too much, just so much that you don't look like you've wandered off the set of *Walking Dead*. Travis," Marcia paused her barked commands. "Why are you here?" She looked around. "Why is he here? Isn't he the ex? Are you trying to stop her? Please tell me you're trying to stop her."

Helen laughed, giddy with the possibility it wasn't too late after all. She might get her happily ever after. "He's not trying to stop me. It was his idea."

"I can't find it!" Ivy shouted, despite the fact that they were crammed into the back of an SUV together. "Do we even know where he's headed?"

"Never mind. We'll figure it out when we get there." Marcia smoothed her skirt. "Ivy find Helen a mirror. If she's going to declare undying love, we want her tragic but in a good way."

Ivy got to work, Marcia harangued the driver for being a grandmother behind the wheel, and Helen tried to gather her thoughts. What would she say? Would Jack be receptive?

When they finally arrived, she didn't wait for the SUV to stop rolling before she'd pushed the door open, stumbling to the sidewalk to the surprise of people standing with their bags outside the entrance. Travelers tugging luggage and small, overtired children gawked as Helen dashed through the sliding doors like Cinderella fleeing the ball.

Her entourage scrambled to keep up.

"Security is that way!" Marcia shouted, but Helen had already seen the signs and picked up the pace, adrenaline coursing through her. He was there. He hadn't left. She could *feel* it.

She skidded to a halt just outside of security and strained to see to the gate area beyond TSA. "Do you see him?" she asked, turning, as Marcia and the others caught up. "Does anybody see him?" She looked at the TSA agent, still out of breath. "Have you seen a man come through tonight? Wearing a blue suit? Blondish hair?" The woman shook her head. "Sandy blondish. Kind of a dirty blond." The woman kept shaking her head and motioned for Helen to move aside to let passengers through. "Because it's really important I find him."

The agent stared at Helen. "Report missing passengers at airport security. They can page him."

"*Yes!* Yes. Thank you." Helen turned to Marcia. "We can page him."

By now a small crowd had begun to form around them, people holding up cell phones. Someone asked if they were a news crew or filming a movie.

Ivy looked at her phone. "Airport security is this way," she said, and they hurried behind her, collecting more curious onlookers in their wake.

"Excuse me," Helen said at the window, breathless from both hoofing it through the Birmingham airport as well as with excitement. "I need to page a passenger. It's vital I find him."

"Name?"

"Jack Daniel Adams," she enunciated.

"Not John?" asked Marcia.

Helen hesitated. "No, I think it's just Jack."

The woman behind the window yawned and clicked a button on the desk mic in front of her. "Would a Jack, maybe John, probably Jack Dannon Adams please report to airport security. Please report to airport security. Your traveling party is waiting."

"Thank you." Helen clasped her hands together and turned. "Well, I guess now we wait."

She blew out a breath and scooted to the side to allow access to the security office.

"I think over here," Nick said.

A security guard pushed through the small crowd in the hallway around them. "Sir, do you have permission to film? You need permission."

Marcia stepped in front of the guard. "He's not filming. He's just carrying a camera."

Helen danced foot to foot. She peered over the crowd.

The security guard asked folks to move along. He told Marcia if they didn't have tickets for flights they should wait in Arrivals. Marcia began to argue with the man.

Ivy put her hand on Marcia's arm. "He's not here," she whispered.

"What?" Marcia said.

"*What?*" Helen breathed.

Ivy glanced at the crowd not-so-subtly leaning in to eavesdrop. "*I don't think Jack's here.*"

"Of course, he's here," Marcia said. "He told Helen he was headed to the airport. Have you checked the outgoing flights? He's got to be on one of them."

"Well, unless he's headed to Ireland or Dubai, he's not on any of them. All the late flights are international. Domestic flights stop flying out mid-afternoon. I don't think he's here."

"*Ohmigod.*" Helen said, her head swimming with disbelief. "He's not here. For real. We came all this way…" She glanced around at the people staring at them. At *her.* "This isn't how this is supposed to go," she said. "This can't be how it ends." She swallowed, biting her lip to keep from freaking out. She grasped Marcia's arm to ground herself.

Okay, yes, she was freaking out.

Hysteria gurgled up like bad seafood from her gut.

"Pull yourself together," Marcia ordered.

"I've watched the movies. This isn't how it's supposed to go. He's supposed to *be here.* He's supposed to wait for me!"

"He never got here to wait for you." Marcia took Helen's arm and propelled her through the crowds. "False alarm!" she called out.

They got to the escalator. Helen gathered her skirts, bunching them in her arms like a mangled cake topper so she wouldn't get sucked into the mechanism.

A thousand eyes watched her descend. "This isn't the way it's supposed to end," she said, her eyes welling with tears *this close* to spilling over. "This can't be how it ends."

"*Jesus,*" Marcia spat as they reached the doors and burst onto the sidewalk outside. The air slammed into them, heavy and damp, the smells of too many vehicles and airport food lingering in trash cans a fitting setting for public disappointment. "Would you hold yourself together? This is only your ending if you stop chasing what you want." She barked at Ivy to call the limo back, and they waited on the sidewalk, huddled, like disoriented travelers who'd landed in the wrong country.

"We came. We tried to catch him. We didn't," Marcia said curtly, like they were discussing an ice cream that had dropped to the ground and not Helen's heartbreak.

"This was supposed to be my romantic moment," Helen cried. She sniffed and wiped her nose with her bare hand. "My *grand gesture.*"

"It doesn't work that way." Marcia swept her arms in the air impatiently. "None of this works that way. Life isn't a movie. Love isn't all grand gestures. Love is all the everyday crap along the way. This—*this*—is a moment. One moment. A crappy moment for you, but it's not the end unless you stop here. So, *don't stop here.*"

"I was going to tell him I love him."

"Then tell him you love him some other way. Some other time. Chasing him down is romantic, but if this is your idea of *love* then you don't deserve to find him until you get your shit together. This is just frosting. Love is… pot roast."

Marcia's words stabbed Helen like a dull kitchen knife that nicked you when you least expected it, but they were all true. Right down to the pot roast. She'd been so desperately clinging to the fantasy of love—as if the fantasy was some magical escape portal—that she'd lost sight of what she wanted at the end of all this.

She didn't want the kind of love that Hollywood made movie moments about. That kind of love was flashy and sometimes funny, but those stories swept relationship hurdles to the side like toilet paper in a gentleman's study. All the crap would still be there when the cameras stopped filming.

No, Helen wanted the kind of romance that quietly chose you when you weren't looking. The kind that stood beside you when you needed to know you weren't alone.

The kind that made you feel, in your heart, that you were number one without ever having to be told.

The SUV pulled to the curb. Marcia mopped Helen's face with Travis's pocket square and yanked open the door. Helen ducked inside in a cloud of blue, punching her skirt down to make room for the others. She clasped her hands tightly in her lap.

"So," she said, as the SUV pulled away from the curb, "Ashley and Emily Robins, huh?"

Marcia slumped in the seat opposite. "Yeah. Score, right? The bosses were thrilled to land the twins instead of having Miss Alabama 2.0."

"I'll bet."

Helen blew out a silent breath and stared out the window.

It seemed she was no one's first choice.

CHAPTER 33

"Thanks for picking me up."

Jack opened the door to the back of his dad's car and tossed in his bag, the déjà vu of the whole thing like reliving an unpleasant Groundhog Day of personal defeat.

"No problem," his dad said. "Good to see you."

Jack wished he could say the same. He knew what was coming.

His father pulled away from the terminal. "Home?"

Jack nodded. As if he had another choice.

His dad waited until they were on I-93 heading north before he spoke again. "You wanna talk about it?"

"No." Talking would involve relating how he'd hit rock bottom in the middle of the Birmingham International Airport without a plan or, apparently, a way out. It would mean he'd have to share how he'd been shooed on his way like a vagrant caught loitering by some security guy with a stick up his ass and then spent a sleepless night in a shady airport hotel knowing that after all he'd been through in the last couple of weeks, nothing had changed.

Except, maybe, him.

They merged onto I-89 north, the passing scenery familiar and foreign. Driving home again felt like squeezing into old shoes you'd grown out of. A part of you wanted them to fit. It'd be easier than shopping for new shoes. With new shoes you had to break them in. You might get friction blisters. New shoes could be a pain. But at least they fit.

His dad glanced at him for the hundredth time. "What are you thinking about?"

"Shoes."

Helen.

Had he given up on her—them—too soon?

"Speaking of shoes, I've had this thing with my toenail growing funny. Do you think that's a problem? Sandi says I'm fine, because it doesn't hurt, but there's this ridge—"

"I'm not talking about shoes," Jack said. "Or feet."

"Oh. I thought we—"

"I'm not talking."

The rode in silence a bit. "So, Phil has been helping out while you've been gone. Fixed the walk-in last week before the repair guy could get out to look, he's taken some shifts on the grill. He's not you, but—"

"That's great."

"Wanda's been training him." Daniel grimaced, his face scrunching up like a displeased leprechaun. "Not sure how I like it, though. He and Wanda have been getting... close."

Jack thought about his father's plump, plain-speaking ex-wife and the lanky Phil. They'd look like Jack Sprat and his wife come to life if they got together. "They're both adults."

"She's nearly twice his age. I don't know. Skye hasn't said much about it."

Skye was Wanda's daughter and Jack's half-sister. It got complicated quickly in their family given Daniel Adams's serial fatherhood.

"Why are we even talking about this?"

His dad shrugged, then rubbed an imaginary pain in his neck. "I don't know. A lot has changed in the last couple of weeks. Just bringing you up to speed."

Jack watched another mile marker speed by.

"So, what's the plan?" his dad asked.

Jack swore. "Do I look like I have a plan?"

"It was a simple question. Don't have to bite my head off. I'd know what not to bring up if I knew what happened down there."

"Let's see, I don't have my car, because it got run into a tree. I don't have a dog, because it jumped off a balcony. And I don't have a..." *What? Girlfriend?* "...plan, because every time I make one, it goes up in flames."

"When's the last time you made a plan?"

Jack didn't want to answer that. "Let's just leave it at: I'm not particularly lucky."

His dad scoffed. "I don't believe in luck."

"You have a literal pub named after it."

"It was a catchy name. Went with the logo." He shrugged.

"That explains why working there the last decade hasn't brought me any."

"I mean, sure, you *can* get lucky by chance," his dad continued, "but your odds improve if you put yourself in the path of luck."

"Is this why you're a hypochondriac?"

"I'm vigilant. Those are two different things. Those were actual kidney stones I'll remind you. *This big.*" He squeezed his fingers together to show the size. "Which doesn't sound very big until you realize where it's trying to fit. Some things don't fit."

Like he and Helen. Except, so much of them *did* fit. They weren't alike, often came at things from opposite directions, in fact. But when they met in the middle? It was perfect.

"How was the wedding?" his dad asked.

"Great," Jack said. And he meant it.

You owe me a dance.

"Mike married Jenna, you know."

Daniel nearly drove off the road over that, but he soon recovered. "That's the kind of news you lead with. How was that?"

Awkward. Gut-wrenching. A relief.

"A shock, but Mike's my friend. I made it work."

"Yup. When it matters, that's what you do."

When it matters.

Sweet mother of sunshine. The old man was right.

CHAPTER 34

Helen carefully cracked an egg against the side of the bowl and watched it slide down with the others. Duke lay on a large, orthopedic doggie bed on the kitchen floor, his brown eyes following her as she padded around collecting ingredients.

"I thought I might find you here."

She looked up at her father and offered a half smile. "I couldn't sleep."

It had been days since the *Happily Ever After* crew had swept up and carted off the last evidence of production like *The Cat in the Hat* come to life. They'd even laid new sod over lawns ruined by vehicles and foot traffic and gifted all the neighbors a new mailbox, bottle of champagne and edible fruit basket for the inconvenience of it all.

"Let me guess," her dad said, taking a tall stool at the island. "Cupcakes?"

"Banana bread," she said. "They were starting to go off."

He smiled, his eyes wistful as he watched her.

"You look like your mother," he said.

"You've always said." Helen slowed her movements as she knocked flour through a sieve into a bowl. Helen tried to recall her mother's face. It had grown harder as the years passed. It made her both sad and relieved to admit that to herself. Still, did getting over grief have to mean forgetting?

"Why did Iris pack up all mom's photos after the funeral?" she blurted. She remembered crying as Iris had done so, but Iris had only turned to her, a haunted look in her eye and said, "It's better this way."

"I think she was trying to help."

Her father avoided her gaze. He traced a circle on the island with his finger. Helen wondered what he remembered. What he had forgotten. She wondered a lot of things.

"Is that why you sent me away?" she whispered, not sure she was prepared for an answer even after all this time. "Because I reminded you too much of mom?"

"*No*. Never. Don't ever think that. I sent you away because… you'd closed in on yourself. You weren't sleeping. Every time I'd wake up in the night, I'd hear you down here mixing and banging around. Like tonight." He shrugged as if uprooting a grieving child and packing her off to school was just something people did. "We thought it would help you move on."

When are you going to stop letting other people make decisions for you?

"I wish you'd asked me what I wanted."

"I know. We did our best. Sometimes we make the right decisions. Sometimes we don't. If we all had crystal balls, life would be easier. But I didn't, so when things went south, I tried something else."

Suddenly so many pieces of her past started clicking into place. "Is that why you pushed the bakeries?"

"When it became clear pageants weren't going to be your thing… I figured you liked to bake, and Travis was a good boy. He had his degree by then. I knew he'd look out for you."

"I don't need him to look out for me, Dad. I don't need you to fix me, either. I'm not broken. I'm just… sad."

All she'd ever wanted was to be left alone to grieve. Not be told she needed to get over it or forget the pain. She just wanted a little time to, heaven forbid, let her mascara run and cry ugly tears and be in the moment of *missing,* because she couldn't accept a loss she wasn't allowed to acknowledge had even happened.

No magic number of casseroles or spring-hued flowers or "thoughts and prayers" flung her way could ever make the fact that her mother had died too soon any better. She didn't want to celebrate her mother's life over a casket. She wanted to celebrate the things that had made life with her mother worth living.

Even cupcakes.

"It's okay to be sad," she said. "I just needed you to let me be sad."

"I know." He fought back tears, blinking, his lips pressed together. "I know. It's just that when you love somebody, and they're hurting, you want to fix things. You got your looks from your mama and your teeth from me, but everything else… that's up to you."

Exactly.

She mashed bananas with a fork.

"You want to tell me what's really got you down here at three in the morning? Because I know it's not, or at least not only, about your mother."

Helen added a portion of the dry ingredients, the flour poofing into the air as she stirred. "I've asked Travis to buy me out of the business. He's agreed."

"I see."

It felt like snipping one of the tethers tying her to her past when she'd asked him, but it was the right decision for both of them.

"I'm also moving."

"Moving? Where?"

"I don't know yet. Boston. D.C..." She waved the spoon as if to encompass the entire Atlantic Seaboard. "I haven't gotten that far."

"But Alabama is your home."

"It's where I was born. There's a difference sometimes. I need to... stir things up."

She stirred in the last of the ingredients.

"Is this about Jack?"

Of course, it was about Jack.

"Don't be ridiculous. We knew each other all of two weeks. It takes more time than that to know if it'll work long-term."

"You were with Travis two years. Was that enough time?"

"It's not about the time." She stopped stirring, looked at her father, and sucked her breath deep into her lungs. *"It's not about the time."*

He half-smiled.

She nodded, her vision blurring.

Her dad got up and wrapped her in a hug, squeezing tight. Then he let go. "Don't forget the nuts," he said. "Your mother loved nuts."

As the kitchen door swung shut behind him, Helen grabbed the bag of walnuts, held it over the bowl, and stopped.

She pulled her hand away.

She hated nuts in banana bread.

She grabbed a bag of chocolate chips, dumped in an unmeasured quantity, and stirred.

This loaf was for her.

CHAPTER 35

Eight weeks later, on a Tuesday afternoon, a man walked into Lucky's Pub, ordered pie and coffee, and handed Jack an envelope and his car keys. Then he asked if Jack wouldn't mind dropping him at the airport.

Jack didn't dare open the letter until he knew the guy was in the air. He didn't want to be tempted to do anything impulsive, not after all the meticulous work he'd put in over the last couple of months.

His family, hearing about the car and the letter were waiting at Lucky's when he got back.

"Are you going to open that envelope, or do we have to steam it and pretend it was an accident?" Bailey, Jack's half-sister, sat on a stool at the counter and glared at him impatiently.

Her fiancé, Ian—the only man on earth who would reject Helen Walker—elbowed Bailey. "Give him a minute."

"He's not doing anything. He'll fossilize if he keeps this up."

Ian gave her a look. "He hasn't stopped moving since he came home."

It was the truth. After talking with his dad, Jack had announced his intention to quit the pub. He'd helped interview, hire, and train his replacement—good practice for the future, his dad had reminded him, found someone to sublet his apartment, and what belongings he hadn't sold, he'd put into storage. He knew he couldn't take his next steps until he unstuck himself, and he could only do that if he let himself imagine himself moving on. It was time.

Jack scanned the faces who'd gathered for the big reveal. His dad. Sandi, Bailey's mother. Wanda, his dad's ex-wife. Skye, Wanda's daughter. More. All family by biology or choice. *His* family. A rag-tag, motley crew of people who'd moved into and out of each other's lives over time but had chosen to stick together out of love. This was the family that had welcomed him with open arms when he'd first arrived in Sugar Falls as a troubled teen.

He blew out a slow breath—something Helen had taught him—and tore open the envelope.

Jack read the letter. Twice. He tried and failed to hide his grin.

"Well?" Bailey demanded. "What does she say?"

"Not much," Jack said.

Bailey snatched the letter from his hand and read it aloud. "Here's your car. Duke misses you. If you're ever in the mood for another road trip, count me in. Helen." Bailey slapped her hand to the counter. "Is this a joke?"

Ian peered at the crumpled paper. "That's all?"

Bailey waved the sheet, exasperated. "There's an address, but that's it. Not even a 'Love'? Why are you smiling?"

"She kept the dog." Jack slid the paper out of Bailey's hand and smoothed it before folding it again to put in his pocket.

He smiled at Bailey as all the scattered pieces of his life finally came together. Jack Daniel Adams had a plan.

"I'm thinking of going on a road trip," he said. "But I need some cash. How'd you like to buy a car?"

~ * ~

Two days later, Bailey pocketed the keys to Jack's car. "If you change your mind..."

"I won't," he said.

"Good. Because I was going to say, you never appreciated this car anyway, and I'm the one that always had to fix it, so it's about time you sold it to me."

"Exactly."

She sobered and lifted onto her toes to give him a hug. "You're my half-brother, but I love you like a whole one."

"Right back at you." He waited for her to let go. "So, is this rattle trap loaner gonna get me there?"

"It should. But I warn you, there's no heat." She looked at him, tilting her head. "Do you know where you're going?"

"I've googled it." He knew what it looked like. A little corner building near a park. A yarn shop and a lawyer's office across the street. A suburb of a larger city he hadn't visited. Yet.

"So. You ready?"

"I'm ready."

Three and a half hours later he slowed to a stop and cut the engine.

289

Cheri Allan

A cardboard sign pasted in a window read:

Sweet Tease
Bakery, Barkery & Sandwich Shoppe
Coming Soon!

CHAPTER 36

Helen swiped her brow and looked around, proud of the work she'd accomplished since leasing the old former pizza shop two weeks ago. She was a long way from weeping into her pillow in her childhood bedroom. After the *Happily Ever After* premier and after the clean-up crews swept up the last of the debris from the show, Marcia's words had had a chance to sink in. Like Jack had said, she was stuck, too. Stuck in other people's expectations of who she should be, what she should become, how she should behave. It wasn't their fault, either, because hadn't she let them make those decisions for her?

She was moving forward now, and part of moving forward meant getting rid of the pieces and people in her life that no longer fit, or that she'd finally outgrown, to make room for the what and whom she wanted in her life.

Between what she'd net from selling her share of the bakeries to Travis and a small contribution from the silent investors who'd helped her negotiate the legalities (thank you, Jamie), she felt, if not ecstatic, at least at peace. Leaving home hadn't been easy. Alabama would always be a part of what made her who she was, but that didn't dictate who she would—and could—become.

Sure, there was more she could have written in that letter to Jack, but the things she had to say to him should be said face to face. If she couldn't say them to his face, it didn't matter anyway.

But that was okay. She was okay.

Duke sidled up to her and bumped her hand with his snout. She snuggled him and ruffled his soft fur. His cast was off, and while the vet had cautioned her to keep him from being too wild, they were so close to the dog park, they'd had a frisbee hit the side of the building more than once. The park had been a selling feature of this location, but it had also given her an idea of the direction she wanted to take her new business by offering a dog-friendly outdoor café and homemade dog treats.

Duke nudged her hand again.

"Stop," she laughed. "I'll never get any work done if you keep this up."

A knock at the front door had her heart leap in her chest, but then she checked the time. "That's probably the contractor." She set the broom to the side, smoothed her hair and prepared to make another decision on the way to, as Marcia would say, "getting her shit together."

She unlocked the door and swung it open, bending to hold Duke's collar so the dog wouldn't slobber all over this man's suit. What contractor wore a suit to a meeting? She blinked at the dress shoes and decided this man must be looking for the lawyer's office across the street.

Then she looked up.

"Hey," she said, as the sight of Jack standing on the stoop stole the breath from her lungs. *Here. He was here.*

"Hey." He smiled. That was a good sign. His eyes crinkled, but he looked nervous, too, under the easy grin. "Can I come in?"

Helen pulled the door wider, wariness and delight warring inside her. Jack greeted the dog, scruffling Duke's fur, but his eyes were on her. "I like the name." He hooked a thumb over his shoulder at the temporary sign in the window. The permanent one wouldn't be ready for weeks, but neither would the interior. She hoped to be up and running before too much time went by, but there was only so much one person could do.

"Thanks," she said, rising to look at him. She gestured to his clothes. "You kept the suit."

"The show gave it to me," he said.

"Looks good on you."

He murmured a thanks and looked around, taking in the wide windows facing the street and park next door. "So, what's the plan?"

"Plan?"

"Doesn't look like you're ready to hop in a car and run away to me."

She shook her head. "No. I'm done running. Only occasional day trips for the time being."

"That's probably just as well, because I'm driving a loaner." He gestured over his shoulder. "I'm not even convinced it could get me back to Sugar Falls. I might have to stay a while. Come up with a new plan." He sobered, the teasing smile fading. "If that's all right with you."

Her eyes searched his features for a clue about whether this was real or not. But why else would he have come? Why would he be here talking about staying and wearing a suit and looking all final-scene-in-a-movie perfect if this didn't mean something?

She found herself hoping for a grand gesture. She wanted to know whether Jack was willing to be here, or wherever, with her for the days in between the big moments. She wanted not only to feel that she was his number one. She wanted to hear it.

"What are you saying?" she asked.

His tongue darted out to wet his lips, and he pulled his hands from his pockets. He did that thing where the man drops down to one knee, and she did that thing where she told him to get off the dirty floor and silently cried through shaking hands as she delighted in his insisting it didn't matter because he wanted to do things right.

Her whole body trembled as he peered up at her. He blinked through the hair that had grown long again and swiped it out of the way with an impatient hand. "I need a haircut," he muttered, and she laughed because in the movies the man proposing never said things so inane in such a moment, but this wasn't fantasy, this was real life.

This was her life. Her *future*. Her number one.

"I'm saying," he said, Duke wandering up to lick his face, because Jack was eye level, and that's what dogs do. "I'm ready now. Wherever we're going. I want to be with you. Duke, *sit*. Thank you."

He repositioned. "I know this is impulsive as hell, and I'm sorry for swearing, I shouldn't have done that, but I've just spent the last two months getting my life in order so I could come to you whole. To tell you that… I love you. That's it. I love you. I know that sounds crazy…"

He paused, and she sucked the air into her lungs and held it, because she understood now why the grand gesture was so important. It was the moment. It was that precious suspension of time between what was and what could be, and it held all the joy and promise and hope of the universe. She felt as if in that one, magical, blink-and-you'll-miss-it moment that she finally had a crystal ball. She could see everything they could be together if they only reached out and snatched this moment from time and held fast to it. Together.

Jack smiled, emotion making his eyes brilliant. "I was sure I was deluding myself that you felt the same way. But, then I got a letter."

"Ask me the question," she said, her voice urgent. "Ask me the question."

"Don't rush me, woman. If I'm gonna be impulsive, I want to take my time doing it."

"Ask me the question," she demanded through laughter and tears, and she knew if he took too long to work up to it, she'd be crying too much to see his eyes when he asked, and that was a moment she didn't ever want to forget.

He popped the little box open. "Helen Walker... Wait. What's your middle name?"

"It doesn't matter!" she all but shouted.

"Helen Walker, will you marry me?"

She hauled him off the floor and threw herself into his arms, not caring that she was getting tears all over his nice suit. "I love you, too, Jack Adams. I know I sound crazy for saying that, but I do."

He cupped her face before she could tug him close again. He kissed her instead and laughed against her mouth. "I take it that's a yes?"

"It's a yes."

"Way to hold your cards close to the vest. You might want to rethink the name, *Sweet Tease*."

"The name wasn't about me." She replied. "You were a little hard to pin down. Kept running away from me."

"I've been busy. I've quit my job, sublet my apartment, and sold my car... Which reminds me..." He stepped back far enough to pull the ring out of the box and slide it on her finger. It was a little loose, but they had time to get it right. Because she loved him. She loved this crazy, opinionated, disarming, charming man with every fiber of her being. And he loved her.

She could not stop grinning. She had no idea how it would all turn out, but she knew it would work out. Because, when you know, you know.

A knock sounded at the door and Helen moaned into Jack's shoulder. "The contractor's here. Shoot. I've already had to reschedule twice."

"It's fine," Jack said, opening the door for the contractor. "We've got time to celebrate. I know you've got this part under control."

"Where are you going?" Helen asked, her heart tripping in her chest.

Jack smiled, his eyes crinkling at the corners in that way that she loved.

"To buy peaches."

Dear Reader,

Like a heroine that didn't want to commit, this is the book that didn't want to be written. Three titles, multiple drafts, and dozens of false-starts later, we have arrived at our destination. Like Jack and Helen, life took me on a detour these last few years. In order to get to the end of this book, I had to let go of what wasn't working and accept where I was—both in the book and in real life.

I had to wave goodbye to children heading out on adventures, mourn multiple losses, and find my calm again in a world that felt much like Helen breathing into a tampon disposal baggie. I had to find the funny in a life that was often moving too quickly to keep up with. I imagine I'm not alone. But I hope—I sincerely hope—that for a little while, Jack and Helen's journey is an escape from real-world stresses for you and a reminder that even when life takes us on a detour, it's okay. Like family you can't disown, we're all in this together.

I'm not done yet. Look for more quirky, fun, small-town romances in the continuing *Lucky Charm* spin-off series: where food, family, and laughter lead to happily ever after!

Plus, don't miss out on exclusive content, info on new releases and other stuff you won't want to miss. Sign up for my mailing list at www.cheriallan.com today!

Love and luck,

~ Cheri

About the Author

Cheri writes kissing books about love and other shenanigans from her charming fixer-upper in rural New Hampshire. She is often distracted by social media, reality television, and a menagerie of cats and dogs. If you find her whizzing down the slopes at the nearby mountain with her family or inadvertently killing perennials in her garden, bring her coffee. She will gratefully provide the conversation and chocolate.

Cheri loves to hear from readers!
E-mail her at cheri@cheriallan.com.
Friend her at facebook.com/cheriallanauthor.
Or, visit her website and blog at www.cheriallan.com.

If you enjoyed this book, please consider telling other readers by writing and sharing a review. (It's ridiculously helpful and makes an author happy!)

Look for other Cheri Allan romances, because life is short, love is funny, and laughter is everything!

Enjoy quirky, fun, small-town romance?
Try the 'Betting on Romance' series!

 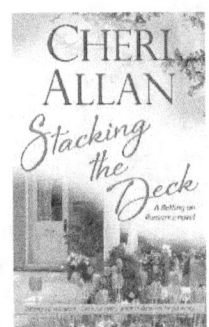  

LUCK OF THE DRAW | If only life had a refresh button...
Kate Mitchell never planned to be a widowed single mom, but when her soon-to-be-EX husband up and dies, her dreams of finishing her degree and moving on are thrown in the air like a game of 52 pick-up.

STACKING THE DECK | Who said coming home is easy?
Liz Beacon has finally put the teenage pounds, dysfunctional family and embarrassingly one-sided high school crush behind her. And then she's called home...

ALL OR NOTHING | When finding Mrs. Right goes, oh, so wrong...
Ian McIntyre suffered through a reality dating show only to return home empty-handed. But what happens when he finds himself more interested in the cute and scrappy hometown girl dusting off his action figures than the audience's favorite southern belle?

DEAL ME IN | Is the game of love worth the price?
Grace McIntyre hadn't planned to lose her virginity in a seedy motel to the hottie with the eagle tattoo, but she *knew* he was The One—until a heart-wrenching good-bye proved he wasn't.

Available in print and e-book. Visit www.cheriallan.com for links to your favorite retailers.

www.ingramcontent.com/pod-product-compliance
Lightning Source LLC
Chambersburg PA
CBHW071255170626
46809CB00001B/223